SISTER OF SHADOWS

THE SCION CHRONICLES, BOOK 3

ERIC KENT EDSTROM

UNDERMOUNTAIN**BOOKS**

To J

1

THE WONDERS OF ANDLEPRIXEN

Trapped again.

Dr. Carlhagen stalked from one side of the small holding room to the other. The blessings of his new young body—which had once belonged to a Scion named Vaughan—had become a curse.

It took just a few paces to cross cold white tile from the locked door to the plain cement block wall. The room was little more than an examination room one would find in any doctor's office, a relatively private place intended for him to hold consultations with Progenitors prior to transferring them to their Scions.

But more recently it had been used as a holding cell. The faux-wood cabinets had been emptied, the body-weight scale removed, the rubber gloves and wipes and sterilizer all carried out. All that remained was the gurney bed with its wad of sheets and blanket from his restless tossing and turning. And him.

A ninety-three-year-old man in a seventeen-year-old body.

So much energy, so little room to move.

The last time he'd been stuck in this little room he'd been strapped to the gurney with an IV dripping brain-numbing sedatives into his blood. Not for the first time he wondered if that might not be better. At least he wouldn't have to suffer such torturous monotony.

He didn't know how long he'd been in there. At least a day. Maybe more. And already he was about to lose his mind. If he had still inhabited his ninety-three-year-old body, he wouldn't have minded it so much.

If he could get some andleprixen, he wouldn't mind it at all. Hell, if he could get enough he could blot out everything. He clenched his fists to stop them shaking. The Scions had not allowed him a dose since locking him in here.

No, not the Scions, he thought. *Jacey* had not allowed him a dose.

He bellowed a curse. The word snapped back at him in the tiny space. "That girl!" he fumed. "That conniving, sneaking, beautiful girl!"

He'd had her strapped down and in the transfer machine, ready for Senator Bentilius to overwrite her mind. But inexplicably, Belle—a Scion who hated Jacey with every cell of her flesh—had taken Jacey's place.

Dr. Carlhagen wrinkled his nose and spun on his heels, adding more force as he stomped across the room. He stopped at the steel door and tried to peer out the narrow window into the corridor. The hall was dark, so all he could see was the trapezoid of light his window cast onto the floor. His own head made a slanted blob of shadow inside it.

He turned his back to the door and leaned against it, suddenly weary.

Even now, all these hours after the senator's transfer,

his skin chilled at the horror of seeing Belle rise from the transfer machine and cross the room toward him. He'd expected Jacey. His final plan to possess her had been to let Senator Bentilius overwrite her. And because Senator Bentilius loved him—or, at least, lusted for him—he would finally consummate his own unending need for the woman he had loved and pined for his entire life: Jacqueline Buchanan, Jacey's Progenitor.

He'd nearly had her once before, though it shamed him to think of it. He was thankful he'd been stopped that time. To have taken her by brute force would have been . . . distasteful.

Maybe it's better this way, he thought. *Jacey's still out there, still intact.* Possessing her body, as enjoyable as that would have been, would be a far sight less rewarding than to have her in his arms with her mind in place. He would much rather have those aqua eyes looking into his with submission than with the pure hatred she lasered at him these days.

If he could get out of this room, maybe he could charm her. If only she could see his brilliance, she might appreciate him.

He laughed, hot and scornful at the thought. Jacqueline had never appreciated his mind. Which is why she had married that idiot, Charles Buchanan.

Dr. Carlhagen let himself slide down the door and onto the floor. Putting his hands over his face, he forced his thoughts to the situation at hand. He needed to escape.

And he absolutely needed to get Senator Bentilius out, too. If he waited long enough, her own people would come to the island. A woman of her political power surely had military force ready to swoop in if they didn't hear from her or her guards soon.

Her bodyguards were all either dead or strapped to

cots in the medical ward—that much he'd picked up from Scion conversations on the occasions he'd been taken to the bathroom. Unfortunately, Senator Bentilius had not revealed the size or timing of any contingency military invasion to him.

It was time to do what he'd been putting off.

It hadn't taken a man of his intellect long to figure out how Belle had gotten into the transfer room. After all, she'd been locked in this very room when he'd last seen her before the transfer.

He got to his feet and looked at the ceiling. She had removed one of the ceiling tiles and climbed above, which allowed her to crawl through the ceiling support beams and then descend into the transfer room. She'd probably gotten down through the storage closet.

That made sense. Jacey would have taken the same route to get out. The shelving in that closet would have made climbing down or up as easy as climbing a ladder.

Jacey must have come down in one of the other holding rooms along the corridor outside. One that was unlocked. Then she'd simply walked out.

Of course, the Scions knew that trick, so all those rooms would be locked now, too. He wouldn't be able to escape using the ceiling. But he could get to the room across the hall where Senator Bentilius was being held.

He would have done so earlier, but she was so aggressively affectionate he was still sore from their first bout of lovemaking. The tile on the transfer room floor was hard and cold.

He'd tried to resist her, tried to remember that she inhabited the pale and morose Belle, a Scion he'd given less than two minutes thought to her entire life. But somehow Senator Bentilius's innate sensuality had transformed Belle into something else. Beautiful, yes. But also frightening.

Dr. Carlhagen worried she'd try to ravish him again if he appeared in her holding room. No. He *knew* she would.

But there was no alternative. He had to know what her contingency plan was.

With the slothful pace of a man walking to his own execution, he climbed onto the gurney and stood. His new body was tall, so he easily reached the ceiling and pushed a tile up and out of the way. The space above was dark as a midnight shadow.

He probed a hand into the darkness until he found a cool steel beam. He started to pull himself up, and had just lifted his head into the blackness when he heard a rapping on the door to his room.

Letting go of the beam, he plopped onto the gurney, heart racing. If a Scion spotted him climbing into the ceiling, they'd take measures to prevent it. His eyes scanned the window in his door, but it was dark and no face peered in.

A flash of movement at the base of the door caught his eye. Dr. Carlhagen gasped and leapt from the gurney. In two strides he knelt and swept up a slip of paper that someone had slipped under the door.

A bit of scratch paper, exactly the kind Nurse Smith had kept on her desk. He unfolded it.

"That traitor," he breathed, recognizing Mr. Justin's handwriting. "What is he up to?"

The note read: *Do you want to escape on Senator Bentilius's chopper? Knock once for no, twice for yes.*

Dr. Carlhagen's eyes narrowed and he pressed his face to the window. He couldn't see anything or anyone out there. Muttering to himself, he resumed his pacing.

Mr. Justin had gone in with Jacey and the Scions when

they'd taken over the school. A betrayal of the worst kind, as far as Dr. Carlhagen was concerned. He'd given that man everything, had even incubated a Scion for the man.

"What's your game, Mr. Justin?" he asked the room.

He crumpled the paper and shoved it into a front pocket of his black Scion uniform pants. He had a decision to make. And it was the worst kind, because every option was bad. The first was to refuse Mr. Justin's offer, which was probably a trick anyway. But that left him with his original plan, to question Senator Bentilius about her contingency force and when they might arrive.

But even that option was mostly downside for him. After the inevitable rescue by the senator's forces, he'd be in a much-diminished position. Senator Bentilius had always been power-hungry. Once her people controlled the island, only a fool would think she'd relinquish that control.

Not that she'd have much choice in the long run. After all, Dr. Carlhagen had his own contingencies in place.

He grunted with dissatisfaction at the lack of a real choice. The timing for this catastrophe couldn't have been worse, as they were just about to start up the next phase of the Scion program. With the facilities on St. Lazarus nearing completion, it was time to scale up—and stream-line—the production of Scions.

He'd had much larger ambitions for the program. Plans Senator Bentilius knew nothing about. If he lost control of the schools, it would be harder to reach his loftier goals. So even if Mr. Justin's offer was a trap, Dr. Carlhagen couldn't see how it would work out worse than waiting for Senator Bentilius's force to come to the rescue.

Decision made, Dr. Carlhagen stopped in front of the door and gave it two sharp knocks. He stood there for several minutes, expecting a response of some sort, a knock in return or maybe another note. Maybe even the door to unlock and the butler to lead him out.

But nothing happened. He resumed his pacing, crossing to the far side of the room, spinning and proceeding back to the door. He'd done a dozen laps before drawing to a stop and staring at the floor.

Another slip of paper lay there, half of it still under the door. Eager as a boy on Christmas morning, Dr. Carlhagen snatched it up and unfolded it.

One word was written in a hurried scrawl: *Wait.*

But that wasn't what drew Dr. Carlhagen's attention. In the dead center of the paper was a small pill, secured by transparent tape.

With shaking fingers he ripped it free and swallowed it, tape and all. It only took a few moments for the familiar heat to spread through Dr. Carlhagen's limbs and the tightly wound coil of anxiety in his mind to unwind.

Ah, the wonders of andleprixen.

2

YOUR TRUE ENEMY

The morning sun already hovered above the spine of the green and brown hills to the east, and the Scions still hadn't finished loading the bus. They came and went in twos and threes, bearing loads on their shoulders or in their arms, sweating and grunting, mouths open under the strain.

Already the day was hot, the air full of moisture from the sea, breezes heavy with verdant odors of inland greenery. The white walled buildings reflected and magnified the sunlight. The quad—a great green space at the center of the Scion School campus—felt claustrophobic to Jacey.

Maybe it was because of the debris left over from the hurricane a few days past. Maybe it was the pressure of time pushing in on her from all directions.

It took all her will not to run to one of the buildings and grab a load and carry it herself. But she knew if she left the bus for more than two minutes, she'd return to find Scions loafing about. So it was better for her to pace alongside the long vehicle and stew.

So much to do. It had become a refrain that repeated again and again in her mind, in conversations, in the dreams that filled the scant hours of sleep she'd stolen over the past couple days. So much to do.

Horace, Constantine, and Kirk emerged from Boys' Hall carrying more pieces of disassembled bunks. They would be reassembled aboard *Aphrodite*, the boat Mr. Justin and his idiot brother Orson had brought to the island of St. Vitus. They had schemed to steal the Scions from Dr. Carlhagen. Only the arrival of Senator Bentilius, and the drama that had come with her, had foiled the plan.

But now, thanks to Mr. Justin's failed scheme, the Scions were in possession of a boat and a bus, and they had Dr. Carlhagen and the senator as prisoners. So if they could just get going, they had a chance to get off the island and away from the Scion School for good.

Jacey fought to control her impatience and not shout at the three boys to hurry up as they trudged past her.

"How many are left, Horace?" she asked the oldest, a boy of fifteen. She felt that she was moderately successful in keeping the impatience out her voice.

"I don't know," Horace said. "Five. Six."

Jacey bit back the impulse to yell. Instead, she put on a syrupy smile. "When you go back, please count."

Horace grunted and mumbled something she couldn't make out.

The boys shoved the wooden headboards and spring platforms of the bunk beds into the back of the long, boxy vehicle. The bus's aqua paint was worn away in many places, revealing an older coat of mustard yellow. According to Sensei, the machine was an antique school bus from North America.

Two Scions inside the bus, the Spider Obu and

Centipede Helen, stacked the pieces between the seats, making sure to use the space as efficiently as possible.

Horace muttered under his breath again. Of all the Scions on the island, he was the only one Jacey actually hated. She'd never forget how he had relished holding her down so that Belle could whip her legs with a thornskipple branch. Even more chilling was the memory of his gleeful expression as he'd stabbed Alice, the senator's huge bodyguard.

But Horace was a Scion. And like herself, he hadn't asked to be born a clone of some stranger, hadn't asked to be grown like a farm animal for the sole purpose of being overwritten. Jacey shivered, wondering what Progenitor had given his DNA to create such a sadistic creature.

"I know it's hard work," she said to him. "But you must move faster. We have to get off this island before the senator's backup forces arrive."

"So you keep saying." He didn't wait for her response before waving to the other two and stalking back toward Boys' Hall. He moved faster, though, and that was enough for Jacey.

In any other circumstance, she would have sent him to Sensei. But this was no time for disciplining sullen Scions.

She was about to turn attention back to the bus when Constantine, also a Centipede of thirteen, broke away from the trio and trotted to the entrance of the dining hall. At first she thought he'd decided to take a break, which surprised her. Not only because she'd just told them to hurry, but because Constantine was as dutiful a Scion as there was.

Others called him Little Vaughan, which always made him beam with pride. Everyone had loved Vaughan; the boys especially had all looked up to him, Constantine more than any other. The boy mimicked Vaughan's mannerisms, his speech patterns, and especially Vaughan's generous kindness.

But Constantine was as dutiful as he always was—he reappeared a moment later, holding the arm of a frail elderly woman with an extraordinarily wrinkled face. Mother Tyeesha. The old woman patted Constantine's hand and beamed at him. He helped her down the steps. In his free hand he carried a bucket. Something Mother Tyeesha had gone to the kitchens to fetch, no doubt.

The woman had raised them all at Children's Villa across the island. Now she and all the little ones were using the Dining Hall as a makeshift dormitory. Constantine said something to her and she let go of his arm. He ran to the bus and handed the bucket to Obu.

When he noticed Jacey watching him, he stopped, dropped his eyes. "Mother found a bucket of rice she wanted us to bring along."

"You did well, Constantine," Jacey said. A bucket wouldn't make much difference, but if Mother Tyeesha wanted something, nobody would deny it to her. "Now get going."

The boy flashed a smile so much like Vaughan's that Jacey wondered if the boy's Progenitor was related to Vaughan's. She made a mental note to check the list of Scions and Progenitors Mr. Justin had shown her.

Jacey turned away from the bus, casting her gaze past the mango grove, down the gently sloping landscape of wild scrub that tumbled in green and brown waves to the sea.

The turquoise waters of the Caribbean seemed to laugh at her with cheerful glimmers of sunlight. The hurricane that had blown through days earlier would have better matched her mood. It certainly would have been a more appropriate symbol of the impending danger threatening the Scions. Somewhere out on that vast blue sea, the senator's contingency force approached.

Just how many soldiers and weapons that force contained, Jacey had no idea. The senator certainly wasn't saying. But if they landed before the Scions got away, all hope of escaping their dark destinies would be swept away, just as surely as the hurricane winds had stripped the leaves from the trees in the quad.

Jacey sensed Humphrey's presence behind her, a warmth that lessened her dread somehow. Without looking, she reached her hand back. He took it in his own strong grip.

"Any luck?" she asked.

His silence was answer enough. Humphrey had been searching the campus for the Artificial Intelligence servers, the computers that hosted Madam LaFontaine. And more importantly, Vaughan and Belle.

"Should I speak with Madam LaFontaine again?" she asked. "She has to know where her own *body* is."

Humphrey snorted a humorless laugh. "She'd hate to hear you call her server her body."

Jacey grinned. "I know."

Humphrey pulled on her hand, drawing her into an embrace. She allowed a kiss, but quickly pulled away. "Not here. It's distracting to the others."

Humphrey let out a disappointed sigh and released her. "I don't see any point in interrogating Madam LaFontaine again. She has every incentive to lie to us. She's loyal to Dr. Carlhagen. And Vaughan is obviously telling the truth about not knowing, because he has every incentive for us to take his server with us."

Dark clouds passed over Jacey's heart. Leaving Vaughan and Belle behind would certainly doom them. Even though both were AIs, someone in the real world could easily wipe them out if they got hold of their servers. After all, Dr. Carlhagen had ordered her beloved old teacher Socrates to delete himself. "We can't give up."

"I'm not giving up. I just think it's time to put some pressure on Dr. Carlhagen."

A new voice, deep and rough, startled Jacey. "I agree."

She turned to find Sensei, the school's martial arts master, approaching, every step precise and calm and yet simultaneously heavy and ominous. He exuded danger, like a quickly burning fuse on a stick of dynamite. Despite this, Jacey always felt safer when he was around.

"Dr. Carlhagen will just have to tell us where the servers are," Humphrey said. "And while I'm at it, he's going to tell me where the other Scion School is."

Jacey willed herself not to slump at the reminder of the other school. Any gesture of exhaustion or defeat would send the wrong message to the Scions still busy loading the bus. If she were alone, though, she would have collapsed in a corner and covered her head with her hands.

During a dinner with Senator Bentilius, Humphrey had learned that Dr. Carlhagen and the senator had been working together to build another Scion School. Humphrey had searched Dr. Carlhagen's office, but hadn't found any more information.

Just hearing Humphrey mention the other school made Sensei's shoulders and chest flex. As usual, he quickly mastered his emotions, letting his muscles relax. "I still can't believe I didn't see all of this for what it was." He waved his hands to take in the whole campus. "I'll go with Humphrey. We'll get the information from Dr. Carlhagen."

He pronounced the headmaster's name with such hatred that Jacey's spine zinged with electric chills. Dr. Carlhagen had "recruited" Sensei from a prison in Brazil where he'd been serving a sentence for murdering a young woman—a crime he had no memory of committing. In return for his release from prison, he had accepted the role of martial arts master at the Scion School. But Dr. Carlhagen kept control of Sensei by threatening Sensei's family if he tried to leave.

For years Sensei had taught the Scions martial arts and kept them in peak physical condition. He'd also been the sole authority at the school during long stretches when Dr. Carlhagen was away from the island. But he hadn't known what the Scions were, hadn't known what their destiny was. And he blamed himself for that ignorance.

Jacey knew that nothing she could say would take away his guilt. It went deeper than self-blame. Dr. Carlhagen, under the influence of andleprixen and his grotesque obsession for Jacey, had recently ordered his paramilitary force, led by Captain Wilcox, to execute "Protocol Seven." Wilcox and his gunmen had forced Sensei and Nurse Smith onto his helicopter, intending to throw them both into the sea.

But Sensei hadn't waited to be pushed, instead choosing to jump into the sea while the chopper was still relatively low. Miraculously, he'd survived and swum to shore. Nurse Smith had not.

By the glitter in the martial arts master's dark eyes, Jacey knew that Dr. Carlhagen might not survive Sensei's questioning. The thirst for revenge burned in his gaze, but not because of the attempt on his own life. No. Sensei wanted justice because Protocol Seven had also ordered the murder of Sensei's family, including his daughter.

Jacey turned to him. A dozen literary quotes about revenge came to mind, all planted there by Socrates during long memorization sessions. But despite the wisdom she found in them, she knew none would have any effect on Sensei. Even so, she could not allow him to go into Dr.

Carlhagen's room. The old headmaster now occupied Vaughan's body, and Jacey planned to someday restore her friend to the world of flesh and blood. She'd do the same for Belle, too. Remembering the icy girl's sacrifice, switching places with her in the transfer machine, firmed her resolve.

Vaughan didn't want to be restored because he didn't want two versions of himself in existence, an AI version and a flesh-and-blood version. Respecting that wish was not prudent. The Scions needed his leadership, and no matter how annoying Belle could be, Jacey needed her in charge of the girls. Leslie was nearly useless and Wanda was stretched too thin.

"Go speak with Dr. Carlhagen, Humphrey," she said. "But not you, Sensei." His fists tightened and his head cocked to one side, furious to be ordered around by a Scion. She slipped close to him, meeting his gaze without fear. "You never taught us girls to fight. But I heard what you said to the boys. 'In every fight, your true enemy is anger.'"

She didn't let her gaze linger, choosing instead to turn away from him. If she challenged him too directly, his pride would stiffen and he'd insist on seeing Dr. Carlhagen no matter what she said.

It worked. Sensei took a step back. "Take someone with you, Humphrey. Dr. Carlhagen is strong and won't hesitate to attack you if he thinks he can escape."

"I'll go," said Sang.

Jacey's head snapped around. She hadn't seen the boy lurking about. Her eyes narrowed. She couldn't be sure Sang wasn't now Mr. Justin.

Thinking quickly, she said, "Thanks for volunteering, but your leadership is needed in loading the bus." She spotted a better choice. "Tytus, you go with Humphrey."

Sang's face scrunched in confusion—or was it consternation?—and he opened his mouth to object. Sensei cut him off. "Do as Jacey says," he said.

Jacey glanced back at the martial arts master. His face was still a storm cloud of fury, but his fists were no longer clenched. He held her gaze for two heartbeats, then dipped his chin in a quick nod. It was slight, but it communicated enough.

Jacey paused a moment, suddenly taken with Sensei's words. *In every fight, your true enemy is anger.*

"I need to remember that," she whispered to herself. And as she watched Humphrey and Tytus head toward the medical ward, she hoped Humphrey would, too.

3

AS YOU SAY

The familiar clang of a bell pulled Jacey from her reverie. She glanced at the top of bell tower, the highest point on campus. Built upon the circular walls of an ancient stonework windmill, the tower's white plank walls reached skyward, tripling the original structure's height.

A perfect perch for her spy to keep watch on the comings and goings of Scions.

She unclipped the walkie-talkie from the waist of her uniform pants and lifted it to her lips. She cast a glance all around before speaking. A group of girls was approaching from the mango grove, but they weren't in earshot. "Anything to report, Livy?"

Static burst from the tiny speaker, then cleared as Livy's voice—calm and precise—came through. "I've been taking notes, but I haven't seen anything particularly suspicious so far."

"Keep watching."

"I'd rather be helping. This is boring."

"Who rang the bell?"

"Rachel. She gave me the notes from her shift. Nothing."

"Thank you, sweetie. Come down in a half hour and bring me what you've got."

"Understood." Livy didn't put any complaint in the response, unlike most of the other girls who'd been assigned various tasks.

Like the group that approached now. Leslie and Wanda carried an insulated white chest between them, both huffing with the effort. Their arms strained, uniform tops stretching tight across their shoulders. Dajeet and Bethancy followed close behind, each leaning under the weight of a twenty-four kilo bag of flour or rice slumped over a shoulder.

"Why—couldn't—we—use—the—Jeep?" Wanda gasped as they trudged the last few meters toward the bus. She had her wild red hair tied back in the requisite pony-tail, but rogue wisps had broken free and fell across her eyes.

"Because Summer took it to the docks," Jacey said.

Leslie's lips pinched together, nostrils flaring as she and Wanda hefted the chest into the bus through the rear door and slid it onto the floor. Releasing the handle, she inspected her hands where a livid mark ran across her palms. At least she didn't complain. Instead, she smoothed her coppery hair and straightened her uniform. "That's the last chest. There's a lot of meat left in the warehouse that's going to spoil unless we can refrigerate it on board the boat."

Bethancy and Dajeet pushed their burdens into the bus and rubbed their shoulders. Dajeet, a round-faced girl with luminous black eyes that made her seem both old and young at the same time, pulled her reader from a satchel and glanced at the screen. "There are six more bags of rice, three of quinoa, and a couple bins of fruit, mostly apples." She swiped a finger across the screen. "By Obu's calculation, with this busload we'll have enough food to last us three weeks at sea."

Obu was a Spider from Humphrey's Nine. His gift for numbers was on par with Summer's gift for mechanical things.

Jacey climbed into the bus through the rear door. The rows of high-backed seats were nearly packed to the ceiling with pieces of bunks, mattresses, food chests, bags and bins full of fruit, nuts, spare clothing, towels, bedding, soap, and other miscellaneous supplies. The Scions had been very fortunate that one of Dr. Carlhagen's resupply crews had replenished the School's stocks of necessities just a day before everything started to spiral down the drain.

Jacey shook her head in disbelief. Less than a week had passed since Dr. Carlhagen had returned to campus—after a four-year absence—to celebrate the first graduating class of Scions. Or so he'd said. And that's when Dante had hidden the radio in his uniform and Vaughan, Jacey, and Humphrey had sneaked to the bell tower to listen in. They'd been so curious to know what happened in the medical ward after graduation. What they'd learned had led to a series of harrowing events that brought them to this day. A chance for escape.

She hopped back onto the grass and looked over Dajeet's shoulder at the reader display. "There's a bit more room in the bus. Do you have all priority items loaded?"

"All that's left on the priority list is Madam LaFontaine's server and the transfer machine. I don't know why you want *that*." She flashed a questioning glance at Jacey. When no explanation was forthcoming, she continued, "We have room on this load for more food. That will give us a buffer. If I didn't have to carry them myself, I'd tell you we should take more bags of non-perishables. The quinoa would be best as it contains more protein than rice."

Bethancy groaned. "Now she's going to make us carry more bags."

Jacey arched an eyebrow at Bethancy. Like Dajeet, Bethancy was fifteen, but she had none of Dajeet's mature poise. And she never caught a joke that wasn't blatant. "Three weeks and one day from now, you'll be thankful for anything extra you carry today."

"She's right," Leslie said. "Let's go." Without waiting, she marched toward the warehouse. Wanda flashed a weary smile at Jacey before following after.

"You go ahead, Bethancy." Jacey took Dajeet by the elbow and pulled her aside.

Bethancy huffed and stomped away, muttering something about someone being a bit too high and mighty. Jacey let it go. If their positions were reversed, she doubted she would have responded any differently.

Dajeet stared at Jacey with her lustrous and nearly black eyes, waiting expectantly for Jacey to speak.

"I need to borrow your reader," Jacey said. "Mine got buried somewhere in the bus when I wasn't looking."

Dajeet handed the tablet to Jacey. "I wouldn't mention that to Sensei. He might let you boss him around most of the time, but old habits . . ."

Jacey made a wry face. "I don't boss him around."

"As you say."

The phrase—one Mr. Justin had uttered many times—made Jacey's eyes snap back to Dajeet's face, studying the girl's expression for any sign of a change.

But no. She couldn't be Mr. Justin. The girl had been

with Humphrey and several others in the hacienda at the time of Mr. Justin's transfer.

Jacey turned her attention back to the reader. "Vaughan, I need to speak with you."

He did not appear.

"Vaughan! I know you're in there."

Her friend's face, an image of male perfection, flickered onto the screen. An odd smile played on his lips, as if he'd just been told a joke.

"Are you the whole Vaughan or one of his many instances?" Jacey demanded.

"It makes no difference."

"It makes a difference to me." Jacey didn't like the idea that Vaughan could split his computer-based consciousness into several identical instances, each doing a different task. She always felt like he wasn't paying his full attention to her. Not that she could tell. But ever since he'd installed Belle on his server, Jacey had the impression he was distracted.

Which made sense, actually. Belle had never been the most pleasant presence in Girls' Hall. And now that she lived in Vaughan's world, maybe she was annoying him the way she'd annoyed Jacey all her life.

"I need you to change your mind," she told him.

"I'm not installing Elizabeth."

"Who's Elizabeth?" Dajeet asked.

"The Progenitor who overwrote Vin," Jacey said.

"Oh. Then I'm with Vaughan on this."

Dajeet's opinion was no surprise. Vin had been the First of Dajeet's Nine before graduation, so naturally Dajeet opposed any resurrection of Vin's Progenitor. At any other time, Jacey would have agreed. But they needed information. Now.

"I need to question Elizabeth," she told Dajeet. "Mr.

Justin told me she lives on an island nearby. I think that should be our first destination once we leave St. Vitus."

Vaughan's brows lifted and a different smile appeared, casting his face in a pose of compassion. It made her think of one of the angels from the Christian texts that Socrates had taught her about. "If I were to install her on my servers, I'd be stuck with her here forever."

"Why can't you just delete her once we get the information we need?"

His mouth gaped at the suggestion. "That would be murder."

Jacey's grip tightened on the reader. She'd rarely been at odds with Vaughan before he'd been overwritten. But since he'd been brought back to life as an AI, they disagreed more often than not. She wanted him to overwrite Dr. Carlhagen and return to his own body, but he kept refusing. And now this issue. "For what that woman did to Vin, she deserves to die. A thousand times over."

"You're beginning to sound like Belle."

Dajeet covered her mouth, but didn't manage to stifle an uncharacteristic giggle.

Jacey glared at her. The giggle cut off, but a tear escaped Dajeet's eye. She wisely turned away, but gauging from her trembling shoulders she was unable—or unwilling—to get her poor sense of humor under control.

"Belle?" Jacey said to the reader, sweetening her tone despite the bitter irritation tightening her throat. "May I please speak with you?"

"How can I refuse when you ask so nicely?" Belle responded as her face flickered into existence next to Vaughan's. Jacey needed an extra second to realize the face really belonged to Belle. The pale skin and delicate features were the same, as was her nearly white hair. But, like Jacey, the AI Belle no longer wore her hair in the school's regulation ponytail. Instead it hung loose on one side, the other tucked behind her ear. And, most shocking of all, she wore a glorious blue hibiscus bloom behind that ear. It gave a softness to the girl's usually icy blue eyes. The habitually pinched mouth had relaxed, as well. And her lips held a sensual blush, as if she'd just been soundly kissed.

It was the mocking notes in Belle's voice that reassured Jacey that she was speaking to her fellow Shark. Despite outward appearances, Jacey doubted Belle had changed all that much since being reborn an AI. Maybe a little. Maybe.

Vaughan had said Belle was learning to love herself, but it seemed an odd notion to Jacey. For their past seventeen years together, Belle hadn't shown anything but self-centered disdain for anyone who *wasn't* her.

Except that wasn't entirely true.

Belle had sacrificed herself to save Jacey.

"Did you just want to see my pretty face," Belle asked, "or did you want something else?"

Dajeet fled around the side of the bus, but her choking giggles carried to Jacey's ears.

"I've explained the situation to Vaughan, but he is hung up on a moral dilemma. I thought you might be more reasonable. You see, we have a boat and we are loading it with supplies, and soon we will be out to sea. But we need a destination. We need to install Elizabeth as an AI so we can ask her where her private island is."

"And what do you want me to do? I don't know how to install that woman on this server."

"I want you to beat Vaughan into submission."

Belle's laugh was so melodic that Jacey had to blink and make sure she was actually seeing it happen. Two rows of perfectly white teeth flashed and Belle's eyes squinted in unguarded mirth. Even Vaughan seemed shocked by the display.

"I'll talk to him," Belle said. "But I can make no promises. He's thick-headed."

"On that, I agree whole-heartedly."

"I'm right here," Vaughan said. "You're talking about me right in front of *me*. A pretty bad strategy."

"We'll see," Jacey said. Once Belle set her mind to do something, very little could stop her.

A tug on Jacey's shirt drew her attention. Livy stood behind her.

"I need to get back to work," Jacey said to Vaughan and Belle. "I don't have my reader, so once Elizabeth is installed, have someone come find me. I want to talk to her."

"Don't concern yourself with it," Belle said. Her voice had returned to its customary iciness. "I'll get the information we need."

Jacey was about to argue, but Belle disappeared in a swirl of white particles.

"You'd better go, Vaughan," Jacey said. "You don't want Belle too far ahead of you, whatever she's up to."

"She's already arguing with another couple instances of me." He grimaced and dissolved in a flash of fire.

Jacey turned to Livy and gave her a hug. She pressed a kiss into the mop of blond curls. Mimicking Jacey, Livy had abandoned the ponytail as well. "What have you got for me?"

Petite for her age, the Dolphin might have been mistaken for a Scion a year or two younger. Except for those wide eyes, green as palm fronds. They held a look of mature wisdom, giving off a sense of confidence not unlike Sensei's.

Livy was all seriousness as she handed a slip of paper to Jacey. "Since you lost your reader, I decided to practice my writing skills with a pen. I can't believe people used to have to do that to just record information they wanted to remember. They must have walked around with their hands curled up like claws from writing all the time."

Jacey scanned the paper without really reading. "No unusual behavior from our suspects?"

"Not really." Livy turned to frown in the direction of the mango grove. "Unless you count hiding in the mango grove to avoid carrying stuff."

"Let me guess. Apollo and Mickey?"

"You got it on the first try," she said with mock surprise. Apollo was nine, a Dolphin like Livy. Mickey was a year older, which made him a Pelican. Both were way too young to be Mr. Justin.

"I'll mention it to Sensei. He can take out some of his fury on them, give them a workout they won't soon forget."

Livy chuckled. "I want to be there and watch. All the boys need an extra hard workout, if you ask me."

Jacey agreed. With the boys' Nine leaders dead, injured, or busy interrogating Dr. Carlhagen, they didn't have the guidance they needed. That would change once they were all aboard the boat. Once Vaughan was back.

But even something as straightforward as restoring Vaughan to his body had proven frustratingly difficult. Setting aside Vaughan's stupid objections, there was still Greta to deal with. The AI in charge of transfers had flatly refused to overwrite Dr. Carlhagen and Senator Bentilius. Jacey thought she could leverage a bit more cooperation from the medical AI once she had control of the AI servers. Madam LaFontaine—the master persona of all the School's AIs—understood self-preservation. Jacey didn't relish making threats, but she would. With the time constraints they faced, expediency always won out.

"I'm hungry," Livy said.

"Mother Tyeesha took charge of the kitchens. I'm sure there will be plenty."

Livy started away, then stopped. "There was one thing Sang did that I found odd. I didn't write it down because it wasn't precisely suspicious."

Sang was the prime suspect on Jacey's list of people Mr. Justin might have overwritten. He was the oldest boy, and he didn't have an alibi for the time period when the transfer had taken place. "What did he do?"

"When Humphrey and Tytus went to the medical ward a little while ago, he stared at the door for a long time."

"Where was he?"

"Across the quad, leaning against one of the tree trunks. I thought he was just avoiding work like Apollo and Mickey, but that didn't really make sense because he's not like that. He stared at the medical ward a long time and then went back to Boys' Hall."

"You said he was leaning against a tree trunk. Would you say that he was hiding behind it?"

"No." She screwed her face up as she reconsidered it. "Maybe. I don't know."

All the other suspects were younger. Obu, Horace, Kirk, and Pedro. She doubted Mr. Justin would have overwritten anyone younger than thirteen. Even fourteen seemed a stretch. No. She was certain it was Sang, Obu, or Kirk. Horace was out, since he was too sadistic. Unless Mr. Justin was a much better actor that she thought he was.

"Thank you, Livy. I'll study these notes in a bit. I need to see to something before we take this bus load to the docks."

Livy dashed off to the dining hall. Even once out of sight, Jacey felt connected to the child, as if an invisible cord ran from the Dolphin's heart to Jacey's. They'd gone through some terrible things together, but Livy had always been a rock of calm and unusual common sense.

Jacey wanted all the Scions to be safe, but above all, she wanted to protect Livy. And she would.

No matter what it took.

4

ABOMINABLE BOY

Dr. Carlhagen hated the silence in his holding room.

He could hear his own heartbeat, his own breath. It reminded him of his father's study, which the old man had decreed a noise-free zone. Dr. Carlhagen had rarely spent time in that dark-paneled, leather-upholstered, antelope-head-decorated gloom. He'd hated how the grandfather clock tocked out the seconds in that stuffy space. An infinity of quietude interrupted by the occasional rub of fabric on leather as his father shifted in his armchair, or the tap of his fleshy finger on a reading tablet.

Dr. Carlhagen recalled an apt quote from *Moby Dick* his father had often recited. "There is no quality in this world that is not what it is merely by contrast. Nothing exists in itself." That had been Melville's nearly incomprehensible phraseology.

But it was true. Sound required silence, cold required warm, open required closed. Old, young. Life, death.

Freedom required imprisonment. Action required waiting.

Waiting. Dr. Carlhagen chafed under the chains of waiting. His life to this point had been action, action, action. Invent the mind transfer technology, build the school, sell the Scions, conduct the transfers. Do. Do. Do.

And why? Because Dr. Carlhagen knew that the world favored only half of each this-requires-that calculation. It valued love over hate, peace over war, amity over enmity. People didn't want balance. And as a result they got more hate, war, and enmity.

So he had chosen to act to offset all the fools out there who had chosen to wait. And here he was, on the verge of claiming all he'd ever wanted. Power to change the world and make it perfect. Yes, people would suffer, people would die, people would be treated unjustly.

But only for a while. In the grand scheme, he was doing the world a favor.

A door in the hallway slammed shut, startling him.

Perhaps Mr. Justin had come to free him at last.

Dr. Carlhagen swung his legs down from the gurney and got to his feet. He hadn't decided yet whether to throttle his old butler to death or to pat him on the back. Truth was, he could still use the man. Not that he could ever truly trust him again.

The light in the hall came on.

The decision came instantly, informed by a raw hatred for Mr. Justin more than any practical consideration. The andleprixen had calmed his shaking hands, but it didn't prevent him from clenching his fists.

The door swung open. Disappointment flushed through Dr. Carlhagen's mind, causing him to sag. It wasn't Mr. Justin at all. It was Humphrey.

"Ah. It's my failure of a Scion," he said.

Humphrey stopped well out of arms' reach. Another Scion, Tytus, stood in the hall, holding the door open.

"You sound disappointed, father. Were you expecting someone else?"

"I'm not your father," Dr. Carlhagen snapped. Humphrey smirked as if he'd won a victory. Dr. Carlhagen forced himself to relax. The boy had wanted to provoke him.

"I know, I know," Humphrey said. "I'm just your pathetic clone. If it's any consolation, I'm as disappointed by our relationship as you are. More, probably."

Dr. Carlhagen returned to the gurney and sat on the edge. "I'd invite you to sit down, but my accommodations are a bit spartan. Perhaps we could go up to the hacienda and continue this irritating conversation."

"I'd be delighted, but I'm afraid I'll have to decline." Humphrey stepped forward, hands clasped behind him in a gesture Dr. Carlhagen recognized as his own. The boy's haughty expression was not his, though. Dr. Carlhagen had always been humble and polite.

"I have a few questions for you," Humphrey said.

"I will not answer."

"What's in the locked room in the wine cellar?"

Dr. Carlhagen snickered and leaned back on his elbows, legs dangling off the side of the gurney, making a show of not answering.

"What's the code to unlock the door?"

"Why should I answer these questions? You offer nothing in return."

Humphrey dug into the pocket of his white trousers and pulled forth a white plastic bottle. He shook it, letting the pills rattle. Andleprixen.

Against his will, Dr. Carlhagen sat up straight. "The whole bottle."

Humphrey popped the cap and dumped out a tablet. He licked his fingertip, dabbed up a pill, and held it so Dr. Carlhagen could see it. "One pill."

Dr. Carlhagen folded his arms across his chest, hoping it would signal intransigence. In truth, he was trying to keep from reaching out and taking the one measly pill. "Five pills."

If he hadn't had the pill Mr. Justin had given him, he would have already eaten the one Humphrey proffered. But he knew in a couple hours the need would return. If he could get a few tablets now, he'd have enough to carry him through the escape.

Humphrey's eyes narrowed in suspicion. "Give me the code for the door, and I'll give you two."

"Five."

Humphrey turned for the door. Tytus stepped aside to let him through.

"Wait," Dr. Carlhagen called. "I'll take the two."

Smiling like a Dolphin who'd gotten an extra serving of ice cream, Humphrey bounced back into the room.

Dr. Carlhagen held out his hand. "Give them to me."

The boy didn't move. "The code first."

"Very well. 3247-5181."

"Put that in your reader, Tytus. I want to make sure we have it recorded."

"My pills." Dr. Carlhagen made a hand-them-over motion with his fingers.

"Once I verify the code, you'll get your two pills."

"Damn you!" Dr. Carlhagen cried.

Humphrey leaned back in mock surprise. "Oh. You wanted the pills immediately? I suppose we can negotiate that."

Clamping his jaw shut, Dr. Carlhagen tried to stare holes in Humphrey's face.

Tricked! The boy played me like a piano.

Keeping his voice even was a Herculean task, but he managed it. "What else would you like to know?"

Looking into Humphrey's cornflower blue eyes was like looking into a magic mirror that showed him his youthful self. And though it pained Dr. Carlhagen to admit it, he discovered in Humphrey's stare a part of himself he'd retained all these years—love of defeating one's enemy.

Humphrey scraped the pill off his fingertip and into the bottle. He swirled the container so Dr. Carlhagen could hear all the lovely little pills inside. "Let's see. What else would I like to know?" His expression brightened. "I've got it! Tell me where the new Scion School is."

The shock of the question broke through Dr. Carlhagen's hard-won demeanor of calm. His lips parted and a question tumbled out. "Who told you about that?"

Tytus cleared his throat. "Do we really have time for this? I say we leave him here. Jacey says it's time to leave for—" The boy's eyes cut to Dr. Carlhagen. Clearly he didn't want Dr. Carlhagen to hear whatever he'd planned to say.

Humphrey shook the bottled again. "Tell you what, dear Progenitor of mine, think about my question while I'm gone. If your answer is satisfactory, I'll give you this whole bottle of pills."

He didn't wait for Dr. Carlhagen to respond before leaving. The door swung shut and the lock snicked into place.

Abominable boy! Hateful villainous cretin!

Dr. Carlhagen leapt from the gurney and slammed into the door. "Come back here! I'll beat you into sludge, you craven lout!"

The door across the hall swung closed as Humphrey

and Tytus went into Senator Bentilius's room. Dr. Carlhagen continued to scream and beat at the door. The rage cleared as pain broke through. His hand ached from the blows he'd rained upon the steel door. Breath rasping in his lungs, Dr. Carlhagen stumbled to the gurney and threw himself upon it.

Pleasure requires pain.

Vengeance requires insult.

"Where is that cowardly Mr. Justin?" he rasped. "What is taking him so long?"

Oh, how Dr. Carlhagen was going to relish his return to St. Vitus. He would crush this childish insurrection. Some Progenitors would lose their Scions, of that he was sure.

As for Humphrey . . . Dr. Carlhagen had thought he might sell the boy to some aging customer who couldn't wait for a Scion to mature. No longer. That boy would suffer. And suffer. And suffer. And only once Dr. Carlhagen had tired of hearing the boy beg for mercy would he be allowed to die.

5

WHAT'S GEORGIA?

The senator's room was the same as Dr. Carlhagen's. Gurney along one wall; cabinets along the other, holding bandages, syringes, antiseptic wipes, and latex gloves. But unlike Dr. Carlhagen's room, which smelled of stale sweat, the senator's held a sweet odor.

Humphrey recognized it. "Who gave you your perfume, Maxine?"

It took concentration to use the senator's first name. Not because he was unused to it. He'd used it plenty during the very uncomfortable dinner he'd hosted for the senator in the hacienda.

The reason using the name Maxine was so difficult now was because the girl lounging on her gurney like a bored cat was Belle.

Or had been Belle, before the senator had overwritten her.

The senator's possession of Belle's body had made a

few noticeable changes. Most obvious was that she wore Belle's straight white hair down, rather than in the school-regulation ponytail. It flowed close to her cheeks and across her black uniform top like a frozen waterfall. Belle's eyes, always blue and icy, had thawed. Somehow, the senator's natural expression broke through, heating Belle's gaze with a bottomless and shameless lust.

At least that heat wasn't directed at Humphrey anymore. He'd been able to fend off her eighty-year-old hands in the wine cellar, but now that she was in Belle . . .

No. Even in her new and beautiful body, Humphrey had no interest in her. For one, he loved Jacey. For two, he couldn't think of Belle as anything but a sister, and a not very fond one at that.

The senator stretched and shifted a narrow-eyed look to Tytus. "How old are you, boy?"

"Fifteen," Tytus answered before Humphrey could silence him.

A lascivious smile blossomed on the senator's lips. "Give it a few years, and you'll be ripe as a Georgia peach in June."

"What's Georgia?" Tytus asked.

"Never mind," Humphrey said, stepping close to the senator's gurney. She sat up and leaned her back against the wall, gazing up at him with such a sullen look Humphrey blinked. The expression reminded him so much of Summer, the senator's real Scion.

But Summer had escaped the campus before the senator's arrival, thanks to Jacey. They had planned to hide and wait it out, as the senator had inoperable brain cancer and very little time left to live.

Dr. Carlhagen had foiled that plan, captured Jacey, and brought her to the campus and offered her body for the senator to overwrite. Inexplicably, Belle had traded places with Jacey.

The senator's childish pout transformed into a thin smile. "Now that you see me like this, I bet you wish you could have me. But I have no interest in you. Not now that I've enjoyed the luscious young body Dr. Carlhagen transferred into."

Humphrey's hand shot out in time to catch Tytus, who leapt toward the senator, eyes blazing with rage. Dr. Carlhagen had transferred into Vaughan. And like everyone else, Tytus had loved Vaughan.

"No," Humphrey warned, "We must not injure Belle's body."

"Why not? Belle's not in there anymore. Belle's an—"

"Enough!"

The last thing Humphrey needed was Tytus blurting out that Belle was an AI. They would give the senator no information she might use later. Just as they'd kept knowledge of the bus and the boat from Dr. Carlhagen.

The senator grinned at Tytus. "I like your vim, young one. Perhaps I'll have Dr. Carlhagen overwrite you in a few years. Variety is the spice of life, after all."

Humphrey shoved Tytus back toward the door. "Don't move, or I'll have Sensei assign you a burpee and deadlift combo you won't soon forget."

He turned back the senator. "I have news for you, Maxine. Dr. Carlhagen has no interest in you beyond the physical pleasures of the moment. He is obsessed with Jacey. So much so he forgets himself and calls her by her Progenitor's name. 'Jacqueline! Jacqueline!' But Jacey hates him, even in his new body. That's why he wanted you to overwrite her. Because then he could at least possess her body."

The senator's pale throat flushed red. "My backup military force will be here soon, boy. I look forward to seeing your broken body at my feet. I hope you'll have the strength to beg for mercy."

Dr. Carlhagen and Maxine were well suited for each other, it seemed. They both intended to revel in his painful demise. Fortunately, they were his prisoners.

"I'm unconcerned about your pathetic squad of guards. If they are anything like the ones you brought with you, we'll handle them easily. Did you know your guards are all either dead or strapped to beds in the medical ward?"

The senator pushed away from the wall and slid forward on the bunk, knees pressing against Humphrey's thighs. He stepped back.

"What time is it, boy?"

"What does it matter?"

"What time is it?"

Humphrey knew the question was a trap, but he didn't see where it was leading. He decided not to answer.

"No matter," the senator said, pushing off the gurney and onto her feet. She took two slinky strides to come close to Humphrey. He tensed, but didn't want to fall into a fighting stance. He didn't think the senator would attack him. She could not defeat both him and Tytus, and a person with a mind like hers would fear reprisals. He stood his ground.

She brought her hands to his shoulders, as if preparing to pull him into an embrace. "I want to be clear with you. I'm not talking about a helicopter and seven bodyguards. I'm talking about an invasion. Hundreds of soldiers coming by air and sea." Her right hand slid down his chest and patted the muscle over his heart. "You should run. Perhaps hide in the forest like my Scion did. You might get a few extra days of life that way. You have no Progenitor waiting, so you are—what's the word? Oh yes. You are useless."

Forcing a smile onto his lips, Humphrey put his hands on the sides of the senator's head. Her eyes widened and she tried to pull back, but he held her there, pinning her gaze with his own. Through gritted teeth he said, "Thank you, Maxine. That's just what I wanted to know."

With a quick jerk he brought her nose close to his, relishing the fear that transformed the pale face. He had no desire to injure her, not physically. But he didn't want her to know that.

"You've been a good girl." He kissed her nose and released her. She stumbled back against the gurney and swiped a hand across her face.

"Bastard," she breathed. "You're just like your—"

"Careful!" Humphrey said, holding up a finger. "Insult me too much and your backup force might have to scour the island to find all your limbs."

He spun and motioned for Tytus to open the door.

"You'll die," screamed the senator. "Both of you! I don't care who your Progenitors are."

Humphrey laughed and patted Tytus on the shoulder as they left the room. He made sure the door was locked and turned to find Dr. Carlhagen's face pressed to the window of his holding room.

Humphrey held up the bottle of pills and waved it. Without another word, he headed out of the medical ward.

He'd gotten some information. Dr. Carlhagen had given him the code for the locked room in the wine cellar. And the senator had revealed the scope of her backup force.

"Jacey was right, Tytus. We've got to get off this island. Come with me to the hacienda. I want to open that door."

Even with an invasion imminent, he felt lighter than he had since he'd kissed Jacey the first time. Manipulating Dr. Carlhagen and the senator had been easy, as both were susceptible to saying too much when they were angry.

It wasn't how he wanted to be, but it was expedient. And at this moment, that was all that mattered.

6

———

A LEVER LONG ENOUGH

"This is the last load," Wanda said to Jacey, brushing her hands together. "Unless you want to give up your seat on the bus."

"That won't be necessary," Jacey said, eyes scanning along the windows of the long vehicle. It appeared to be packed floor-to-ceiling now. "We'll load in some more on the final trip when we take all the Scions to the boat."

Leslie huffed forward, a glaze of sweat on her brow. She dumped her sack of rice on the ground. "And when will that be? I thought it was urgent to get off the island."

"Soon," Jacey said.

Leslie's tone reminded Jacey how wonderful it was to have Wanda as the Second of her Nine. Leslie had always been—Jacey searched for a gracious term—unextraordinary.

Not that Leslie was ignorant. Like all the Scions, she was intelligent. It just seemed that when Leslie wasn't in class or doing an assignment, she didn't have many thoughts at all. The stress of recent events had brought out a different side of the girl, though. Leslie was a now a bit of a complainer.

Dajeet and Bethancy came along under their burdens and circled around Leslie, who was standing with her hands on her hips staring at the bag she needed to carry four more meters to get it to the bus.

"Where's Sensei?" Leslie asked. "I thought he had to drive this thing."

"He'll be here when I need him."

Leslie frowned at the vehicle and absently patted the coppery bun she'd made of her hair. She'd always been a bit vain. "I don't see why we didn't load all this stuff yesterday. We could be taking all the Scions to the boat now."

Jacey sought patience and found none. "Because I said so!"

Wanda returned at that moment. Her brows knitted together and she flicked a stray lock of red hair—almost orange compared to Leslie's—out of her eyes. She gave Jacey a questioning look, clearly not approving of her tone of voice.

"I'm sorry, Leslie," Jacey said, patting the girl's shoulder. "I'm just tired, managing all this."

"So what's the answer to the question?" Dajeet asked. "Why did we lose a whole night if things are so urgent?"

A fair question, and they deserved an answer. "Because Summer is trying to figure out how to drive the boat."

The reaction that followed was as bad as Jacey expected. Mouths dropped open. Not in surprise, but in disgusted disbelief.

"You're kidding!"

"Summer?"

"She's just a Spider!"

The last was from Bethancy, who at fifteen was only

one year older than Summer.

Leslie folded her arms across her chest. She had prominent cheeks and expressive lips that were usually on the verge of disapproval, no matter what was going on. Unlike Belle, she didn't try to hide her feelings and fail. She *broadcasted* her feelings and succeeded. "Why on Earth is Summer even on the boat right now?"

Jacey understood the girls' confusion and irritation. Just days ago she would have thought Summer's assignment utterly absurd, too. But once Jacey had helped Summer escape campus and had spent time in the rainforest with her, she'd learned that Summer had a gift for all things mechanical. The girl had crafted water bowls out of leaves, designed a snare out of wire and caught a mongoose, and she'd started and driven a motorized skiff they'd found at the docks.

"She's as good tinkering with machines as I am memorizing Shakespeare," Jacey said. "I know it's hard to believe, but I've seen her do it."

Leslie's skeptical look deepened as her eyelids half-concealed her pupils. "If she's so good, then she's had plenty of time to figure out how to move the boat."

"You haven't seen the boat." Jacey gestured to the bus. "This thing will fit on the top deck with a lot of room to spare. Summer says she knows the principles of the boat's operation, but she doesn't know how it behaves under power, or how to navigate certain underwater obstacles to get out to sea."

"What about Orson?" Wanda asked. She had none of Leslie's whininess, but she still seemed doubtful about Summer. "He drove the boat here, didn't he?"

"He won't cooperate."

Orson was Mr. Justin's brother and partner in the scheme to kidnap the Scions from under Dr. Carlhagen's nose. Together they had planned to gouge the Progenitors for more money than they'd already paid. That, or sell the Scions to the highest bidder.

Fortunately, Jacey and the others had been ready for them. Orson and his two thugs were strapped to cots in the medical ward, but so far Orson had refused to help the Scions at all.

"He should be *made* to cooperate," Leslie said. "Let Horace go in there. He'll get some results."

Wanda blanched at Leslie's suggestion, and Bethancy and Dajeet stared at her in horror. Horace was problematic. He'd always gotten thrills killing lizards and bugs, something Sensei had brought to an end with a string of horrendous workouts as punishment. But during the fight with Senator Bentilius's bodyguard Alice, Horace had gotten ahold of Alice's knife.

A horrific image flashed in Jacey's mind of Horace gleefully stabbing Alice to death, eyes bright with bloodlust.

"I'm not willing to torture the man," she said finally.

"I didn't say torture him," Leslie protested. She dropped her arms to her sides and looked to the other girls for support. "But you can threaten to do it, can't you? Orson won't know you don't really intend to follow through."

"Horace would be very convincing delivering threats like that," Dajeet said, looking away from Jacey. "But I know someone even scarier."

Sensei stalked out of his villa and strode toward her. Jacey smiled at the sight of him. With his face, burdened with rage, he'd be a far more intimidating presence than Horace. She wouldn't have thought to ask him, since such techniques were counter to his teachings. Except when it came to Dr. Carlhagen.

"You two," Jacey said, taking Leslie and Wanda aside,

"go back to Girls' Hall. Make sure everyone showers and changes into clean clothes. Then go to the Dining Hall and help Mother Tyeesha and her staff keep the children entertained."

"Why don't *you* go babysit them?" Leslie demanded.

"Because she's going with me to the boat," Sensei said.

This declaration cut off all argument. Jacey dismissed Leslie and Wanda. She caught Bethancy and Dajeet trying to leave, too, and stopped them with a raised eyebrow and a shake of her head. "I need you two to come along to help unload the bus."

Their shoulders sagged, but they climbed onto the bus.

Jacey started toward the medical ward. Humphrey had wasted enough time interrogating Dr. Carlhagen and Senator Bentilius. If he was coming with them, he needed to come now.

He came out before she got halfway there. She waved him to her. "Come on. The bus is loaded."

He trotted over, Tytus on his heels like a shadow. "I'm not going."

"What?"

His grin told her everything she needed to know. "You got the code! How?"

Humphrey shook a bottle of andleprixen. In a fair imitation of Socrates, he said: "Give me a lever long enough and a fulcrum on which to place it, and I shall move the world. Absent that, give me drugs and an addict and I'll get the unlock code for a mysterious door."

Jacey smiled. "I didn't know Archimedes said that last part."

Humphrey snorted and wrapped Jacey in his arms. "I might have added a little something of my own to the quote."

The embrace was welcome, but filled Jacey with a flush

of sadness. She had to get going. And there was so much left to do. "I'm considering using a different kind of leverage to get Orson to cooperate. Did you happen to find out where the other Scion School is?"

Humphrey's grin fell. "Not yet. But the old man is breaking. I don't think it'll be much longer before he starts talking."

Jacey pulled free of his arms. "I don't suppose you thought to ask him where Elizabeth's island is."

"No. I didn't want him thinking about why I want to know. Isn't Vaughan looking into that?"

Jacey didn't bother answering beyond a noncommittal shake of her head. She'd have to check in with Belle soon to see if she'd made any progress twisting Vaughan's arm.

She went up on tiptoe and kissed Humphrey, taking momentary refuge in the warmth of his lips. Pulling away, she started toward the bus.

Humphrey caught her elbow. "Wait. I got something from the senator, too."

Jacey raised an eyebrow. "I thought she was too handsy for you." His story of the senator's amorous advances before the transfer had left Jacey panting for air she'd laughed so hard.

Humphrey ignored the comment. "She told me her contingency force is hundreds strong and will come by air and by sea."

Her lips parted, mouth going dry. "Hundreds?" It wasn't a specific number, but at that scale it didn't need to be. The Scions could never fight off a force of even ten armed soldiers.

The news sent her trotting to the bus. Dajeet and Bethancy sat together on one of the bench seats, their knees pressing to their chins due to the bags of quinoa on the floor beneath their feet. Kirk and Conrad, a Crab who was big for his age, had climbed atop two mattresses so close to the ceiling they had to lie on their stomachs. Only their faces peeked out.

"Let's go, Sensei," Jacey said.

He gunned the motor and the bus lurched forward. He turned a huge circle in the quad and headed for the gate. Jacey sat in the only open spot left in the huge machine, a wicker chair stolen from the hacienda and placed right next to the driver's seat.

As they rolled through the gate, she told Sensei what she'd learned from Humphrey. Whatever the martial arts master thought of the news, he kept his expression blank. The bus's engine suddenly strained harder though, and the island whipped by a bit faster.

They rode in silence for a while, mostly out of necessity as Sensei concentrated on guiding the bus up the precipitous switchbacks climbing the southern hills.

On the descent, the road was wider and straighter. Sensei glanced at Jacey, seeming like he wanted to say something. When he didn't and turned his eyes back to the road, Jacey pulled out the slip of notes Livy had given her.

Written in a childish but neat hand were the names of each Scion suspected of being Mr. Justin.

"Has your spy network uncovered any clues?" Sensei asked. His eyes flicked to the round mirror overhead that let the driver see everything behind him. Jacey doubted the others could hear their conversation over the rumble of the bus.

Jacey chortled at the term "spy."

"Nothing. Obu, Kirk, Constantine, and Pedro were all busy loading the bus. Livy did mention Sang loafing by a tree in the quad. She said he stared at the medical ward when Humphrey and Tytus went in to question Dr. Carlhagen."

"Anything else?"

"No. But that's the most we've got. It could be any of them. Mr. Justin knows we know he transferred. He's trying very hard to fit in."

"That's his greatest strength. Even in his old body you hardly ever knew he was there most of the time."

"The thing I can't figure out is what he's planning to do. As soon as he does anything out of the ordinary, we'll be all over him."

They were quiet for a while, and the rocking of the bus made Jacey very drowsy. She hadn't slept more than three hours in the past forty-eight.

Just as she had nodded off, Sensei spoke. His voice was quiet, but thick. "Thank you, Jacey."

She turned her heavy eyes on him. "For what?"

"Back there, when you stopped me from going into the medical ward to help Humphrey question Dr. Carlhagen. You reminded me of who I am. What my principles are." He kept his eyes ahead, but his lips pressed hard together and Jacey saw something unsettled in his profile, in the way his nostrils flared.

"Dr. Carlhagen deserves to die," Jacey said. "He deserves worse. But not while he's in Vaughan's body."

After a long pause, Sensei said, "Many people deserve to die. So many I doubt I'll live long enough to enjoy justice when it finally comes."

"Does one enjoy justice? Isn't that really just revenge?"

Sensei laughed and nodded in concession. "You always draw such fine distinctions, girl. Perhaps when this is all over you can be a lawyer or a philosopher."

Jacey settled herself deeper into the chair. "When this is all over? We don't even have a place to go yet."

They didn't even know if they could get off this island.

7

OUR BELOVED HEADMASTER

Humphrey typed the numbers into the keypad next to the steel door in Dr. Carlhagen's wine cellar. His breath heaved from running up the path. His heart slammed with anticipation.

Nothing happened.

"Read the numbers to me again," he ordered Tytus, his voice booming under the arched concrete ceiling.

Tytus rolled his eyes. "Three two four seven five one eight one."

Humphrey pressed the plastic buttons on the keypad and waited.

"Maybe you need to press the red or green one afterward," Tytus suggested.

Humphrey tried the code two more times, but nothing happened. "I should have known the old man would lie."

Tytus lowered his reader and studied the keypad. "Maybe he just remembered it wrong. This doesn't seem like a place Dr. Carlhagen would come very often."

That was one explanation, Humphrey supposed. Tytus

was a bit naïve, though. Not his fault. He hadn't been directly involved with the old man and his manipulations and cruelty. "I'll have to go back to our beloved headmaster and see if he realized his mistake."

Humphrey glanced up to the shadows above the wine racks behind him where his reader leaned against the wall, camera facing the door. He'd left it there a few days ago, hoping that Mr. Justin would come to the room.

He considered taking it with him but decided against it. There was still time. If the room held anything important, he was sure Mr. Justin would make a move to collect it. When the time came to leave for once and for all, Humphrey would come down and grab it.

"Let's go, Tytus."

"Are we going back to see Dr. Carlhagen?"

"No. Let him stew for a while. He knows he gave me a bad code. He probably wants me to come running back so he can gloat over his tiny victory."

"What are we going to do?"

"Let's head down to Boys' Hall and make sure everyone is ready to depart."

Tytus started for the stairs. Humphrey followed along, running his hand along the wine racks, wondering if the senator's contingency force would ransack the place.

Probably. He hoped it gave them the worst headache of their lives.

8

———

APHRODITE

The murmuring among the Scions in the back stilled as the bus emerged from the thick canopy of the rainforest and into the clearing around the docks. Soft cries of amazement filled the bus as the Scions spotted the boat. Though Jacey had seen it before, she couldn't help but smile at the sight of it.

"It's humongous," Bethancy said breathlessly.

Sensei gave a soft laugh as he turned the bus onto a concrete pier jutting into the bay. The boat's rusty hull towered above them like the face of a steel cliff. "This old scow is nothing. Wait until you see a tanker or a cruise ship."

"What's that machine on the other side?" Tytus asked, pointing to a truss tower angling over the pier. Cables ran up the structure and dangled from a pulley at the top. A hook hung from the cable, so heavy it barely stirred in the stiff wind coming off the sea.

"A crane," Jacey said. "It's going to lift the bus onto the boat."

Sensei brought the bus to a stop between the crane and the boat. The Scions tumbled out the door, all pointing and shouting at once as they took in the boat. Jacey smiled wanly at Sensei as she stepped down the stairs and onto the concrete.

The boat stretched forty meters along the pier; the top deck rail was ten meters above. Ropes as thick as Jacey's arm drooped from round ports in the side and curved where they wrapped around iron bollards embedded into the concrete. The hull pressed tight against the pier, cushioned by orange, balloon-like bumpers mashed between steel and concrete.

When Jacey had first come to see the boat, she'd walked to the very end of the pier and looked back at the rear of the vessel, expecting to see the motors. She'd been surprised to learn from Summer that they were internal to the boat, with huge propellers deep underwater jutting from the end of the keel. But she'd discovered something else there. The ship's name in block letters, each as tall as she was: *Aphrodite.* The Greek goddess of love and beauty. Jacey doubted they could have selected a less appropriate name.

Far aft, an aluminum gangway ramped from the pier into to a gaping hatch in the hull. The boys raced toward it, but Sensei whistled them to a stop. "Conrad, come help me rig the bus hoist."

"Do you need my assistance, too?" Jacey asked. "I'd like to go speak with Summer right away."

The martial arts master glanced at the bus. "I need spotters on deck for when we lift the bus. Could you guide Kirk and Dajeet up there and give Dajeet the walkie-talkie?"

Jacey beckoned to the two Scions and headed for the gangway. Bethancy and Conrad stayed to help Sensei rig the straps and chains under the bus that would then connect to the huge iron hook dangling from the crane. The idea of lifting the entire bus onto the boat still made Jacey queasy. Summer had assured Jacey that the crane's steel cable could support the weight. It made no sense, but Jacey trusted Summer's judgment. Besides, Orson had obviously used the machine to get the bus off the boat.

She guided Dajeet and Kirk into the dark interior of the boat, wrinkling her nose at the heavy smell of oil and diesel fuel that hung in the passageway.

Jacey scowled at the dingy plastic-paneled walls and ceiling. They'd probably been white in some distant epoch, but were now a urine-yellow. "Watch your step," she cautioned as she stepped over a puddle of hazy water.

"This is . . ." Dajeet's tone carried the gist of what she left unsaid. Disappointment. Disgust.

Kirk let out a huge sigh. "Can you guess what Sensei will be making us do while we're at sea?"

"Cleaning," Dajeet said.

The passageway narrowed in the distance. It spanned the entire length of the ship. Jacey took the first door to the left, where a companionway climbed to the upper decks. Their footsteps rang on the metal-grated staircase as they ascended, and the air freshened the higher they climbed.

Pushing through a swinging door, they came onto the top deck. Jacey squinted against sunlight glancing off the steel decking. Behind her stood a blocky structure Summer called "the bridge" which held the controls for piloting the boat. Metal-grated platforms stuck out from the side of the bridge, giving a view down to the deck fore and aft.

Directly ahead, the deck lay mostly empty, except for a smaller hoist mechanism mounted to the deck itself. To the left and right were rectangular hatches in the deck. Once opened, cargo could be lowered by the hoist into the cargo holds.

"Doesn't look like these sailors have ever heard of paint," Kirk said. "I'd be embarrassed to let things fall into such a state."

Jacey and Dajeet both glanced at him. Kirk had never been known for neatness.

"Sounds like you just volunteered for painting detail," Jacey said smiling. She meant it as a joke, but Kirk nodded and breathed deep through widened nostrils. The look was so serious she had to laugh.

Amazing how a few days of crisis could mature a person. And Kirk had transformed more than most. He'd gone from being the boy who helped hold Jacey down during Belle's "punishment" with the thornskipple to being one of the more dependable and thoughtful Scions on campus.

Jacey handed Dajeet her walkie-talkie. "Tell Sensei you're ready. I'm going down to talk to Summer."

She left the two Scions at the rail, looking down at the pier and the bus. Sensei, Conrad, and Bethancy had already gotten it rigged.

Shielding her eyes, Jacey studied the bridge, but glare on the windows kept her from seeing inside. She doubted Summer was up there, though.

A quick hike down the stairs and then aft led her to the engine compartment. The space was as big as the Scion School's dining hall, but with a ceiling so low Jacey had to duck to keep from smacking her head on the leg-thick pipes mounted to the ceiling. The sound of cursing, punctuated by the sharp clangs of a metal tool on a hollow metal object, came from starboard. Or was it port? Jacey couldn't remember. Didn't care, either.

She followed a metal-grated walkway toward the

sounds, amused at Summer's creative combinations of swear words. She found the girl glaring at a cylindrical tank with a domed top. A gauge attached to a short metal pipe stuck from the top of the dome. To avoid a tedious lecture, Jacey didn't ask what the tank was.

"Sensei is hoisting the bus aboard," Jacey said. "I brought a team along to unload and begin setting up bunks in the cargo hold."

Summer dropped a wrench into a beat-up red toolbox that had grimy and torn pictures of half-naked women taped to the inside of the lid. With a grease-blackened thumb, she tucked a few stray wisps of black hair into a filthy cap. The hat had once been green, Jacey thought. An emblem above the protruding bill in the front showed a leaping deer on a field of yellow. Beneath the image the words "John Deere" were embroidered in green thread.

In the shade of the oversized cap, Summer's sweltering brown eyes glistened. Her mouth, usually configured in a cute pout, had thinned to a bloodless slash of irritation. "It won't matter if we can't pilot this rusty old heap away from the island." She kicked the tank she'd been struggling with, producing a hollow bong. "It's a wonder it runs at all. Only one engine is working up to spec and all the repair equipment needs repair."

"Is that what you were doing? Fixing an engine?"

Summer's features relaxed as her mind engaged with the problem. "Fix? I'm nowhere near fixing that engine. I need to cut the bolts off this housing so I can see what the problem is."

"We don't have time for that," Jacey said, irritated by Summer's compulsion to optimize every mechanical device she came across. "What about piloting the boat? Do you think you can do it?"

"Of course I can," Summer snapped.

Jacey raised a warning eyebrow. Summer looked away before continuing, "The problem is not how to make it go forward or turn it left and right. The problem is *where* to turn it. Only an experienced pilot can get us out of this bay safely. If you leave it in my hands, there's at least a seventy percent chance I'll run it into a reef and tear a hole in the keel. You need to lean on Orson a bit more."

Jacey flashed back to Leslie's idea of sending Horace in to intimidate Orson. As much as she hated the idea, she didn't see a better way. Not with time running out.

But she wouldn't use Horace. She'd do it herself.

"I'll work on Orson. What else do you need?"

Summer let out a long sigh. "You'd better come with me."

9

ZERO REMORSE

In the computer-simulated version of the Scion School, time passed in weird fits and starts. It didn't bother Belle much. It was more of a curiosity for her now.

At the moment, she sat in the middle of the quad, legs crossed, taking long, deep breaths through her nose and exhaling more slowly through her mouth. It reminded her of the deep breathing exercises Sensei had Scions learn when they were young. She had never found the practice very valuable. But Vaughan insisted that if she were to get in touch with her true self, she needed to spend more time alone with herself.

But *not* thinking.

It didn't make any sense to her, but she trusted Vaughan. More importantly, she loved him. She hoped that one day he would love her back. And not in the brotherly way he did at the moment.

She opened her eyes and gazed to the western horizon, where the gloriously huge sun, glowing a fiery red and amber, had half-disappeared behind the hills. Its lush rays painted the white stucco of the campus buildings with a wash of topaz and russet. Vaughan had made the magnified sun for her. Fortunately, it gave off no more heat than it should.

With a thought, she stopped the sun where it was. Unless she or Vaughan changed it, the world would stay locked in perpetual sunset. The breeze would stay just as it was. Time would seem to freeze. If only she could *truly* stop time.

Inside of her chest, the pulse of impatience beat like a clock.

She suddenly knew the cause of her impatience, and it surprised her. She was worried about the Scions in the real world.

They had to get off the island before the senator's backup force arrived. She just hoped Humphrey would find her and Vaughan's computer server before he had to leave. She didn't relish being left behind, even though her day-to-day existence would be no different no matter where her server was.

Thinking of her reliance on computer hardware turned Belle's thoughts back to the more pressing problem at hand. Vaughan had refused to install Elizabeth on their server.

Belle had nearly changed Vaughan's mind. But he had one condition that Belle found utterly intolerable. Vaughan said he absolutely would not delete Elizabeth once they got the information Jacey needed. And that meant that Belle and Vaughan would have to share this existence for all eternity with a woman Belle hated on principle—a Progenitor who had overwritten Vin.

So Belle sat there, torn between an incomprehensible desire to help protect the Scions in the real world and her very clear and unmistakable jealousy to keep her isolation with Vaughan intact forever.

She decided to stand, and so by the next heartbeat she was standing. She no longer bothered with the in-between stages, the way Vaughan did. If the simulation gave her magic-seeming powers, why not enjoy them? With another thought, her hair was pulled back into a ponytail. She didn't prefer it that way, but she liked to dress and manage her hair to match her mood. Vaughan needed to see that she meant business.

She always knew where all the various Vaughans were in this world. Why he felt compelled to divide himself into so many instances, she didn't know. He claimed it helped him multitask. One Vaughan could be researching something, another could be exploring somewhere, another could be swimming. She had tried it herself, but found it very disconcerting to have all those copies of her mind wandering around the island and being aware of what all of them were experiencing.

"Vaughan?" she said into the air. He materialized in front of her, and she knew instantly that he was the only instance currently in existence.

"What have you decided, Belle?"

Seeing him made her chest ache. She wanted to reach up, pull his face close to hers, and kiss his lips and flow into him so that she wasn't even a separate entity. But she couldn't do that.

"Install Elizabeth," Belle said.

"You accept my condition?"

Belle drew in a deep meditative breath, held it, and even in that moment still didn't know what her decision would be.

She spoke and discovered. "Yes, I accept. But I can't promise I'll always be nice to that woman."

Vaughan nodded, his face grave. She wondered if he felt any hatred toward Elizabeth in his own heart. She doubted it. Vaughan seemed incapable of hatred.

No, she mused. If anything, he probably feels sorry for the woman.

"I think we'll bring her back by the beach," Vaughan said.

Belle remembered her own rebirth, coming awake afloat, naked, in the water just off of Isaac's Beach. It had been a strange but peaceful experience. The realization of where she was and what she was had come very slowly, gently, because Vaughan had designed it that way for her.

He had never spoken about his own birth as an AI. That fact alone told her enough. It must have been jarring, perhaps excruciating. And though she had always been a loner, she knew that if she had come to life in this existence with no one to talk to, no other person around at all, she might have gone mad from loneliness.

"I'd like to walk there," Vaughan said.

"All right."

Vaughan held out his hand and she took it. They walked down the path toward Isaac's Beach, a route she'd taken countless times in her real life on St. Vitus.

"It's just as well you made the decision you did," Vaughan said. "Elizabeth is already there."

Belle yanked him to a stop. "You installed her before we talked?"

"Yes," Vaughan said.

Belle reached out with a sort of sixth sense, the one that told her where all the Vaughans were. She found a new mind, a new entity. She had never met Elizabeth in real life, but this new presence had a strangely familiar feel. One that felt like Vin.

She said as much to Vaughan, and he nodded sagely.

"It's like when someone you know walks into a room, but you're not looking. You know who it is by just the sound of their footsteps, or something in the air."

That was exactly what it was like.

They crossed the final stretch of path and out onto the promontory of Jacque's Point. From there, they saw a figure in the distance, small and naked, just trudging to shore, gazing around in wonder.

Belle's heart froze. "You brought her back as young. As Vin."

"Vin was Elizabeth's clone," Vaughan said. "That's how Elizabeth looks."

"But she should be an old woman. You're rewarding her for what she did."

Vaughan's brows bunched together. "You know as well as I do a person can appear however they want in this reality. I could bring her back as an old woman or a troll or a bird, but every person has her own concept of what she looks like. Elizabeth sees herself this way."

It was true. Belle knew it in her heart, but she felt the shadow of jealousy cloud her already unsettled mood. Perhaps Vaughan had wanted to bring this other girl here. Perhaps he had always found Vin more attractive.

But no, Vaughan knew who this woman was. She was a Progenitor, someone who had purchased a Scion to overwrite. He would never be attracted to such a person.

And yet . . . he stared down at the form, who had materialized a towel out of nothing and had begun wrapping it around herself. Just as Belle had done when she'd been reborn.

Belle couldn't read what was in Vaughan's gaze. She wasn't like Jacey, who pried into people's minds by analyzing their faces.

"Let's get this over with," she said. She no longer

wanted to walk. In a blink, she teleported a few meters from Vin. Vaughan appeared beside her less than a millisecond later.

This was not Vin, Belle reminded herself before she spoke. "Hello, Elizabeth, welcome to St. Vitus."

Elizabeth gave Belle and Vaughan a passing glance before her eyes turned up to the sky. She kept turning—gazing all around—taking in the surroundings. Finally, she asked Belle, "Where am I? I don't remember this beach."

Belle was about to answer, but Vaughan stepped forward, wearing a pleasant smile. He held out a hand to Elizabeth. She took it and gazed up at him with glistening green eyes. "My name is Vaughan," he said. "I was once a Scion at the Scion School at St. Vitus."

Elizabeth tried to jerk her hand away, but he kept hold of it. "Just relax," he said, voice soft yet earnest. "You are the Progenitor of a Scion named Vin. You came here to overwrite her, and you did."

Elizabeth turned her eyes to her own hand and body. "I'm young!" she said. "It worked!"

"It did," Vaughan said. "But you are not the Elizabeth who overwrote Vin. This world is a computer-simulated reality. You, Belle, and I—we are all artificial intelligences. Belle and I have brought you to life here to ask you a few questions."

Elizabeth's brow knitted in confusion. "I don't under-stand what you're saying."

Belle stepped forward, barely resisting the urge to yank Elizabeth's hand out of Vaughan's. "You are a computer simulation. I am a computer simulation." She flung her arm out. "This whole world is a computer simulation. We brought you here to ask you where your private island is. Where is it?"

"How do you know anything about—" Elizabeth

stopped. "The transfer machine. I remember Dr. Carlhagen explaining how the transfer machine worked. He said my old body would die. How can I be an artificial intelligence if my mind was transferred into another, younger, body?"

"Because the transfer machine control AI has a habit of making a copy of every Progenitor's mind," Belle explained. "Vaughan can access those copies. So here you are—born again. Now, where is your island?"

"I'm not telling you anything," Elizabeth said, snatching her hand out of Vaughan's and stumbling away from him. She drew the towel closer around her and crossed her arms across her chest. "Stay away from me. Where is Dr. Carlhagen?"

"He's not here," Belle said. "We're the only ones."

"I have to get out of here," Elizabeth said. "I have to get out. I want to be in my new body."

Vaughan waved his hands and a map appeared in them.

Elizabeth gaped, "How . . . ?"

He moved close to her and held the paper so she could see it. "This is a map of the Caribbean. Where is your island?"

She shook her head slowly. "The scale is too large. I can't . . ."

Belle circled round to look over their shoulders. The map zoomed in, centering on St. Vitus. "Can you see it now?"

Elizabeth's face grew grim and she said nothing.

"She's not going to tell us," Belle said to Vaughan.

"Why do you need to know?" Elizabeth demanded.

"Because in the real world the Scions are about to escape St. Vitus, and they need somewhere to go."

Elizabeth laughed. "And you think I'll help them do that?"

Vaughan dropped the map and it disappeared before reaching the ground. "I had hoped you would feel some sympathy for the Scions' plight. Especially now that you've met one of them and overwritten one of them."

"Why would she, Vaughan?" Belle said. "You restored Elizabeth from a state right before the transfer. She still wants to transfer. This woman has no remorse."

Vin raised an eyebrow and tilted her head back so she was looking at them down her nose. "She's right. I have zero remorse. Right now I'm quite upset. Let me speak with Dr. Carlhagen."

"Go ahead and find him," Vaughan said, walking away.

Belle was not content to let the woman simply refuse to tell them what they wanted to know. It was time to show the woman how the simulated world worked. For starters, she dropped the sun below the horizon.

Elizabeth gasped and nearly fell on her butt.

Belle grabbed her hair, then imagined them both two miles up.

And they were. The entirety of the island lay below them, a view not dissimilar to the map Vaughan had just shown Elizabeth. But they were not flying, nor were they standing on anything. They were just there.

Elizabeth's eyes bugged out and she shrieked. Wrapping her arms around Belle, she cried out. "Put me back on the ground."

Belle gave her the coldest smile she could manage. "Very well."

With a thought, Belle let Elizabeth fall. Arms flailing, hair flying, she tumbled toward the island far below. The wind tore the towel from around her body.

Belle closed her eyes and took a couple deep breaths. The screaming was barely audible.

She stopped Elizabeth's plummet and moved her onto the beach. An AI could pass out, apparently. That was interesting.

But not very useful.

Sighing, Belle gathered up the unconscious girl in a swaddle of air and pulled her along behind her.

"That was a bit excessive, Belle," Vaughan's voice spoke in her mind.

"Yes. I see that now." But it had been damned satisfying.

"Let her sleep it off. We'll get her to cooperate."

"Yes, Vaughan."

Belle knew Vaughan planned to reason with the woman. But Belle intended to take her right back up in the air. If necessary.

If Elizabeth was anything like Vin, it probably would be necessary.

10

I'M A SPIDER

The kitchen—which Summer insisted Jacey call the "galley"—was amidships on a middle deck, wedged between the infirmary and a cramped crew cabin. Each compartment was smaller than one of the hacienda's walk-in closets.

Flickering tube bulbs bathed the galley in harsh glare that gave a greenish cast to Summer's skin. A stainless steel counter ran along one wall; pots, cooking utensils, and a wooden block of knives, were lashed under elastic webbing, presumably to keep them from clattering to the floor in rough seas.

Opposite the counter stood a freezer and refrigerator. A gritty hum emanated from one of them.

"Is it supposed to sound like that?" Jacey asked.

Summer rolled her eyes. "No. The compressor unit is about to fail. The refrigerator is already out. I had to toss out some spoiled food." She waved a hand in front of her nose.

The state of the boat puzzled Jacey. There was no

evidence of maintenance anywhere. The engines weren't performing optimally, pipes leaked water in the passageways, and even food preservation had been neglected. "If Mr. Justin went to so much trouble to scheme to steal us from Dr. Carlhagen, why would he use such an unsafe vessel?"

"I can think of one reason," Summer said, leaning against the counter. "He didn't plan to take us very far from St. Vitus."

Of course, Jacey thought, impressed yet again by Summer's logical thinking. "Did you find any maps on board? Any indication of where they planned to take us?"

"There's a navigation system on the bridge. It's like a reader screen, but bigger. The interface is locked with a password. Orson has to know it or he wouldn't be able to pilot the ship anywhere. There are some paper maps, but I couldn't even find St. Vitus on them."

It always came back to Orson. The answer to what Jacey needed to do seemed simple, in a way. After all, Orson had planned nothing but bad things for the Scions. And now the safety of all Scions depended upon his cooperation. Wasn't the ethical choice to force him to help?

Jacey's stomach soured. But did that mean she could use any means necessary to compel him? What if it went beyond mere intimidation?

"Is something wrong?" Summer asked. Then, as if hearing her own question, she made a silly face. "I mean is something *else* wrong? Something beyond the fact that we're all doomed to be overwritten if we don't get off the island pretty soon in this rattletrap bucket?"

Jacey snapped out of her thoughts. Smiling at Summer's uncharacteristic humor, she said, "Do you really want to know?"

"I suppose not. I have enough problems of my own."

An urgent need to get back to campus swept through Jacey, making her limbs buzz with impatience. She didn't want to wait for the bus to be unloaded and hoisted back down to the dock. She didn't know how to drive the Jeep. But Summer did.

"Do you need to supervise the unloading?" Jacey asked.

Summer smirked and rolled her eyes. "You don't really think things through sometimes, Jacey. I'm a Spider, remember? Would you really want me to 'supervise' Snakes and Eagles?"

"But I thought you said they had to distribute the cargo evenly so the boat doesn't tip over."

"I said so the boat doesn't list too much. That's not at all the same thing."

"Come with me, then. *Consult* with Dajeet about the unloading and then drive me back to campus."

Sighing as if she'd just been asked to carry the boat on her back, the girl yanked off her hat, letting sheets of black hair tumble free. "Whatever you command, Boss, I do."

Jacey let the comment slide. Everyone was under stress and Summer tended to fall into sullen disrespectfulness when the pressure was on.

"Once we're at sea, you can spend as much time down there tinkering with the engines as you want."

Summer perked up at that and disappeared toward the exit. She knew her away around the space better than Jacey. By the time Jacey got to the stairs, Summer was already a flight up. She stood there, tapping her toe impatiently. "I need to get that elevator working, too. Just another thing for my list."

"Elevator?"

Summer pointed at a vertical gap in the wall across from the stairs. "Behind those doors. It's a lift mechanism.

You step in, press a button and a cable pulls the car up or lets it down to move between decks."

"Why would they need it if they have stairs?"

Summer threw up her hands. "I don't know. But it doesn't *work*."

A boom far above thundered through the boat. The deck shivered under Jacey's feet.

"What the hell are they doing to my boat!" Summer cried, looking up.

"They must have finally gotten the bus aboard."

"They're supposed to lower it, not drop it." Summer set off up the stairs and Jacey had to take two at a time to catch up. They pushed into the brightness of day and found the bus sitting perfectly centered on the deck. Scions scrambled to remove the chains and straps.

Summer tore into Kirk, demanding to know if he was incompetent or merely stupid. She ripped off a string of facts about the tensile strength of steel and force vectors, which sounded like an unknown language to Jacey's ears. Dajeet met Jacey and was about to explain what had happened when a new sound cut the air.

The beat of helicopter blades.

Summer stopped mid-curse and spun. Jacey followed her gaze out to sea.

A black speck hung in the air, approaching fast. Jacey's heart fell into icy blackness, like a stone dropped into the deepest reaches of the ocean.

The senator's contingency force?

But if so, where were the rest of them? Humphrey said they'd come by air and by sea. She saw no boats on the horizon. And the aircraft was alone.

It buzzed straight toward them and passed twenty meters overhead, its roar so loud Jacey couldn't help but duck and cover her head with her hands. The sound faded as the helicopter crossed over land and disappeared beyond the green hills.

"It's headed toward campus," Jacey said. "Dajeet, warn them."

Dajeet turned her eyes on Jacey, expression blank. Jacey yanked the walkie-talkie from the girl's hand. She twisted the dial to a different broadcast channel and mashed the transmission button. "Humphrey! Are you there? Chopper coming. Humphrey!"

Summer's hand closed over Jacey's and brought the walkie-talkie away from her mouth. "The radio doesn't have the range to reach campus."

Jacey's eyes went from the hills in the direction of the Scion School toward the sea. Why was there only one helicopter? Where were the ships? "Come on, Summer. Get me back to campus as fast as you can."

11

THE UNMISTAKABLE SHAPE

At Vaughan's insistence, Belle left Elizabeth lying in a bed in the hacienda. He said he would tolerate no more cruelty.

Let her stew in her own twisted psyche, Belle thought. *She deserves worse than I gave her.*

Belle had admonished Elizabeth that if she so much as left the hacienda, Belle would throw the woman into the pit, lock the grate, and never let her out again.

Reaching out with her senses, Belle found Vaughan. He was in Dr. Carlhagen's office. She appeared there next to him and found him speaking with a hologram of Humphrey projected above Dr. Carlhagen's mahogany holodesk. Humphrey was looking at a reader in his hands.

"No, Elizabeth isn't talking yet," Vaughan was saying.

It struck Belle as funny that she and Vaughan lived in a simulation that was simulating a holodesk, when it could just as easily have simulated an entire life-sized Humphrey anywhere they wanted. It had something to do with human psychology, keeping Humphrey out of the simulation helped the mind stay . . . sane, she supposed.

Humphrey's brows scrunched together as he studied the map Vaughan had sent to his reader. "We're running out of time. If we don't find your server soon, I—"

"Just get the Scions off the island, Humphrey."

Oh, sure, Belle thought. Worry about the living and just leave us to be deleted.

"You should forget about finding Elizabeth's island," she said. "She has no incentive to help us Scions. If anything, she has more to gain by turning you all away and telling the senator's backup force where you are."

"Belle makes a good point," Vaughan said.

Humphrey nodded vaguely as he studied the map. "There are a lot of other islands here. Do you suppose they all have people living on them?"

Nobody answered because nobody knew. Except Elizabeth. "I can go talk to our guest again," Belle said. "She just needs a little more pressure and she'll spill everything."

Humphrey looked up and away. His little hologram seemed to be peering up at the ceiling fan whirling in Dr. Carlhagen's office. "There's a chopper coming."

"The senator's force?" Vaughan asked.

"It sounds like just one. But they can carry several armed men. I need to go."

Humphrey's image disappeared.

A second later, a chime sounded in the air and Vaughan's head snapped up, eyes going wide. "It's that reader Humphrey left in the wine cellar. Someone's down there."

"Who is it?"

Vaughan gestured like a magician, and a window opened in mid-air above Dr. Carlhagen's desk. It showed a video feed, mostly dark.

The beam of a flashlight pierced the blackness and

shone on the steel door in the wine cellar. Enough light reflected from the metal to highlight the vague shape of a figure holding the flashlight, nothing more than a lighter shadow against the blackness.

"Can't you brighten the picture?" Belle demanded. "Or turn on the lights down there?"

"Wait. I want whoever it is to unlock the door first. Before they know they're being watched."

Anxiety felt odd to Belle's AI body and mind. It didn't register as sweaty palms or heart palpitations. Instead it was like a keen sound, a rising tone of alarm that only she could hear.

A hand reached out to the keypad and jabbed in a sequence of numbers.

Vaughan mumbled along: "577-157-325. Got it."

Sound came through as well, but it was just the scuffing of shoes on the cement floor. Something beeped. Then a click.

A thin strip of light appeared at the bottom of the door, and it grew as the figure pulled the door open.

Light spilled into the wine cellar, casting the figure in silhouette. But only for a flash, then they slipped into the room and shut the door.

"I didn't catch it," Belle said. "I thought there was a moment where—I don't know. Play it back."

Vaughan rewound the video and played it in slow motion.

"There!" Belle snapped. "No. You went too far."

With extreme patience, Vaughan backed the video frame by frame, stopping at the instant the figure had turned to glance back into the wine cellar.

The unmistakable shape of a ponytail hung in silhouette. Light from inside the room limned a feminine nose and one cheek. It glinted in her eyes.

Belle looked at Vaughan, expecting to see the same shock in his face as she felt. Instead she saw grim fury as he confirmed what she saw so plainly but couldn't believe. "It's Leslie."

It was.

As the truth sank in, Belle found herself shaking her head. Leslie had been the Second of her Nine. Not the sharpest thorn on the bush, but a loyal girl. Not much of a leader, but not disliked. Belle couldn't say the same for herself.

"So Mr. Justin overwrote Leslie," she said. "What a stupid, stupid girl. Why would she allow that?"

Vaughan's face softened. "Mr. Justin must have tricked her. I'll install the backup of Leslie. Maybe she'll remember what happened. But first I have to warn Humphrey."

While Vaughan called for Humphrey at the holodesk, Belle paced the room. Two fears sent slick tendrils into her mind, each shrieking into the ears of her consciousness like terrified birds. The first fear was on behalf of the Scions who did not even suspect Leslie. The second fear was for herself.

If Vaughan installed Leslie here, there would be three young women in the simulated St. Vitus. Yes, he could split into a thousand instances. She'd never have to know what went on between him and the other two girls. But part of her would know anyway.

Belle wanted all of him.

"Humphrey's not answering," Vaughan said, interrupting her anxious thoughts. She felt a rush of shame at her selfishness. "That helicopter he heard must have been trouble."

"Just leave a message. We need to get Leslie going."

Vaughan's mouth quirked and his head cocked to one side. "Do you hear that?"

"What now?"

"It's Madam LaFontaine."

"You can hear her?" This was news to Belle, and she did not like it. But at least the over-dramatic AI persona wouldn't be likely competition for Vaughan's affections.

Vaughan was nodding vaguely. "You can hear her if you know what to listen for. But . . . she's in a panic." His face transformed. Belle could have sworn it was terror that made his eyes sag and cheeks sink in.

"What is it?"

Eyes widening, he glanced at Belle. "Oh no."

"What?"

"Mr. Justin is shutting our server do—"

12

MORE OR LESS TWITCHY

Humphrey stood in the doorway of Boys' Hall, ears bent to better hear the approaching helicopter. Scions milled about in the quad, most with nothing to do until the bus came to take them to the boat. A few had turned to look southeast.

The wind was strong, bending the tops of trees in the mango grove. A fringe of gray clouds hovered above the southern hills. At first all Humphrey heard was an occasional thump, but then it became clear at the same time a dot emerged above the green hilltops.

"It must have flown right over *Aphrodite*," Tytus said. "Do you think the senator's force is already there?"

The thought filled Humphrey's stomach with hot fear. And they had absolutely no way to get the Scions to the boat. The best they could do would be run for cover outside the fence. "Get everyone together on the quad. Tell the Nine Leaders to be prepared to take their Nines in different directions out the front gate."

The helicopter continued its approach. Humphrey

clenched and unclenched his fists. Nothing good had ever come from such an aircraft. It had been Captain Wilcox a few days before, and that had nearly ended in catastrophe for everyone. And then the senator had arrived.

He would not let disaster strike a third time. He ran toward Sensei's villa, where he knew the martial arts master had stashed the guns they'd taken from Senator Bentilius's guards.

Wanda got to the door first. She barred the doorway with her body. She put a hand on his chest to stop him from shouldering past.

"There's only one helicopter," she said.

"I don't care if it's one guy on a donkey. If he's armed and we aren't, we lose."

She didn't budge. But she didn't frown or challenge him with her eyes the way Jacey might have. Instead she held her ground with patience and said softly, "You said there were hundreds coming. This one helicopter cannot be the invasion we fear."

"It doesn't matter. Or are you expecting some *friendly* people to just show up?"

Humphrey became aware of a number of Scions gathered behind him. Apparently they'd ignored his instructions to assemble.

Wanda grabbed his arm. She pulled him close, her lips close to his cheek. "If *you* got off that helicopter and saw a bunch of people with weapons, would your trigger finger be more or less twitchy?" She let him go and stepped back. "This could be an emissary of the larger force. They don't want to fight us or kill us. They probably want to give us an ultimatum. Let's keep the guns concealed until we really know what's going on."

Humphrey glanced over his shoulder. Obu, Tytus, and Dansha had gathered round. Horace stood behind them.

He could read their concern in the tense postures of the first three. They would follow his decision. He knew they must be wishing Vaughan were there, though. Because at that moment, Humphrey wished it, too.

The helicopter had circled wide of the school and was approaching straight into the wind. It flew low, nose slightly tilted down. And fast.

Obu glanced southeast. "There really don't seem to be more of them."

Humphrey made his decision.

13

—————

BLOOD BLOSSOMING

D r. Carlhagen read the new note for the twentieth time: *Come out when you hear the chopper. Not a second sooner.*

He crumpled the paper in his fist and began to pace back and forth in the small holding cell. How much longer was this going to take?

He stopped abruptly. If the sound of the helicopter was the signal, then the door must already be unlocked. He cursed himself for not trying the handle before. In two steps, he was to the door, gripping the handle and cranking it down. The door pushed open. In the doorway directly across from his stood Senator Bentilius. Their eyes met, hers narrowing in momentary suspicion.

Just as quickly, the look disappeared and a lascivious smile spread across her lips. "So the butler is still on your side, Christof. Interesting."

He decided not to tell her Mr. Justin remained a traitor. Instead he grunted a noncommittal acknowledgement. "Let's go."

As they pushed through the door into the main ward, Senator Bentilius split away from him and headed toward the patient cots.

Dr. Carlhagen heard the beat of a chopper. "Come on, Maxine. We don't have time to visit with the convalescents."

She ignored him and approached a man bound to a cot. Dr. Carlhagen followed after, ready to drag her out by her hair if he had to. The guard Senator Bentilius stood over was bald, his face black and blue, one eye swollen entirely shut.

"Tinlon," she hissed at him, "Wake up."

The un-swollen eye fluttered open. It took a moment for him to focus on her. "Get the hell away from me," he croaked.

"What happened to you?"

"Your friends jumped me."

"What?"

Dr. Carlhagen grabbed her elbow. "He doesn't recognize you in your new body. The Scions did this."

She shrugged him off and turned back to her guard. "I'm Senator Maxine Bentilius, Tinlon. I transferred into this body."

The bruised face twisted into an even more grotesque configuration as the single eye swept over Senator Bentilius's new figure.

She glanced around the ward. "Where's Alice?"

"Dead," Tinlon said.

Senator Bentilius took a step back, jaw dropping in shock. "Impossible."

The thump of the helicopter was closer now. It sounded like it was directly outside.

"Come on, Maxine," Dr. Carlhagen said, backing toward the door. "We've got to get out of—"

His eyes fell on three faces he did not recognize. All three men were bound to cots like the Senator's body-guards. They were gagged and unconscious. "Maxine."

Ignoring him, the lithe and pale senator dashed to a medical supply cart and rummaged through the drawers.

"Maxine!" Dr. Carlhagen shouted.

"Stop bossing me around. I need to take care of some loose ends." She plucked something from a drawer and went back to the bald guard. "This is for the pain," she said to him.

The man grunted. "Just loosen these straps so I can get up."

Dr. Carlhagen crept closer to one of the strangers, an unshaven lump of a man who smelled vaguely of cigarette smoke. He prodded the man's shoulder. The man did not wake up.

Tinlon said, "I'm not in much pain. They already have me so drugged I can't think straight."

Light glinted from something grasped in the senator's fist. "Well, now you'll feel even less."

With a quick and deliberate stroke, she drew it across Tinlon's throat. His mouth gaped and a choked moan cut through the air. The whole cot shuddered as his body shook against the straps.

Dr. Carlhagen gasped at the sight of blood blossoming from a slit across the guard's throat.

With robotic efficiency, Senator Bentilius turned to the cot where her other guard lay. That man appeared to be unconscious. With a swipe of her blade, she dispatched him.

He made no noise. Didn't struggle or appear to awaken at all as blood spilled from his gashed throat.

Senator Bentilius's eyes scanned the room, pausing momentarily on the Eagle boy. Elias. Dr. Carlhagen strode toward the woman, hands out. "You mustn't kill that one. He's too valuable."

"You don't say," she said with a humorless smile. Her hand still clutched the scalpel. It did not tremble in the slightest.

Dr. Carlhagen looked at the three strangers. "I don't know who these men are."

Senator Bentilius moved to the closest one. "They're not my guards. Not in uniform." She turned back to Dr. Carlhagen. "I say kill them."

Dr. Carlhagen's eyes went to the scalpel. Drops of blood splattered the floor at the senator's feet.

He weighed his choices. The thump of helicopter blades beat against his brain with an insistent demand: Run. Run. Run. Run.

"What if they're representatives of a Progenitor?" The possibility made his heart chill. "One of these might even *be* a Progenitor."

"Wouldn't you know?"

"I don't meet them all face-to-face. Most of the deals are done through intermediaries."

"Why would a Progenitor come here unannounced?"

Dr. Carlhagen smiled grimly. "Why would a Progenitor come here to transfer early?"

"I see your point." Senator Bentilius pushed him aside. "But it doesn't matter. They're in the wrong place at the wrong time."

"Stop!" Dr. Carlhagen said, sickened by the senator's cold willingness to murder. "At least let me talk to this one, find out who he is."

It was her turn to show impatience. She pointed the dripping scalpel at the ceiling, in the direction of the approaching helicopter. "We've got to get going!"

She drew back the white sheet tucked under the last man's chin.

Dr. Carlhagen grabbed her elbow, pulling her away from the cot. "If he represents a Progenitor, killing him would do irreparable damage to our program."

She yanked her arm free and spun on Dr. Carlhagen. The hand holding the scalpel raised momentarily and her ice-blue eyes narrowed to slits. A flush of red bloomed on her pale neck and cheeks. Looking more like Belle than she had since transferring into the girl, the senator seemed poised like a snake in the last still moment before lashing out.

Dr. Carlhagen dropped his voice. "Leave these men. They're unconscious. They haven't seen anything."

He reached out, slowly, and placed a hand gently on her shoulder. Stroking her like a cat, he drew her away from the man.

Senator Bentilius seemed to uncoil then, let her hand drop. Turning back to the last stranger, she carefully set the scalpel on his chest. Blood from the blade wicked into the white sheet and grew into an amorphous stain. "So he will know he was spared." She wiped her hands on the corner of his bed sheets.

"Let's go," she said and started for the door.

Clamping his lips against rising nausea and cursing the woman for her rashness, Dr. Carlhagen trailed after her. If he'd had any doubts about the limits to which she'd go to secure her own safety, they were gone now.

He wondered how many people had she disposed of in similar ways—if not by her own hand—in her rise to power. Even more chilling was the question of how close Dr. Carlhagen himself had come to being one of her victims.

14

BLADES STILL BLURRING

The helicopter hovered over the quad and slowly descended, its downdraft flattening the grass and flinging the branches of the trees to and fro. A thick smell of exhaust, completely at odds with the lush aroma of the island, swept over the assembled Scions.

Humphrey walked and shouted with confidence he did not feel. "Move everyone to the front of the dining hall. Wanda, Tytus, come with me to greet our guests. I'll pretend to be Dr. Carlhagen and see if we can't get them to see this as a big misunderstanding. Maybe we can get Summer back here and show them that Senator Bentilius has transferred into her and get them to back off."

Wanda actually smiled at the idea. Humphrey was beginning to think the red-haired girl liked all the games and deceit of the past few days.

The Scions moved to follow his instructions while he, Tytus, and Wanda went to the edge of the quad near the bell tower.

He left Sang in charge of the Nines. It was the only real

choice, since Elias was in the medical ward and Kirk was with Jacey by the docks.

Humphrey took a moment to study Sang's face. He was fidgeting with his sleeves, a nervous habit he'd always had right before a sparring match.

The helicopter settled onto the grass, blades still blurring, wind sending Wanda's hair flying.

"That's the senator's helicopter," Tytus said as it landed. "I remember those white markings on the side."

Humphrey strode forward, already wearing Dr. Carlhagen's jovial smile. For the first time ever, he wished he were wearing the old man's clothes. He didn't know how he would explain why he was dressed like a Scion.

The side hatch of the helicopter slid open and the stairs unfolded. Two men in black leapt out, holding machine guns in their hands. They immediately pointed the weapons at Humphrey.

"Hold!" the taller one shouted. He had a thick black mustache and dark glasses concealing his eyes. The other was slimmer, but his taut limbs spoke of wiry strength.

Humphrey held his arms out. "Welcome, boys. Senator Bentilius told me she planned to stay another week or so. What's with the early arrival?"

The mustached man fired three rounds into the dirt at Humphrey's feet. The Scions screamed and Humphrey jerked back a few steps, heart leaping. "Stay back. I know you aren't Dr. Carlhagen. Justin warned me about your tricks."

Mr. Justin. So *he* was behind this.

"Where are the rest of your men?" Humphrey called, looking toward the hills and then north to the sea. "Are you the entirety of the senator's backup force?"

The man just laughed, then said something to the

slimmer soldier that Humphrey couldn't hear. They looked to the medical ward.

Humphrey wasn't the only one to cry out when he saw Dr. Carlhagen and Senator Bentilius step through into daylight.

15

LEVERAGE

Squinting against the bright sunlight, Dr. Carlhagen trotted down the steps. Senator Bentilius came after him. Scions stood in front of the dining hall, eyes on the great, black helicopter crouched upon the quad less than twenty meters from the medical ward.

Four other Scions, including Humphrey, stood nearer.

Two of Senator Bentilius's guards stood waiting, postures tense, holding machine guns in their black-gloved fists. The helicopter blades did not slow. Dr. Carlhagen waved to the men as he trotted toward them. They swung the barrels of their weapons from Humphrey to him.

"I'm Dr. Carlhagen," he said, holding up his hands, "And this is Senator Bentilius." He waved toward his companion. The men stared at them with steely eyes and did not lower their weapons.

"What's the pass phrase?" growled the one on the right. He had a ridiculously large black mustache.

The question stopped Dr. Carlhagen with his mouth

open. Smile faltering, he raised his hands in a shrug. "I don't know."

"'Oh, happy blade!'" Senator Bentilius shouted.

At once, the barrels of the guns fell and the men waved Dr. Carlhagen and Senator Bentilius toward the open hatch of the chopper. A commotion beyond it drew Dr. Carlhagen's attention. A group of Scions were running toward him.

The guards noticed and immediately raised their weapons and shouted for the Scions to stop. Seeing the Scions gave Dr. Carlhagen an idea. He scanned their faces, but couldn't find Jacey. His eyes fell on the Dolphin. Livy.

She stood near Bethancy, at the front of the throng massed before the dining hall.

Dr. Carlhagen tapped one of the guards on the shoulder. "That one," he said, shouting over the roar of the chopper's engine. He pointed at the Dolphin. "Bring her to me."

The guard looked at Dr. Carlhagen like he was crazy.

"Do it," Dr. Carlhagen insisted.

The man didn't move and instead shifted his gaze to Senator Bentilius. Her eyes blazed at Dr. Carlhagen. "Why do you want that girl?"

His answer wasn't a total lie. But it wasn't the whole truth, either. "Leverage."

16

———

COUGH AND SHUDDER

Jacey thrust her feet against the floor of the Jeep as jounced over the twisting road toward the Scion School. Next to her, Summer sat tall to see over the steering wheel clutched in her grease-covered hands.

The thick foliage bordering the road blurred by, a wall of green. Wind whipped at the girls' faces, making their hair swirl around them like Medusa's snakes. Jacey wished —for the first time in several days—she had a rubber band to tie it back with.

The vehicle lurched over a pothole. The world tilted before Jacey's eyes, then righted itself as the Jeep recovered its stability.

Summer drove with more abandon than Belle had when she and Jacey had been trying to elude the senator's bodyguards. And that had been the most harrowing Jeep ride of Jacey's life.

But Jacey didn't care now. She wanted more speed.

Please don't let it be the backup force, she thought.

They were so close to having the *Aphrodite* ready. All they needed was for Sensei to bring back the bus and load everybody on.

They topped a hill and the island fell away to the south in a tumble of green and brown scrub. In the distance, the red roofs of the Scion School campus shone like hibiscus blossoms in the morning sun. There was no sign of the helicopter from this vantage. It must have landed in the quad.

Summer jammed the brakes at a sharp turn in the road, making the tires cough and shudder on the rutted gravel. She battled the steering wheel, turning, turning, as the Jeep made the curve, then revved the motor to send them charging down a straightaway.

Jacey held on, knowing that Summer's smallest error in judgment would send them tumbling two hundred meters down the slope. With the Jeep's top down, neither of them would find out how that fall ended.

As they lost altitude, the Scion School disappeared behind a low rise. Jacey dreaded what she'd find when they finally got there. Because she knew one thing for sure:

Outsiders always brought guns.

THE LUCKIER THE MAN

M r. Justin hustled out of the server room and into the wine cellar, Senator Bentilius's suitcase rolling behind him, heavily laden with servers. Strictly speaking, he hadn't needed Socrates's old server. But since Vaughan and Belle were on board and knew far too much about what he was up to, he chose to bring the extra box.

Besides, who knew how such AIs might be useful to him in the future? Waste not, want not.

His distraction—the chopper—would only last for a while longer. He needed to put on some haste and get the suitcase stashed where it would eventually make its way onto the bus and to *Aphrodite*.

Three steps into the darkness of the wine cellar and an odd gleam to his left caught his attention. It was unlike the glassy roundness shining off of the wine bottles in their crisscrossed racks.

It was from the light of the server room reflecting off a flat surface.

He released the suitcase handle and crept toward the shiny object. His body was shorter than he was used to, but he was able to leap high enough to snatch it down.

A reader. And look, it was set to record video of anything moving in front of the door to the server room.

"I almost got caught," he said under his breath. But almost will get you no cookies, as his father used to say. He shook off the chill of what might have been and grinned. The Scions were smart, but Mr. Justin was smarter.

Snatching up the suitcase, he made his way out of the hacienda. No time to lose.

He trundled down the path toward the quad, wondering whose reader he'd discovered. Jacey hadn't had time to bother going down to the wine cellar. But Humphrey had been nosing around in the hacienda earlier with Tytus in tow. Yes. Humphrey had also been searching high and low for the AI servers.

Clever. Vaughan had surely been monitoring the video feed. And that meant Mr. Justin had narrowly escaped discovery. A lucky break, indeed.

As any self-respecting butler knew: the better the plan, the luckier the man.

A minute later, he scrambled to the bottom of the path from the hacienda. He shuddered every time the suitcase bounced on the path. The servers were hardy, but they weren't designed to be jarred and jounced this way.

No one had spotted him so far, of that he was sure. They were all busy staring at the helicopter.

Even so, Mr. Justin breathed a sigh of relief as he came off the path and the bulk of the medical ward building hid him from everyone on the quad. He left the suitcase and crept to the corner, pressed his hand on the sun-warmed stucco, and peeked out.

Chopper blades still blurred above the aircraft, which

filled the air with its roar. The Scions stood well back from it. He couldn't make out their faces, but in their postures he saw nothing but distress. Old ones held onto younger ones and boys paced and threw furious glares at the helicopter.

Dr. Carlhagen and Senator Bentilius stood motionless before two armed men. It appeared they were just standing there having a staring contest.

What's the old man doing?

Whatever it was, Senator Bentilius was none too happy about it. She swung out an arm and pointed toward one of the younger Scions. Dr. Carlhagen answered, firmly.

The Scions were watching them. Nobody had even spared a glance for the medical ward. Good.

Seizing upon the distraction, Mr. Justin retrieved the suitcase and slipped away from the quad. He crossed the path and skirted behind the bell tower. It was slow going once he stepped into the tangle of brush and grass. The suitcase wheels were not made for such terrain. He leaned into the effort, cursing to himself.

It didn't surprised him that Dr. Carlhagen had decided to dawdle once set free. The man was ridiculously single-minded about doing things his way. A bit of luck, actually. As long as the Scions weren't looking, Mr. Justin could easily get the suitcase into position. Chest heaving, he yanked the unwieldy baggage around a thicket of thorn-skipple and raced past Boys' Hall.

18

BUTTERFLY WINGS

The senator's pale face flushed bright red and her mouth twisted in a snarl. She stepped close to Dr. Carlhagen and tapped his chest with a finger. "I want to make one thing clear. I am *not* babysitting that child."

"I'm not asking you to," Dr. Carlhagen said. "Livy is perfectly self-sufficient."

"Who's her Progenitor?"

"A very important person. That's all I can say."

"They're all important. Why *her?*"

Dr. Carlhagen hesitated. He couldn't tell Senator Bentilius the whole truth—that he wanted Livy because she was leverage over Jacey. The pair of them shared an inexplicable connection, probably because both were inveterate rule breakers. On arrival, the Dolphin had refused to throw her stuffed toy in the burning barrel and Jacey had helped her hide it.

But telling Senator Bentilius about his need to control

Jacey in particular would only produce more questions, more suspicion.

"She's the ideal insurance policy," he said. "Until this island is secure, I want leverage over the Scions. This particular Dolphin is very popular with all of them."

Senator Bentilius paused for a moment longer then gave a curt nod to the guard, who then strode toward the young Scion. Dr. Carlhagen scurried after him. The fact that some Scions had killed Alice and brutalized the other guards put him on his toes. He straightened and painted a scowl on his face to warn off any Scion who was thinking of playing the hero. Which was probably all the boys.

While Vaughan had been the best fighter on campus, few of those skills had transferred to Dr. Carlhagen. Fortunately, the Scions didn't know that.

Dr. Carlhagen held his hand out toward the Dolphin girl. "Come along, Livy." The other Scions cried out. Some of the older boys started to creep toward the guard.

Livy looked at his hand and took a step back, chin lifting, green eyes hard. "I'm not going with you. Do you think I'm an idiot?"

Two Centipedes, Pedro and Constantine, edged closer, their thirteen-year-old bodies in the loose but tense fighting stance Sensei had trained into them. Humphrey was shouting at them to stop, but they ignored him.

"This man will shoot!" Dr. Carlhagen warned the approaching boys. He cocked his head toward the guard. "I know you think you're important, but I will order you killed if you interfere."

The boys stopped, but they didn't relax.

Livy took another step back. The guard lunged for her. She spun away, but he got a hand on her blond curls and yanked her roughly back. Her cry shrilled above the pulse of the helicopter blades. Several Scions echoed her in anger.

The two boys moved closer.

Turf kicked up at their feet as the other guard fired off a burst from his weapon.

With one hand keeping his gun trained on the boys, the mustachioed guard flung Livy over his shoulder. Her tiny fists pummeled his back, but had no more effect than butterfly wings against a windowpane.

Dr. Carlhagen watched the boys' faces for signs of attack as he retreated. He didn't dare turn his back on them.

The thought occurred to him that he might be able to regain control right now. The Scions were not armed, for some reason. He smiled inwardly, realizing that Sensei was behind that. What a fool.

Dr. Carlhagen had no more chance to think, though. Pedro flew at him, a flurry of fists and feet. The boy was smaller than Dr. Carlhagen, but he made up for it with speed and skill.

Despite Vaughan's expertise in the martial arts, Dr. Carlhagen was completely outmatched. Blows struck his abdomen, his arms.

Stumbling back, he covered his face. More blows rained down on him. The grass struck his back, driving the breath out of him.

Gunfire rang out. Someone shrieked.

Hands grabbed him and pulled him to his feet. His lungs tried to suck in air, but couldn't quite catch it. He was being dragged.

The roar of the helicopter and the draft of its great propeller tore at his Scion uniform.

More gunfire. More cries.

Air returned to his lungs in an exquisite gulp. He

shrugged off the hands dragging him. It was one of Senator Bentilius's guards.

"You better not have killed any of them," Dr. Carlhagen shouted.

He turned back. Constantine lay on his back, Pedro kneeling over him, pressing his hands to the boy's side. Humphrey was sprinting toward the fallen Scion, followed by Obu, Sang, and Wanda.

The guard tugged Dr. Carlhagen's shoulder. "The senator demands that you get in the helicopter."

"She does, does she?"

Curse that old hag, ordering me about like one of her lackeys, he thought. "If that boy dies . . ."

Gunfire erupted from across the quad. The air sizzled as bullets passed overhead.

The guards returned fire.

Scions fell to the grass. Some ran for the dining hall.

"Stop!" Dr. Carlhagen shrieked.

"Get in the chopper!" the guard cried.

The moment hung thickly. All of Dr. Carlhagen's plans were bending, just on the verge of snapping into pieces.

The guard next to Dr. Carlhagen spun suddenly and dropped to the grass.

Half his face was missing. The other half was still. Blood soaked the remaining bit of his thick mustache.

Instinct propelled Dr. Carlhagen toward the helicopter. Already the stairs were retracting. He leapt aboard as the machine's engines revved.

The hull pinged with bullet impacts.

The chopper strained. Bullets struck like hail, loud and clanging. Dr. Carlhagen flattened himself on the floor as the chopper climbed out of range of the Scion's weapons.

And then it was over.

Senator Bentilius was already strapped into a seat.

Face pale as alabaster, she pointed to the seat next to her. It was the only forward-facing one free, so he plopped himself into it and buckled the five-point harness. A moment later, the wiry guard thrust Livy into Dr. Carlhagen's lap.

He wrapped his arms around her squirming body and pressing his lips against her ear. "Be still, child. It's a long fall into the ocean and I wouldn't want you to slip."

The words had their intended effect. Her struggle ceased.

He peeked through a window as the chopper banked. Scions swarmed across the quad, pointing and shouting. A few covered their mouths with their hands. Two older girls shook their fists, faces masks of fury. Most of the Scions had circled around Constantine. The aircraft turned and they were gone.

The guard handed him and Senator Bentilius headsets. Dr. Carlhagen pulled the padded cups over his ears and caught the last bit of the pilot's question: " . . . a particular destination?"

Before Dr. Carlhagen could answer, Senator Bentilius spoke. "St. Lazarus."

She ignored his pointed glare. Clearly these men would take orders only from her. As the chopper spun away from the campus and headed toward the sea, Dr. Carlhagen's eyes followed the long, twisting line of the gravel road that led away from the school. A plume of dust rose from it in the distance. A flash of red broke into a clearing in the trees. It was the Jeep speeding toward the gate. It had to be one of the Scions driving it.

Dr. Carlhagen gritted his teeth in a humorless smile. St. Vitus was boiling in chaos at the moment, but soon all would freeze into order.

He hoped Constantine lived. The boy's Progenitor

wasn't known for his patience, as his political enemies could attest. If any of them still lived.

Livy started to struggle again and he loosened his grip. She squirmed to the window. He watched with interest as she pressed her small palms to the plastic. Her ponytail had come loose, and her blond curls tumbled over her face.

"Get away from there, child," Senator Bentilius snapped.

The girl turned her eyes away from the island below and stared at the senator, giving her a look of absolute defiance. Dr. Carlhagen marveled at how short a period the child had been at the Scion School and how quickly she had taken on Jacey's attitudes, right down to the look of hatred in her eyes.

19

A DARK SWELL

"Come on! Open!" Jacey shouted at the chain-link gate in the Scion School fence. The gate shivered as it slid in its track. Red lights flashed on posts to either side. An alarm whooped, stark and shrill in the growing quiet as the helicopter shrank toward the coast.

"Why are they leaving already?" Summer asked.

Jacey didn't know. "Humphrey!" she barked into the walkie-talkie. "What's going on?"

No answer. He hadn't responded to any of her calls the whole ride from the docks. Unusual for him, which made her stomach grind.

Finally the gate opened wide enough for the Jeep to pass. Summer stomped the accelerator and they burst through. The Jeep tore up the path, mango grove blurring to one side, Boys' Hall a smear of white on the other.

Scions crowded the quad, some hugging each other, some still watching the helicopter as it flew into the distance. Sang spotted the Jeep and waved his arms. He ran to meet them as Summer skidded the vehicle to a stop.

Jacey had already unbuckled and she leapt out. "What happened?"

Sang pointed in the direction of the helicopter. "Dr. Carlhagen and the senator got out. They flew away."

Jacey closed her eyes and let out a sigh of relief. "If that's the worst of it, I think we lucked out."

"That's not the worst," said a new voice. Humphrey. His narrowed gaze lingered on Sang before turning to Jacey. "One of the guards shot Constantine. And Dr. Carlhagen took Livy."

His words hung in the air. Jacey understood them, but they didn't mean anything. They couldn't mean anything. They were crazy. "What was that about Livy?"

Already her body buzzed with rage.

"Dr. Carlhagen took her," Humphrey said. "Constantine is—" his voice broke.

Humphrey blurred. The island titled. Jacey pressed her fingers to her forehead, trying to keep a sudden internal pressure from making her head explode.

He took Livy!

"How could you let this happen?"

"There were two guards," Sang said. "They both had guns. When they took Livy, Pedro and Constantine tried to attack Dr. Carlhagen. And then Horace . . ."

The world snapped into focus as a cloak of chilled air curled around Jacey's body. Her bones felt heavy, as if suddenly transformed into iron. She climbed out of the Jeep. "You people *let* him take Livy?"

"It wasn't like that," Sang said. "No one could have—"

"Shut. Up," Jacey said between clenched teeth. She stepped toe to toe with Sang and shoved his chest. "*You* did this! You called in that helicopter. You let Dr. Carlhagen go."

Sang stumbled back, jaw slackening in shock. Or, at least, the appearance of shock.

She shoved him again. "Admit it. You *are* Mr. Justin!" Her palm cracked into his cheek. Sang's head jarred to the side. He brought his hand to the hot red mark on his skin.

Jacey drew her arm back for another strike, palm on fire from the first blow. But Humphrey caught her wrist. He squeezed his body between her and Sang. "Stop."

Jacey yanked her wrist free and spun to glare at all the Scions gathering around. "You let him take her!" she shouted. Several blanched at her accusation; most turned away with reddened faces, whether from shame or anger Jacey couldn't tell.

"We couldn't *do* anything," Humphrey said. "Did you want more of us to get shot?"

"How can you even ask that question? They *can't* shoot any of us." She smacked her chest with the palm of her hand. "We're clones of powerful people. The whole point of this place is to keep us alive."

"But they did shoot someone," Tytus said, striding forward. His voice was soft but firm. The Snake's sharp features gave him an elfin air. Over the past few days, a permanent tight-mouthed scowl had banished his usual easy smile. Jacey knew the boy hadn't grown physically, but his presence surely had.

But that was true of all the Scions. The stress of recent events had hardened them, molded them, stolen their innocence.

Dansha, a Spider, moved to stand beside Tytus. She nodded in agreement, fixing Jacey with a determined stare even as tears streamed down her cheeks.

Tytus met Jacey's gaze with calm confidence. "You didn't see Constantine go down. You don't know what you're talking about."

Jacey turned her eyes to where the helicopter had disappeared. It had flown somewhere to the south, somewhere beyond where the sea met the sky.

Humphrey put an arm around Jacey. She let her body sag into his. His voice was soft. "If Dr. Carlhagen was going to harm Livy, he had no reason to take her with him."

"But why Livy?" Dansha asked as she, too, stared out to sea.

Jacey knew. Dr. Carlhagen planned to use Livy to get her cooperation. He'd done it just a few days before, when he'd put Livy in the pit.

"Did he make any threats?" Jacey asked. "Did he leave a message for me?"

She got only head shakes in reply.

Drawing in all her anger and fear, Jacey focused it on the task at hand. "We've got no time to waste. The senator and Dr. Carlhagen will contact the senator's backup force immediately. We must evacuate today. You two," she said, pointing to Tytus and Leslie, who were hanging back by the Pelicans, "see that everyone finishes packing personal items and then get everyone fed. Quickly."

She turned in Humphrey's arms. His old sour frown had returned. "Come with me," she said. "It's time we deal with Orson."

She broke free from his embrace and headed for the medical ward.

Humphrey moved to follow her, but made no reply. Clearly she'd hurt him with her outburst.

The sounds of sobbing drew her attention to a crowd of Scions huddled in a circle upon the quad.

She pushed through them. Pedro sat on the grass, uniform askew and soaked with blood. He held Constantine's head in his lap. Someone had fetched a blanket. A dark swell of blood stained a spot over Con's stomach.

The boy's face looked peaceful, as if he were asleep. Jacey squatted and gently stroked the pale cheek. Only thirteen and just showing the firming of jaw that hinted of a man's face. A face he would never get the chance to grow into. A quiet, sweet boy.

Vaughan would be crushed.

Pedro's eyes were as vulnerable as open wounds. "What should we do with him?"

She didn't know. What did one do with a dead body besides put it in the freezer in the medical ward? But the thought of leaving poor Con among dead Progenitors sickened her.

"We'll take him with us aboard *Aphrodite*. We'll bury him at sea."

There wouldn't be time for anything else. They had to leave. Now.

She stalked toward the medical ward, jaw clenched. Orson would cooperate. He would pilot the boat, and they'd be long gone before the invaders arrived.

She nearly ran over the senator's nurse, Miss Dayspring, a woman so meek she was nearly invisible. But not now. The dark-skinned woman's face was streaked with tears. Horror drew her smooth skin back from her mouth. "Oh Lord God!" she cried, trying to squirm past Jacey and through the door.

Humphrey stopped her. "What's going on?"

The woman shuddered and turned in slow, jerky movements back toward the ward. She lifted a trembling hand and pointed toward the cots. "Murder."

20

――――

IT LOOKED LIKE RAGE

The vaguely metallic smell of blood swirled in the air of the ward. It mixed with the cloying stench of urine and feces. Jacey held a spare pillowcase to her nose and tried to ignore the sound of Humphrey's retching. She leaned over Tinlon's dead body and examined the wound crossing his throat.

A clean slash.

Jacey turned away and Miss Dayspring drew the sheet back over the man's face. "I don't understand this. Why would Senator Bentilius murder two of her own men? And why leave Orson and his men alive?"

Orson's eyes flicked toward her, and he mumbled something into his gag. He looked paler than usual. Afraid. Not surprising, given the presence of a bloody scalpel on his chest.

Good. Let him soak in fear.

Humphrey wiped his mouth on his sleeve. "Maybe the senator was mad at her men's failure to keep us in line."

"Maybe." She glanced at Elias, who sat up on his bunk,

his stricken, pale face haggard with confusion and horror. The senator had left him alive. But that made sense. Elias was a valuable asset, from the senator's perspective.

"I can't believe I let them get away," Elias said, voice full of recrimination. With shaking hands, he threw aside the bed sheet and swung his legs over the edge of his cot.

"Don't try to get up!" Miss Dayspring squawked.

Elias ignored her and rose unsteadily to his feet. He was bare-chested, but a huge white bandage puffed out on his left flank. It covered the grazing bullet wound he'd received from Alice.

Miss Dayspring rushed to his side and took hold of his arm. He tried to shake her off, but as small as she was, she easily guided him back down to the bunk. He collapsed with a pained sigh.

"Did you see anything?" Jacey asked him, gesturing to the dead men.

"No, I was asleep. I woke to a commotion, but I was confused." He glared at Miss Dayspring. "This woman keeps giving me pills for the pain and it clouds my thinking."

"You can't blame yourself, Elias," Humphrey said. "You were in no condition to fight them anyway. It's just as well. If you'd put up any resistance, they might have done the same to you."

The second dead guard was just a body-shaped lump under the sheet Miss Dayspring had drawn over it. Jacey didn't need to inspect it. Miss Dayspring had already said the wound was the same.

"And Senator Bentilius did this? She killed these men? Not Dr. Carlhagen?"

"Yes. I'm positive." The small woman left Elias's side. She wrung her hands in front of her.

"You saw her do it?"

The nurse's eyes fell. "Yes."

"Why would Senator Bentilius kill her guards and leave you alive?"

"She didn't see me. I don't think she remembered I existed."

Jacey stepped to the middle of the room and turned a slow three hundred-sixty degrees. "Where did you hide?"

Miss Dayspring scurried to the opposite side of the ward. She sat on the edge of a cot then slipped under the sheet. "I was right here, taking a nap. I awoke when I heard a conversation. Dr. Carlhagen was urging the Senator to leave, but she insisted on stopping."

"And you didn't say anything to her?"

"No."

"Why not? She's your employer. She was your patient for so long. I would think that as soon as she came out of her holding cell, you would have jumped up."

"Something was off," the nurse said. She rose from the cot and smoothed the blankets down. "When you work for Senator Bentilius for any amount of time, you get a sense about these things. I could hear in her voice that she was in one of her moods. And when I saw what she did, I held my breath and stayed as still as I could."

Jacey studied the nurse, allowing suspicion to roil in her mind, waiting for some conclusion to arrive in her gut. She did have a few reasons to trust the nurse. Miss Dayspring had done everything she could to care for the injured Scions, especially Elias. And she had made no attempt to let Senator Bentilius and Dr. Carlhagen out of their holding rooms. She was a meek woman and seemed willing to accept the authority of whoever asserted it.

On the other hand, Mr. Justin had come through the medical ward to transfer into a Scion. Miss Dayspring claimed to have no memory of seeing him or another

Scion enter, even though they must have passed right by her.

A warning buzzed in Jacey's mind. She stepped closer to Miss Dayspring, studied the woman's mud-brown eyes. She saw no artifice in them. The tiny woman carried herself as if she bore some great burden. Jacey had no idea how old she was, but she thought she was probably younger than Sensei, maybe by ten or fifteen years.

"Are you sure you didn't see Mr. Justin come through here the other day?"

No flash of tension tightened the woman's face at Jacey's change in the line of questioning.

"I told you," Miss Dayspring said. "I didn't see him. The truth is, I might have been napping then, too."

Jacey's gut didn't arrive at any sense of certainty about the woman, but she found herself leaning toward trusting her.

"Miss Dayspring," Jacey said, "I want you to prepare Elias to travel."

"And what about me?" Miss Dayspring asked. "Are you going to leave me here?"

"No. We need your medical expertise."

Miss Dayspring sagged with relief. "Thank you! I don't know what I would have done here all by myself."

Jacey turned her attention to Orson. He was the reason she'd come to the medical ward in the first place. The murders had shaken her, to be sure. But they'd also given her perspective. The senator was a monster, cold and ruthless.

What Jacey intended to do was equally ruthless, equally cold.

She ambled toward Orson's cot. "And why did Senator Bentilius leave you alive?" she mused in a singsong voice.

Orson grunted and tried to move his head.

Jacey paced around the cot with deliberate steps, trying to think up some threat, some way to scare him into cooperation. Her eyes fell on the scalpel resting atop the man's barrel chest. She pointed at it. "What's this?"

She plucked it up between her finger and thumb and held it up to the light streaming in the window. Dark stains marred the blade.

Her free hand went to one of the straps binding the man to the cot. "You don't look comfortable, Orson. Would you like to get up?"

He managed to nod a fraction of a centimeter, eyes widening in hope.

"Should I cut you free?"

Orson nodded more vigorously, making his body shake and his belly wobble.

Miss Dayspring croaked, "You don't need to cut the straps on Mr. Orson's cot. There are buckles."

"I'm not going to cut the straps."

She said this staring into Orson's eyes. They went wider, and the remaining blood drained from his face.

Heat rose up the back of Jacey's neck, and she was sure her face had gone red. She hoped it looked like rage, rather than the sick shame she felt.

This is for the greater good, she reminded herself.

"Are you sure you want to do this?" Humphrey said quietly. "Maybe Sensei could pilot the boat. And what good would Orson be to us, anyway, when you're"—he seemed to choke for a moment—"when you're done with him?"

She realized he was playing along. And it had the intended effect. Orson's eyes had locked onto the blade and his beard and mustache crumpled together as he clenched his teeth on the gag.

With a swift jerk, Jacey yanked off the sheet covering

Orson's body. He still wore the clothes he'd arrived in. Straps over his ankles, knees, thighs, waist, torso, shoulders, and forehead kept him immobile. His shoes were off, though.

She began a slow inspection of his body, starting with his feet. He wore ratty wool socks, with holes worn in the heels. She just stared at them while spinning the scalpel between her thumb and forefinger.

Miss Dayspring hissed in a sharp breath. "What are you doing, girl?"

"I'm deciding." She trailed her eyes to his prominent belly and tilted her head, as if considering how best to slice into a roast chicken.

"Jacey, don't," Humphrey said, a hint of desperation in his voice.

She finally turned her gaze to Orson's face, which had turned a greenish yellow. His eyes, large as pelican eggs, darted from the scalpel to her face. Breath sucked into his nose, and he let out a gibbering tumble of grunts and groans.

"Be silent!"

A final squeak erupted from him before he got himself under control. A tenuous control. His body vibrated with bottled fear.

"Jacey, please," Humphrey said, "at least give him a chance."

"He had his chance. How many times have I asked him nicely? We don't have time to wait for him to come around." She pulled up the hem of his shirt to expose a hairy lily-white belly. Running a fingertip across it, she mused, "I think I'll start right here . . ."

Humphrey shouldered her aside. "At least let him talk." He yanked Orson's gag down.

The man erupted in sobbing shrieks. "Please! I'll help

you. I'll pilot the boat. Wherever you want to go. Don't cut me!"

Jacey squatted next to him. With his head strapped down, he could barely turn his eyes far enough to meet hers. "I'm heartened to hear this. But I'm not convinced. I think I need to give you a permanent reminder so you don't get any ideas once we're at sea."

"No! I promise! I promise. Please—" A fit of coughs cut off his pathetic oaths. Tears streamed down his cheeks, dampening his beard.

Jacey stood and moved out of his line of sight. Hot swirls of nausea doubled her over. Shame shouted at her.

But she'd had no alternative. Nostrils flaring and jaw quivering, she straightened and tossed the scalpel aside. It clattered against the wall, making Orson flinch.

Orson's two thugs were awake now, too. Their eyes were wide with terror. Good.

"I expect you to keep your word, Orson. And if one of your men steps out of line, I'm coming for you." Her eyes shifted to the two men. "And if you think I'm cruel, you have no idea what would happen to you if I turned you over to Horace."

Even making the threat sent thrills of horror down her back. She shook them off. The Scions needed to get off the island. Her method had been expedient. She'd have plenty of time later to reflect on it, to atone for it. But only if she lived. Only if the Scions found a safe haven in the world beyond the shores of St. Vitus.

Orson's whole body seemed to sink into the cot a few centimeters as the tension washed out of him. "We'll all be straight as an arrow. I swear it!"

"Good," Jacey said. "I will inform Sensei, and he will release you. We will be keeping a very close eye on you."

"You have nothing to worry about from us," he said. "We just want out of here."

Jacey spun away from him, fearing that her sudden urge to smile with relief would spoil the intimidation. "No more sedation for these men, Miss Dayspring. We'll want their help moving the transfer machine."

"What about the dead?" asked the meek woman.

"Leave them in the cots. Let the senator's people deal with them." She headed for the door, and stopped to turn back to the nurse. "And gather what supplies you can. Bandages, antiseptic, painkillers."

Jacey had no idea what the Scions would face in the future, but she wanted to be prepared.

She and Humphrey stepped outside and nearly ran into Leslie. Behind her, Horace and Tytus carried Sang. The Eagle had clearly lost a very rough fight and his head lolled in unconsciousness.

Horace had a machine gun strapped over one shoulder.

21

EXPEDIENT

"What happened?" Jacey demanded, glaring at Horace.

Leslie gestured vaguely toward Sang. "Somebody let Dr. Carlhagen and Senator Bentilius out. It had to be Mr. Justin. I knew you suspected Sang. When I questioned him, he got defensive. Then he ran."

"Now that we have him, we should lock him up," Tytus said, "just to be safe."

Horace sneered and patted Sang's face. "I say we strap him down. Make him talk. Constantine is dead because of him."

Humphrey's face went red and he shook a finger in Horace's face. "Constantine is dead because you disobeyed me and started shooting."

"They had guns. They were kidnapping one of ours."

Jacey doubted Horace cared a spit about Livy. And seeing him armed made her skin crawl.

"Tytus is right," Leslie said, obviously changing the

subject, "let's lock him up for now. Once we leave, we'll have time to interrogate him."

Jacey didn't like it. Yes, Sang was the most likely suspect, but attacking him, threatening torture—after what she'd just done to Orson—it all felt wrong.

But it was expedient.

"You say he was uncooperative?" she asked. "Do you have specific evidence that he is Mr. Justin? Did anyone see him come out of the medical ward in the moments before Dr. Carlhagen and the Senator escaped?"

Leslie folded her arms across her chest in what looked like an imitation of Belle. "No."

The boys glanced at each other before shaking their heads.

"So you took it upon yourselves to accuse him, and you're surprised that he ran?"

"Jacey," Tytus said quietly, "we have good reason to suspect Sang. It won't harm him if we keep him locked up for a while."

He was right, Jacey knew, but she didn't like it. Everything they were doing had a good justification. To protect the Scions, to help them escape. And yet it seemed each step took them closer to Senator Bentilius's way of doing things.

She stepped aside from the medical ward entry. "Put him in Dr. Carlhagen's holding room and lock the door. Do not strap him down. Do not try to sedate him." She jerked her head at Humphrey. "Come on, I need to ask you a favor."

Jacey strode around the medical ward building and started up the bougainvillea-lined path leading upslope to the hacienda. Humphrey walked beside her. She sensed a heaviness in his steps. No surprise, considering all that had happened.

"We have to get that gun away from Horace," he said.

"Yes. And count the rest of them, make sure he hasn't stashed them somewhere."

"I don't think he'll turn it over to me. It'll have to be Sensei."

She nodded, but was already past the issue. She didn't look at him when she spoke. "I need you to do something for me."

"No. I won't do it." His voice was soft but firm.

"I haven't even asked it yet."

He stopped walking, forcing her to stop, too. He turned his blue eyes on her and just stared for a moment. "You're not the only person who can read people. I've made a study of you my entire life. You're planning to go after Livy. What you want me to do is order Captain Wilcox to fly you out of here. The only thing I haven't figured out yet is where you want him to take you."

Humphrey's very accurate guesses irritated her. "You can't expect me to let Dr. Carlhagen keep her."

He clamped his lips together, then sighed. "No. But he is using her to get to you."

Jacey knew that, but it made no difference. Even if she didn't go after Livy, Dr. Carlhagen would eventually contact her. Somehow. And then Jacey would be forced to give in to Dr. Carlhagen's demands. He'd want all the Scions back on campus, and he'd want Jacey in the hacienda, wearing a dress and scanty underthings and . . .

Jacey shivered and banished the thought. "It's better for me to go after him quickly, before he can prepare."

"But you don't even know where he is."

"I'll find him. There are at least seventy Progenitors out there. One of them has to have a way to contact the old man. I just need Captain Wilcox to get me off this island. Today."

Humphrey caught her arm and turned her toward him. "I swore I would never wear that stupid white suit again. Don't you know how it makes me feel? To pretend to be him?"

Jacey let him vent his frustration. Her mind was made up. "This isn't about you, Humphrey."

"You want me to ask Captain Wilcox to sweep you off into danger, on a mission I completely disapprove of. What kind of idiot do you take me for?"

Jacey tried to loosen her fingers, which had curled into fists. "Don't lecture me," she hissed. "You're more upset about having to put on Dr. Carlhagen's suit than me leaving."

"That's not true! How could you say that? Just saying that proves—" He turned his head away and picked up his pace. His legs were longer, forcing Jacey to race to keep up.

"I'll see you in Dr. Carlhagen's office," she said, and fell into a trot. She ran the rest of the way to the hacienda. Humphrey wouldn't run to keep up with her because that would make it look like he was chasing after her.

In the walk-in closet of Dr. Carlhagen's bedroom, she found three dresses. Mr. Justin had told her the headmaster had intended to surprise her with them.

She shook off a wave of unease at the memory of how the old man had touched her shoulders, the way his warm fingers had lingered against the skin of her neck as he'd clasped on a necklace.

She chose a dress at random and yanked the protective cover from it.

"What the—?" The entire garment sparkled like red stars. Squinting, she slid a hand over the odd fabric. It was covered with thousands of shiny red discs. She tossed it away from her. No way was she going to wear anything that red or that short.

She grabbed another dress. This one was black and sheer, but it seemed more suitable even though it was far too long. At least it would cover most of her legs.

In a few seconds, she'd slipped out of her uniform and put on the gown. Despite the plunging neckline and dinky little cap sleeves, it fit perfectly. Contorting herself to zip it up produced a string of curses, but she managed it. No way was she going to ask Humphrey to help her.

The silky black fabric draped over her hips and swept to a pool around her feet.

It was going to get dirty real quick, but she didn't know how to prevent it.

A stack of shoeboxes stood on the closet floor beneath the remaining dress. She figured one of the pair of shoes was meant to go with the dress. She rejected two pair that had precarious stilt heels. The third pair were flat-soled satin little nothings that looked like ballet slippers.

She decided to keep her Scion uniform shoes, which were more durable, more comfortable, and would be much more suitable for running, if the need arose.

She went to the bureau, pulled open a drawer, and flung aside the dainty underthings Dr. Carlhagen had insisted went better with her gowns than her standard-issue ones. She certainly wasn't going to need those. At the bottom of the drawer was the necklace Dr. Carlhagen had clasped around her throat during an excruciating dinner just days before. She left it there.

She checked the mirror, surprised to discover how the gown aged her, made her more . . . womanly. That was the only word she could come up with.

She hoped the gown would help her to blend in. She absolutely couldn't wear a Scion uniform out in the world.

Her Shark pin sparkled on the collar of her uniform top. She removed it and turned to the mirror. With a strange sense of sadness mixed with pride, she pinned it to the bodice of her dress. It didn't quite go, but she wanted it, wanted that connection to the Scion School as a reminder of where she'd come from, and of the family that she'd sworn to protect.

Most of all, it reminded her of the day she'd received the pin. The very same day Livy had arrived on campus.

A door thunked down the hall. Humphrey going into his room to change. At least, she hoped he was changing. It'd be a real challenge to talk Captain Wilcox into coming for her without his help, and he couldn't do it dressed as a Scion.

Jacey shook her hands at her side, trying to shed her weird mood, and hustled down the hallway to Dr. Carlhagen's office.

Less than a minute later, Humphrey swept in wearing the top half of Dr. Carlhagen's white suit, but still wearing his Scion School trousers. It didn't matter. The holodesk cameras wouldn't pick up that part of him if he stayed in his chair.

He didn't look at her as he went to the seat behind Dr. Carlhagen's great mahogany desk. Heaving a huge sigh, he said, "Where do you want Captain Wilcox to take you?"

"Elizabeth's island. I'm going to tell Elizabeth that I've been transferred, but that I did not have a good cover story in place because I transferred early. Mr. Justin said that Elizabeth had offered to help Janicka with the same problem. It never happened because . . ."

She didn't finish. Humphrey already knew Janicka's fate.

"Beyond that," she continued, "I want to see if Elizabeth's island will be a good place for you to take the Scions."

"Me?" His face snapped toward her, blue eyes drilling into hers. "And what about you?"

"I'll be trying to track down Dr. Carlhagen and Livy. You'll have to get everyone aboard *Aphrodite* and out to sea as fast as you can. Elizabeth will have a holodesk. I'll contact you on the boat and let you know whether Elizabeth's island is safe or not. I got the impression from Mr. Justin that it's a very quiet place. And even as a temporary stop for the Scions, I think it's best to get them off the boat as quickly as possible. Once Senator Bentilius's forces realize no one's here, they're going to begin searching all the boats in the area."

Humphrey gave a grudging nod. "Let's get this over with." He put his palms flat on the desk. "Captain Wilcox."

It took a while for the captain's holovid to appear above the desk. Even as a 15-centimeter-tall image, the man intimidated Jacey. She stayed out of view of the holodesk's cameras, but sat close enough to see the grim expression on the soldier's face.

"Good morning, Dr. Carlhagen," the man said. He stood rigid, with his hands clasped behind his back.

"Ah, Captain Wilcox, good to see you. I need you to come to St. Vitus."

Humphrey was putting on his Dr. Carlhagen impersonation, which always spooked her because it was so perfect.

He continued. "I had a Progenitor arrive for an early transfer due to an illness. It was quite an emergency. Unfortunately, her cover story isn't well developed and she needs some assistance in preparing the way back into the outside world."

"And where do you want me to take her? The range of the helicopter isn't that great."

"Elizabeth Burnell's island. She has offered to assist

Progenitors who find themselves in such predicaments. Do you think your aircraft has the range for that?"

Captain Wilcox smirked, as if responding to a bit of sharp sarcasm. "I think it will make it, sir." There was a wry quality to his response. Jacey had the impression the soldier thought Humphrey was making a joke.

"How soon can we expect you, captain?" Humphrey asked. He let his eyelids fall into a haughty, bored expression. He was done with this conversation and he wanted Wilcox to hurry up.

Jacey had to admire the performance. He certainly knew how to play Dr. Carlhagen. And even though Humphrey didn't want Jacey to leave, he put on a show even Madam LaFontaine would've approved of.

Captain Wilcox managed to stiffen his posture even more. "Give me thirty minutes. As always, I have the helicopter fueled and ready to go. I'll muster the pilot. Do I need to bring the full contingent of soldiers?"

"No," Humphrey said, "You don't even have to get out of the helicopter. The Progenitor will come to you, and you'll recognize her by her clothing." Humphrey's gaze ran up and down Jacey's gown with great disapproval.

"Very well. Captain Wilcox out." The hologram disappeared.

Humphrey slumped back in his chair, hand immediately going to his bowtie and tugging it loose. "There, it's done."

"Thank you. I know how hard it was."

"The problem is that it wasn't hard at all. I'm too damn good at it."

Jacey went behind him, wrapped her arms around his chest, and kissed his cheek. "I don't know how long it's going to take, but trust me, I will find Livy. And we will find a safe place for the Scions."

"I wish I had your confidence." His hands rose to cover one of hers, pressed it to his heart. "This is a dangerous game. Once we leave the island, we won't be able to see any of the pieces on the board."

Jacey had no answer for his worries except to kiss him again. He swiveled the chair and drew her into his lap. His hands wove into her hair as he drew her down for a longer kiss.

A cough startled them both.

Leslie stood in the doorway, face grave. She held up a reader. "The network is down. Madam LaFontaine won't come to the studio mirrors. Chax isn't on any of the security panels, and Newton won't come to the holodesks in the classrooms."

Jacey tried to summon Vaughan on Dr. Carlhagen's holodesk. No response.

"Dr. Carlhagen must have shut down the network before he left," Jacey said.

"But how?" Humphrey asked. "The servers are not in the medical ward."

Jacey bit her thumbnail as worry began to churn in her mind. "Maybe he gave a command through Chax's security terminal. What I don't understand is why he'd bother."

"To put us at a disadvantage when the security forces arrive," Leslie said. "Now we can't use the network to communicate with each other."

Humphrey shrugged. "That doesn't make sense. He knows we have walkie-talkies."

Jacey walked around the holodesk and looked out the window. The red roofs of the Scion School shone beneath the blazing sun. It looked like any other day on campus. Nothing gave any indication that everyone's fate lay in the balance. "Maybe Dr. Carlhagen meant it to be a distraction, to make us waste time looking for the AI servers."

"Maybe," Humphrey said.

"Why are you dressed like that?" Leslie asked.

"I'm going to scout a location for the Scions. Captain Wilcox is picking me up."

Leslie's brow furrowed and she stood in the doorway, as if she planned to keep Jacey from leaving. "That is stupid. You'll get caught."

"I'm not going to debate my plan with you."

Nostril's flaring, Leslie looked about to rush at Jacey. But instead, she spun and stormed out.

"She's not handling this well," Humphrey said. "I think she's trying so hard to be like Belle, but she's just too scared to pull it off."

"She'll be fine once you're out to sea. Will you come with me to the bell tower while I wait for the helicopter to come?"

"Do you really have to do this alone?"

"Yes."

Jacey smoothed the skirt of her dress and took a last look around the office, as if searching for some item she couldn't do without while off the island. There was nothing.

It was time to go.

But now that it came to it, she hesitated. As terrible as her fate would be if she stayed, she had no promise things would be better off the island. She recalled a saying Socrates had often repeated: *Better the devil you know than the devil you don't.*

She'd never understood the phrase until this moment.

But then another of Socrates's sayings popped into her mind. An answer to the fear the first one produced. *Nothing ventured, nothing gained.*

In thirty seconds she was out of the hacienda and striding down the path toward the quad. Humphrey walked with her, silently. But his dread was louder to her than any shout.

"This is going to work."

He took her hand and gave her a fake smile. It was the best he could give her, she knew. But she needed so much more.

22

PEOPLE AS TOOLS

The roar and vibration of the helicopter's engines lulled Dr. Carlhagen into a state of exhausted relaxation. It magnified the effects of the andleprixen Mr. Justin had slipped him. Still, he fought to keep his eyes open rather than slip into numb oblivion.

And that was because everything was wrong.

Even with his painkillers, his body ached from the beating that Scion had dealt him. At some point he'd have to contact the boy's Progenitor.

He'd have to say the boy's death was an accident.

He dragged his thumbs over the slip of paper Senator Bentilius had handed him in response to his question about why she had killed her guards. She had received the note from Mr. Justin, slipped under her door. It included all the same business about being ready to leave at the sound of the choppers. But there was an extra line at the bottom, scrawled in a different color ink—red—and in a hurried hand: *Your guards have been talking.*

Senator Bentilius's actions made more sense in light of

the note. But the note itself bothered him. Why would Mr. Justin tell her about her men talking?

What was Mr. Justin playing at? The question would have driven Dr. Carlhagen mad, except he had yet another issue to deal with.

Senator Bentilius kept glaring at him and Livy.

The girl sat on the floor, hugging her knees, back pressed to the hatch door. The cramped compartment quickly grew sour with sweat and the acrid tinge of engine exhaust.

Senator Bentilius's mood hung over it all, like the constriction one feels upon entering a room and interrupting an argument between two friends. Dr. Carlhagen had experienced many such moods, often of his own creation. Rarely had he been subjected to it by others.

The woman sat very still, icy blue eyes fixed straight ahead. She'd drawn her hair back so that the headset could better cover her ears. A smear of blood streaked through her snowy locks, stark as Tinlon's slashed throat. She hadn't gotten all of it off her hands, it seemed.

Occasionally she spoke, but so softly Dr. Carlhagen couldn't hear the words. An intercom mic jutted from one side of the headset. She had to be speaking with the pilot on a separate channel. Probably giving him directions.

The woman had mutinied on him. She hadn't even asked his opinion about going to St. Lazarus.

On most navigation charts, including military ones, the island of St. Lazarus appeared as nothing but a tiny green blip in the sea. Nothing special. All databases listed it as uninhabited, too small to sustain any sort of community. Which was true, except that once the new Scion facility was up and running there, regular supply boats would import all the necessities for survival.

But why the hell did Senator Bentilius want to go there?

Puerto Rico was closer and offered more luxurious accommodations, no questions asked. And if that was too high-profile, the Virgin Islands—the parts that hadn't been washed away by the asteroid tsunamis forty years earlier— were even closer, and would provide more convenient headquarters to oversee the invasion of St. Vitus.

The only reason to go to St. Lazarus was to inspect the construction or to manage the startup of the facility. The only other reason he could think of was to hide.

And there it was. Senator Bentilius couldn't go anywhere until she'd laid new groundwork for her entry into the world. He didn't know how many people in her organization knew about the Scion program, but none of them would be ready for her reappearance as a slender, icy blond girl of seventeen. She'd have to contact them, one by one, and get them prepared.

She'd already told him she wouldn't be returning to politics in any public way. No doubt she intended to pull strings from behind the scenes. And now it all made sense.

The strings she intended to pull were the ones Dr. Carl-hagen himself intended to pull.

Whoever controlled the Scion program controlled everything. If only she knew how much leverage he had.

His gaze drifted back to Livy. She stared straight back. Her earlier defiance was gone, replaced by a chilling curiosity. If the girl had been ten years older, the look wouldn't have given him pause. But in the eyes of a nine-year-old, the stare was downright creepy.

He jumped as the senator's voice blared in his ears. "We'll make good use of her." He fumbled for the volume control on the right side of his headset, twisted it down a few notches. The senator must have switched comm chan-nels again.

He thumbed the transmission button bulging from the

headset cord. "Yes. Threatening her will subdue whatever rebelliousness remains among the Scions. And without shooting any more of them." He threw a dark look at the guard. The man either didn't hear him or just ignored him.

"That's not what I meant," Senator Bentilius said. "I was thinking that since the cryopods are ready and the medibots have all been checked out, we could use this girl as a guinea pig."

"She's too old. The pods are intended to start the infants."

Livy seemed to sense they were speaking about her, for her eyes tracked their conversation. Dr. Carlhagen knew she couldn't hear anything over the roar of the engine, though it wouldn't matter. Livy certainly had never heard the terms "cryopod" or "medibot."

Senator Bentilius nodded as if he'd agreed with her. "And the pods have room for those infants to grow into fourteen-year-olds." Senator Bentilius cut off his rebuttal with a slice of her hand. "There's no reason this child shouldn't go in. Besides, if she gives me as much leverage over the Scions on St. Vitus as you say she will, it would be foolish of me to return her to them."

Me. Me. Me. Yes, everything was becoming clear to Dr. Carlhagen. Senator Bentilius was taking charge. Did she really think he'd allow that?

"Maxine, my dear, you seem to be suffering from the misapprehension that you have the slightest authority over the Scions. You do not." He smacked his palm against his chest. "I invented the technology for mind transfer. I created the Scion School. I sold each and every Progenitor on the idea, including you."

Senator Bentilius pursed her lips and her eyelids drooped with cool disinterest at his statement. "And you seem to believe I won't order my guard to shoot you."

A slight movement in his peripheral vision drew his attention. The guard had raised his weapon. The end of the barrel formed a perfect circle that seemed quite large when aimed at Dr. Carlhagen's face.

"I enjoy your company, Christof," Senator Bentilius said lightly. "I look forward to long days and nights enjoying our young bodies together. But I don't need you for the Scion program. As it is, I don't have any faith in your ability to manage the facility on St. Vitus. And certainly not the new one on St. Lazarus. And since my body's youth forbids any return to politics for many years to come, I've decided to take over the day-to-day operation of both facilities."

Despite the fury smashing in his heart, Dr. Carlhagen strained to maintain an outward calm. He would not reward the senator with an outburst. It took no genius to see his position at this moment was weak at best. He shifted slightly in his seat and made an effort to lean back and appear relaxed. "Very well, my dear. I've worked hard enough to get the program off the ground, why shouldn't I leave the clerical work in your very competent hands?"

He closed his eyes and forced his breath to deepen. *Let her think I've given up. Let her drop her guard.*

After all these years, nothing had changed about Maxine Bentilius. She still used people as tools. For her pleasure. For revenge. For leverage. For fun. Dr. Carlhagen respected that. After all, her ruthlessness was the primary reason he'd allied with her when it had come time to expand the Scion program.

He would play along with this little coup of hers. Humor her. What difference did it make if Livy were put into a cryopod for six or seven years? Assuming she survived the drawdown and suffusion procedures, she'd be as good as new when she came out.

He kept the smile from his lips as he ran through the list of Progenitors who had already sponsored Scions. Yes. Senator Bentilius had figured out who some of them were. But not many. Because if she had, she wouldn't be so cavalier about taking control of the school. With all her years in politics, she thought she was well-connected. She thought she could flout any law she wanted. And she'd broken scores of them by helping him expand the Scion program.

Yes. She was important. Powerful. But if she knew who else was keeping an eye on the Scion program, she'd be fighting the guard for the chance to jump out the door right now.

The chopper banked to the right and started a gradual descent toward a blob of green on the horizon.

The island of St. Lazarus.

A sharp mountain peak jutted from the eastern side of the island. It looked as tiny as the point of a thumbtack from this vantage.

For the past six years, a construction crew composed mostly of Pakistanis had been excavating a secure compound deep into the guts of the mountain. The construction company's managers had believed they were building a seed vault, intended to preserve plant seeds from future catastrophes like the Kille-Tine asteroid impacts.

The Chinese teams who had later installed the cryopods thought they were installing hydroponic grow-beds for underground seed starters. The medibots had gone in as automated pea shuckers, since the robots themselves were general-purpose devices. What made them special was the AI that controlled them, an installation that Dr. Carlhagen had handled himself.

He fluttered his eyelids and passed a glaze-eyed look at the guard. He hoped the wiry man saw his look as the temporary wakefulness of person sleeping in an uncomfortable position. Dr. Carlhagen took in the man's body armor, weapons, his stature. He sat like a stone statue. Strong. Immobile. Dangerous.

Dr. Carlhagen would watch his step. He might even have to put Livy into the drawdown hibernation of a cryopod. But at the time of his choosing, he would strike. The guard first. Then the senator.

The important thing was that he had Livy in his possession.

That would force Jacqueline to come to him.

23

ABOUT TO FLY

Jacey paced back and forth in the entrance to the bell tower as she waited for the helicopter.

Humphrey sat on the first of the aged wooden steps that led to the top of the tower. He had his head in his hands, but his left toe tapped nervously on the dust on the floor. "We should talk to Sensei about this," Humphrey said. "Maybe he'll have another idea, another place we could go once we're on the boat."

"If Sensei knew of a place, he would have told us. Besides, it's better I leave before he gets back from the docks. He would just try to talk me out of going."

"Of course he would," Humphrey said.

And he might be successful, Jacey thought. She just wanted to get out of there, get going, get Livy.

Humphrey stood and brushed off the seat of his white pants. Jacey had convinced him that he needed to at least walk with her onto the quad when the helicopter arrived, wave at Captain Wilcox. And he couldn't have done that wearing only his uniform pants and the white coat.

"When the bus arrives, get everyone loaded, turn it around, and get back to *Aphrodite*," she said. "And don't forget to get the transfer machine on board. It's essential that we have it."

"I know what to do." He shoved his hands in his pockets. "But it's not going to be that easy. We have to get the bus all the way to the hacienda."

Jacey stopped her pacing and spun on him. "What do you mean you have to take the bus to the hacienda?"

"The holodesk," Humphrey said simply. Jacey looked at the rough plank ceiling overhead and sighed. She had completely forgotten. The boat didn't have a holodesk built in, and so they planned to take Dr. Carlhagen's.

"That's assuming it even works once it's powered up," Humphrey said. "I honestly have no idea how to connect it to the boat's communication systems."

Jacey sighed and waved her hand, dismissing the whole topic. "Summer will figure it out. Can I borrow your reader? I want to talk to Wanda about something."

"I don't have my reader," Humphrey said. "It's still in the wine cellar so Vaughan can—" His face drooped in shock. "Of course."

He rushed to Jacey, put his hands on her shoulders and kissed her. "I can't wait for the helicopter. I've got to get to the hacienda. Contact me as soon as you arrive at Elizabeth's."

"But I don't even know if she'll let me in her house."

He smiled a rakish grin that reminded her of Dante, one of the Scions who had been overwritten. "Then break in." He dashed away, the tail of Dr. Carlhagen's white coat streaming behind him.

Jacey stood just inside the archway of the bell tower, trying to keep out of sight. The Scions had all gone indoors to make final preparations, but in case one came out she didn't want questions about why she was dressed the way she was.

A rumble sounded to the west. She recognized the grind of the bus's engine. Sensei and the others must have hoisted it off the boat in record time. That was good. Humphrey would have them loaded up and headed back to the boat in an hour.

The helicopter flew in from the west, the sight of it filling Jacey with gut-clenching anxiety. She was about to leave St. Vitus. She was about to put herself completely in Captain Wilcox's power.

She was about to fly.

Jacey didn't wait for the skids to touch the grass before grabbing fistfuls of her skirt and trotting into the open. A black-gloved hand extended from the hatch. She grasped it and was pulled into the relative stillness of the helicopter.

Captain Wilcox guided her to a seat and strapped her in. She looked up into his face, fighting the urge to punch him. This was the man who had thrown Nurse Smith to her death, and who would have done the same to Sensei— if Sensei hadn't jumped out first.

The man had steel gray eyes and a jaw of granite. "You?" he said, leaning away from her. "You can't have transferred. Your Progenitor is dead."

Jacey stifled a curse and busied herself with checking her buckles. Dr. Carlhagen must have told Captain Wilcox about her Progenitor, a woman named Jacqueline Buchanan. Apparently she'd died in a boating accident with Vaughan's Progenitor. It still seemed strange to her that her and Vaughan's Progenitors had been married.

Thinking quickly, she pasted on a smile and patted Captain Wilcox's knee. "I'm not supposed to say anything about how it works. But Dr. Carlhagen made a backup of my brain before I died. He did the same for—"

Shut up, Jacey. You're talking too much. That's what liars do.

She clamped her mouth shut and gripped the seat straps crossing her shoulders. Captain Wilcox frowned at her, but signaled to the pilot to go. The engines wound up to a higher pitch and the helicopter tilted to one side. A childish cry escaped Jacey's lips and she gave Captain Wilcox a sheepish grin.

"My first time in a helicopter," she shouted to the man.

His brows came together. "You piloted a helicopter in my favorite film of yours: *Geishas Seven.* I suppose that was all just special effects, though."

Jacey had no idea what he was talking about. She berated herself for offering more information than necessary and snaring herself in a trap of her own making. Giggling to cover her embarrassment, she said, "I meant it was my first time on this kind of helicopter."

"You need to work on your lies." He bent closer to her. "Did you know you were getting *her* body when you arrived?"

Something in his tone sent a sizzle of warning through Jacey's mind. What had he meant by emphasizing *her* body? He seemed to be suggesting that she wasn't Jacqueline at all. Yes. That was it. He thought she was someone else, someone who had overwritten Jacey the way Senator Bentilius had overwritten Belle.

Jacey decided to temporize, offering a response that didn't answer the question. "When you're dying, you don't complain about the cure."

He seemed satisfied with her answer. His eyes went to the skirt of her gown. "You really came ready to dress the part. Going to a red carpet somewhere?" His laugh was a gravel-crushing rumble in his throat.

Red carpet? It had to be a euphemism, but Jacey had no idea what it meant. Still, she wanted to encourage his joviality, so she let out bubbles of laughter. "Maybe someday."

The helicopter tilted again and Jacey swallowed hard, trying not to let her fear show. The machine carved a circle in the air around the school. Captain Wilcox pulled a headset from a clamp on one bulkhead. He pressed an ear cup to the side of his head, brought the mic to his lips and spoke. Jacey didn't hear what he said.

The hard-eyed man dropped the headset and scrambled to the hatch. He peered through the side window. His curse resounded in the small compartment. Spinning, he threw himself close to Jacey.

She flinched, fearing he was going to strangle her.

Instead he pressed his mouth to her ear. "Why is there a boat at the docks? Why is there a bus approaching the Scion School gate?"

Keep calm, she told herself. She wanted to beat her forehead with her fist. Why hadn't she thought this through? Of course the pilot would see the boat and the bus. She'd been lucky that Captain Wilcox hadn't spotted them on his way to the school.

"Dr. Carlhagen said something about bringing kids from Mother Tyeesha's to the campus so they could get some familiarity with the school. I only saw the old woman once while I was there. I was preoccupied with other things. Ha ha."

The helicopter continued to circle. The pilot waved to get Captain Wilcox's attention. The soldier picked up the headset and had a short conversation with the pilot. The helicopter leveled and gained altitude.

Captain Wilcox seated himself and buckled in. He did not speak to Jacey again; his eyes stayed pasted to the window, even though there was nothing to see through it but blue sky.

She could tell by the way he held his body he wanted nothing more than to gather his gunmen and go back to St. Vitus.

She closed her eyes for a while, let the hum and vibration of the aircraft soothe her. An odd noise broke through her light dozing, and she opened her eyes to find Captain Wilcox watching her. A humorless smile twisted his mouth and he shook his head side-to-side. He was laughing.

It seemed calculated to get her to ask what was so funny. She kept her mouth shut.

Her mind returned to what he'd meant by asking about "her" body. He'd said it as if it was an undesirable body to have.

An insidious question kept repeating in her mind: what's wrong with my body? What's wrong with my body?

She had no idea.

24

WHO IS MARILYN MONROE?

The rubber soles of Humphrey's canvas shoes skidded on the tile in the hacienda hallway as he stopped breathlessly at the wine cellar door. If what he suspected was true, there was almost no time to act.

He yanked on the handle, flipped the switch, and took the steps two at a time.

At the bottom, he sprinted among the crisscross wine shelves straight to the back of the cellar, his footsteps echoing off the arched ceiling.

The odd steel door at the rear of the cellar was closed. He spared it the slightest glance before going up on tiptoes to grab his reader, which he'd left leaning on top of one of the wine racks in the shadows.

It wasn't there.

It must have fallen flat atop the rack. He felt around, hand slapping up dust that stung his nose and made him sneeze.

He ran around the cellar in search of a stool. An old

metal bucket, turned upside down, gave him just enough height to discover his worst fear had come true.

The reader was gone.

Mr. Justin had come for the servers and somehow had noticed the reader spying on him. What a stroke of bad luck.

Humphrey went to the door, pressed his forehead against it. Jacey had certainly left by now, and a pang of regret filled his heart at how they had parted ways so abruptly and with so much unresolved. Time was clicking by fast, and he had to get everyone to the boat and off the island.

So much to do before that. Most importantly, he had to make sure the holodesk was loaded onto the boat.

Warring with the pressing need to get away from St. Vitus was the insistent certainty that Mr. Justin had recently been through that damned door. Maybe he had left some clue about who he was or where he might have stashed the servers. Maybe he hadn't even taken them.

Humphrey pounded on the door. Infuriated, he grabbed the handle, twisted and yanked. The door swung open without resistance and he nearly fell on his butt.

When Mr. Justin had left the room, he hadn't locked the door. Humphrey was glad nobody had witnessed his stupidity.

The room beyond was dark. Humphrey struggled to his feet, panting.

Light from the cellar painted across rough stone walls and ceiling. It was the same material as the wine cellar, but unfinished, as if the room had been a hasty addition. It was small, no bigger than a closet.

A metal rack stood along the rear walls. Empty screw holes ran down each side of the front risers. A thick bundle of cables lay on the floor next to it. Numbers from 1 to 14 were written on tape labels starting at the top and going down the side of rack. Each position was empty.

He squinted at the screw holes. Only the top four showed any signs of wear. It was obvious that some equipment had once been mounted to the rack in those spots. Madame LaFontaine's computer server. That meant Vaughan's server had been there, too.

Mr. Justin had come to collect them. But why? And where had he taken them?

The only answer was that Mr. Justin knew Senator Bentilius's force was on its way, and for some reason he wanted the AIs out of their grasp.

There was nothing else in the tiny room, so Humphrey left, not even bothering to close the door behind him.

As he stormed down the gravel path toward the quad, he heard the whoop of the campus gate alarm. That could mean only one thing. Sensei had returned with the bus.

THE BUS GRUMBLED to a stop in the middle of the quad. Acrid exhaust fumes carried to Humphrey's nose, making him cough.

The door folded open and Sensei stared out. "Where's the helicopter?" Kirk and Dajeet were sitting in the front two seats. The rest were empty.

"Gone," Humphrey said, climbing aboard. "Go straight to the hacienda."

"That's a lot of sharp turns," Sensei said, eyeing the path.

"Don't worry about the turns, go through the damn hedges. We have to get the holodesk."

"What happened?"

Wanda, Tytus, Leslie, and Obu appeared at the door of

the bus. Questioning looks all around. Humphrey waved them aboard. "Just drive, Sensei. I'll tell you on the way."

Sensei frowned, but he gunned the motor, turned the wheel and headed up the path. He didn't run down the hedges the way Humphrey wanted him to, which he supposed was smart. If the bus got stuck, they were done for.

Humphrey didn't know how to break the news to Sensei about any of what had happened, so he just blurted it all out. He told the story in short bursts—interrupted by cries of horror, outrage, and disbelief.

Kirk seemed struck numb by the news of Constantine's death. When he learned that Horace had started it, he buried his face in his hands and wept. Dajeet moved next to him, rubbed his back, and murmured tearful comforts to him.

From the way Sensei's knuckles whitened on the steering wheel, Humphrey was afraid the man was going to rip it right out and chew it in half. "Horace must be punished. Severely."

"He still has the gun."

"I'll take care of that." The look in Sensei's eyes brought a burst of sympathy for Horace. But it only lasted a moment.

Humphrey finished the story. "Jacey decided to go after Dr. Carlhagen. She had Captain Wilcox take her to see a Progenitor who lives nearby, a woman named Elizabeth."

Sensei's head snapped around. "You're kidding. Elizabeth is one of them. She's never going to help Jacey. She's not going to help any of you Scions."

"Jacey considered that. She's going to tell Elizabeth that her Progenitor came to transfer early. The way Senator Bentilius did."

Sensei brought the bus to a stop and turned in his seat.

"That won't work." He was half-grimacing, half-laughing, though humorlessly. Humphrey had never seen the martial arts master's face so gaunt, so haunted.

"What do you mean?" Humphrey asked, suddenly defensive on Jacey's behalf. "It's a sensible cover story. Elizabeth has no reason to doubt it."

"You don't understand. Jacey has one of the most recognizable faces on earth."

It was Humphrey's turn to laugh. "This isn't a time for a joke. How can anybody know who Jacey is? We've never been off the island."

"I'm talking about her Progenitor, Jacqueline Buchanan," Sensei said, pausing and pressing a thick palm to his face. "She was the most famous actress who ever lived. Somebody did a poll of famous faces about ten years ago. Jackie B was the most recognized by a nine point margin over Marilyn Monroe."

"Who is Marilyn Monroe?" Obu asked. Sensei didn't answer.

Humphrey sank into one of the vinyl seats. The other Scions stared at each other, each falling into the same shocked reverie.

Sensei just laughed, but there was only bitterness in it. "Jacey doesn't know what she's getting into. It doesn't matter if Elizabeth helps her or not. Even if she gets off that island and into North America, there's absolutely nowhere she can go anonymously. She'll be hounded by paparazzi."

Humphrey stared out the window but didn't see the hacienda or the thick foliage or Bird of Paradise blooms. He only saw Jacey in her black dress, furious at him for arguing with her.

"There's nothing we can do about it," Wanda said softly. "Jacey had to go after Livy. We all know that. And she will have to take care of herself. Let's go get the holodesk and get out of here."

Wanda's soft and sensible words seemed to pull Sensei out of his odd mood and he lurched out of his seat. He called for Kirk and Obu, and together they headed into the hacienda.

Humphrey had no experience consoling anyone, but he felt he should say something to Kirk. "Con got some good blows in on Dr. Carlhagen."

Kirk swiped his sleeve across his nose. "He did?"

"I wish you could have seen it. He knocked him onto the grass. The old man's going to have some bad bruises."

The Spider didn't smile. In fact, his lips trembled. But he nodded, as if taking this as good news. His shoulders straightened and he lifted his chin. "I hope to leave some bruises on him myself. Someday."

Humphrey let Kirk walk ahead of him, feeling defeated in his effort to comfort the boy.

He felt a pat on his arm. Wanda walked next to him, eyes glistening. "Well done."

Behind him, Dajeet sniffled. A moment later she appeared on his other side and gave him an awkward hug. It ended the second it began. She didn't look at him.

Their acts of support made his vision blur, and he forced himself not to blink and let the tears fall.

It took a lot of grunts, groans, sweat, and a fair amount of cursing from all involved, but they managed to move the heavy mahogany holodesk, trailing a bundle of wires behind them. In ten minutes they had it wedged into the back of the bus.

Humphrey's thoughts were so much with Jacey and

what she was walking into that he remembered very little of the process. By the time they got back to the quad the Scions were all lined up and ready to board the bus. Humphrey didn't even get out.

"She can think on her feet," he said aloud to himself. "If anyone can navigate this situation, it's Jacey." She was the best actor he knew, which admittedly wasn't saying much.

"Damn Dr. Carlhagen," he said. "Damn him to hell."

Sensei heard this last bit and nodded. "Amen." He stood and squeezed out of the bus, past the stream of younger Scions trying to board. He waved for Humphrey to follow.

"We need to get going," Humphrey said.

"We need a boat captain, don't we?"

Humphrey rolled his eyes. He wanted to slap his own face. He'd forgotten Orson.

"Coming." As he trailed Sensei toward the medical ward, he wondered what else he was forgetting. And then he saw.

Leslie had commandeered a bunch of younger Scions. Together they were carrying bits of equipment from the medical ward. When Terrel and Conrad, two twelve-year-old Crabs, backed out carrying a huge white circle, he realized what it was.

The transfer machine. Jacey had told him not to forget and he had. Fortunately, Leslie hadn't.

Mother Tyeesha tottered from Girls' Hall, a trail of little ones behind her. Her two adult staffers carried infants, as did two of the eight-year-olds.

Miss Dayspring emerged from the medical ward, arms full of a white bundle. It looked like a bed sheet. It bulged with the various medical supplies she'd collected at Jacey's insistence.

Horace pushed Sang ahead of him. Humphrey noted

the gun was gone. The Snake's face was full of grim fury. He took it out on Sang, mercilessly shoving and cursing the boy. Sang's face was puffy and blackened from the beating he'd taken.

Less than five minutes later, Humphrey was back aboard a bus overstuffed with Scions and children. Orson and his two men were in the front seats, none looking too well. The air smelled of sweat. Faces were drawn, voices low. Older Scions snapped younger ones to silence.

Wanda met his gaze and nodded.

"Let's go, Sensei. Let's get off this damned island."

25

______

FRENCH FOR BEAUTIFUL

As the helicopter began its slow descent, Jacey unbuckled her harness and shifted across the cabin to look out the hatch window. Captain Wilcox made no move to stop her.

The island below was a blob of green surrounded by an endless blue sea. Just like St. Vitus, hills rose in scrub-covered ridges along the middle of the island. To the west spread the canopy of a thick forest. Slashes of beige beaches hugged the shores here and there.

A compound of metal-roofed buildings huddled near one inlet. The structures looked like garages, except for the windows and doors. A trail of men in uniform ran along a coastal path. A square landing pad sat atop a hill, the top chopped off as if with a giant knife.

"That's our base," Wilcox said. "We'll be neighbors."

Jacey realized how odd Humphrey's orders to Captain Wilcox must have been, requesting he take Jacey to "Elizabeth's Island." No wonder the man has been amused.

Nothing to be done about it now. And maybe it was good he was based so near. If things didn't go well with Elizabeth, Jacey could get a ride back to St. Vitus. Or somewhere. Surely Captain Wilcox knew how to get in touch with Dr. Carlhagen.

She watched the island pass beneath her, amazed that a single person could own such an area of land. The coast grew rougher, the cliffs more jagged.

And there, set atop the cliffs surrounding a docile bay, stood Elizabeth's home: a sprawling mansion of concrete, steel, and glass. The design reminded Jacey of the building blocks she'd played with at Mother Tyeesha's a lifetime ago. The whole house was structured from huge square and rectangular pods interconnected in pleasing proportions.

The helicopter circled and approached a concrete pad set atop a barren rise overlooking the house. At the mansion, a tiny figure in white stood on a patio facing the ocean. Whether it was a man or woman, Jacey couldn't tell. But the figure had an arm raised to shield their eyes from the sun.

Jacey noticed more people arranged around the pool, all topless—or nearly so—and lying on reclining chairs. The helicopter twisted away, but not before she'd counted at least seven other people.

And just like that, the flight was over. The skids touched down on the landing pad. Captain Wilcox thrust open the hatch door and hopped down. Jacey took his hand and jumped out after him.

"That's the path to the house," he said, pointing to Jacey's right. "I hope she's expecting you." He didn't wait for an answer before climbing back into the aircraft. No sooner had the hatch slammed shut than the blades spun back up, downdraft whipping against Jacey's body and blowing her hair across her face and plastering the drapes of her dress to her body.

Ducking, she shuffled for the path, cursing her confining outfit.

The helicopter passed directly overhead, then charged west toward its home base.

Jacey made it twenty meters down the path, then stopped in her tracks. Standing in her way, dressed in loose-fitting pants and tunic of white, was a ghost from her past.

Dante.

He'd been Vaughan's best friend and frequent co-conspirator. Not long ago, on Birthday, Dante had hidden a radio transmitter in his uniform when he'd gone into the medical ward right after graduation.

Jacey, Vaughan, and Humphrey had gone to the top of the bell tower, where they'd listened to Dante's transmission. And that's when everything had changed.

They'd heard the Scions meet adults that Dr. Carlhagen called Progenitors. From that point forward, Jacey's life had been nothing but turmoil.

But this isn't Dante, she reminded herself. This was the man who'd overwritten Dante's mind. This was the enemy.

"Jesus Christ!" Dante-who-was-not-Dante said, smiling lazily. "If I'd known *you* were in the Scion program, I would've stuck around a few more days. Nice dress, by the way."

"Um, thank you," Jacey said, confused by the fact he recognized her. "I came to see Elizabeth."

"She's back at the house. I've been appointed as the greeting committee for her big to-do. So what the hell are you calling yourself these days, Jackie?"

"Jacey. And who the hell are you?" she asked, courteously returning the curse. Inside, a sense of foreboding curled around her heart like a python. He'd apparently known her Progenitor well enough to use the familiar form of Jacqueline's name.

His smile widened and he pressed a hand to his flat belly as he laughed. "Don't you recognize me, Jackie? But I don't suppose you would remember a mere billionaire from Brazil who wrote checks to all your charities."

Jacey's blank look made him frown. He approached, one hand out. His smile was fake now. "I was Silvio. But call me Dante from now on. New identity, and all."

Jacey took his hand, remembering a vid she'd seen that showed clasping of hands as a formal greeting. Silvio put his other hot hand over hers and drew her close. He pressed his lips to her knuckles. "Charmed."

She pulled her hand free and took a step back. "Are you going to escort me to the house, or shall we stand here for the rest of the day?"

Chuckling, Silvio guided Jacey along a well-worn path among an explosion of hibiscus and frangipani. The flowers were too sweet, the air too hot.

She found the man's insistence in helping her down the gently paved steps irritating. He was always bounding down ahead of her, then taking her hand, as if she might trip over her own feet. Then he'd place a hand firmly against the small of her back and gently steer her. The hand often curled around her waist and wandered down the side of her leg.

"I can handle walking quite easily without you pushing me around, Silvio."

"It's Dante," he snapped irritably. But he made no move to distance himself from her. The hand-holding and back-steering continued as the path descended and twisted through a canyon-like passageway in the bedrock of the island. Once past the turns in the path, he leaned into her shoulder and put his face close to hers.

"So, my darling. Mind telling me how you pulled it off?"

Jacey glared at him. She'd learned her lesson about saying too much during her conversation with Captain Wilcox. "I have no idea what you're talking about."

His whole chest moved as he laughed. But the mirth faded quickly. Eyes narrowing, he considered her face as if reassessing a prior judgment. "Hmm. Maybe I shouldn't be surprised that you're good at playing dumb. Acting is pure deceit, is it not?" He gave her a conspiratorial leer. "So, the whole boating accident thing. That was your cover story, eh?"

Acting?

Dr. Carlhagen had mentioned Jacqueline had been an actor.

Silvio thought Jacqueline had faked the boating accident to prepare the way for her Scion to come out into the world. Seizing on the idea, she turned her head away, pretending to mask a smile.

"Ah, my darling. No need to play coy with me." He snaked an arm around her waist and pulled her close, which threw off her gait and made her stumble. He caught her and suddenly she was engulfed in his arms. "We Progenitors must help each other, no?"

She stiffened and pushed at his shoulders until he released her. "Help each other, yes. Manhandle, no."

He burst into more laughter. "Accept my apologies, my lovely. It's this new virile body of mine. A blessing and a curse." Though nobody was around to overhear, he put a hand to his mouth and whispered to her. "Elizabeth and I have spent half our time in bed since transferring. And most definitely *not* sleeping!"

"Seems a waste of time, if you ask me. I want to get back out into the world as soon as possible."

His humor vanished, and a look like fear darkened his eyes. "But my dear Jacqueline, is that wise?"

She nearly tripped again, but this time she had her hands out to push away his overly fond rescue attempt. "My name is Jacey." She put as much indignation into it as Silvio had when she had used his Progenitor's name. It did the trick.

"Oh. Of course. *Jacey*." Silvio smacked his lips and made a sour face, as if her name tasted sour. "I named my Scion Dante. A joke, really. But I just love it. What better name for a man who's made a life's work plumbing the depths of depravity?" He hummed and chewed on her name again. "Jacey. Are you quite sure about that name? Jacey sounds a bit low-rent, if you know what I'm saying."

She had no idea what he was saying, but she nodded noncommittally. "Do you have a better idea?"

He thought for a few moments, inhaling dramatically through flared nostrils as if drawing inspiration from the warm sea breezes. "You need something appropriate, something that fits." He held up a finger. "I've got it! How about Belle? That's French for 'beautiful.'"

Jacey choked and had to pat her chest with the palm of her hand as she coughed. Wiping a tear from one eye, she fixed him with a hard stare. "Um, no."

He sighed and waved a hand, giving up on her. "Jacey it is, then."

The path opened upon a span of flat rock that gave an unobstructed view of the mansion, which now stood a hundred meters uphill.

It was perched upon a massive slab of black rock that thrust into the sea like the prow of a gargantuan ship. Jacey imagined that in some distant epoch a great upheaval in the very crust of the earth had split a mountain, toppling this formation into the water.

The cliff fell fifty meters into a swirl of mist where waves crashed against the face of the island.

Nothing could have been more at odds with the natural magnificence of the location than the house. Whoever had designed it had chosen to stack box-shaped pods of glass, concrete, and rusted steel atop each other in a random-seeming configuration. When taken together, the pods formed an edifice of supreme artificiality.

Wind gusted across the exposed observation point, making Jacey rub her elbows despite the sun.

"Magnificent, isn't it?" Silvio said.

Jacey shrugged and followed him to a path leading from the rock. It curled along a grassy slope and ended at a course of steps hewn from the bedrock. Jacey's heart hammered as she followed Silvio into a shady, covered gallery bordering a courtyard leading to the entrance.

The open area was filled with fine white sand. Black boulders, placed just so, punctuated the expanse, which had been raked with flowing lines all around. The effect might have been calming if Jacey hadn't been so nervous about meeting Elizabeth.

The walkway tunneled between two pods before opening again into sunlight at the edge of a crystal blue swimming pool twice the size of the one at Dr. Carlhagen's hacienda.

To Jacey's left a carpet-like lawn stretched toward the sea, ending at the rocky drop off. To her right towered the house of boxes, vast glass fronts reflecting the green and blue of the outside world. Jacey couldn't see in, and had to shield her eyes against the brain-piercing light glancing from the pool and windows.

Silvio's hand tugged at her. "Quickly now. This way." He hustled her away from the pool and to a set of glass doors. With a soft hiss, they slid aside as Jacey approached, letting out a wash of cold air that smelled like the inside of a refrigerator.

"I'd like to speak with Elizabeth right away," Jacey said, turning to watch the glass doors slide closed behind her. "I have urgent things to discuss with her."

"Of course. Soonest possible moment. This way."

Silvio led Jacey across white marble tiles. Their footsteps reverberated in a grand hall of ice. Or, at least, that's how Jacey thought of it. Every surface was cloud white—from the marble floors, to the painted concrete walls, to the ceiling ten meters above. In the center of the space stood a cluster of sofas and chairs of creamy white leather. Nearby, a low glass-topped table rested on weirdly bent white plastic legs. In one wall, blue flames lurched behind glass, a decorative fireplace giving off no heat.

In contrast to the pool deck, the air inside the mansion raised goosebumps on Jacey's skin. She rubbed her arms as Silvio led her up a steel staircase made of white planks cantilevered from one frigid wall. No support structure beneath it, no rails.

"Watch your step," Silvio called over his shoulder. "And definitely take the elevator when you're drunk."

The staircase made a ninety-degree turn before coming to the second floor mezzanine. This did have a railing made of taut steel cables stretching between steel uprights. Jacey peered into the main hall below. Its beauty was undeniable, though it made her uneasy. It was a room designed to be seen as a work of art rather than a functional place to live.

"Not exactly your style, is it?" Silvio said, placing his hands on the railing and peering down at the white expanse below. "It isn't Liz's either, but she told me she tore down the old villa and put this up to signify her new start. Truth be told, she wants to like this kind of thing, but doesn't really."

"Then why keep it this way?"

"Because she's putting on a big show. And you, my love, are just in time."

"In time for what?"

Silvio nudged her with his shoulder. "For Liz's big coming out." He sucked air through his teeth and shook his head. "I mean for *Vin's* big coming out."

Hearing Vin's name made Jacey's skin flush with rage. Vin had been Sarah's age, and the First of Belle's Nine. Jacey had known Vin just as long as she'd known Dante. "What do you mean by 'coming out?'"

Silvio leveled a skeptical gaze on her. "You of all people should know. Vin is announcing her existence to the world. Secret granddaughter of Elizabeth Burnell. Stepping forward into the public eye, et cetera, et cetera. There will be helicopters arriving throughout the day, bringing members of the press and VIP guests to witness the press conference. And then the party, of course."

"So that's why you're here," Jacey said. She barely paid attention to her own words as she absorbed what Silvio had told her.

Voices sounded below, followed by bubbles of laughter.

Silvio tugged her elbow and guided her away from the balcony. "Come."

He led her along the mezzanine to a hallway. Windows

on the left overlooked the sand garden. Doors stood in ranks to the right.

He stopped at the end of the hall and spoke to a screen next to the door. No avatar of a security AI appeared, but Jacey supposed it was the same sort of system that kept the medical ward locked. The door released and Silvio pushed through.

The room beyond was not nearly as stark as the rest of the house. For one, a red hibiscus-patterned bedspread covered a stilt-legged four-poster bed. Windows filled two entire walls, offering views of the coast and the pool deck. Half-naked people still lounged in chairs. One young woman floated on her back in the pool atop a small inflatable raft of some sort.

Noticing Jacey checking out the walls, Silvio nudged her shoulder. "Since I decided to stay a few months, I had one of the servants paint the walls. I couldn't bear all the white, white, white."

The walls were a buttery yellow. Lamps stood on side tables next to the bed, their glass shades as turquoise as the sea. A display monitor hung on one wall, tilted slightly out to face the bed.

"There's a bathroom in there. Towels. This cabinet has a refrigerator. Have a beer. I'll be back in a while."

"Where are you going? I need to speak to Elizabeth immediately."

"I told you. She's preparing for a very big event. She doesn't have time to speak with every guest."

"But I'm not a guest. I came here uninvited. And I have a favor to ask her. A very important and time-sensitive one."

Silvio smiled and cupped her shoulders with his hands. His eyes twinkled just as Dante's had when he'd been up to some mischief. "Don't worry. You know she'll be thrilled to have you here. I mean, come on. Jacqueline Buchanan!"

"I have urgent things to discuss and she'll—"

Silvio clicked his tongue. "Just be patient, my darling. I know a diva like you is not used to waiting, but trust me, you don't want to be seen here just yet. Now. Make yourself at home."

He stepped into the hall and closed the door.

26

AN UNCANNY CREATURE

As the helicopter descended toward St. Lazarus, Dr. Carlhagen pressed his face to the hatch window and indulged in a moment of pride. Everything he'd accomplished to this point—the current mess notwithstanding—was all prologue to a much larger plan.

Much of his progress toward that goal would occur here in the heart of his new and much improved Scion facility.

He could almost summon a feeling of fondness for the years he'd spent working with Michael—the old business and science partner he'd tricked into uploading into a computer server—but in the grand scheme of things, the invention of True Cloning (as opposed to the zombie-like carbos everyone else was making) and the mind transfer technology had only rewarded Dr. Carlhagen on an financial level.

Dr. Carlhagen's ambitions were greater than mere money—or even fame. Which is why he hadn't concerned himself with publishing his discoveries and inventions in scientific journals or politicking for meaningless Nobel Prizes. That making clones was illegal was another factor in his silence, though less important.

Michael had been the first to realize Dr. Carlhagen's true aims, which was why it had been necessary to upload him to a server, where he could be controlled.

The new phase of the Scion program had begun twelve years earlier. Dr. Carlhagen had recognized that the world's political leaders were not going to solve the real problems facing the human race, which was hanging onto existence by a thread. Rising sea levels, the Kill-Tine asteroid, nuclear proliferation. The world was tumbling downhill.

What the world needed was one man in charge of it all. Someone who would make the tough choices, decide how scarce resources should be allocated, and cull the Earth of deadweight, noncontributory people.

In short, the world needed a benevolent dictator. But who could do it? Who could consolidate power? Mere military might would not work. Heavens knew how many had tried.

But with the godlike power to bestow immortality, Dr. Carlhagen had the key. Immortality is a wonderful and persuasive gift to offer to politicians in power. Dr. Carlhagen could take his pick of world leaders. He'd started at the top, then worked his way down to people like Senator Bentilius. Along the way, he had picked up celebrities and billionaires as well.

The helicopter circled around the peak of St. Lazarus, a long-dead volcano overgrown with greenery and shrouded in mist. Even now a line of rain clouds blotted half the island. The helicopter flew into them and the window went white.

"What are you looking at?" Livy asked. She'd crept up

beside him and was peeking out at the murk. "Oh, it's your conscience."

"Are you going to let her speak to you that way?" Senator Bentilius asked.

Dr. Carlhagen hadn't intended to, but he wasn't about to snap at the girl on the senator's command. The urge to grab the old bag and hurl her out of the chopper made his nostrils flare and the window fogged with his breath. "Responding to such little impertinences at all is to reward them, I've found."

Livy giggled and grinned at him. It wasn't a friendly look, and it chilled him.

What an uncanny creature she is. Like an adult in a child's body.

The chopper dipped below the cloud ceiling, revealing mist-shrouded treetops. Though he couldn't see it from this vantage, Dr. Carlhagen knew they were on final approach to the landing field. He'd forbidden any paved landing pads, or any permanent docks, for that matter. The island of St. Lazarus was officially uninhabited, and even the most suspicious spy satellite would uncover nothing to suggest otherwise.

There were many in the North American government who knew better, of course. But they all thought the installation here—carved into the guts of Mt. Lazarus—was part of their own intelligence operation. That was a big part of why Dr. Carlhagen had needed Senator Bentilius in the first place. She'd diverted government funds to the project, hired South American contractors to excavate it, and imported Pakistani and Egyptian construction crews—all undocumented and highly illegal—to build the facility.

That last bunch, some fifteen hundred men, was now entombed in a subterranean cavern of their own making. Regrettable that so many had to die to keep St. Lazarus a secret, but that was the price of saving the human race in the long run.

The chopper slowed to hover above a clearing in the rainforest. The pilot brought them down. The skids came to rest on a broad patch of grass among the trees. One of the guards grabbed the hatch handle and pushed the door open. It unfolded, stairs deploying. The guard climbed down, his weapon up, eyes scanning the tree line.

Dr. Carlhagen urged Livy down the steps, keeping a hand on her shoulder so she didn't bolt. He turned to study the terrain. He hadn't been here for a few months and needed to get his bearings.

"Are you going to help me or not, Christof?" Senator Bentilius stood at the top of the steps.

"Have you forgotten that you are barely seventeen years old, my dear? I think you can handle walking down a few steps."

"I don't care if I'm young or old, I expect you to mind your manners and hand a lady down from her chopper."

Dr. Carlhagen took her hand. She descended with slow, graceful steps, a queen making a grand arrival. He barely restrained the urge to throttle her.

The pilot appeared a second later, eyes scanning the tree line. "Are you sure you'll be okay? The charts say there's nothing here."

Dr. Carlhagen waved at the trees. "There's a cache of supplies nearby. We'll be fine."

The pilot shrugged. "Okay. I'm based at the San Juan Skyport, so it'll take me two hours to return if you need me."

Dr. Carlhagen was sick of chatting with the man. "Go on, then. We'll call if we need you."

"Can I ask why you wanted to come here?" The question was directed to the senator, which made sense. She was his boss, after all.

"No. You may not," she said.

"You," Dr. Carlhagen barked, jabbing a finger at the armed guard, "go back with the pilot."

The man looked to Senator Bentilius. She stepped close to Dr. Carlhagen and pressed her hand to his chest. "Christof, you're delusional if you think I'm going anywhere with you alone."

The guard's face hardened.

"Fine," he whispered to her. "But you know he can never leave, right?"

"I'm not an idiot, Christof." Her thin smile chilled him. If he hadn't felt the warmth of her body, he'd swear she had no blood at all.

Dr. Carlhagen prodded Livy forward, not waiting for Senator Bentilius or her guard. The hidden entrance to the Scion complex lay at the end of a footpath that started somewhere in the trees ahead of him.

The senator keeping her gunman was a stroke of bad luck. He'd have to step very carefully until he could get rid of the man. But no rush. He still needed Senator Bentilius, for now. And if her usefulness wore off, he could do with her as he pleased. Several options occurred to him. He could strangle her with his own hands. He could push her from a cliff, or shoot, stab, or drown her.

All of those options were distasteful when he considered the actual doing of them. But it didn't matter, because he had one more trick up his sleeve. It was the linchpin behind his greater ambitions for the Scion program. The thing that would give him complete power over every Progenitor.

He called it Protocol One, and even now it was in full effect.

27

METALLIC THUMP BONGED

The Scions tumbled out of the school bus and onto the dock, each carrying what meager belongings they had, mostly readers and spare clothes. Humphrey raised an arm to help Mother Tyeesha totter down the steps. Her deeply lined face was set with determination, and her claw-like grip on his forearm belied her age. Her four adult staffers followed, carrying the babies. The two- and three-year-olds glommed onto some of the older children.

This was the first time at the docks for most of them. They stared wide-eyed at the boat that would carry them into the wild unknown of the outside world. Five Scions were already on board, having taken the Jeep ahead. They should have assembled the bunks in the cargo holds by now.

Humphrey's walkie-talkie squawked and Summer's voice blared through. "Where is my pilot?"

Humphrey yanked the walkie-talkie from his waistband and lifted it to his lips. "He'll be coming aboard soon. Should he go to the engine room or the bridge?"

Summer swore. "I don't want him anywhere near my engine room. Take him to the bridge."

More Scions piled out before Orson finally appeared. His legs wobbled a bit, whether from weakness or fear Humphrey didn't know, or care. Elias came down after him, making a great show of being dangerous even though just hours before he could barely stand.

"Straight to the bridge," Humphrey said to Elias. "But don't let him touch anything."

Elias prodded Orson with a fist and the man trudged forward. Jacey's intimidation efforts had transformed him, brought out his meek side.

Elias leaned close to Humphrey as he passed. "It'd be nice to have one of the Senator Bentilius's guards' weapons."

Humphrey shook his head. Sensei had locked up all the firearms and wouldn't allow anyone to handle them. Said it was just as likely that the Scions would shoot each other by mistake than any attackers.

Sensei was right. If it did come to a confrontation with the Senator's forces, shooting first would be a huge mistake, since those forces would surely be under orders not to kill Scions unless attacked.

Elias swayed. Humphrey caught his arm and straightened him. "Are you okay?"

Elias nodded, though his pale face contradicted him. He grabbed Orson's shoulder and steered him toward the boarding ramp near the stern of the ship.

Tytus and Obu came out next, guarding Orson's two men, Dickie and Rosales. Their hands were bound behind them, and their eyes hammered at Humphrey. "Take them to the top deck. Have them unload the heavy stuff off the bus once the bus is secured."

"But then we'll have to untie their hands," Obu said. He wasn't as confident a fighter as Tytus, and their combined weight didn't match Dickie's alone.

"Find something you can use as a club. If they so much as look at you wrong, give them a whack."

The boys nodded, though Tytus seemed troubled. Humphrey understood why. Sensei deplored violence, and he'd instilled that into them.

But these men were dangerous, and they had meant to do harm to the Scions. Even so, threatening them bothered Humphrey.

Pedro and Kirk came out, bearing a long white bundle between them. They had fashioned a litter out of branches. The sight of Constantine's form, even shrouded under a sheet, struck Humphrey like a blow to the throat.

"Find a shady spot on deck. We'll do it as soon as we get beyond the reefs."

It was only practical. In the heat, Constantine's body would soon sour. He didn't want anyone to remember "Little Vaughan" that way. The boys carried their friend toward the boat. When the other Scions saw them coming, they stepped aside. More than a few paused to wipe their eyes.

Humphrey did the same, then shook himself. There was no time to grieve.

A team of Scions set about preparing the chains and straps to hoist the bus onto the deck. Humphrey had wanted to leave it behind, but Summer had insisted they bring it, arguing that wherever they ended up they would need transportation.

A familiar form stumbled down the bus steps and onto the dock, followed by Sensei, whose massive arms flexed as he clenched and loosened his fists. He'd insisted on guarding Sang himself, after relieving Horace of that duty. Sang was not nearly as strong as Sensei, but Sensei had trained Sang, knew what he was capable of. Nobody knew if Mr. Justin had trained in the martial arts or not, but Sensei wasn't about to risk it.

"To the left," Sensei said to Sang. The boy's uniform was disheveled. His Eagle pin had been torn off, leaving a ragged hole in his Mandarin collar. His left eye was swollen shut where either Horace or Tytus had struck him unconscious.

"Where are you going to put him?" Humphrey asked Sensei.

"There are crew quarters near the infirmary. I've had some of the boys remove anything dangerous from one of the rooms. We'll lock him in there for now."

"Wait a moment." Humphrey approached Sang, stood nose to nose with him. Sang refused to meet his gaze. "Where did you put the AI servers?"

Sang merely looked at the pocked concrete of the dock.

"Mr. Justin," Humphrey said to the boy, "where did you put the AI computer servers? Did you smuggle them aboard somehow?"

Sang lifted his head, slowly bringing his one good eye to bear on Humphrey. "I'm not Mr. Justin."

Humphrey turned his back on Sang and nodded to Sensei. The martial arts master barked orders, and Sang complied.

Wanda stepped down from the bus, eyes lingering on Sang's back for a moment. "I've been thinking about why Mr. Justin would want to take the servers."

Humphrey had always liked Wanda, though they'd never had much of a relationship. She'd been too gregarious, or at least that's what he'd thought all these years.

Now he considered her more levelheaded than most, with an intellect as keen as a kitchen knife.

In fact, he'd learned a lot about his fellow Scions he never suspected, the talents that had lain dormant in them, just waiting for an opportunity to blossom.

Wanda understood biology the way Summer understood mechanical things. Wanda had shown herself to be calm under pressure and a natural leader. He was going to need both of those qualities in the future.

"What's your theory?" he asked.

"Mind transfers. The AI controls the transfers. If Mr. Justin intended to steal us, he certainly didn't intend to kill us. He planned to sell us. For him to make good on those deals, he would have to be able to perform transfers for whoever was the highest bidder. For that he needs the AIs. And that means . . ."

"He needs the servers," Humphrey said, nodding grimly.

A Dolphin girl named Vestana called to Wanda. She turned to go, but stopped and leaned close to Humphrey, rested her hand in his arm. "I'll keep an eye out as we unpack supplies in the girls' cargo hold."

"Understood. I'll check the boys' hold."

Humphrey waited until the last Scion came off the bus, then followed them up the ramp and into the side hatch into relative darkness. The oily smell of machinery, salt water, and rusty iron hit his nose.

He'd only been on the boat twice before, and not for very long, but he knew the layout well enough to find his way to the central staircase. It had once been painted white. Most had chipped away, and the little paint that remained had turned a grimy yellowish-brown. Rust covered the treads and handrail like a rash.

Humphrey took the steps two at a time, eager to get to the bridge and make sure Orson was cooperating.

A metallic thump bonged in the stairwell, followed by a string of curses. He turned at a landing and found Leslie dragging a suitcase behind her. She saw him and swore. "I don't know why I have to be doing this. Elias just went up these same steps empty-handed."

"He was guarding Orson," Humphrey said. "Besides, he can barely stand, let alone carry stuff."

"I don't believe that big lump needs that much watching. He's old and out of shape from what I've seen. I could have guarded him and I don't even know how to fight." As she said this last, she glowered at the ceiling.

Like Jacey, Leslie often complained about Dr. Carlhagen's rule against girls learning fighting skills. It might have been a blessing that she hadn't learned it, Humphrey reflected. She was the one who had instigated the confrontation with Sang.

She'd never been very warm-hearted. Humphrey attributed her recent icy attitude to Belle's influence. That, or the pressures of the past few days had gotten to her. Each person had reacted differently, that was for sure.

Humphrey glanced at the suitcase and recognized it as Senator Bentilius's. "Where did you find this?"

"I didn't find it. One of the girls found it in the garage when she was doing a final sweep for things to bring to the boat. She noticed the tag."

A paper tag wrapped around the handle read "bridge."

"What's in it?"

"I don't know." She flopped it on its side, making a louder racket. She unzipped it at the top and reached in. "Ah." She pulled out a wrench. And then a hammer. "Looks like tools Summer couldn't bear to leave behind." Leslie said this last with a wry twist of her mouth. She'd been quite vocal about her skepticism of Summer's new-found skills as an engineer.

She stuffed the tools back into the suitcase and zipped it shut.

Humphrey nodded absently. He wasn't about to question what tools Summer might need.

Leslie brushed her hands together. "Well, if you're going to take it up, I don't need to go with you. I've got better things to do. I shouldn't leave Wanda in charge for a second longer than necessary. The girls' cargo hold will be chaos if I don't get down there soon."

Humphrey suppressed a laugh. Leslie's high opinion of her own leadership skills was not shared by anyone else. He also didn't point out that he hadn't offered to carry the suitcase.

"By the way," she said as she started down the steps. "Exactly where is this place Jacey went to scout out for us?"

"She found out about an island nearby. She went to see if it's a good location for us to hide."

Leslie grunted. "Both of you are keeping too many secrets from us. How did Jacey know about this other island when the rest of us did not?"

"Dr. Carlhagen told her about it. One of the Progenitors owns it. She lives there, I guess."

Leslie threw her arms up. "And why on earth would one of the Progenitors want to help us? If anything, they'll report our location to Dr. Carlhagen and he'll be waiting there when we arrive."

"That's why Jacey's going there. To make sure that doesn't happen."

Leslie stopped at a turn in the stairs and frowned. "That's the stupidest thing I've ever heard." Then she trotted down the steps and out of view.

Humphrey hefted the suitcase and climbed the stairs. As irritating as Leslie's final comment was, he couldn't help but agree with it. Especially after Sensei's revelation that Jacey was famous. At least, her face was famous.

"She'll be fine," he said to himself. "She has to be fine."

The words didn't comfort him at all.

Humphrey found Summer on the bridge. Her huge eyes sucked in every motion Orson made as he pointed out the controls of the ship and explained the procedure for leaving the dock. She brought a walkie-talkie to her lips and barked an order to two Scions standing on the dock. Humphrey dragged the suitcase to the back corner of the bridge to keep it out of the way, then went to a side door. It opened onto a steel platform that Summer called a "wing." It gave a clear view toward the front and back of the ship. He leaned against the rail to watch their departure from St. Vitus.

On the pier below, two Scions lifted the thick ropes looped over the bollards. The Scions dashed to the ramp, ran aboard, and drew the ramp in after them.

"Boat is free," blared a voice from Summer's walkie-talkie.

Orson jabbed a green button with his chubby thumb while his other hand thrust forward on a black-handled lever. The boat shuddered to life. As the engines fired up, he pursed his lips in thought. "The engines sound different."

"That's because they're working better," Summer said.

"You did that?"

Summer ignored the question. Orson shrugged and shifted another lever and grabbed a dinner-plate sized wheel and spun it.

The boat rocked slightly under Humphrey's feet.

"That's the bow and stern side thrusters," Orson said, then shoved the first lever forward.

The vessel drifted away from the dock as the sea foamed and roiled all around the hull.

From Humphrey's perch, he could see Scions lining the rails forward. Several cheered, others shook their heads doubtfully. Humphrey understood both sentiments.

The sounds and vibrations changed, and the boat began to creep forward, slowly at first but then she picked up enough headway to create enough wind to ruffle Humphrey's hair.

They were leaving St. Vitus. Actually leaving.

Humphrey marveled at how an event he'd wanted for so long could fill him with such dread. The boat turned southward to skirt around what Orson said was a reef that could tear a hole in the keel.

Orson seemed happy at his post, piloting the boat, but Summer stared at everything he did, watching with great suspicion and asking many, many questions.

Huge breakers crashed to either side as they passed through a narrow gap in the reef. Once the danger was past, Orson pushed a red lever forward and the boat shook so hard Humphrey thought the steel plating of the hull might fall off. The motion settled as *Aphrodite* picked up speed.

The deck pitched and rolled beneath Humphrey's feet as he moved back into the enclosed area of the bridge and out of the wind. He widened his stance and gripped the back of a chair bolted to the floor.

"Okay, boy," Orson said to Humphrey, "where're we headed?"

"I'm awaiting word on that," Humphrey said. "We brought a holodesk aboard. Where is a good place to connect it to the network?"

Orson made a snuffling sound that turned into a choke. His face turned bright red. "Network?" he said, voice rising in pitch. "There hasn't been a working data-feed aboard this bucket for twenty years."

Summer's head snapped around, and a wry smirk twisted her mouth. "The network aboard this ship is broken? Why am I not surprised."

Orson just shrugged. "My job is to drive the damn thing. Justin was the one who found her. And if there's one thing I know about my brother, he's cheap as a—" He cut off, as if realizing what he was about to say wasn't fit for a fourteen-year-old girl to hear.

"I'll just add it to my list of things to fix," Summer mumbled, trudging off the bridge.

Orson scratched his head. "So until you get word, which direction should we go?

"Give me a map," Humphrey said.

28

ONE BIG, POUNDING THROB

The knob wouldn't turn. Jacey pounded on the door. "Let me out!"

The realization that she'd been lured into Silvio's room in order be kept away from Elizabeth slowly sank in. And as it did, panic bubbled to the surface. She kicked the door. Swore at it. Demanded to speak with the AI.

She might as well have been yelling at the sea.

Giving up on the door, she went to the huge plate-glass window and pounded on it, trying to get the attention of one of the sunbathers. None of them so much as looked at the house.

Jacey eyed a chair tucked next to a small desk. She took hold of the back and rolled it into the room. Breath heaving through her nostrils, fury burning in her body, she heaved the chair over her head and threw it at the window.

The glass bonged like a deep bell, and the chair clattered onto the tiles.

Jacey looked out. This time there were people staring

up at the window. She waved and shouted. But after a few seconds they returned to their sunbathing.

Jacey remembered how the glass mirrored the sky and sea. They couldn't see her at all. She threw the chair again and again. Eventually one sunbather called over her shoulder. A bald man in white linen hustled to her lounge and bent to listen to her. He glanced at Jacey's window and then darted toward the house.

"That's it," Jacey said. "Come check on the racket upstairs."

She waited by the door, trying to keep her breath even. It wouldn't do for the man—a servant, Jacey guessed—to find a raving madwoman inside the room. She didn't have to wait long before she heard footsteps and a voice.

The door opened.

Silvio stood there. Alone. He arched one eyebrow. "My darling, you really must behave yourself. Being a diva will get you nowhere here."

Jacey tucked her chin and lunged, driving her shoulder into his gut.

He let out a surprised grunt and flailed to wrap her in his arms. Jacey wriggled free, stumbling away down the hall.

She jerked to a halt as Silvio grabbed a handful of her dress. He yanked, making the stitching in the sides tear. She fell to her knees and twisted, ready to kick. But he was already on her, hands scooping around her waist, lifting her.

Her scream cut off as the air rushed out of her lungs. The floor pressed into her face, and a pain shot through her shoulder. Silvio stood behind her, twisting her arm behind her back.

"Let me go!" she rasped through gritted teeth.

"I will," Silvio said, panting. "But not until the time is right."

He applied a slight bit of pressure and Jacey came to her feet. It was cooperate or have her shoulder dislocated. Dante had been very strong due to Sensei's unrelenting training regimen. And apparently Silvio had retained some of the boy's skills in the martial arts.

He urged her into back into his room and shoved her onto the bed. "Stay there, my dear."

He released her arm and she brought it around to cradle in her other one. From shoulder to hand, her arm was one big, pounding throb.

Silvio busied himself collecting all moveable objects that Jacey might throw at the window. "You disturbed the guests with your tantrum. One of them sent Elizabeth's man O'Brien to investigate. Fortunately for you, I intercepted him."

"Why are you keeping me prisoner?" Jacey demanded. "I need to talk to Elizabeth. It's urgent."

Silvio turned as he stepped into the hall. "Liz—*Vin* and I are just as eager to hear your 'story' as you are to tell it. But your timing could not have been worse. Someone might have seen you. Trust me, you don't want anyone seeing you."

"But I *don't* trust you."

"Pity." Silvio smiled and made a mock bow. "Because I'm all you've got."

He closed the door, leaving Jacey slumped on the bed.

29

IF MADAM PRESIDENT ONLY KNEW

Finally, a moment to rest, to relax.

Mr. Justin stood at the railing of *Aphrodite* and watched the shoreline of St. Vitus shrink away. They were going to escape.

He didn't know how close it would be. Maybe the senator's backup force was a day away. Maybe a week. It didn't matter. The only thing that did was that Mr. Justin had all the Scions exactly where he had wanted them from the start—on the boat and headed away from St. Vitus.

Perhaps it had worked out even better than planned. This way there was no kidnapping involved, no direct coercion of Scions. From Dr. Carlhagen's point of view, the Scions had escaped on their own.

Thinking of Dr. Carlhagen sparked a flash of anger in Mr. Justin's chest. He hated the man. Not violently. Not in a way that could drive a man into a red-faced fit of rage. His was a deep and old hatred, like an ocean of magma beneath the roots of a mountain.

Mr. Justin's father had been Dr. Carlhagen's butler. Dr.

Carlhagen had even paid for Mr. Justin's education, all for the purpose of raising up a successor to his most loyal servant. And when Mr. Justin's father had died, the job opening had been too convenient to pass up. Besides, Justin had felt obligated to both his father's memory and to Dr. Carlhagen.

He'd taken over just as Dr. Carlhagen and his partner Michael had made the technological breakthroughs that led to the Scion program. He vividly remembered the day Dr. Carlhagen had called him into his office and explained what the Scions were. The old man had chuckled and promised to create a Scion just for him. "That way," Dr. Carlhagen had said, "you can serve me for another lifetime or two."

Mr. Justin tightened his grip on the railing and spat into the water.

Wanda gasped in horror. "Did you really just *spit?*"

Wanda stood next to him, wind fluffing the many stray red hairs that had escaped her ponytail. Of course, Wanda had no idea *who* she stood next to.

"I think I swallowed a bug," he said, covering quickly. The girl's eyes lingered on his before turning back to the horizon.

Mr. Justin's thoughts snapped back to the cause of his inopportune spit of disgust. The idea of serving Dr. Carlhagen for another lifetime—and another lifetime after that—revolted him.

On the other hand, the chance to enjoy a virtually endless lifespan . . . That had a definite appeal. It had gotten Mr. Justin thinking.

He immediately saw the opportunity to supplant Dr. Carlhagen as master of the Scion School. It would make him rich and ensure that he was the last of the generations of butlers in his family. And so began years of planning and scheming.

He'd run into obstacle after obstacle and disaster after catastrophe. And yet here he was, with the Scions on board his boat and soon to be headed where he wanted them to go.

There was still much to be done, including getting rid of Dr. Carlhagen. Letting him escape had been a calculated risk, but the diversion had been utterly necessary. Fortunately, Mr. Justin knew where the headmaster and senator had gone. Right where he'd manipulated Senator Bentilius to go.

The trick now was to get the Scions there, too. Once everyone was in place, he'd be able to run the new Scion facility and no one would ever know it wasn't Dr. Carlhagen running it.

Why? Because he had Humphrey.

What an inspired bit of improvisation it had been to put Humphrey forward as the doctor, first with Captain Wilcox, and then with the senator.

Humphrey thought he could put away the white suit forever, now, but that was pure fantasy. The boy was eminently easy to manipulate. And if he grew a spine? There was always the transfer machine.

And then there was Senator Bentilius. How she had managed—as a mere senator of the North American Union —to command segments of the North American military evaded Mr. Justin. Clearly, the government was more corrupt than he'd suspected.

Liberating her from the island had been a necessary evil. But without her helicopter, there wouldn't have been a diversion at all.

Remembering the image of Dr. Carlhagen and Senator Bentilius arguing in the quad brought up another source of worry. Why had the old man taken the Dolphin Livy with him?

On the Scion/Progenitor list, Livy's Progenitor was listed with an obvious pseudonym: Juanita Smith.

Mr. Justin wondered if perhaps Livy's Progenitor was famous or powerful. The way Jacey's was, for instance. Or Leslie's.

No, he decided, chuckling to himself. Nobody was as powerful as that. Leslie's Progenitor, the President of the North American Union, commanded more power than anyone had in the history of the world.

If Madam President only knew where her precious Scion was now!

Mr. Justin giggled again at the thought of it.

"What are you laughing about?" Wanda asked, giving him a weird look.

"I just had a funny thought. It's hard to explain."

Wanda rolled her eyes, but said nothing more.

Whoever Livy's Progenitor was couldn't be *that* important. But maybe she was important to Dr. Carlhagen personally. Or, now that Mr. Justin thought about it more, maybe Livy was important only to the extent she could be used as leverage against Jacey.

Yes, that had to be it.

This reassuring thought was interrupted by Sensei's voice behind him, ordering some boys to finish securing the bus to the deck.

Sensei had hoisted up the Jeep as well, and it was tied down just to the rear of the bus. Both vehicles were pointed toward the bow. Given the roll and pitch of the boat, Sensei's orders were sensible.

Gauging from the position of the sun, Mr. Justin noted that the boat was heading southwest. Excellent.

His thoughts returned to Jacey, who had sped off to Elizabeth's island to secure a safe harbor for the Scions.

Mr. Justin shook his head at the stupidity of the idea. Elizabeth would be the least cooperative of the first group of Progenitors.

If the truth came out about that woman and what she'd done, it would destroy her legacy as the beloved television personality who had interviewed every important political leader and holovid star of the past fifty years. She was noted for her great charity works and her deep dive into spiritual awakening. If it was learned that the great Elizabeth Burnell had purchased a carbo to transfer her mind into . . .

Mr. Justin didn't finish the thought. That potential scandal awaited all the Progenitors who had a high profile.

Sensei barked again, and Mr. Justin turned to lean his back against the rail. He watched the martial arts master stomp around the deck, pointing and ordering people about.

A shout drew everyone's attention. Humphrey stood on one of the wings just off the bridge. The wind plastered his uniform against his body. With his hands to his mouth, he shouted, "Sensei! We need you on the bridge."

The martial arts master waved an acknowledgement and threw a few more stern glances around before trotting to the outside staircase leading directly to the bridge.

Mr. Justin watched his progress, keeping his face as blank as he could. Inside, his brain steamed. Why hadn't Captain Wilcox just finished the job when Dr. Carlhagen had called for Protocol Seven? Was it that hard to kill one man?

Apparently it was. So now it was up to Mr. Justin to finish him off. Sensei was too strong, too dangerous to be allowed to live, especially once they got to their final destination.

And that brought up another problem. He needed to keep the boat heading in the right direction.

But Mr. Justin had a plan. He just had to make a few preparations and then strike when the time was right. He stared down at the waves, thinking about the hidden depths beneath the surface.

That depth was also inside him. And since his identity was still a secret and everyone believed he was Sang, he had the opportunity to act with absolute impunity.

"I'm going below," he said to Wanda. "I'll see you later."

30

YOU'RE ALL CARBOS

The gentle side-to-side roll of the *Aphrodite* had morphed into a pitch and climb that made Humphrey's stomach bubble with unease. Only the urgency of their situation kept him focused on the map.

Orson jabbed it with a fat finger. "That's St. Vitus."

Humphrey studied the battered spread of filthy paper. It looked like it had been walked on with muddy boots, folded a hundred times at random angles, unfolded and then wadded into a ball and soaked in coffee. The green spot Orson indicated was no wider than the man's dirty fingernail.

And if St. Vitus was only as wide as that, then the body of water surrounding it was unimaginably large. Humphrey struggled to get his head around how big the world was. Socrates had discussed the size of the world in kilometers, but numbers were abstract. Seeing the relationship between the island and the rest of the world . . . now *that* gave perspective.

Sensei stood next to Humphrey, stance wide, hands gripping the table as tightly as the table itself was bolted to the floor.

Humphrey also had a death grip on the table. The boat tended to pitch and yaw in a way his legs had not yet learned to predict. Orson had no such trouble, standing and swaying with every shift of the deck as if it weren't moving at all.

"Which way did Wilcox's helicopter go when Jacey left?" Sensei asked.

Humphrey tapped the island. "If the Scion School is here, that means this little speck is Turtle Island. I remember it flying over Turtle Island and disappearing in this direction." Humphrey dragged his finger southwest, stopping when he came to the first island. "So Elizabeth's island could be this one."

Orson snorted and poked three other islands. "Or that one, or that one, or that one. All of these are southwest of St. Vitus."

And each was over three thumbnails apart, which in the real world translated to a hundred kilometers or more.

The boat suddenly pitched and Humphrey had to grab the table or fall over. His stomach quivered. "We'll have to check them all."

Since there was no network on board, Humphrey had no way to contact Jacey. He berated himself for not checking on that little detail before they left.

Not that it would have mattered; they couldn't have stayed on St. Vitus much longer anyway. Even now he felt they were too close to it, though the island had receded beyond the horizon over an hour earlier.

"If only I could talk to Vaughan," he said, more to himself than Sensei or Orson. Jacey had put Vaughan on the project of finding out where Elizabeth's island was. But since the servers had gone missing, he had no way to find out if Vaughan had been successful or not.

"How would we know if we found this woman's island or not?" Summer asked from where she sat at the controls of the ship. Since Orson had shown her the basics, Humphrey hadn't been able to pry her away from it.

Orson nodded in agreement. He seemed to have developed a grudging respect for the girl. "I doubt this Elizabeth woman is going to have a sign posted saying 'Here's My Island.'" He made air quotes with his fingers.

"Even if we find it, we don't know if we'll be welcome," Sensei said. He pointed at a string of larger islands. "St. Croix. St. Thomas. I know these are inhabited. Puerto Rico has millions of people. But I doubt any of these places would offer us much sanctuary. The Scions don't even have passport chips. We'd have to try to sneak to shore in the dark. But then there's the problem of your faces . . ."

"What about our faces?" Humphrey asked, sensing there was another huge problem about to erupt into his life.

"Many of you would be recognized by people out there. Many of your Progenitors had a very high public profile. Not as big as Jacey's, but big enough. With so many of you together, it won't be hard to figure out you're all carbos."

"Carbos?"

"Clones. It's short for carbon copies. Carbon is the basis of all life, so it's sort of a slang term."

"Is there something wrong with being a, uh, carbo?"

Orson made a disgusting sucking noise through his sinuses. He spat into a handkerchief and wiped his mouth. "Carbos are illegal."

Sensei's face had gone very cold. There was more to all this. Something he didn't want to tell them.

"What is it, Sensei?"

"It's the policy of most countries in the world to destroy carbos."

"Why?" Humphrey noticed Summer had lost interest in the ship's controls. Her eyes had gone wide and she had clamped her teeth on her lower lip.

"Fear. The carbos that people are used to are not really fully human. They're like eerie robots made of flesh and blood. None of them have much intelligence. Dr. Carlhagen's system is light years beyond what everyone else is doing."

It wasn't much comfort to hear that last bit. But Humphrey also saw the conversation was a trap. Being distracted by it would paralyze them. It was time for decisions.

He turned back to the map. "Let's just check all three of these islands. Jacey is counting on us."

Sensei met Humphrey's stare. There was a challenge in this look, as if Sensei was about to dismiss Humphrey from the bridge. Humphrey tensed. Jacey was counting on him to get the Scions headed in the right direction.

"Make up your mind soon," Orson said, huffing out a huge breath. "We've only got two choices at the moment. Northeast or southwest."

"Why only those two?" Sensei said.

The vibrations in the ship suddenly changed and the boat lurched to port. Humphrey grabbed the table to keep himself upright.

Orson swore and studied his controls and gauges. He rapped a knuckle on one. "Engine Two just went offline. It never was very reliable. You should let Rosales go down and check it out."

Humphrey would never let one of Orson's men anywhere near the engine room, but Summer's indignant swearing got out before Humphrey could say it.

She grabbed the throttle and backed it down, then fixed Orson with an imperious glare. "Do not increase speed until I've had a chance to check things out." She headed for the door to the stairs, saying something about torque and screws and gaskets.

Humphrey shared a very different sort of glance with Sensei this time. The last thing they needed was to be adrift. Hopefully Engine One would hold up. Even not knowing much about boats, Humphrey knew that losing half their power would slow them considerably.

Orson hovered over another display. "We do not want to tarry in these waters for long."

"Why?" Humphrey asked, a knot tightening in his belly.

"As I was about to say, we only have two choices of direction because we've got some weather coming. We can try to skirt away from it northeast, or slip by it to the southwest."

"What do you mean by weather?" Sensei demanded.

Orson hunched up one shoulder, though his face looked extra pasty. "Well, it *is* hurricane season."

Humphrey studied the map. Nothing lay to the northeast except the vastness of the Atlantic Ocean. "Southwest, Orson."

Sensei trailing a finger across the filthy paper, skipping over the islands to the southwest and stopping on the mass of the South American continent. He stared at it for a long time, not even blinking.

"Sensei?"

The man snapped out of his apparent trance and gave a quick nod. "Southwest."

"We'll need more speed than this." Orson adjusted the wheel. "I hope that girl's got a miracle up her sleeve."

31

DO. NOT. USE. OUR. OLD. NAMES.

Flat on her back in a strange bed in a strange cold mansion, Jacey rubbed her aching hand. As feeling had returned, needling pain came, too.

She sucked air through her teeth and cursed Silvio. And herself. How could she have been so stupid as to trust a Progenitor?

The thump of yet another helicopter drew her eyes to the window. The aircraft angled like a wasp along the coast, then disappeared from view as it descended toward the landing pad. It was the third in the last hour.

Jacey massaged up and down her arm and berated herself for getting trapped. Coming to Elizabeth's island had been a mistake. And with all the people arriving for this "coming out" event, Elizabeth would be much less receptive to the idea of a boatload of Scions imposing on her hospitality.

"Here you are, my lovely."

A squawk of surprise burst from Jacey's mouth. She squirmed upright, heart hammering. Silvio stood at the door, holding a bundle of clothing in his arms. His smile might have been charming if she hadn't wanted to smash his teeth in with her fist.

A young woman followed him in. Her high heels clicked on the tile.

She was Vin.

But this wasn't Vin anymore, having been overwritten by Elizabeth less than a week before.

In the handful of days since the mind transfer, Elizabeth had altered Vin's appearance. For one, the considerable area of exposed skin on display was suntanned a creamy cocoa color. She wore a flowy sleeveless top that ended above her navel. Matching shorts clung to her hips in a way that enhanced the very curves they concealed.

Vin's once-lovely long brown hair now hung in a loose auburn fringe that barely reached the nape of her neck. Even stranger were the dark spectacles over her eyes that made her look inhuman, even insectile.

Vin's head swiveled until the gold-rimmed lenses pointed in Jacey's direction. The woman lifted a hand, nails painted pearl white, to the spectacles and drew them down to the tip of her nose. Vin's eyes, at once familiar and strange, peered over the top edge of frames and swept up and down Jacey's dress. "Going to a red carpet, my dear?"

Another figure entered the room. Male, gauging by his build, but slightly built. He wore baggy trousers with many pockets and a zipped jacket of navy blue. It was hooded, like one Sensei sometimes wore on cooler days, and the hood drooped over his face, shrouding his eyes in darkness.

"I didn't hear you come in," Jacey said, pressing her hands to her chest to keep her heart from popping right out. "Announce yourself next time."

Silvio cocked his head to one side and shrugged. "This

is my room." He presented the bundle, a stack of white linen garments. "I thought you might appreciate more appropriate attire. You're not going to a red carpet, after all."

All this talk about red carpets confused Jacey to no end. As far as she could tell there wasn't a single carpet in the whole frigid house.

When she made no move to take the offering, Silvio unfolded a white blouse and held it up. "The current fashion for the tropical scene. Straight from our hostess's closet."

He checked a tag on an inside seam and whistled, eyeing Vin appreciatively. "Nina Schön. You have expensive taste."

Light cut through the fabric. Jacey said, "I can see right through it. Why don't I dispense with clothing all together?"

"Why don't you?"

Jacey met his mischievous leer with as much ice as she could muster, but it only provoked a laugh.

Vin smirked, removing her spectacles and strolling around the room, looking here and there as if she'd never seen it before. Once her inspection was complete, she said, "Keep your red carpet look if you wish. I'm frankly astonished that you arrived with no luggage whatsoever. Why is that, exactly?"

Jacey put the question of red carpets out of her mind. And she did her best to ignore the weirdness of seeing Vin behaving so oddly. The question had cut right to the heart of Jacey's plight. And she was not prepared to answer. She had thought these clothes were normal in the outside world. Obviously, that wasn't the case.

It was time to lie. And fast. "I was a bit rushed when I

went to St. Vitus to transfer. I didn't have time to pack all my things."

"Rushed?" Vin said. "You've been 'dead' for nearly a year. What have you been doing this whole time that you couldn't plan ahead for your transfer?"

"The accident was planned, but an illness forced me to transfer early."

Silvio shook his head, a knowing smile splitting his face. "I knew that whole sinking ship routine was faked. I told Janicka at the Scion School. I said, 'Just you watch. Before the decade is out, we'll see some mysterious new heir to the Buchanan fortune come out of the woodwork. And won't that cause a mess?'"

Jacey kept her laugh of relief tightly bottled in her belly. Silvio's brag lent credibility to her story. Finally, a break. Dr. Carlhagen had told her Jacqueline and Charles had died in a boating accident. It made sense—from a Progenitor's point of view—that the accident had been faked.

Silvio thrust the blouse into her hands and plopped next to her on the bed. "I have to presume the bodies they recovered were someone else's. You'd think the authorities would have been able to identify them as the wrong people. But who am I kidding? My old friend Charles is as well-connected as a rich man can be. If he wants to fake a death, he can pull it off easily enough. No questions asked." He emphasized "fake a death" by poking Jacey's shoulder.

Whatever satisfaction Jacey had derived from Silvio filling in her own lies vanished like smoke in the wind. He spoke about Jacqueline and Charles as if he'd known them.

Whatever the case, Jacey couldn't retreat. "So clever of you to figure out something so obvious."

This brought a humorless laugh from Vin. The smile that came with it seemed haunted.

The hooded figure had moved across the room to sit in an armchair, back to the window so he was just a black, ghostly shape against the panorama outside. "I think we've had enough small talk."

Jacey recognized the voice instantly. "Ping?"

Delicate hands pulled the hood back. The boy who had been the First of Humphrey's Nine sat before her, face passive, smooth. He did not smile in greeting. Of course, he *wasn't* Ping. Jacey tried to recall whose name had been across from Ping's on the list of Progenitors and Scions Mr. Justin had showed her.

"Han Xi," she said after a moment. "I didn't expect to find you here."

Hearing his name caused all three of the Progenitors to gape momentarily. Jacey wondered if she'd made a mistake. "There's no one here but us," she said quickly. "I think your secret is safe in this room."

Ping shot to his feet. "In this room maybe. But not anywhere else in this house. The first rule is: Do. Not. Use. Our. Old. Names."

He slashed a hand through the air before him and glared at the other two Progenitors. "This is exactly what we feared."

Though his voice was soft, it contained steely fury. He directed his glower, eyebrows scrunched, mouth turned down, at Jacey. "So what are you calling yourself?"

"Jacey."

Vin clasped her hands in front of her. "Let's all try to stay calm. Clearly, Dr. Carlhagen means to send us a message by having Wilcox deliver such an esteemed guest on the eve of my big announcement."

Ping spoke through clenched teeth. "He didn't need to send a message. This is just him toying with us. And he told her my name! Can you believe that?" He returned to the chair and slumped into it.

Jacey kept her mouth shut and her ears tuned. There was so much in what they were saying, but she was struggling to put the pieces together. Clearly, they were not happy with Dr. Carlhagen. And not happy to see her, either.

She needed to keep her mind clear. She did not want to alienate any of them. That meant she had to get her thinking straight.

She resolved that from now on she would think of them only by their Scion names, which they each seemed to have adopted. Now that she thought of it, they had probably chosen their Scion names when they'd signed up for the program.

So here was Ping. Jacey knew nothing about his Progenitor, Han Xi. She'd seen Han's corpse in the freezer of the medical ward. He'd been very old. Perhaps a hundred years or more. He looked like an eighteen-year-old boy now. And he was angry with Dr. Carlhagen. He was nervous. His knee bounced as he sat in the chair, and he huddled in an unconsciously defensive posture. He looked at Jacey with suspicion—and hate.

And here was Vin. Her Progenitor was Elizabeth. Rich enough to own this island and mansion. Hadn't Mr. Justin said something about her being famous, too? She interviewed people, Jacey remembered. Vin was exactly the same age as Ping and Dante, but she looked older. It was her hair and clothes, her demeanor. Jacey saw now the girl—the woman—wore coloring on her eyelids and cheeks. It was very craftily done, barely noticeable. The effect was striking, though. Vin's mood was hard to gauge beyond the general impression she wasn't pleased by Jacey's presence. But unlike Ping, Vin's eyes held calculation. She was curious about Jacey. That could be good.

Finally there was Dante. It burned Jacey's heart to have to call Silvio by that name, even in her thoughts. But she had to or risk mistakenly calling him by his Progenitor name at the wrong moment. He still had Dante's mischievous look, the slight smile. The boyishness might have been attractive if it didn't seem so insolent. At the moment, he seemed more intent on Vin's and Ping's reactions than on Jacey herself.

"Do you believe me now?" Dante asked Vin.

Vin breathed in through her nose, lifting her shoulders and chest. She let it all go. "Yes. This proves you correct. Damn you." A sadness drew her brows down.

"I feel like I've walked in on a conversation here," Jacey said, trying to be jovial, but feeling her stomach quaver. "Can you enlighten me about what Dante might have gotten right?"

"Surely, you understood all along what we only now have come to learn," Vin said, taking slow, clicking, steps toward Jacey. She lifted a tanned hand and slipped a stray lock behind Jacey's ear, dropped her palm to cup Jacey's chin. It was like something Mother Tyeesha would have done. And yet, it wasn't grandmotherly the way Vin did it.

"Otherwise," Vin continued, patting Jacey's cheek, "you would have asked the good doctor to change your looks. But you couldn't do that, could you? You are just too addicted to the attention to give it up."

"Carlhagen chose her specifically for his scheme," Ping said. "It's kind of a stroke of genius, actually."

"He chose her because he wanted her," Silvio said. "Everybody knows about his infatuation. I saw him at a dinner party the Buchanans threw for one of their charities. You should have seen how Carlhagen fawned over her."

"I remember that party," Vin said. "But Carlhagen always has more than one reason for the things he does. Let's think this through." She counted off on her fingers. "First, he knew we'd figure out our predicament as soon as he gave us our allotment of ATR meds. Second, he wanted to send us a message—a reminder—by dropping Jacey in our lap. The dress was his idea, wasn't it dear?"

She didn't give Jacey a chance to answer. "He wanted to demonstrate his new power by sending Jackie B as his messenger girl. Third—"

"Names!" Ping barked. "We must have discipline with our names."

Vin spun on him, waved a finger at his nose. "What the hell difference does it make? There's no secret to keep."

Her hand dropped to her side, but her body trembled with rage. "Carlhagen knows I'm making my first appearance as Vin tomorrow. He knows there will be press here. He knows I'll have to deal with all the 'oh-my-God-you-look-just-like-your-grandmother' comments. And so he sends her here—looking just like she looked in *Hamlette*—making it so we have to explain how two recently-deceased celebrities happened to both have secret heirs who look exactly like their grandmothers."

"Not to mention two other semi-famous faces lurking in the crowd," Ping said quietly. Apparently, he meant himself and Dante. "We might have gone unnoticed for a while longer, but once the press starts looking . . ."

Dante saw Jacey's confusion. "I don't think our guest has put two and two together." He slid close and took her hand between his. They were very warm. He looked down at her with warm brown eyes. "My darling, Carlhagen wants the world to know about the Scion program."

Jacey felt like her brain was three minutes behind everything they were saying. What predicament were the

Progenitors in? What was an ATR med? What was *Hamlette*?

Finally, Dante's words registered. And they didn't make any sense. "Dr. Carlhagen wants the world to know about the Scions? But I thought he was trying to avoid that, for fear that somebody would put a stop to it."

"Who would put a stop to it?" he asked.

"Somebody . . . the government?"

She had no idea what government existed, except that Senator Bentilius was powerful in the North American Union. It clicked then, what Dante was really asking. Why would a government made up of Progenitors put an end to a program that benefitted them?

Her instincts told her she needed to change the balance of the conversation. They knew all kinds of things she didn't, but she knew things they didn't.

"Senator Bentilius must have known about all this," she said, as if musing to herself.

"What did you say?" Vin grabbed Jacey shoulder and turned her about. "Senator Bentilius has been missing for a few days now."

"She was on St. Vitus. Dr. Carlhagen was upset that she had come to transfer early, too. Apparently her Scion was not mature enough for a safe transfer."

Ping moaned and put his face in his hands.

Dante looked stricken. "So there it is. Can there be any doubt he has the Scions of many more powerful world leaders growing at that school?

A knock on the door. The latch rattled.

The Progenitors looked at each other, terrified expressions on their faces.

"I'll get rid of them." Dante motioned them toward the bathroom. Jacey scurried in after Vin and Ping and closed the door.

Dante's voice boomed out. "Lovely to see you again, my dear. No. I was just preparing to take a nap."

A female voice responded, but it was too low to make out.

"I'm flattered," Dante said. "Perhaps we should meet up later this evening."

Vin huddled next to Jacey, ear to the door. She gasped in exasperation. "I can't believe how they throw themselves at him." Jacey noted a tinge of jealousy in it.

Dante's voice was closer now, just on the other side the door. "No. I just like to keep the bathroom door closed."

The woman's voice came through clearly. "Would you mind if I just freshen up?"

Something bumped into the door. Dante's voice, louder, with hint of embarrassment. "You caught me, Meow Meow. I do have another guest here. But I would love to spend some special time with you. Later."

Vin grumbled something very unflattering about the girl Meow Meow.

"Is it our hostess? I would love to meet her."

The girl's voice slithered through the door. Jacey could picture a slender hand stroking Dante's shoulders, a slim body pressing close against his as she spoke. "If she's pretty enough to entice you, I wouldn't mind if she joined us."

The sound that came from her next told Jacey why she went by the name Meow Meow.

"That skank!" Vin whispered.

It *was* jealousy. Perhaps Vin's objections to Jacey's presence were about more than Dr. Carlhagen's schemes.

Ping did something that made Vin wince. She had to clamp her hand over her mouth to keep from letting her pain slip out. Jacey glared at them. For old folk, they were acting like a couple of foolish Spiders on kitchen duty.

There was a long silence beyond the door. Eventually Dante cleared his throat and sort of coughed. "I, uh, if you'll excuse me."

Meow Meow made the purring sound again. A moment later, the outer door clicked shut.

"You can come out," Dante called.

Vin pushed past Jacey, rubbing her buttocks and throwing dagger glances at Ping.

Ping ignored her. "You see what Carlhagen has done to us? We were hiding like first-year schoolchildren sneaking smokes in the bathroom. And from who? A pop star!"

"Meow Meow prefers the term 'entertainer'," Dante said, making the air quotes and smirking. His face grew more thoughtful. "I'll admit, she has her charms."

Vin stalked back and forth, shaking her hands at her sides as if trying to fling cookie dough off her fingers. "I can't tolerate this. I can't *endure* it!"

"We need more time," Ping said. "Vin, you have to cancel this stupid party. If Carlhagen wants the Scions to be public, let him step forward and make the announcement. Why should you take the heat?"

"Why should any of us?" Dante asked. "I know a guy in Brazil. Dr. Faccion. Does amazing work. I sent my second ex-wife to him several times. He's why she ended up being my third ex-wife. I'm sure he could alter our appearance so nobody would notice more than the faintest resemblance to our former selves."

"Unless you can materialize both him and an operating table into this room, that does us no good now," Vin spat. "I can't cancel this event. The press already knows the story. I'm the secret granddaughter. Elizabeth paid for my upbringing, private tutors, kept me anonymous for my own protection so I could have a normal childhood, blah, blah, blah."

She went to the mirror, pulled at the skin beneath her eyes. "Maybe with the right makeup I could de-emphasize the resemblance."

"You'll have to keep *her* hidden until they're all gone." Ping was looking at Jacey. He'd pulled the hood back over his head. His eyes were only the faintest glimmers. It reminded her of how sea turtles hid when threatened. She wondered if he had been a frightened man all his life.

"Obviously," Vin said.

Dante sprawled onto the bed, folded his arms across his chest. Of the three, he seemed the most relaxed. There was a carelessness in his personality, as if he wasn't able to take the world too seriously. "She can stay with me in here as long as she likes."

Still looking in the mirror, Vin tousled her hair and slipped her spectacles on. She pursed her lips and turned her head side to side. Satisfied that she was gorgeous, she said, "Ping, please come along and make sure the halls are clear. I don't want anyone seeing me until my grand entrance tomorrow."

The hooded boy grumbled and sighed, but he went to the door and peeked out. "It's clear."

Vin patted the clothes Dante had left on the foot of the bed. "You're a bit bigger boned than I am, sweetie. I'm afraid this is all I've got that will fit."

She slipped out of the room, Ping following close behind.

Dante whistled, a long note that fell in pitch. "I've known her for thirty years and I have never seen her so jealous." His eyes lingered on Jacey's.

Crossing her arms, Jacey retreated to the armchair Ping had vacated. It was still warm, which felt good. But the warmth bothered her, made her squirm uncomfortably. Ping was a Progenitor.

Dante was still watching her.

She had accomplished exactly none of her goals. If anything, she was farther from Livy than ever. And bringing the Scions here seemed a ridiculous notion.

She couldn't even get off the island now. Assuming she could get ahold of Captain Wilcox—which she doubted—Dante wouldn't let her leave this room.

"You're thinking a lot of thoughts over there," he said.

Her mind scanned over everything she had learned. The only piece that was certain was that the Progenitors felt betrayed by Dr. Carlhagen.

The old man wanted the Scion program made public. She followed that logic like Hansel and Gretel after a trail of crumbs.

Vin had said something about world leaders. "So, you think Dr. Carlhagen will use powerful people like Senator Bentilius to make the Scion program legal?"

"Legal, yes. Tolerated?" He shrugged. "It'll be a long time before carbos like us are welcomed. But yes, powerful people like the senator will make it legal. And that's all that matters."

Dante stood, demeanor changing, becoming more businesslike and less boyish. "Dr. Carlhagen's a chess master. Did you know that? I never ranked, but I recognize the way he thinks. Politicians, dictators, thugs in power, they're all pieces on the board. He knows how they move, how they think. He knows they will all want to control access to the Scion program. They will all understand the power that being able to grant or deny immortality could give them. Carlhagen has been playing them all against each other to keep them from invading the island. All he needs are a few of the really big dogs to transfer into their Scions. With them dependent on the ATR meds, he's won."

Something in her expression gave her away. Maybe her

earlier confusion had tipped him off, made him look for the ignorance she didn't even know to hide.

"He didn't do it to you, did he? Didn't saddle you with the ATR meds." Dante laughed, a deep-throated, genuine laugh. "That explains why you showed up here looking like an little lost puppy. He couldn't do it because he loves you."

"That's not it," she said. "If there were a chance to make me dependent on him, Dr. Carlhagen would have done it with great enthusiasm."

Dante tilted his head slightly, conceding her point. "So where do you keep your bottle of ATR? Got it tucked in your cleavage, do you? I didn't see you carrying so much as a clutch when you arrived."

"You're right. I don't need the ATR. I don't even know what it is."

"But you said . . . Wait a minute, you said Carlhagen 'would have done it'. But he didn't . . ."

His eyes grew very intent, more like Vaughan's than Dante's. It made Jacey's heart ache. She would have given anything to talk to either of her real friends. She felt a sudden longing for Humphrey, to feel his comforting arms around her.

"Jacqueline, what's going on?"

"That's not my name."

"Come now. Ping isn't here to berate us about meaningless rules."

"It isn't meaningless." Heart pounding, vision narrowing from fear, from the risk she was about to take, Jacey clutched her hands to her chest. "My name isn't Jacqueline. It never has been. I've only ever been Jacey."

Dante's face slackened, lips parting just slightly as the unbelievable truth fought to rise in his consciousness.

"Jacqueline is truly dead," Jacey said. "I am her Scion. And I have escaped St. Vitus."

He stood in shocked silence for a long, long time. Jacey felt as if she were balanced on a strand of rope stretched above a pit of fire. She had just confided her deepest secret to a person she didn't trust.

"That's incredible," Dante said, laughing.

But she was desperate. She took a step closer to Dante, dropped her hands, clenched them into fists. "Oh, there's much more."

32

NONE OF WOMAN BORN

Senator Maxine Bentilius was starting to straggle, and it was no surprise to Dr. Carlhagen. The heat on St. Lazarus was unrelenting. Even in the shade beneath the rainforest canopy, the air verged on boiling. Or so it seemed. But that wasn't her problem.

Because he was ahead of them all, he allowed a smile. Maxine was feeling the effects of Protocol One.

He glanced back. Her cheeks were flushed red and her breath was coming too hard. Her guard stayed with her, nervously scanning the trees for threats and keeping an eye on his struggling employer.

Dr. Carlhagen wiped a sleeve across his brow to keep sweat from dripping into his eyes. The three of them had just begun the final ascent along an overgrown service road, which in another year would be completely obliterated by the irrepressible plant life that covered the entire island. In short order, all evidence of man-made activity on St. Lazarus would vanish.

"A pity we couldn't come by boat," Dr. Carlhagen said. "It would have saved us this hike."

Along the north shore was a sea entrance to the compound, a hidden series of caves—ancient lava tubes formed at the very birth of the island—leading to a cavern. Dr. Carlhagen had installed docks there so supplies could be brought in.

"How much farther?" Livy asked.

The child's cheeks glowed from exertion, and her ponytail hung askew, stray strands plastered to her face with perspiration. Dr. Carlhagen didn't deign to answer the child, choosing to save his breath for the final climb.

The path switched back a few more times, though it still remained concealed beneath the mossy trees. As he topped the rise, he followed the trail under a monolithic stone overhang jutting from the side of the mountain.

The air became instantly cooler in its shade, and he came to a stop in front of a steel door twice his height and wide enough to admit a Jeep. An access panel to the right flashed to life at his approach.

The others came into the shade behind him. Maxine leaned against the stone, gasping for air.

The face of the facility's AI peered out at him, but this wasn't like Chax at the Scion School on St. Vitus. The AI he had grown and installed here had none of the personality quirks of Madam LaFontaine and her alter-egos. This AI was all business, which suited Dr. Carlhagen perfectly. He didn't need any AI teachers for the Scions here. No ballet instructors. No professors.

Because of that, he'd grown a much simpler and less human-like AI to run the operation. He'd named it Lazarus, after the island. The avatar's face was only vaguely human, with a sharp nose, no ears, no eyebrows. No hair at all. Flat brown eyes expressed the perfect balance of politeness and boredom. Rather like Mr. Justin, Dr. Carlhagen reflected. Thinking of his turncoat butler brought up a rush of irritation.

"Access code," Lazarus prompted in an expressionless baritone.

Dr. Carlhagen's skin chilled with anxiety. Hidden weapons were trained on his head at that very moment. A wrong answer to the prompt would end with Dr. Carlhagen's blood and brains all over the ground. He cleared his throat and gave the code, taking care to enunciate each word: "None of woman born."

"Welcome, Dr. Carlhagen." Lazarus's face disappeared from the screen.

A moment later, a series of thumps and hisses sounded from behind the door. Air sucked beneath a gap at the base as it began to rise straight up into the mountainside. Its bottom was serrated with long-toothed prongs like the portcullis from some ancient castle.

Dr. Carlhagen slipped under it and waved to Livy and Maxine. "Come along." His voice echoed hollowly in the circular tunnel beyond.

Livy didn't obey. Her wide eyes were fixed over Dr. Carlhagen's shoulder, as if trying to see into the darkness beyond the doorway. "I'm not going in there."

"Yes you are, child," Maxine said, coming up behind her. She prodded the girl forward. When Livy refused to go in, Maxine nodded to her guard. He hooked his hands beneath the girl's arms and lifted her.

Livy started to flail, kicking her feet and screaming.

But the guard easily carried the girl through the doorway. Maxine followed after, frowning at the wriggling child.

As soon as they passed through, the door began its slow grind closed. The rumble filled the tunnel, which was perfectly circular, except where the floor had been flattened for ease of moving vehicles up and down during construction.

Light fixtures flickered to life one by one down the corridor, the passageway so long that walls and ceiling converged to a pinpoint in the far distance.

The final boom of the closing door echoed for several seconds before leaving the tunnel silent and still as a held breath. The scent of damp rock mingled with the tinge of ozone produced by the air purification system, making the tunnel heavy with expectation, as if a thunderstorm might erupt in the narrow confines at any moment.

Dr. Carlhagen ran a hand along the black lava-rock wall. It had been polished and sealed with a glassy polymer finish, making it smooth as marble. The floor had been left rough, with nice grip for traction.

"We're almost there," he said to Livy, his voice ringing in the odd acoustics in the tube. He didn't know why he bothered trying to comfort her. Just a bit of left-over paternal instinct surfacing. The thought amused him.

"At least it's cooler in here," Maxine said. She was starting to catch her breath.

Livy faced the door, chest heaving. She was clearly teetering on the edge of panic.

Dr. Carlhagen resisted the urge to put his hands on her shoulders and ruffle her hair.

The girl's uncanny maturity always made him uneasy, but to see her struggling with this helpless animal instinct bothered him. She was just a child, after all.

"Shall we?" Maxine said.

Dr. Carlhagen started down the slope, not checking to see if his companions followed. Their footsteps—and Livy's half-muffled sobs—reverberated behind him. He glanced back to see Maxine trudging behind her guard, who had the girl by her collar.

Maxine was muttering something he couldn't quite hear. The guard kept his face stony.

The tunnel leveled off and came to another door. Again he gave the access code. The door opened and he entered the new Scion facility.

The layout and underlying concept of the Lazarus facility represented a complete reimagining of the Scion program, one that required much less space. And once it was fully operational, it needed very little human supervision.

The top level provided living quarters for adult attendants. He anticipated most rooms would remain empty. He'd only need a medic and a physical trainer, preferably a martial arts master like Sensei. Perhaps he could fill the role with a single individual, assuming he could find the right candidate.

He'd installed a personal suite for himself at the end of the hallway. Three more suites broke off left and right.

"Let's put her in cryo now," Maxine said. "I'm sick of dragging her around." Even wearing Belle's face, the senator had an air of authority that only came with age. But the dark circles under her eyes belied the creeping weakness taking over her muscles.

Dr. Carlhagen gave her a flat look. "Do you really think I brought Livy here just to put her in stasis?"

"I don't care why you brought her," she said. "But that's what we're going to do." Maxine had tapped into some reserves of energy, for her demeanor was very much like Belle's at that moment: icy stare, disdainful expression, tense posture, eager for confrontation.

Dr. Carlhagen considered his moves. It wouldn't harm the girl to put her in stasis. And yet that would take time.

And Dr. Carlhagen didn't anticipate staying at St. Lazarus very long.

Once the senator's military force regained control of St. Vitus, he intended to return there with Livy. And then he expected Jacey to present herself with a much more accommodating attitude.

"She needs to be prepared first," he said. "For now she can rest in one of the suites while we attend to more important things." He went to the first door on the left and opened it up.

Lights came on inside the luxuriously appointed living quarters.

Livy walked in, hands held close to her sides, eyes wide as she gazed all around.

The living room was as big as Dr. Carlhagen's bedroom back at the hacienda. Thick carpet covered the floor. A plush leather sofa and armchair gathered around a low coffee table of stainless steel.

"The bathroom is through there," he said pointing at a door across the room. "To your left is the kitchen. You'll find water and glasses. I'm afraid it has not yet been stocked with food, but we'll address that in an hour or so. Right now, the senator and I need to make contact with her backup force."

Without another word, he left the room, forcing Senator Bentilius to follow after him or be locked in with the girl. He rapped a knuckle on the monitor outside her door. "Lazarus, keep an eye on the child."

"Of course," came the baritone reply, though Lazarus didn't bother to show his face on the screen.

Maxine was staring at him, jaw clenched. Her guard seemed especially tense.

"Please, Maxine. Let's go to my suite. I have a holodesk

there. You can contact your commander and see what progress he's made on reclaiming the Scion School."

She didn't say anything for a long moment. Finally, she motioned for the guard to stay in front of Livy's door.

Dr. Carlhagen kept his face calm while he seethed inside. The main question was whether he would have the discussion about ATR now, or wait until she noticed the problem.

He smiled. No rush. She wouldn't feel the full effects for another day.

33

CHAIN REACTION

Humphrey stepped over a puddle in the dim hallway leading from the engine room to the forward storage compartments they were now calling Girls' and Boys' Holds. The black water rippled and sloshed with the rock of the boat; the surface glistened with the rainbow swirls of petrol. The smell of mildew and grease filled the companionway.

His conversation with Summer just now hadn't alleviated his fears, even though she had gotten engine two running again. The silly girl had wanted to shut down the other one and "optimize synchronization for better balance," whatever that meant. Only the reminder that worse weather was coming shook her out of her must-fix-every-machine-I-see mindset.

The puddle he'd stepped over seemed to chase him as *Aphrodite's* bow pitched down. Humphrey stopped and grabbed the doorjamb leading to the stairwell. The queasiness in his stomach grew as the vessel shook, plunged into the trough between two huge waves, then began its ponderous shift upward.

He needed to get abovedecks so he could keep his eyes on the horizon for a while. But first he had to check Boys' Hold for the AI server Mr. Justin had sneaked aboard.

He started up the corridor again, now walking uphill as the ship climbed the next wave. Ahead, the single working ceiling light flickered off, leaving a whole section in darkness.

When it came on again, Wanda was stumbling toward him. Though her face was drawn from exhaustion, she didn't seem seasick in the slightest.

"I've been looking for you," she said, stopping to block his progress. She had to grab on to his arm to keep upright.

"We've been having engine trouble. I was just talking to Summer."

"I've searched Girls' Hold from top to bottom. No servers." She brushed a stray red curl from her forehead. "You said they'd look like a box of some sort." She spread her hands indicating the width.

"Yes. Without mounting brackets on the front. Screw holes."

Her lips pouted as she shook her head. "Well, no such thing in Girls' Hold. Have you checked—"

"I'm just on my way there now."

Aphrodite topped the next wave and Humphrey felt his stomach lift as his weight dropped momentarily. The boat swung even farther to starboard as she plummeted, sending Wanda into Humphrey. They crashed against the starboard bulkhead, her shoulder jamming into his sternum.

"Ow," she said, rubbing her shoulder. "Your chest is bony."

Humphrey kept his comment about her sharp shoulder

to himself, but he was sure he'd have a bruise on his chest. "Sorry. I can't seem to steer the boat *with my mind*."

Wanda's face jerked up, eyebrows forming a V over her nose. But then her expression relaxed. "No. I'm sorry. It's just so damned tense on this bucket. Half the girls are puking from motion sickness and the other half are puking from holding the first half's ponytails while they sick up. It's a vomit chain reaction down there."

Humphrey swallowed. Hard. Wanda's vivid imagery wasn't helping his own stomach one bit.

The redheaded Eagle patted his shoulder. "You're looking a bit peaked."

His hand went to his belly. Jaw clamped tight.

"You should go see Mother Tyeesha. She has some ginger. It's worked wonders for about six of the youngest. And Mother is at ease as if she were lounging in a hammock."

"What about Miss Dayspring?"

Wanda rolled her eyes. "Trust me. Mother Tyeesha is the one you want to see."

Humphrey smiled wanly at thought of going to the old woman and feeling her rough hand on his forehead and hearing her quiet comforting murmurs. In truth, he would love to do that. But there simply was no time. But the ginger . . .

Yes. He'd stop there for a bit of medicine and then he'd go on to Boys' Hold.

And then he'd go back to the bridge and not think about throwing up. Not think about—

Aphrodite leaned to port, making him stumble.

Wanda caught hold of his waist as he convulsed and dropped to his knees. She rubbed his shoulders and patted his back while he brought up the little he'd eaten that day.

The boat pitched bow-first downhill, bringing oily

water rushing down the companionway to wash the mess away.

Wanda helped him to his feet, but didn't let go of him right away. She looked into his eyes, squinting. "You need to go lie down. I'll fetch some ginger for you from Mother Tyeesha."

Humphrey was not used to gratitude, and the flush of it made him stammer.

Wanda shoved him gently back toward the stairwell. "I'll find you on the bridge."

"But the servers. I have to search Boys' Hold."

"Leave that to me."

As Humphrey stumbled up the steps, clenching his mouth shut against a revived bout of nausea, he couldn't help but wonder: if it was this bad now, what would it be like if they got caught in the hurricane?

34

AN UNREACHABLE ITCH

Summer took off her John Deere cap and smacked the elevator button with it. "Stupid. Useless. Junk!"

The tantrum had no effect, of course. It didn't even relieve her fury. She could barely hear her own shouts above the rumble of the boat engines. Especially the clatter of engine two. She cast a hateful glance at it. She had got it running again, but it simply refused to tell her what was really wrong. And that worried her.

As if in answer to her thoughts, the boat listed hard to starboard. Summer stumbled sideways, shoulder crunching against the rusty bulkhead. Her eyes locked with Elias's as they both held their breath, willing *Aphrodite* to recover.

Slowly, the old ship swung back. Already they were in the ragged edge of the approaching storm. And with the ship under less than full power, they were likely to see much worse.

Elias's voice was barely audible over the racket. "You've done all you can for now."

She clicked her tongue. Elias was right. But the short-cuts and patchwork fixes she'd resorted to made her skin crawl. All she needed was a dry dock and a few months and she knew she could have *Aphrodite* back to like-new condition.

No chance of that. Humphrey had just left, and he'd made it clear that they needed the speed now—not in a few weeks.

Summer had put up a good argument, but he'd aced her with the hurricane info. She was supposed to keep that to herself, which also made her jittery. Entrusting her with a secret was like stoking an overworked boiler with no bleed valve.

"I'll get back to you, mister," she said to the engine. "Don't you doubt that for one second."

She turned back to the elevator and waved her hat helplessly at it. "Maybe this thing's problem is electrical. I'm going to have to pry these doors open and check the cabling."

"Does it really matter if the elevator works?" Elias waved a wrench at the doors. "The stairs seem to serve the purpose of moving us between decks."

He sat on the grated metal catwalk of the engine compartment, sorting through the toolbox, removing the stray screws, washers, bits of wire, and other unidentifiable bits and pieces that Orson had tossed in. What a disorganized buffoon that man was. No wonder the boat was in such a deplorable state.

Despite her general dissatisfaction with the boat, Elias's presence had stoked a warm glow in her heart. She loved, loved, loved Elias. For one, he was the most beautiful person who ever lived. And for two, he'd volunteered to help her fix things. That he was utterly incompetent when it came to mechanical stuff was kind of cute, too. Of course, with the wound in his side, he wasn't much practical use to her anyway.

She was content to have him sort washers and be there to look at.

She shoved the hat back onto her head, carelessly stuffing as much of her hair into it as she could.

"The elevator matters," she said to Elias.

He just did not understand. For her, a broken machine was like an unreachable itch. Which meant this whole ship was like a rash. She wouldn't be able to rest until she got it ship-shape. And that meant she'd probably never rest again.

Elias shrugged and tossed a handful of screws into one of the empty plastic pill bottles Summer had swiped from the infirmary. "Then pry the doors open and fix it."

"I will. Give me that chisel." She snapped her fingers and opened her palm.

The boy handed her a flathead screwdriver. Close enough.

She jabbed it between the elevator doors and gave it a wriggle. Once the gap was wide enough she got her fingers in and pulled it open.

Aphrodite plunged, but she was ready for it. She didn't understand why so many of the others were getting sick. Humphrey had been so weirdly green she wondered if he had a disease. He swore he didn't, but he retched like he'd swallowed a jumbie bean.

A waft of fishy air blew back at her as the elevator shaft balanced air pressure. She plucked up a flashlight and shined it into the blackness. The bottom of the elevator car hung four meters up, stopped at deck two. It opened on the main landing of the stairwell.

The shaft was not large, basically a closet. She had no idea why the boat even needed an elevator. As Elias had so intelligently pointed out, there was no reason a person couldn't use the stairs. The elevator wasn't big enough to move large equipment. Maybe that was why no one had bothered to fix it.

She shined the beam down. The bottom of the shaft was half a meter below the grate she stood on. Big rubber bumpers and pulleys for the lift mechanism lay half-submerged in filthy water. The sight of the fetid pool made her stomach lurch, but not from nausea.

It was fear. "Umm, Elias?"

"What."

"The bilge pumps are not keeping up."

"What's a bilge pump?"

"It pumps water out of the bottom of boat so it doesn't collect in places like this."

"Shouldn't the water stay out of the boat in the first place?"

"In general, but there's always some water coming in through small holes in seams of the hull panels. The deck is awash from the storm, so some is probably working its way down from up there. The bilge pumps should detect it and start pumping it out automatically."

She scanned around the edge of the elevator shaft. While rusty, it wasn't damp. "If water has risen to this point, the bilges must be full. No wonder Aphrodite draws so deep."

Elias came to stand beside her. "I understood almost nothing you just said."

She patted his pretty face, then went to the master control screen mounted on a panel between the engines. A few taps brought up schematics for the ship. She located the pumps and swore. She'd have to check each one, which would be nasty business since they were submerged in the most disgusting water she'd ever seen.

Scratch that. The pit back in the Scion School quad was worse. But not by much.

"Elias, close the elevator doors. I can't stand the smell coming out of there. I need to deal with these pumps."

The control screen had a diagnostics function that was supposed to show the operating status of all the equipment. But there was no data to indicate which pumps were broken. For that matter, the diagnostics for the engines didn't work either.

"Summer?" Elias called. "I think you need to see this."

The curious tone in his voice sent a pleasant shiver through her. She hustled back to the elevator, found him in the shaft, shin-deep in water. He held up a coil of blue cable, a frayed end exposing shiny copper wire. Not the kind of cable used to lift elevators. It was a data cable.

"Good job, Elias. You just found out why the diagnostics don't work. The network cable's been severed. It's also probably why the elevator doesn't work." She tapped her temple. "It *was* electrical after all."

"Can you fix it?"

She yanked off her hat and gazed up at the immobile elevator car. Clearly the shaft was serving double-duty as a chase for the data cables. But if she couldn't get the elevator out of the way, she wouldn't be able to rewire the network. She was going to have to come up with another work-around.

Elias sloshed his way back onto the grating and sat to put his shoes back on.

Aphrodite leaned hard to starboard again. Summer kept hold of a support strut and waited for ten heartbeats for the ship to right herself.

Bilge pumps first, she reminded herself. If *Aphrodite* sank, she'd never get the rest fixed.

She extended a hand to help Elias to his feet. He

grimaced and put a hand to his side as she hefted him up. The gunshot wound.

Without thinking, Summer wound her arms around his neck.

The kiss lasted for an unknown span of time—possibly several decades—before rational thought returned. Summer broke free and snatched her hat off. She fanned her face with it and looked around, trying to remember what she was going to do.

"The bilge pumps," Elias said in a husky voice.

"Ah. Yes. The pumps."

35

TURKEY FLOAT

Being forced to stay hidden in Dante's room was not what Jacey had expected when she'd boarded Captain Wilcox's helicopter that morning. In fact, she had figured that by now she'd be helping prepare for the Scions' arrival.

She snuggled deeper into the cushy four-poster bed. She had to admit that at least she was comfy. Her cot back in Girls' Hall had nothing on the lush, thick, cloudy mattress with which Vin had furnished her guest rooms.

Dante had left her alone while he went down to entertain the guests. Apparently he wasn't as concerned about being recognized as Vin was. And he had volunteered to play host until the big coming out the next day.

"I was famous in Brazil," he had said. "Especially among my circle of subsetters."

At her blank look, he said, "it comes from 'sub-orbitals'. It's a kind of spaceplane. Flies real high, goes real fast. Chicago to Moscow in a couple hours. The tabloids call us subsetters because we all travelled that way. Some of us—"

he nudged her shoulder with his, indicating it was Jackie B who he was talking about—"had our very own sub-orb."

Before he'd left he'd asked whether she minded him bringing back Meow Meow to share their bed. He'd said he was kidding, of course. But he had such a rascally look she wasn't convinced. She'd thrown a pillow at him, but he'd closed the door in the nick of time.

She wondered if he realized he was going to be sleeping in the armchair tonight.

He'd stocked her room with food. She'd eaten it without really tasting it. And now, to avoid going crazy with worry about Livy and the rest of the Scions, Jacey decided she needed a distraction.

"Power on," she commanded the monitor mounted on the left wall of the room.

It didn't turn on. Maybe she had to tap the screen.

She grumbled as she climbed from beneath the warm covers. Her dress lay across the foot of the bed, slinky and smooth as pool of black oil. She'd discarded it in favor of the "resort wear" Silvio had brought. It wasn't as see-through as she'd feared and the light fabric was comfortable.

Her bare feet chilled as she tiptoed across the tile. She tapped the monitor.

Nothing.

She wondered if Silvio had disabled the device to keep her from learning anything. But no, he'd suggested she use it. Her eyes fell on a small object clamped to one edge of the monitor. It was rectangular and had an array of rubber buttons on it.

She unclipped it. A green button at the top invited her thumb.

The monitor lit up and a woman's voice boomed out so

loudly that Jacey stumbled backward. Fumbling with the button device, she found a volume control.

Once the volume was at a level mere humans could withstand, she returned to her bed. What a marvelous little device, she thought. As she slipped back under the covers, she decided it made more sense to press buttons than to shout at a monitor clear across the room.

What would Madam LaFontaine say to the idea that a Shark was lazing about, watching videos on a big screen, in bed?

Jacey snorted a humorless laugh.

There was a woman on the monitor. She stood in front of a background of blue lines that swirled slowly as she talked. Occasionally the image would cut to different video while she spoke. At the moment there was parade of weird vehicles streaming down a city street. People in heavy coats lined the walks to either side.

The camera fixed for a moment on a formation of people in uniforms. They all played instruments. Horns. A line of drummers beat upon their drums with sticks. A few had huge mallets in both hands, pounding out a resonant beat as they marched.

The video cut to a slow-moving vehicle shaped like a huge turkey. A man and woman sat atop it in the oddest clothes Jacey had ever seen.

The woman was talking about it: ". . . in the first Thanksgiving Day Parade in nearly five decades. The event lasted three hours, and throngs from all over the Indy-Minnie corridor flocked to Chicago's Michigan Avenue to witness it. From today forward, the holiday will be celebrated on the fourth Thursday of every July. In celebration, the Parade Council funded the creation of an exact replica of the famous Turkey Float, a sight not seen since the Kille-

Tine asteroid tsunamis wiped out the eastern seaboard of the United States."

Jacey had no idea what Thanksgiving was or why the turkey was famous.

Cutting back to the woman's face, the program changed tone. Background music turned mournful. "And now for our daily Tent City Update."

Video showed an aerial view of a barren stretch of land. Brown straggles of grass grew in clumps surrounding a fenced in encampment. The tents had probably once been white, but were now a sandy brown. They weren't arranged in any sensible way, just placed next to each other in random clumps. A street of brown dirt, rutted with vehicle tracks, and littered with paper, bottles, and unidentifiable garbage, wound through the camp.

Just looking at it made Jacey clamp her mouth shut against the smell—the taste—the images brought to her mind. The garbage outside the kitchens at the Scion School often grew so ripe in the sun Sensei made them bury it. She imagined the whole encampment stank of it.

And now a shot from street level. Children in dirty clothes, rags really, kicked a ball around while other children tried to steal it. Their breath plumed, as if they exhaled smoke. But no, it was just from the chill. Some of them wore long coats or scarves. A few had boots. Most had no shoes at all, just holey stockings.

Their white-toothed grins were at odds with their gaunt faces and frail limbs. They reminded Jacey of marionettes Socrates had shown her once. And their movements were just as jerky.

"The plight of the plague refugees worsens by the day," the announcer woman said. "Officials report that twenty refugees arrive each day, mostly children."

Video cut to a close-up of a muddy pair of kids not old

enough to be Dolphins. Their eyes, huge and brown, stared into the camera without emotion.

"Just yesterday these twins arrived, brother and sister Hil and Ana. They claim to be six years old and came from the town of Chilton over seventy miles away. They walked the entire way, hiding during daytime and walking at night to avoid snipers."

The music changed, swelling into a major key, suggesting hope. "Today the TCK was toured by Ollie Montgomery and her team of inspectors."

Video showed a squad of people wearing yellow jump-suits, hands encased in thick gloves. The suits had integral hoods and clear plastic visors. Protruding from the lower portion of the visors were long filter canisters.

"Infection rates in the camp remain at a steady 80%. No one knows why the 20% are immune, but even the immune people carry and spread the marrow plague."

The video flashed to a close-up of a central figure. A woman, Jacey thought, based on her relative size and the suggestion of femininity in her eyes, the only feature visible through the mask. She wore a violet scarf around her neck, over her protective suit. It fluttered in the breeze, thin and delicate and lovely.

A graphic appeared below her image, reading: Ollie Montgomery, Philanthropist/Refugee Advocate.

Someone off-camera thrust a microphone at Ms. Montgomery's face. "Are you satisfied with what you're seeing, in terms of medical attention for refugees, and food and shelter provisions?"

What a stupid question, Jacey thought. Why ask that? Just look at those poor people.

Ms. Montgomery seemed to share Jacey's thoughts. "I am not at all satisfied. My team and I were just in the supply depot outside the fence. It is very clear that what food is available is out of date and of low quality. In discussions with government supply coordinators, it is clear something is holding up delivery of new supplies. Clearly, with the absence of Senator Bentilius, someone—or some group—has decided to redirect funds intended for the care of plague victims and refugees."

Jacey sat straight up, jamming the remote control to raise the volume.

"Are you suggesting there is a conspiracy to deny these people care? That Senator Bentilius's disappearance is not the long holiday her staff claims it is?"

"I'm not suggesting anything. I'm just pointing out the obvious. People are suffering. And the people in positions of responsibility have decided to cut off assistance. They have decided to give up on these lives. There are people—"

The person holding the mic—a man, gauging by the size of the gloved fist clenching the thing—interrupted Ms. Montgomery. "In a statement today, President of the North American Union Annabelle Rochelle claimed just the opposite. She stated that the government is committing an additional $300 billion to aid efforts."

The video cut to a handsome woman of perhaps fifty years. She stood at a podium, two flags behind her, one red-and-white striped, the other white with a black band across it. Her hair was pulled back in a severe coppery-colored bun, but her brows were elegant, and her eyes . . .

"You've got to be kidding me." The words tore from Jacey's throat.

The view of the woman snapped away. Ms. Montgomery answered the reporter with sharp waves of her gloved hands. Though she wasn't yelling, passionate outrage came through her voice. Jacey was no longer listening, though.

She searched the buttons on the remote control. She

found one with triangles aimed to her left. She pressed it. The video backed up. After three tries, Jacey found the button to freeze the video.

She got up from the bed, paying no attention now to the chill of the floor tiles.

With trembling hands she touched the screen, outlined the President's brow, her jaw, her nose.

What was this world Jacey had emerged into? This odd society of extreme wealth and extreme poverty, of vast cities and turkey parades, of "coming out" parties for Progenitors and videos about plague cities?

The floor seemed to shift under Jacey's feet. Not literally, but her balance faltered nonetheless.

She stumbled back to the bed. She lay there, hands squeezing her temples, needing the pressure to contain the hurricane of thoughts shattering her world apart.

President Annabelle Rochelle was a Progenitor.

Leslie's.

36

WE'RE ALL SMALL

The trick was to watch the horizon. That way the brain had a reference point and could then understand the wild motions the inner ear detected. Or so Sensei had told Humphrey.

The problem was that the horizon was either lost in mist or hidden behind enormous swells of the sea. And the roiling waters surrounding *Aphrodite* matched the rise and fall of Humphrey's stomach.

He groaned and heaved over the railing of the starboard wing, just off the bridge. There would be no mess to clean up below. For one, the deck was awash from huge waves crashing over the bow every 45 seconds. Second, he had nothing left in his guts to bring up. Wind pummeled him, but he sucked it in. At least the air was fresh. The chill mist felt good on his face, too.

But if he lingered, he'd get soaked through. And then he might really get sick. He couldn't afford that.

Wind threatened to blow the door into the bridge right

out of his hand, and it cut through the small room, sending the map curling and tumbling to the floor.

Humphrey pressed his back to the door and latched it shut. His hair wasn't long enough yet to get in his eyes, but he had to run fingers through it to unwind the tangles the storm had woven in it.

Tytus stood guard duty across the bridge, leaning against the door to the port-side wing. He gave Humphrey an empathetic smile. He'd eaten some of Mother Tyeesha's ginger and seemed to be bearing the motion better than most. The plunging of the ship seemed to unnerve him, though. He gripped the edge of the control console every time the vessel dove into a trough, knuckles whitening with the strain.

Orson sat on a swiveling stool mounted to the floor in front of the ship's controls. He leaned into the climbs and leaned away from the falls without seeming to think about it. Apparently computers did most of the steering, for the lump of a man did very little. Occasionally his hands went to the breast pocket of his dingy shirt, patted it and then dropped to his lap. This was always followed by a huge sigh of disappointment.

"Did you lose something?" Humphrey asked. He didn't actually care about the answer, but he'd try anything to distract himself from his misery.

Orson's beard and mustache crumpled around his mouth as he bit his lip and nodded. "I hanker for a cigar. I have more down in my stateroom, but your kung-fu master won't let me smoke 'em. I said I could just as well chew on the end, but he just gave me one of those looks he gives." Orson shivered and rubbed his arms.

Humphrey knew the look Orson was talking about. "You actually light those things on fire and inhale the smoke?"

"Aye, I do, indeed. And my stash is the best Cuban varieties still available." The man tilted his head thoughtfully. "You know, I always found a good cigar cut right through a sick stomach."

Humphrey bit his lower lip. Damn the man for bringing it up.

And there was a little nasty smile parting the beard. Orson had said it on purpose. Humphrey was starting to think his puking was a form of entertainment for the man. Diabolical old blob.

The door at the back of the bridge banged open. Tytus spun, dropping into fighting stance.

It was Wanda.

Tytus relaxed his muscles by a fraction and returned to his grip on the console.

Wanda crossed to Humphrey, reaching him just as *Aphrodite's* bow nosed over the peak of a wave and started her slide into a valley. They both grabbed onto the map table and braced. Wanda kept her eyes fixed on the bow, eyes intent. She'd redone her ponytail, so no strays were falling into her face. Humphrey watched her mouth compress, knew the moment of impact was moments away as her eyes squinted shut.

The boat shuddered as it wallowed in the trough and the propellers fought to keep her going forward. The roar of water and spray pouring across the decks subsided, and slowly the boat began to climb the next swell.

"This is insanity," Wanda said under her breath.

Humphrey caught it though, and in the quaver he detected a hint of fear. Wanda had kept it hidden well, but now that he knew it was there, he could see it in her eyes and in the way her shoulders tensed.

No, he thought, reconsidering. The tension was anger.

"What happened?" he asked.

She regarded him a moment. She seemed irritated he'd seen through her mask. The thought amused him. Wanda had been through a lot. They all had. But when it came to masks and hidden motives, she was a rank beginner compared to Humphrey. And Jacey. Especially Jacey.

"I went to Boys' Hold to search for the server. I had a run-in with Horace."

It was Humphrey's turn to be irritated, but he had no compulsion against showing it. "What did he do now?"

"He invited me to join him in his bunk."

"That is intolerable. I'll inform Sensei."

"You think it's the first time he's said something like that? You should talk to all the Spider, Snake, and Eagle girls. We've all had to deal with worse from him."

Humphrey gaped at her. "Does Sensei know?"

Wanda said nothing. She didn't have to. Her stiff jaw told him. They hadn't told the martial arts master anything.

Aphrodite topped the next swell.

"You never noticed that girls haven't gone off campus alone in the past week or so? We always, always go in pairs?"

Humphrey had not noticed. But the thought that it was because of Horace sickened him. And in a different way than the ridiculous climb, dive, and roll of the ship did. It sickened his heart.

"It started after Birthday." Wanda braced for another impact. Once it passed, she continued. "When Dante and Ping left. And then Vaughan was knocked out . . . Horace became very forward."

"Why didn't you say anything to me?"

Her green eyes flashed momentarily to his. "You were distracted."

Fair enough. The drama with Dr. Carlhagen and Jacey

had been a bit consuming. But still. "I could have put a stop to it. I could have locked him up."

"Yes. You could have. All you boys could have saved us *weak* girls." She spat the last bit. Before he could object, she patted his hand. "I know you mean well, Humphrey. But you don't understand how hard it is to talk about. You don't know how small it makes me feel to talk about it even now."

"But you are talking about it now."

Wanda motioned to the raging sea with her chin. "Out here we're all small. I figure, what difference does it make?"

"I'll talk to Horace."

"No, you won't."

"But I won't allow him to continue harassing you."

Horace had always been a problem. Wild, undisciplined, and with a penchant for torturing insects. Humphrey would never forget seeing the boy firing the machine gun at Senator Bentilius's guards, wild rage in his eyes.

Wanda sighed through her nose and smiled, tight lipped. "I don't think he'll be doing much harassing any time soon."

"Why?"

The door to the bridge opened again and Leslie strode in. She wore a self-satisfied look, as if she'd just won an argument. She glanced at Wanda. "He's in the room opposite Sang's."

"Has the bleeding stopped?"

Leslie shrugged. "I don't know. Don't care."

Wanda smiled and nudged Humphrey with a sharp shoulder. "Leslie punched him in the nose."

Leslie grunted. "A good thing Sensei didn't teach me to fight. I might have done much worse."

Orson waved a paw to get Humphrey's attention. "I want to send Rosales to—uh, assist—Summer. We need to squeeze more out of the engines."

Humphrey could only imagine how Summer would react to that. And from what Humphrey had learned, Orson's mechanic hadn't kept the engines in very good repair to begin with.

"Why, are the seas growing?" Humphrey couldn't imagine plowing through bigger waves. He thought it might be better for them to just sink beneath the surface and put an end to their queasy misery.

"No. But there's a fleet to the southeast."

"A what?" Humphrey said.

Orson's eyes flashed momentarily to meet Leslie's. Just as quickly they snapped back to Humphrey's. "A fleet. You said something about getting away from the island before a backup force arrived?"

The man swiveled in his chair and pointed. "Fifty miles that way." He checked a display on the control console. "Make that forty-nine."

"How many ships?" Leslie demanded.

"Impossible to say. The storm is generating a lot of noise for our radar. At least ten ships. Big ones. With big guns."

37

I KNOW MY CHILDREN

Motion sickness was for the unprepared.

And a good butler was never unprepared.

Mr. Justin popped another motion sickness tablet and hummed quietly to himself. The storm was making a mess of the boat, especially in the holds, where the Scions were taking turns tossing up their meals.

Fortunately, Sensei had trained into them a sense of hygiene. Beat it into them, more like.

The butler laughed, realizing he was still worrying about housekeeping problems. Old habits die hard, as they say.

The Scions could take care of themselves. And it seemed the worst of their sickness was waning as they collapsed into insensible slumber.

Obu, a very clever Spider from Humphrey's Nine, had showed everyone how to fasten themselves into their bunks with some spare rope he'd found lying about. He'd helped secure the bunks so they would stop sliding and tumbling as well.

Mr. Justin wondered—with only the slightest bit of actual interest—who Obu's progenitor might be.

With everyone hunkered down in the holds and Humphrey suffering on the bridge, Mr. Justin had the run of the ship as long as he stayed off the weather deck. Only a fool would go out in that.

He stumbled down the Deck One companionway, heading aft toward Orson's stateroom.

He stopped momentarily to peek into the staterooms where Sang and Horace were locked up. The latter boy's nose had stopped bleeding after all. Pity.

Of all the Scions, Horace was the only one Mr. Justin would actually consider killing rather than selling. But that would be an unnecessary waste. Once overwritten, nothing of the boy's weird sadistic nature would remain.

He considered how to weave Horace into his plan, but since everyone thought Sang was Mr. Justin, Sang would have to serve. Also a pity, as Sang was truly a nice boy.

"Shouldn't you be with your Nine?"

Mr. Justin managed not to jump out of his skin. He turned to find Sensei emerging from the small galley kitchen a few doors down. The martial arts master held a can of beans in one hand, tin lid cocked up. In his other he held a plastic spoon.

Fast thinking was just normal everyday thinking for Mr. Justin. The lie he conceived on the spot made him smile. Working among these people was like a chess master playing against three-year-olds.

"Mother Tyeesha was concerned about Sang and Horace. She sent me to peek in and discover whether they were as ill as everyone else. I have ginger." He held up an empty fist.

Sensei shoved a spoonful of beans—cold, it appeared—into his mouth and mushed them around for a moment before swallowing. He had gained his sea legs faster than anyone else. He merely shifted his weight to remain rooted where he stood as *Aphrodite* climbed and plunged over the raging swells. A dangerous man, indeed.

"Odd. I was just speaking with Mother Tyeesha. She expressed to me the same concern. Didn't mention sending you to do the same task she assigned me."

Mr. Justin smiled and stepped closer. He'd spent a fair amount of time before a mirror, practicing various expressions with his smooth feminine face. He put on one that he knew expressed exasperation. "That poor old woman. She's so forgetful these days. And she's absolutely convinced Sang is not Mr. Justin. I explained the evidence we've gathered, but she wouldn't hear it. She kept saying—"

Sensei interjected, filling in Mother Tyeesha's words: "'I know my children. Sang is as innocent as a newborn babe.'"

"Yes. Exactly that. I have to admire her affection for us, even if I think it's a bit blind."

"So how is Sang?" Sensei took another spoonful. He seemed casual, but there was something in the flicker of darkness in his eyes that warned Mr. Justin. The man was suspicious.

"I didn't see any vomit on the floor." He said it lightly, with a smile. "Horace, on the other hand . . ."

"I heard there was an altercation. I extracted from Kirk that Horace has been a bit of a menace recently."

Sensei went to Horace's door, peered in the window, mashing another spoonful of beans in his mouth. His shoulders were like balls of iron, his thighs, thick logs. Too dangerous to keep around.

"I had warned Vaughan about it," Mr. Justin said. "Humphrey, too. But everyone was so distracted by

Birthday. And then everything with Dr. Carlhagen happened."

Sensei nodded slowly, scraping the spoon around the inside of the can.

Mr. Justin wished he had everything in place. Right here. He could get rid of the man and it would be so easy.

But everything was not in place. And a good butler knew patience, knew preparation, planning, double-checking, thinking of contingencies, and then striking when all aligned as it should. This was not that time.

"I want to go check on Summer in the engine room," Mr. Justin said. "She sometimes forgets to eat when she's absorbed in mechanical problems. And on this ship, that means she'll starve to death."

He almost turned to leave, but in the last instant remembered that Scions do not just leave Sensei's presence without being dismissed. Maybe Jacey could get away with that, but *Leslie* could not.

Not yet.

Sensei eyed him for what seemed like fifteen seconds before nodding a dismissal.

Mr. Justin let a grin replace his polite and attentive expression as he walked up the companionway and into the flickering dimness toward the engine room. Just short of that were Orson's quarters.

Mr. Justin had led the search of Orson's room himself so he could report to Humphrey that nothing untoward was in there, nothing Orson could use to hurt a Scion or the ship.

That was untrue, however. There was something in there that could most definitely hurt a Scion.

More importantly, it could kill Sensei Rosa.

38

IN A BAR, MAC

Sounds of festivities rumbled through the door of Jacey's room.

Bass notes and drums thrummed and made her windows resonate. Above that noise came shrieks of laughter, shouts, and the occasional clash of breaking glass.

Jacey kept the lights off now, except for the video monitor. Every so often she crept to the window to watch people come and go alone or in couples. They'd stroll around the pool, most of the women wearing versions of what Jacey wore. A few had on short dresses.

The pool glowed with eldritch blue light from bulbs below the water level, a haze of blue colored the bottoms of palm trees nearby. To the right, a path wandered away toward the cliff, now lost in darkness.

Jacey wished the windows had louvers so she could let in some fresh air. Warmer air would be welcome, too. She wondered why Vin kept the place so cold. It made her think of the freezer in the medical ward. Perhaps the Progenitors were all dead and they just walked around with no blood in their hearts.

No. She'd been close enough to all of them to feel the warmth of their bodies. Her friends' bodies. They were now dead, overwritten, gone, lost. Destroyed.

The news program she'd been watching continued to drone in the background. It was on a channel called Survivor News Network. And it looped the same handful of stories over and over.

Every time the Tent City segment came on and showed Ollie Montgomery and the President, Jacey watched, letting it sink in. She had known that the Progenitors were powerful people. The richest, the wealthiest. And though she had no understanding of the structure of nations in the outside world, she knew what the title of "president" meant. Socrates had taught her about the Democratic ideals of the ancient Greeks. He seemed to love that topic above all others, even more than Shakespeare. And that was saying something.

The fact that Leslie was the President's Scion reinforced Dante's argument that Dr. Carlhagen was gaining sway over the most powerful people on earth. What Jacey couldn't understand, yet, was what he planned to do with that power. What did he want?

She had always attributed his actions to greed. And lust.

And his addiction, she reminded herself, remembering Dr. Carlhagen's insatiable need for andleprixen.

She hadn't told Dante about that yet. Hadn't told him a lot of things.

Already she'd confided more than she'd planned. Desperation had made her do it because she wanted to get off this island and find Dr. Carlhagen.

Warring with that desire was her need to contact

Humphrey. Dante said he'd help her get to a holodesk later, once everyone went to bed. The party had already raged for hours, and the sun had set long ago. She feared the sun would come up before they finally slept.

Frustrated, she snatched up the remote control and scanned through more channels.

The wealth of non-stop information astonished her. The dramatic productions alone filled hundreds of channels. Then there were the sporting events where people in colorful shirts and shorts kicked a white ball around a vast green field. She'd seen Sensei lead Scions in games of football before, but this was something on a much higher level. And the people! The arena was filled with over seventy thousand of them.

Another channel showed a young man in a suit standing in front of a map. It had a red and yellow swirl on it. "Hurricane Ignatius is building up in the Caribbean. Right now it's approaching the uninhabited islands east of Puerto Rico. Computer models predict with high certainty it will turn north and graze the Florida stub, then continue up the coast. Salvage divers on what was once the eastern seaboard are heading to sea, hoping to avoid the worst of it."

Jacey didn't know the geography well enough to know where on the map she was. She knew the words Caribbean and Puerto Rico, though.

She needed to talk to Dante. Now.

If *Aphrodite* was caught in this storm, she'd soon be at the bottom of the sea.

At some point she'd gotten out of bed. She found herself back at the window, considering whether to pound on it.

And why shouldn't she? Who was she protecting by staying hidden? Didn't she want the truth to come out?

The sooner the better, actually. If the world learned of the Scion program now, before the president—and who knew how many other world leaders—transferred, wasn't it more likely some force would sweep in and put a stop to it?

As wishful as that thinking was, she couldn't convince herself it was true.

Everything she'd seen so far had showed her that any force that took St. Vitus was likely to use the Scion program for their own advantage, not to shut it down.

She remembered that Dr. Carlhagen had another Scion School somewhere. Humphrey hadn't been able to find out where.

And then there was the carbo problem. Jacey's very existence was illegal, apparently.

Returning to bed, she flipped away from the weather news and kept scanning. Her eyes weren't even focused on the screen. Her thoughts were far away, imagining Humphrey and the rest thrashing through towering waves, their boat lost beneath them.

Her own voice coming from the screen pulled her from the waking nightmare. "I found him in a bar, Mac. Where else? Looks like he was there all day. Drunk. He smelled like piss."

Eyes focusing on the screen, Jacey felt the world tilting again.

She was on the screen.

She was sitting in a plain room, walls of concrete block. A battered table sat in the middle. She was on one side, wearing a sort of suit, but cut for her curves.

She had a strange necklace on that looked like a shoelace. A plastic placard dangled from the end in place of an actual piece of jewelry.

Jacey was leaning back in a chair, haughty expression

on her face. Her hair was pulled back in the familiar pony-tail, but the color was wrong. It looked sort of red. And she wore makeup, darkening her eyes, making them more mature, more sensual.

The real Jacey, the one sitting on the bed in the cold room in Vin's mansion, swore. It was guttural, passionate, and breathless.

It was the first time Jacey had ever seen Jacqueline Buchanan.

39

NAWK FLEET COMMAND SHIP

The storm passed just before dawn, the seas mellowing into long gentle swells that rocked *Aphrodite* and her long-suffering passengers to sleep.

Humphrey was still up. He hadn't slept for over twenty-four hours and it felt like twenty-four days.

Both bridge wing doors were braced open, letting in the fresh breeze. Sun-fire burned just beneath the horizon to the east, casting a burnt orange light onto the ragged tail of storm clouds scudding away to the northeast.

The air smelled clean. Humphrey's stomach had settled once he'd been able to keep Mother Tyeesha's ginger down long enough. And with the settling sea, the edge of hunger was working its way into his belly.

Orson scratched his beard as he studied a display on his console. "The fleet drifted east over the past few hours, but radar shows them bearing straight for us."

He flipped a few switches and turned a knob. Static hissed from a metal-grated speaker next to a radio handset on a curly black cord. "Haven't heard a peep from them yet."

"Is that bad or good?" Humphrey asked.

Orson shrugged. "A military fleet in radar range is never good."

Sensei was taking a turn at guard duty. He stood at the map table, frowning it at and clenching his jaw. "The islands we were headed for are beyond our reach at the moment, not that we could hide there anyway."

"Should we turn back?" Humphrey asked. "Or maybe turn toward them?"

"*Toward* them?" Orson and Sensei said together.

Humphrey held his hands out. "I don't know. I thought maybe we'd look less suspicious if we just casually went in their direction. What moron trying to escape their notice would do that?"

"Apparently you," Orson said.

The comment stung, but only a little. Humphrey was confident they had to do something to mislead the fleet. Make them think *Aphrodite* was anything but a boatload of Scions.

"We don't know they are the senator's force," Sensei said.

"What else could they be?"

Sensei clasped his hands behind his back and walked to and fro, head down in thought. "I don't know. But we must be clear on what the objective facts are versus the ones we make up."

The radio crackled and a tinny voice blasted out. "Freighter ship bearing southeast, this is NAUC fleet command ship *A. Rodgers*, please identify yourself, your port of departure, and your port of destination."

Humphrey's skin chilled despite the balmy air whirling through the bridge. "What's a nawk fleet command ship?"

Orson stared at the speaker, tip of his pink tongue peeking from his whisker-shrouded mouth. "That's N.A.U.C. It stands for North American Union—Caribbean Fleet. The *A. Rodgers* is an aircraft carrier. Fighters. Bombers. Sub-orbs. Missiles. Dozen gun turrets. A detachment of marines, probably. She's got a whole slew of other ships with her."

The message repeated. And then again. The next time the voice added, "you, with the bus, I'm talking to you."

"You'd better answer," Sensei said. "Remember, we don't want to look suspicious."

Orson lifted the handset and put it near his mouth. He didn't thumb the transmit key though. "Just remember, they probably won't kill you," he said to Humphrey. "But they'll have zero hesitation to put a bullet between my eyes."

Humphrey raised his eyebrows and smiled. "Then I guess you'd better be convincing."

Orson straightened in his stool and clicked the button. "This is Captain Santana of freighter *Aphrodite*. Sorry for answering slow. Three of my able-bodied seamen got arrested at our port of departure, Nassau. Anyway, we stopped for a couple salvage dives around Cuba, then at Puerto Rico to take aboard the bus to deliver to a school in Mexico. Gotta make a buck, you know what I'm saying?"

"You're very far south for the run you're describing. By chance did you stop at any of the little islands on your way? St. Vitus?"

"No, sir. Damn storm caught us with an engine down, so we got a bit off track. She's back up and humming now. Just bad luck, is all."

"St. Vitus?" Humphrey said to Sensei. "How's that for an objective fact?"

It was a little impertinent, but the martial arts master

either didn't notice or didn't care enough to make an issue of it.

The voice replied, "Admiral Wanish commands you come about and maintain station at your present location. We are sending a boarding party to inspect your cargo."

Orson jumped from his stool, surprisingly agile for a man as heavy as he was. "Negative. We are already way behind schedule."

Humphrey and Sensei had moved next to Orson. They exchanged tense glances as they awaited the reply.

It was not long in coming. "Admiral Wanish commands you to come about. This is not a request. Repeat, this is not a request. You are required to comply by WhemSea Treaty Section Five. If you do not comply, you will be fired upon."

"Western Hemisphere Sea Treaty," Orson said, explaining the lingo. "WhemSea."

"Would they really shoot at us if they thought Scions were aboard?" Humphrey asked.

"Would you like to find out?" Orson asked flatly.

There was no choice but to obey. Besides, there was no chance of outrunning a military fleet. Especially one with missiles and airplanes at its disposal.

"Come about, Orson," Humphrey said.

Sensei nodded his agreement. "Tell them you'll comply with all requests."

The man hadn't been the least bit queasy during the heaviest seas, but now he looked green.

Humphrey couldn't take any satisfaction in it. Sure, Orson's life was forfeit if it was discovered he had helped the Scions escape. He might endure even worse if Senator Bentilius learned he had been working with Mr. Justin to steal the Scions. But the same was true for Sensei.

"You need to hide," Humphrey said to the martial arts master.

"I will. But not how you think." He didn't let Humphrey ask the obvious question. "We need Summer up here right now."

It only took Humphrey a second to understand why. If anyone aboard could stash all the Scions away, Summer could.

Orson held binoculars to his eyes. "You two might want to hurry with your schemes. I see one hell of a wake fanning behind a gunboat heading this way. They're moving fast. And there's a chopper on the horizon."

Humphrey forgot his sleepiness, his physical exhaustion, and his hunger. He flew down the stairs, shouting for Summer.

40

TRANSFIGURATION BENTILIUS

Dr. Carlhagen's quarters in the Lazarus facility were not as relaxed as those in his hacienda on St. Vitus. But that was good, in a way. The move to this facility was a signal—as much to himself as to his clients—that the Scion program was a business. That he was here much earlier than he anticipated didn't bother him at all.

The fact that the Scions were running amok on St. Vitus did bother him. A great deal.

As confident as he was that all would be set aright soon, something nagged at him. He decided it was Mr. Justin. The man was very competent and he had betrayed him. And Dr. Carlhagen hadn't seen it coming.

Dr. Carlhagen stretched in his comfortable bed and observed the faux sunrise just now making the wall screens glow. He'd made up for the lack of windows in his rooms by covering the hewn stone walls with nano-pixel paint.

Unless he smacked the wall with his hand, his brain

could not tell there wasn't a great stone arch giving a magnificent view of the sea to the east.

Nano-fans embedded among the paint pixels created breezes scented with floral perfumes. The scents were made on demand by manufactory nanites of his own design.

The overall effect of the scene and scents pleased him. He recalled how his father had complained about every new technology that had come along, from autonomous cars to VR eye implants. The man truly had been born a century or three too late.

Dr. Carlhagen felt tremendous satisfaction in defeating this disadvantage of living underground. It was confirmation that man could—and should—conform the world to his needs, not be conformed by the world. That went for his windowless room the same way it did for his new, young body.

With the pixel walls he could enjoy all the sunrises, sunsets, and moonlit nights he wanted. The swimming pool three levels down was never fouled with leaves, bugs, and iguana scat, or dead frogs. Weather had no impact on his day, hurricane or heat wave.

If necessary, he could live here for years on end without going stir-crazy.

Of course, he had no plans to do that. And some of the furnishings reflected that. Oh, it was all expensive, luxurious. But none of it meant anything to him. The artwork was not precious, the wine collection modest. The furniture was solid, craftsman style from the early twentieth century —a bit of an obsession he'd had at the time he'd bought it all.

None of those deficiencies really mattered. The only thing he really missed was having a man to wait on him.

He grumbled a curse as the topic of Mr. Justin reappeared in his mind.

Maxine stirred next to him. She had slept poorly in her ever-weakening state. The sheets were tangled around her, and dark circles made her eyes look bruised. She threw an arm over her eyes and swore at the growing light of the sunrise.

She didn't find the mountain hideaway nearly as comfortable, it seemed. All the previous evening she had kept arms wrapped around herself, her shoulders hunched, as she paced the floor. Occasionally she looked up at the high ceilings, as if worried the weight of the mountain would squash her.

She had recently claimed to have overseen the final construction of the facility, but apparently that hadn't involved actually being on-site.

"I'm going to try Colonel Vikisky again," she said. She let her covers slide away and she slid from the bed. The orange sunrise painted her lithe naked body gold. The effect was remarkable. She looked like a golden goddess, flaming hair falling over her face and shoulders.

But then she stumbled as she struggled to slip on the silk pajamas Dr. Carlhagen had given her.

She had told her guard to burn the Scion uniform she'd worn for the past few days. So far she hadn't thought to ask why Dr. Carlhagen had women's clothes in his quarters. But then, Maxine was a worldly woman. She couldn't be too surprised that Dr. Carlhagen would have a few items ready in case he chose to entertain a lovely guest or two.

Dr. Carlhagen dressed and followed her through the general living area, past the cushy leather sofas and geometrically rigid wooden chairs and tables.

Lazarus anticipated their destination, turning on the light in Dr. Carlhagen's office. A holodesk, this one of steel and glass, occupied one side of the room. The rest of the space was dedicated bookshelves, mostly old medical texts. One area held choice items Dr. Carlhagen had plucked from Michael's things before having the rest destroyed.

Remembering his old partner and former teacher of Scions, Dr. Carlhagen wondered what he would think of this new facility. Aside from hating the idea of overwriting Scions, old Socrates—as the Scions had known him—would have loved it. So much interesting technology. And who wouldn't love a mountain fortress?

Dr. Carlhagen followed Maxine as she stumbled into the office, at once admiring her figure while restraining himself from strangling her. The latter impulse didn't take much effort to control since her guard followed her as well.

Wearily, she placed her hands on the desk. "Transfiguration Bentilius," she said. A moment later Lazarus's emotionless voice replied: "Prepared."

Because they had transferred into young bodies, it was necessary to use the AI to show outsiders images they were expecting. After all, Colonel Vikisky wouldn't take orders from a pale eighteen-year-old girl he'd never seen before.

And if such a girl claimed to be Senator Bentilius, well . . . it would be better to explain that once they were able to meet face-to-face.

Vikisky had a Scion of his own, of course. One didn't get high-level military personnel to do your bidding without paying.

Actually, finding such a person had been much more challenging than Dr. Carlhagen had anticipated. It seemed most of the military valued honor above self-interest. He'd needed Senator Bentilius to feel out the officers' ranks.

She'd come through for him. Two generals, an admiral, and Colonel Vikisky.

Captain Wilcox had been Dr. Carlhagen's find, but that man had never been more than a mercenary to begin with.

"Colonel Vikisky," she said.

It was the eight or ninth or twentieth time she'd tried to summon the colonel's holo to this desk. Dr. Carlhagen had lost count during the first hour they'd been there.

A whole night had passed and still they had not heard one word from the man leading Senator Bentilius's backup force. Dr. Carlhagen wasn't too worried. The weather around St. Vitus was terrible, and he doubted the satellite communications were reaching the command ship.

Maxine leaned on the table, face damp with the effects of transfer rejection. She thought she'd caught the flu.

Dr. Carlhagen was about to suggest they give up when the colonel materialized as a fifteen-centimeter-tall holo-gram standing upon the desk. He wore military fatigues, sleeves rolled up to the elbows. His cap sat forward on his head, the wide bill nearly obscuring his eyes, which gleamed with furious intensity. Dr. Carlhagen fought the reflex to step away from the man.

Without any greeting, the man spoke. "Senator Bentil-ius. I can't tell you how relieved I am to see you're well. The fleet is approaching St. Vitus now. Should I call off the invasion?"

"Absolutely not! St. Vitus has fallen into absolute chaos. The Scions have taken over. I barely escaped with my life. Frankly, I'm appalled you haven't subdued the situation there yet."

"We're still two hundred nautical miles from the island. We won't have boots on the ground until late tomorrow morning."

"Why the delay?" Senator Bentilius asked, clearly

displeased. "If I hadn't escaped, I'd surely be dead by now."

"Four factors, ma'am. First, we were delayed by the remains of the hurricane that came through the region a few days ago. Second, we waited for twenty-four hours after you missed contacting us, as was the agreed-upon protocol. Third, Fleet Commander Admiral Switty had to do some fancy political dancing to explain to Pentagon-Chicago her reasons for repositioning the fleet to the Eastern Caribbean. Fourth, we got caught in the fringe of yet another hurricane. We're coming out of the worst of it now."

Senator Bentilius gritted her teeth, but she apparently didn't have any answer to Vikisky's rational excuses. Gauging by the flush in her cheeks, she wasn't happy about them.

The delay soured Dr. Carlhagen's mood, too. Trying to put a good face on it, he decided that having some freedom would give the Scions hope. Just when they started thinking they were in control, the senator's force would bring down the axe of discipline. Spirits broken, they would be much more compliant going forward.

Vikisky glanced away from them, as if listening to someone off-camera. "Where are you, Madam Senator? We can't seem to trace your call. Should we detach a squadron to fetch you?"

"I have transportation available. Just secure St. Vitus. I expect the Scion School to be under your command by noon tomorrow."

Maxine leaned forward. "Use force if you need to, Colonel. But don't kill any of them. One might be yours."

"Understood. I would be remiss if I didn't mention a small freighter nearby we mean to check out. Its path suggests it came from St. Vitus or skirted near to it."

"Do what you must, but get that school under control!"

The man nodded. "Vikisky, out." The hologram disappeared.

Maxine lifted her palms from the desk and collapsed back in the office chair. After a brief moment of slow breathing with her eyes closed, she crossed her legs, folded her wrists across her knee and tilted her head as she regarded Dr. Carlhagen. She was putting on a good show of strength.

"What is it, Maxine?"

"I'm just studying you. Trying to figure you out. When I first transferred, you were so loving, so concerned. But as soon as we escaped, all of your attention went to that child."

She was speaking about Livy. Dr. Carlhagen had insisted the girl be allowed to sleep a full night before being committed to a cryopod.

"It seemed so random that you picked her out of all of them. Odder yet was that you thought it necessary to have a Scion to use as leverage. I have 100 soldiers with machine guns. I have navy ships, fighter jets, and helicopters, all headed to that island. And you knew it. Yet you felt it necessary to have her. I can't help but wonder why that is."

She uncrossed her legs and stood. She needed a side-step to maintain her balance, which ruined the illusion she was trying to maintain. Dr. Carlhagen admired the effort it must have taken.

The natural iciness of her Scion's features solidified, made her face a talking sculpture. "There's something else going on here, Christof, and I want to know what it is. And don't tell me it's a contingency plan for the contingency. There's something special about that girl. I've noticed the way you look at her, and I've noticed how she talks. Not like any nine-year-old I've ever heard speak."

Dr. Carlhagen smiled and tried to force his body to relax. "I can't get anything past you, can I, Maxine? Livy's Progenitor is one of the most important people who ever lived. Obviously, I've signed non-disclosure agreements, so I'm afraid I cannot tell you more."

It was a lie, but Maxine wouldn't know that. She didn't know the identity of most of the Progenitors for the current crop of Scions. She might suspect some, but she couldn't know unless they'd confided in her. And given Senator Bentilius's reputation, nobody was rushing to tell her their secrets.

Dr. Carlhagen continued, "Let me just say that if all the other Scions were to die, this one can keep my neck out from under the headsman's axe. Your neck, too," he hastened to add.

Another lie, but he knew Senator Bentilius would appreciate that kind of thinking. She understood the necessity of having a backup plan to protect oneself from the worst-case scenario. Hell, Dr. Carlhagen had learned that lesson from her many years ago.

But it would also stoke her curiosity. And that could be dangerous.

Maybe it was time to put her in her place. Maybe now was the time for the ATR conversation.

But no. He wanted that to be a special moment. He wanted to catch her at the moment it would have the most impact. Then he would bring her crashing to the ground.

He moved to stand toe-to-toe with her and put his hands on her shoulders, working his thumbs into the tense muscles at the back of her neck and along her shoulders. She stiffened at first, then slowly began to relax, her head lolling from one side to the other.

He bent close, brushed her ear with his lips. "Come to bed, Maxine. You need to rest."

The sultry eyes came back, as did a hungry smile he instantly recognized. She took his hands and led him back into the bedroom. "Yes, Christof. Let's rest. And then we're going to take that girl to the cryo chambers and put her into a very, very deep sleep."

41

IF MADAM PRESIDENT ONLY KNEW

D ante had not returned to his room the night before, a fact that simultaneously pleased and infuriated Jacey. She didn't want to sleep in the same room with him and his lecherous eyes, but she needed to talk to him about the storm.

She hadn't told him about the Scions escaping to sea. Not yet. But if that's what it took to get him to take her to a holodesk, she would tell him now.

The man in the suit who knew all about the weather said the storm had continued along its predicted track, leaving behind St. Vitus's section of sea. If Humphrey and the others still lived, they would be frantic to hear from her.

Worry spoiled her appetite, but she forced down some leftover bread and cheese from the night before. Keeping her strength up only made sense. The view out her window still showed a hazy sky and restless seas. But the palm trees no longer leaned over so far and birds had returned to the air. Even now, a pelican glided along the cliff edge then dove out of view toward the water.

A small army of liveried servers—mostly men in black trousers, white shirts, and black vests—scurried upon the lawn between the pool and the cliff. They set up rows of chairs. A four-wheeled vehicle with knobby tires pulled a flatbed trailer. The driver, a swarthy man in shirtsleeves and straw hat, unhitched the wagon. He'd barely driven away before the servers swarmed over the trailer, transforming it into a stage. Before long, two stands holding up loudspeakers were in position and a podium had been placed atop the stage.

Vin was going through with her coming out. At least Jacey would be able to see it from her prison.

A knock at the door.

Dante hadn't ever knocked, so she knew it wasn't him.

She went to the door. "What?"

Silence.

A fast burst of three raps.

The other two Progenitors knew she was locked in. They wouldn't be knocking.

She doubted it was Meow Meow. Dante's absence meant—as far as Jacey could guess—that he'd spent the night with her. He probably was still with her.

It had to be one of the other guests, maybe. Or a servant.

Another rapid series of knocks, these louder.

Indecision paralyzed Jacey. But only for a moment. Her famous face be damned. She had to talk to Humphrey.

"Help!" she called through the door. "I got locked in."

She thought she heard a voice, but it was very faint.

She grabbed the knob and twisted. It moved. The door swung out.

Standing before her, arms crossed, was Ping. He was

dressed in dark trousers and a button-down shirt. A black leather belt with silver buckle and dark, shiny black shoes gave him a polished look. His hair was short, still growing out from the Scion close-cut that Dr. Carlhagen required. But it was thick and black. His eyes burned with fury.

"I knew you'd betray us." He put a thumb and pinky in his mouth and gave two short, shrill whistles.

Two men with boulders for shoulders and tree trunk thighs stepped out of a room down the hall. They wore black suits and ties and shaded spectacles.

"Grab her and bag her," Ping commanded.

Jacey stepped back into the room, pulling the door shut.

Ping thrust his body through. Jacey yanked harder. The door clunked into his head. He grunted.

She kicked his stomach, but he got hold of her ankle. With sharp twist, he pulled her from her feet. The tile smacked her cheek.

Thick hands, strong as steel, gripped her waist and lifted her.

Her scream cut off the second it started as a meaty hand clamped over her lips. She tried to bite it, but the fingers squeezed, dug into her cheeks.

Legs flailing, she squirmed and moaned, screams muffled through her nose.

"Get her legs," Ping said.

Her kicks stopped instantly as the second man gathered her legs in his arms.

She'd been subdued as easily as a child. Only her continued moans and groans expressed her terrified fury. Those cut off too, as Ping pinched her nostrils shut.

"You will silence yourself, or you will suffocate."

She was being held between two giants. An arm of iron

clamped around her body, trapped both her arms. The other hand gripped her entire face.

Ping leaned close to her, eyes penetrating her panic. They held a malicious intensity that turned her bones to ice. "Do you understand?"

She nodded in fast little jerks.

Ping released her nostrils and she drew in rapid breaths. The room was spinning. Her heart pounded from a rush of adrenaline. The hiss of her breath was loud in her ears. Through will alone, she slowed her breathing.

The men carried her down the hall and ducked into another room. This one was laid out like Dante's except the bathroom was on the other side.

The walls were a stark white. The windows offered the same view. But that was all she was able to take in. Her attention was drawn to the body bag lying across the bed. Its zipper was down, the opening pulled aside. Ready to embrace her.

Her breath faltered a moment, then moans started anew. She could not, would not, control them. Every fiber of muscle in her body strained to break free from the men holding her.

Ping barked something at her. She didn't register any meaning in it.

Suddenly the room was full of music. Loud, thumping drums and the sound of alien, wailing instruments.

Ping had turned on his video monitor and turned the volume up to mask what noise did escape her.

He was hovering over her again. "You can go in voluntarily and stay awake and unbruised, or you can go in unconscious and very, very hurt."

The decision was no decision at all. A part of her mind that she had no control over—the part that was pure animal fear—would never willingly go into the body bag. She renewed her groans and kicks.

Her struggles had no more effect than a fish struggling in a gull's beak.

The blow fell quickly and without warning.

At first there was no pain, just a hot pressure on her right temple.

Strange silence filled Jacey's mind, as if all thought had been knocked right out of her.

The ceiling moved, the walls tilted. The face of the man holding her legs spun around and around. Nighttime was falling in the room, the morning sunlight spilling through the window turned gray.

"Zip her up. I'll send for a server cart. We'll get her out through the service elevator down the hall."

"Someone will wonder why we're going down the dock," said a husky voice in Chinese.

"Tell them I sent you to check the boat for damage from the heavy seas we had last night."

"And the bag?"

"There will be some produce boxes in the kitchens. Put the bag in one and say it's supplies for the boat."

Jacey tried to move her legs. The pressure of hands was gone, but her limbs were restrained.

The man let go of her mouth. Breath came in and out, but thoughts were still struggling to surface from the black depths of her consciousness.

A new sound cut through. The zipper.

It tore into the silence of her mind like a machete through flesh.

She drew in a great breath and let out a scream that began in the very depths of her animal instincts.

She did not hear it, or anything else, after that.

42

TOO STUPID TO HIDE

Humphrey studied the radar display. Once Orson had explained it to him it was easy to understand. A line swung around a center point like the hand of an analog clock. At the northernmost point in its cycle were a bunch of bright blobs, each representing a ship the radar was detecting.

"A mini carrier? What is that?" he asked Orson.

The fleet's voice—a man called Lieutenant Smythe—piped over the radio speaker: "Freighter *Aphrodite,* please come about to zero-zero-zero and drop your speed to five knots."

Orson raised the radio to his furry lips. "I'll send a hand to the starboard aft boarding hatch to receive your men."

"Negative. Sergeant Jin is commander of the boarding party. He requires you to assemble your crew on the bridge. He'll come to you."

Orson glanced at Humphrey, who was now watching the approaching speedboat through the binoculars. "He wants the crew contained. We'll need to bring my men up here."

"Will they keep quiet?"

"They aren't stupid."

Humphrey gauged they had no more than ten minutes before the boarding party arrived. The speedboat was still too far off for him to count heads. "That thing is fast."

"That ain't no waterski boat, that's for sure. That's a fast-attack gunboat. It'll carry at least fifteen marines. We'd be boarded whether we slowed down or not. If they find a bunch of kids in black uniforms and collar pins hiding in our cargo holds, this little escape mission will be dead in the water. Pun intended."

He held out his hand and Humphrey relinquished the binoculars.

Summer burst onto the bridge. Humphrey had given her the problem and ten minutes to solve it. He sensed only about five had passed.

"I can hide them," she said, panting. "All of them. Sensei, here." She grabbed the P.A. microphone and pointed at a button on the side. "Tell everyone to come to the engine room. Babies and all."

Sensei took the mic, but didn't speak for a moment. His dark eyes bore into Summer's. Humphrey understood the hesitation. All of their lives depended on Summer's plan.

"Trust me," she said.

Orson was scanning the sea through his binoculars. "Whatever you're going to do, you better hurry."

Sensei clicked the button on the mic. "Attention. This is Sensei Rosa. All Scions and staff immediately report to the engine room on deck one. You have four minutes."

Summer dashed from the bridge before the martial arts master had finished. Sensei put the mic back in its holder and began to unbutton his top. "Do you have other clothes around here?" he asked Orson.

"You'll find some overalls in my cabin."

Sensei started for the stairs. "Humphrey, you better get to the engine room."

"Who's going to watch Orson?"

"I'll watch myself," the crusty man said. "Trust me, I don't want the marines to catch me with a boat full of Scions." He made a cutting motion across his throat. His skin had gone pale and a sheen of perspiration covered his forehead. "But you have to send my men up here. The marines'll never believe I'm running this rig alone."

There wasn't much choice. Humphrey decided trusting Orson to protect his own skin was fairly low-risk. "How are you going to explain all the supplies and bunks in the cargo hold?"

Orson's nostrils whistled as he heaved out a huge breath. "I'll think of something. Probably. But it won't matter if they find you because you were too stupid to hide when you had the chance."

Out to sea, the attack boat was easily visible as it raced ever closer. Behind it, and quickly gaining, was the black speck of the helicopter.

Humphrey sprinted down the clanging metal stairway again, heart racing. This wasn't going to work. He knew it in his gut. They were going to get caught, and they would all be sent back to St. Vitus.

43

IT WASN'T JUST PANIC

Blackness suffocated Jacey, enveloping her in her own hot and stale breath. The lack of fresh air made her light-headed and nauseous. The side of her head throbbed.

She'd stopped struggling after the initial panic had exhausted her. It was useless.

Her arms had been bound at her sides with a strap over the body bag. Another cinched her ankles tightly together. And still one more was wrapped under her thighs and over her shoulders, pulling her into an immobile fetus position.

She couldn't open her mouth.

Something held it shut. She wriggled her lips and cheeks as best she could. Something pulled at the skin of her face.

Tape.

The only air she could get came through her nose. She had to slow her breathing or pass out again.

Her body did not want it slow. Her heart beat out a

rapid, insistent drumbeat. Run. Run. Run. Fight. Fight. Fight.

She had to override that impulse. Use her reason.

Sensei had taught her breathing exercises, ways to calm her mind. She'd never been very good at them.

Wetness ran down the side of her face, pooled alongside her nose.

Tears.

Focus, Jacey. She screamed it in her mind, recruiting the anger that lay beneath the fear.

She started counting her breaths. Slowly in. Slowly out.

She remembered Ping saying something about a box. Yes. She was in a body bag, but she was in a box, too.

Had one of the thugs said something about the docks?

She didn't remember seeing docks on the flight in. But that didn't mean there weren't any.

Ping had bodyguards. That made sense. He was a cautious man.

He doesn't want to kill me.

She clung to that. It had to be true.

Yes. If Ping had planned to kill her, he would have done so already. He could have done it in his room. It would have silenced her. They wouldn't have needed to bind her up.

Think, Jacey. What does Ping want?

What had he been most upset about during that weird conversation among the Progenitors?

Her head ached, her stomach quivered.

Her pulse continued to race, but her inhalations became less panicked. The sense of being on the verge of losing her mind retreated.

It was dark. But she had other senses.

She investigated them one by one.

She lay on a hard surface, the body bag providing no

real cushioning. It was cold, too. Perhaps most disconcerting, the floor moved.

So it wasn't pure dizziness that disoriented her. She was on a vehicle of some sort. A muffled engine rumble engulfed her senses. It strained as the floor tilted one way and eased as the floor tiled another. Going up and down a hill.

When it started an ascent, the floor tilted behind her. That meant she was lying on her side, facing forward.

That was new information. Good. She couldn't see, but she had other senses.

Aside from the faint smell of her own sweat, the only scent reaching her was vaguely citrus. But it was the stale, cloying aroma of fruit long rotted. It was probably from the box she was in.

Her hands were numb, but her fingers were free. The straps were all on the outside of the body bag. They'd done it after zipping her inside.

The one keeping her arms immobile was cinched tightly across her abdomen, trapping her forearms across her belly. She could wiggle her fingers, but not much. And when she did, it sent pins and needles through her palms.

It was the strap keeping her nose within a few centimeters of her knees that kept her immobile. It was wrapped over shoulders and under her knees, with her forearms sandwiched between her belly and her thighs.

No wonder it was so hard to breathe. It wasn't just panic.

If she could loosen the one keeping her bent over, she could at least stretch out. That would be a small blessing in itself.

Her ankles were bound, but she still had the ability to move her knees apart. Just a little.

The strap keeping her in fetal position was tucked right

under her thighs. She pushed against it, felt the strap dig in across her shoulder blades.

She visualized her predicament. It was as if she'd bent to touch her toes and someone had looped a strap over her to keep her in that position. If she could get that loop to go over her head, she'd be able to unfold.

Didn't know you'd hogtied a ballerina, did you, boys?

Madam LaFontaine had announced to everyone on three occasions that Jacey's flexibility was acceptable. High praise indeed.

Exhaling, Jacey straightened her legs so she was folded over on her left side, knees unbent. Her left shoulder and ear ground painfully into the floor of the vehicle.

The strap passing under her knees grew tighter as her torso naturally tried to lift.

She inhaled deeply, felt the strap tighten, digging into her flesh like steel bands. With a deep exhale, she folded herself more deeply, spreading her knees just a fraction of a centimeter, letting her take the tension off the band.

It slackened completely.

She moved her shoulders in circles, walking the strap farther up her back.

With a grunt, she braced her shoulder and head on the floor and tried to roll forward to get the strap to fall over her head.

But she needed air. Relaxing, she drew in slow breaths and reassessed. This strap was higher now. It had also worked itself below her left knee. That was good.

She exhaled again and continued to wriggle her shoulders, drawing her head down as far as she could.

The exterior surface of the body bag was slick. Surely if she got just the right spot . . .

She strained to fold deeper still, putting enough slack

into the strap that she couldn't even feel it. Her hands and forearms jammed into her gut.

Needing air again, she relaxed and sucked in a great breath through her nose. Sweat dripped into her eyes, soaked through the linen top Vin had loaned her.

"Big-boned, am I?" Jacey said. She exhaled and rolled forward, onto her shoulder and left cheek. The strap slipped forward, along her neck, then it was gone.

Jacey stretched out fully, and lay on her back. Straightening awakened many strained muscles, sending fiery pain through her back and down her legs. She desperately wanted fresh air. The heat in the bag robbed every breath of life-giving oxygen, it seemed.

But now that she was straight, the strap around her middle had slackened. She thrust her arms back and forth, working them until she felt the strap over her wrists.

She had to roll onto her stomach and then onto her side, but soon she had the strap over her hands. They were free in the bag.

Electric with nerve pain, her fingers sought the zipper mechanism. There was no pull-tab on the inside, but a fatter part of the metal zipper mechanism was there. She snagged it with a fingernail and pushed it down.

Fetid spoiled-fruit smelling air fell through the opening and into her nose. But it was so much fresher than the air in the bag that it tasted sweet and cool.

Hands trembling, Jacey found the corner of the tape covering her mouth and worked an edge up. With a tug, she yanked it free.

Her skin might as well have come off with it. She barely stifled the scream of agony tearing through her throat as fire lit up her face.

Between her groans of pain, great gulps of air came into

her mouth, filling her lungs with rotten, but wonderfully deep breaths.

She lay there, gasping for a minute. Involuntary sobs shook her ribcage.

No time for that, she scolded herself. She sat up, worked her ankles loose.

The vehicle was still moving. It rounded a curve at top speed, sending her tumbling sideways. She struck the inside wall of a cardboard box. It was thick and moist.

She flung her arms up, hit the box top. She punched it and it flew aside.

Dim light showed her the interior of a cargo truck. Several other boxes, all marked with drawings of oranges and, written in a fancy script, the words "Florida-like Citrus."

Trembling, she climbed out of the box and stumbled to the rear door. Windows looked out on a retreating stretch of dirt road. Wheel ruts ran along it. The landscape was different than she'd seen at Vin's. More trees. Vines and moss hung from their heavy boughs.

Rainforest. She remembered seeing the same species when she and Summer had fled the Scion School. It seemed every island had a rainy side.

She found a door latch, pulled it. The door swung open.

The road blurred below her. Too fast to jump. Even if she lived, she'd be too injured to run. They'd find she was missing and backtrack for her.

Feeling was returning to her legs, and with it came more pain. The sensation of pins and needles made her gasp. She closed the door and rubbed her calves, her thighs.

She needed the truck to stop. Now. Before the men ever got her where they were taking her. If it was heading for the docks, then they'd likely be putting her on a boat. Who knew where she'd end up if that happened?

She wasn't a strong enough swimmer to dive overboard and try to return to Vin's island.

She shut the door and looked back at the stacks of fruit boxes. The plan that came to her seemed utterly stupid. But what choice did she have?

She scrambled deeper into the truck, pushing aside her empty box. She opened one that was full of oranges. The smell that wafted from it made her gag. The top was still on and the whole thing was wrapped with a clear plastic.

Good. It would stay together.

It was heavy, but the floor was bare metal. Once she got it going, she was able to shove it against the rear door.

The thing to do now was simple: Don't think. Just do it.

She pulled the latch and flung the door open. It swung wide. Jacey put her shoulder to the box and shoved it from the back of the truck. It fell and toppled and rolled.

It came to a stop in the middle of the road.

A shout came from the front of the truck. Jacey was already braced against the rear wall when the driver slammed on the brakes. The rear door slammed itself shut. Her empty box slid forward until it came to rest against a crate of rotten bananas.

Once the truck had stopped, Jacey crept to the back and peered out the window. With a gentle pull, she unlatched the door, but she did not open it.

Two doors from up front slammed. Voices cursed at each other.

Ping's guards rushed toward the box in the road. The instant they moved past Jacey, she eased the door open.

Her feet touched dirt. Never before had she been so thankful for her Scion shoes. If she'd been in those insane high heels, she wouldn't have a chance.

She slipped around the truck. The driver's door stood open. She got in.

She'd watched Summer drive the jeep. It was as simple as sliding a lever to align with D.

The truck didn't have such a lever.

She closed the driver's door, but didn't try to latch it. No sound. No sound.

Eyes scanning the dashboard, she found an array of letters and numbers that looked similar to what was on the Jeep. Several levers stuck out from the steering wheel column. She tried one. A light flashed on one side, and made a clicking noise. That wasn't it.

A cry rose from behind her. Glancing at the side mirror, she saw Ping's men charging the truck.

She tried another lever. The N lit up. She pressed it again. The D lit up. Her foot stomped the gas pedal—the way she'd seen Summer do it. Dirt flew from the rear wheels as they spun.

The truck lurched forward.

Jacey gave a whoop and made a gesture with her middle finger at the mirror. She'd seen one of Orson's men do that to her when he thought she wasn't looking. She didn't know what it meant, exactly, but it felt appropriate in the moment.

The road twisted before her and her focus turned to guiding the machine over the road. Once the men had fallen far behind her, she tested the brakes.

She learned quickly that one didn't have to stomp on them. The resulting skid aged her twenty years in three seconds. Fortunately the road had widened there and the truck careened to a stop before going into a fringe of thin trees and thorny bushes.

But now where could she go? Surely not to the docks. She didn't know what awaited her there. Intuition told her that the farther she got from the mansion, the more danger she was in.

"Fine." After a minute of revving the engine and unskilled backing up, she turned the beast around.

She took it slowly this time, winding her way back up the rutted road.

Ping's men were where she'd left them. They stood in the road. One held a pistol in his hand. The other held some sort of handheld radio.

A cool calm fell over Jacey then. She pressed the accelerator to the floor and aimed the truck right for the man with the gun.

"Decide, you idiot," she said through clenched teeth. "Decide."

He did. Dodging away from oncoming death, he fired as the truck went by. Jacey counted two shots.

Nothing happened.

In the side mirror she saw a cloud of dust. The radio man was shouting something. The gunman was sitting on his butt.

Ping had some explaining to do. That was as sure as the sunrise.

The question now was whether Vin or Dante had known his plan.

Jacey slowed to a stop at a fork in the road. A sign pointing right read "Burnell Estate." The other read, simply, "Barracks."

The barracks had to be where Captain Wilcox and his men were posted.

Now it was Jacey's turn.

Decide, you idiot. Just decide.

VINYL GREEN

By the time Humphrey got to the bottom deck a throng of Scions blocked the way to the engine room. The companionway was dark and stifling as fearful children and sweaty Scions crowded forward.

Mother Tyeesha's four adult staffers carried infants in their arms. They wore grim expressions and cooed softly to the children in their care. The older Scions wrangled the one- and two-year-olds. The babies squawked and wriggled. Toddlers gripped the hands of older Scions, tears and snot streaking their fear-reddened faces.

"What's going on?" Wanda called to Humphrey.

"We're going to be boarded."

"Then why are we going to the engine room?"

All eyes were on him, most tense, some fearful. "I don't know. Summer has an idea."

The Scions around him burst with questions and doubts. Humphrey raised his arms and whistled. "Summer knows this boat better than anyone. Just keep going. She can tell you what her plan is."

He hoped she could. He had no idea.

A few continued to shout questions, but Dajeet and Wanda hissed something at them Humphrey couldn't hear. Whatever it was, it shut up the malcontents.

The throng continued to shuffle forward until they'd all made it into the crowded engine room. Since Orson had slowed the boat, the racket in the low-ceilinged compartment had fallen to merely deafening. A metal grated walkway surrounded the massive engines, and Summer was arranging the Scions into their Nines. The children from Mother Tyeesha's were kept together on another walkway along the starboard bulkhead.

Summer held what looked like a white horn in her hand. She put the narrow end to her lips and spoke. Her voice came out amplified. "Nine leaders, count your Scions. Mother Tyeesha, please count your kids and staff."

Humphrey counted his group and his stomach gave an acid flop.

He'd forgotten about Sang, who was the Eagle in his Nine. "Tytus! You're in charge of your Nine. I've got to fetch Sang and Horace."

Wanda, Leslie, and a very pale Elias waved to Summer. All were accounted for in what remained of their Nines. Humphrey shouldered past Leslie's Nine and whispered to Summer. "I'll be back in three minutes."

She gave him a grim look and waved him away before lifting the horn to her mouth. "You are all standing on the metal grating. It's made of one-meter panels resting on a steel platform. You can lift up one side of a panel and drop into the crawlspace beneath it. Mother Tyeesha, I have a different place for your group. Please guide them to the elevator doors at the rear of this compartment."

Humphrey didn't hear the rest. He had a vague burst of gratitude for Summer. Who would have thought such a flirty and flighty girl would turn out to be so essential to their survival?

He sprinted out of the engine room and toward the stairs. The marines had to be close by now. He took the stairs two at a time and plowed through the deck-two doors. A sign pointed the way to the infirmary. He hadn't spent much time on this deck and didn't know the layout very well.

White letters stenciled onto a steel door announced the infirmary. Across the passageway was another door marked RADIO. He skipped it and tried the next door on the left. It swung in to a narrow cabin with a bunk and narrow desk.

Empty.

Light streamed in through a porthole. Humphrey pressed his nose to it. He squinted against the glare of the sun on the sea.

The attack boat buzzed by right beneath him. Gray and sleek, it was loaded down with soldiers in helmets and black visors. Each wore a bulky vest loaded down with bulging pockets. Machine guns were strapped close against their chests.

Humphrey retreated and closed the door. He went to the next one down. A makeshift latch secured the door from the outside. This had to be it. He unlocked it and opened it.

Sang lay on the bunk, apparently asleep.

"Get up and come with me," Humphrey ordered.

Sang didn't move.

"Now!" Humphrey grabbed Sang's arm and yanked, nearly pulling him off the bunk sideways.

"I'm coming. I'm coming. What's going on?"

"We're being boarded by soldiers from Senator Bentilius's contingency force."

Sang swore and followed Humphrey into the passageway.

Humphrey opened the door across from Sang's. Horace was pressing his face to the porthole.

"We need to move," Humphrey said.

Horace glanced over his shoulder, lips twisted in a smirk. "No. I want to watch the helicopter."

"They're looking for us. If they find any of us, we'll all be heading back to the Scion School. And then they'll post so many guards, none of us will have a chance to escape."

Horace squinted at Humphrey. "Fine. But I'm not going anywhere with him." He pointed at Sang.

Sang didn't seem very keen about being in Horace's presence either. For obvious reasons. Horace had beaten him to a pulp when Leslie had confronted him.

"He may be Mr. Justin. But for the next half-hour we're on the same side. None of us wants to be caught by Senator Bentilius's forces. I'm not asking you to link arms and sing songs."

"I'm *not* Mr. Justin! How many times do I have to say it?"

In three long paces, Horace moved to within a foot of Sang. "Then where were you when Senator Bentilius and Dr. Carlhagen were escaping from the medical ward?"

"I was on the quad!"

"Nobody saw you."

"But—"

Humphrey pressed between them, pushed on their chests to keep them from tearing each other's throats out. "Stop it! You will both follow me. We have to get to the engine room. Summer has found a good hiding spot there for everyone."

The staredown continued, Horace's eyes wild, Sang's furious. A boom from above made them both jerk away and look at the ceiling. Moments later, the sound of foot-steps rang out. Lots of them. Heavy and urgent.

Humphrey grabbed a fistful of both boys' shirts. "They're heading for the stairwell. We have to beat them there."

He shoved Horace toward the door. The boy intention-ally shouldered Sang out the way.

Humphrey caught Sang's wrist as his fist punched at the side of Horace's face. With a twist, Humphrey turned the momentum away. He pressed his hip into Sang's and used the boys' energy to lift him and drop him to the floor of the companionway.

Sang's breath went out of him.

Humphrey dropped a knee onto Sang's throat. "I will personally throw you over the side if you do that again. You too, Horace."

Sang nodded, but he looked over Humphrey's shoul-der. He tried to say something, but it came out strangled.

Humphrey lifted his knee, ready to hear Sang's vow of total obedience.

Instead, Sang struggled to his feet. "Horace is gone."

Humphrey spun. The sound of running faded toward the bow. Horace had gone the wrong direction.

"Let's go." Humphrey couldn't chase Horace down. Not with Sang in tow. Though it sickened him, he decided the best course was to return to the engine room, hide, and hope that Horace found a different place to lie low.

"If anyone can find a hidey hole, it's Horace," Sang said bitterly. "He always got out of work, leaving Tytus and me to do it all. Even Vaughan couldn't inspire him to do his share."

True enough. Horace's primary skill was avoiding work. And inventing elaborate excuses. Only Sensei's threats of punishment had motivated the boy.

The boots above them had stopped their racket.

Humphrey stopped at the door to the stairwell to listen. He raised a hand to keep Sang quiet, then held his breath to focus his hearing.

Nothing.

Orson had slowed the boat, so the engine noise and vibration were noticeably less. The boat's motion no longer bothered Humphrey at all as it slowly swung side to side in fairly calm seas.

He nodded to Sang and stepped through the door.

Sang grabbed his shoulders and yanked. Humphrey stumbled, but Sang caught him, pulled him back through the door and jammed him into the wall. The boy's hand covered Humphrey's mouth.

Sang made a shushing motion with his other hand. He pressed his mouth to Humphrey's ear. "They're on the landing above."

Humphrey relaxed a tiny bit. For a moment he'd thought Sang was attacking him.

Sang dropped his hand and mouthed, "Sorry."

They backed away from the stairwell door, toe to heel, toe to heel. As they stepped back into Sang's room, the boy whispered. "How many are there?"

"Fifteen, according to your brother."

"My brother?"

Humphrey saw only confusion on Sang's face. An act? It had to be. But then, Mr. Justin was always calm under pressure. "Orson. You know, the man driving the boat?"

"He's not my brother."

At the moment it didn't matter. "We need to get out of here. Come on."

They left the infirmary and cabins behind. The hallway turned ninety degrees as it met up with the bulkhead at the rear of the cargo holds. A companionway led left. Two hatches with spoked wheels were on the right wall. Each would open into one of the forward holds, where the bunks had been set up.

If they went in either one, they'd be cornered once the soldiers searched the holds. And there was no place to hide, unless they trusted marines not to bother looking under the bunks. That didn't seem likely.

Sang's voice, soft but firm: "They're coming."

It was the first time Humphrey was glad the lights in the companionway weren't working.

There was no way forward except the cargo holds. Humphrey decided to go into the Boys' Hold. Maybe he and Sang could get out through the overhead deck doors without drawing attention.

He went to the hatch wheel. Spokes stood out to give grip. The whole mechanism had been painted at some point. Big globs of dried paint lay on the floor beneath them.

The wheel wouldn't budge. Paint and years of rust had seized the mechanism.

Sang was already trying the hatch to Girls' Hold. He was obviously having the same problem.

Humphrey peeked down the main companionway toward the stairwell. He saw no movement at all. Just flickering lights on the ceiling.

Sang tapped his shoulder. "Where did Horace go?"

A great question. If Horace hadn't gone in either hold, he had found some other way out. Looking back down the corridor, there were no other cabins or rooms he could have gone in without Humphrey and Sang seeing him do it.

"Look!" Sang tugged Humphrey's shirt and pointed at the ceiling.

A hatch.

But there was a problem. "There's no ladder."

There had been one at one point in time. Bolt holes on the wall showed where it had been mounted. And a pattern of dirty lines on the wall showed where rungs had concentrated dust and grime in years past.

Horace couldn't have removed it so quickly. It must have been moved long ago. Maybe one of Orson's men had needed it elsewhere in the ship. He'd have to ask Horace how he'd gotten up there after he caught him.

A man's voice boomed from the main companionway. "Move forward. Check those cabins left and right."

"Get on my shoulders, Sang." Humphrey braced himself on the wall and cupped his hands.

Sang put a foot in Humphrey's hands, then stepped onto his shoulders.

The sound of a latch grating against metal.

A waft of fresh air.

Sang's weight lifted from Humphrey's shoulders. He looked up in time to see Sang's feet disappear and the hatch fall shut.

The boom echoed down the hall.

Voices, sharp and tense, tumbled down the corridor. "Loud bang on deck two main companionway forward. Checking now."

The sound of boot-stomps and the clink of soldiers' equipment grew louder. Humphrey's mind flailed for a plan.

He could think of only one thing. The thing he was born to do.

Be Dr. Carlhagen.

He tried to put on the jovial smile. Tried to get himself into the superior attitude that seeped from the old man's face.

But he wore a Scion uniform. And what reason could

he have to be aboard this ship? Even if they believed he was Dr. Carlhagen—which he doubted, since the real Dr. Carlhagen and Senator Bentilius had escaped and certainly had spoken with these men—how could he ever expect to get rid of them?

A door clanged shut down the corridor. The boot stomps slowed.

Humphrey heart fluttered in his chest. His palms sweated. His throat went dry.

A wash of fresh air and sunlight descended on him as the hatch above swung open. A second later, Sang's upper body appeared. He extended a hand.

Humphrey clasped the boy's forearm and jumped. Sang pulled, groaning softly with the effort. Humphrey's belly caught on the lip of the opening, but Sang was leaning back now, pulling with both hands. Humphrey slid through and onto the deck.

Fire raced across the skin of his abdomen where it had scraped on the sharp, rusty metal.

He didn't care. In seconds, he had turned himself around. Sang was already there, lowering the hatch door down.

He held it with his fingertips, grimacing under the weight of the steel. Humphrey grabbed hold and helped him lower it into place. They had to slip their fingertips out together, causing the hatch to fall the final centimeter, producing a clang that Humphrey was sure was heard around the world.

The sound of a helicopter buzzed somewhere behind him. His spine thrilled with prickling sense of being watched.

More voices. Footsteps tromping closer, these from somewhere on deck.

"Come on!" Sang said, crawling away. Humphrey

followed, and found himself squeezing under the school bus. Face pressed to the deck, he looked past the front left wheel and at five pairs of heavy black boots stomping by.

The thump of a helicopter sounded off to his right. By stroke of fortune, the bus had masked their emergence from the hatch.

Humphrey glanced back at the hatch. The door was swinging up, a black-gloved hand pressing it from below.

He patted Sang and urged him toward the back of the bus. They squirmed on elbows and knees under the rear axle and differential. No matter how hard Humphrey tried to control his breath, he couldn't keep it from rasping with his effort. Surely the soldiers would hear him.

He heard a boom, the hatch slamming onto the deck. Sang rolled out from under the bus and disappeared. Humphrey squeezed out and felt a hand on his collar.

Sang hoisted him to his feet, then yanked him up into the air. They fell backwards into the bus through the rear door. Humphrey lunged forward, grabbed the door, and swung it shut.

They lay there in the aisle, the vinyl green seats above them. Their breath was even louder here. Humphrey started to cough, but shoved his nose and mouth into the crook of his arm to stifle the sound.

Sang broke the relative silence with a nervous laugh. "That was close."

Boot stomps and rough commands sounded outside the rear door. A man's bold voice announced: "All clear up here." A pause. "Roger. Lindson, you and Dexter check the starboard cargo hold. Bentley, you and Smith take the port-side hold."

Humphrey got to his knees and peered through a window toward the starboard side. "They're going to find bunks in there. I don't think we're going to get out of this."

"Bunks without Scions don't mean anything," Sang said. "Where is everybody, anyway?"

Humphrey lowered himself and rested his back against the side of one of the seats. "Hiding. Just like us."

Sang raised his eyebrows and shook his head doubtfully. "I hope they found a better spot than we did."

45

NÃO COMPREENDO

Sensei Mario Rosa had not worn coveralls since prison. Hadn't missed them, either. In fact, the last time he'd worn them, he'd had an electrical cord tied around his neck and looped over a light fixture in his cell.

The desperation he felt now was similar to what he'd suffered that night in a faraway prison somewhere in Brazil. But instead of longing for death, he wanted to live. Not only live, but to survive long enough to bring justice to those who had it coming.

"Stay in control, Mario," he said to himself. Even after all these years, he couldn't think of himself as Sensei. It would be too presumptuous to give himself that title.

Mario rolled up the dingy gray sleeves—the disgusting garment was at least two sizes too big—and stepped out of Orson's cabin near the engine rooms. The Scion voices in there had stilled.

He climbed the stairs and padded toward Sang and

Horace's holding rooms. There were soldiers' voices coming from far down the hall.

The doors to both boys' rooms were open, swinging in and out with the slow rock of the ship.

Both Scions were gone. There was no way they could've opened the doors themselves. Someone had let them out. The marines would have raised a ruckus if they'd found them. It must have been Humphrey.

Mario backed out of Horace's room just as a squad of soldiers ran down the corridor from the direction of the bow.

"Down, down, down!" the lead man cried, aiming his weapon at Mario's face. Like all the soldiers, the man was dressed in black from head to toe; a bulky bulletproof vest made his thick arms look stubby.

Mario feigned shock and dropped to his knees. Another overeager soldier jammed a boot into his spine and pressed him onto his stomach. Hands frisked him, then flipped him onto his back. A helmeted head eclipsed the flickering ceiling light. The man lifted a glove and flipped his visor up. "What. Is. Your. Name?" He shouted each word in a gravelly monotone.

"*O que?*" Mario said, putting a tremble into his voice and lips.

"Your name! Your name!"

"*Não compreendo.*"

"Do you speak *Anglaise? Anglaise!*"

"*Non, non. Portuguese.*"

"Dammit! Havert, take this prisoner to the bridge. The sergeant might want to get a fleet translator on the radio."

"Yes, sir."

Mario was lifted and prodded toward the stairs.

"These rooms are all empty," shouted a soldier.

That meant the marines hadn't gotten to Sang and

Horace first. Mario kept his smile of relief hidden. Someone else had come to fetch them. Not a surprise. The Scions were a smart bunch.

Another soldier grunted a few curses. "There have to be more hands on this bucket than a fat captain, two know-nothing goons, and a Brazilian mechanic, don't there?"

"Not necessarily," the squad leader said. "With fuel costs as high as they are, they operate these tubs with skeleton crews to keep their costs down."

Wanting to hear more, Mario slowed his pace. Havert jabbed him between the shoulder blades with what could only have been his machine gun.

Mario picked up his pace. Antagonizing these men wouldn't gain him anything but delays. The main goal at the moment was to get them to wrap up their search and get off the boat.

He just hoped Humphrey had gotten the two prisoners hidden somewhere not even a motivated marine would search.

If there was such a place.

46

HAIRLINE TO CHEEKBONE

The road turned from rutted dirt to smooth pavement as Jacey approached Vin's mansion. She'd left the rainforest behind more than twenty minutes before. Apparently she'd been unconscious in the fruit box longer than she'd thought.

By the look of the green hills in this region, she could still be on St. Vitus. Rough grasses and thorny bushes covered the slopes, tumbling toward a ragged coast of black pebble beaches. Gauging by the sun, it wasn't yet 10 a.m. The sky was nearly cloudless and a deep blue.

To her right, the turquoise Caribbean cheerily played with white-topped waves that coursed toward the shore. Further out, a pair of tiny islands humped out of the sea, like the spine of a great serpent.

At last, the mansion came into view.

The weird construction of steel and glass blocks was still as alien to Jacey's eye as the first time she'd seen it.

She pressed fingertips to her temple, wincing at the tenderness. A glance in the side mirror had shown her the black-and-blue bruise covering half her face from hairline to cheekbone.

If there was an advantage to being a Scion, it was that they healed fast. Or so Jacey had been told. These bruises would put that to the test, for sure.

But it presented a problem for her. What would she do once she got back to the mansion?

Vin's coming out event would be starting any minute. The house would be full of guests and journalists. It would be one thing to try to keep her head down and slip back to Dante's room while everyone was distracted by Vin's unveiling. But a young woman with a huge bruise on her face was sure to draw notice.

Her confidence as a driver improved with every mile. If she hadn't been so terrified, she might have enjoyed it. As the road wound up the steep slope toward the house, she tried to figure out her next move.

By returning here, she had chosen not to seek Captain Wilcox's help. The man was already suspicious enough. If she showed up at his base with a big bruise on her face, he'd ask questions she couldn't answer. She could not forget that his loyalty was still with Dr. Carlhagen.

But Dante's was not.

The truck's engine roared as it climbed the steepest part of the climb to another fork. One headed toward the side of the house and a garage. A sign reading "All Service Vehicle's. No Exception's!" pointed her toward the other road.

Cringing from the misuse of apostrophes, she went that way. The road descended slightly as it curved around the back of the house. She passed through an open gate into a large gravel lot. More vehicles were parked here. Two were nearly identical to the Jeep Dr. Carlhagen kept at the Scion School.

To her left stood a butter yellow metal-sided garage.

One of its two huge overhead doors was open, the parking spot inside empty. It looked exactly big enough for the truck Jacey was driving.

She spun the steering wheel and pulled into the garage. She'd already identified the button to turn off the truck. She pressed it and the engine went quiet.

A quick scan showed her the building was empty. Another truck of the same type and size sat to her right. Various tool cabinets and workbenches hugged the walls.

A chain-link cage of some sort jutted from the rear wall. There wasn't anything in it.

Jacey climbed down from the truck and pushed the door shut as quietly as she could. The air was cooler in here. It smelled of grease and petrol.

She padded to the edge of the open door, keeping her body out of the sunlight just starting to angle onto the concrete pad of the floor. The white gravel of the parking lot blinded her, and she had to squint to see anything.

A span of open space—perhaps forty meters—separated her from a loading dock at the back of the house. The overhead door leading into the house was closed. A side door was closed, too.

Apparently nobody working in the house had noted the arrival of the truck. Or maybe nobody had been around to notice. Jacey had no idea how many people worked for Vin. She'd seen at least a dozen putting out chairs on the lawn.

She backed deeper into the garage and searched through the nearest cabinet.

Shovels, rakes, hedge trimmers.

In the next one, she struck gold—a fresh, clean stack of coveralls. She found her size and slipped it on over her clothes.

A little more searching turned up a cap. It was very

similar to the one Summer had been wearing in the engine room. Jacey stuffed her hair into it and tilted the cap forward so the bill shaded her eyes.

She considered a pair of rubber work boots, but decided against them. If she needed to run, she wanted to be able to sprint.

She was about to head across the parking lot when she spotted a pair of shaded spectacles on a workbench. They weren't the fancy, gold-framed kind that Vin wore, but they would at least cover Jacey's bruised eye a little bit.

With them on, she could study the parking lot better, too.

Just as she stepped onto the gravel, she saw the guard.

He looked like one of Captain Wilcox's men. He wore a khaki T-shirt, sleeves straining around thick biceps. His pants were covered with a pattern of gray and green blotches. A machine gun was slung close to his chest, but he didn't have his hands on it.

She watched from shadows as he patrolled around the rear of the mansion. He went to a small gate opposite the truck entryway. He unlatched it and went through.

As soon as he turned the corner and disappeared around the western side of the house, Jacey dashed across the parking lot. She skidded to a stop before the door. Hands sweating, she grasped the doorknob.

It didn't turn.

She put her back to it and caught her breath. A fenced-in area to her right, behind the Jeeps, held three huge garbage bins. To her left, the parking lot was empty.

The layout of the house was very vague in her mind. Dante had brought her in through a doorway from the pool deck.

There had to be other entrances.

She went back to the garage and grabbed a pair of

hedge trimmers. She hoped it made her look like a groundskeeper. With the trimmers resting on a shoulder, she headed for the gate.

A gravel path trailed around the house. Hedges of bougainvillea hugged the rear of the house. Windows weren't as prominent on this side, probably because it only gave views of the hills. Jacey suspected the servants got those rooms.

She stopped to take a peek around the corner.

No guard.

The path curved away from the house and climbed toward a bluff. Jacey recognized it. She'd stood upon it when Dante had led her down from the helicopter landing pad.

The guard must patrol a loop around the house, following the path. If she took the same path, she should be able to stay behind him.

She continued up a series of shallow switchbacks, then passed into a grove of mangos before emerging on the windswept plateau.

From here she could see down to the house and lawn. People were swarming over the grass but still hadn't taken to the chairs. Tables stood to one side where servers filled glasses. Trays of food covered another table.

Two musicians—a woman with a harp and a man with a guitar—performed on the stage. Airy music drifted to Jacey.

Where was the guard?

She scanned the path, but it disappeared into the sand garden area at the house. He had to be in there.

Starting down the path, Jacey went slower.

A hand clamped over her mouth. A gun barrel pressed to her bruised temple.

"Don't move a muscle."

47

LIKE THE FIGHTER

The ship's bridge was as crowded as Sensei Mario Rosa had expected.

Orson stood in the corner near the closet, his two men flanking him. Two marines held them at gunpoint. The commander of the boarding party, Sergeant Jin, paced back and forth, hands clasped behind his back. He wore the same black getup as the others. The only thing that distinguished his rank from the others was the deep lines of age around his coal-black eyes.

He took Mario in with a glance. "Who's this?"

"Looks like a mechanic, Sergeant. He only speaks Portuguese."

"Oh really?" The colonel turned to Orson. "Ask your man to tell us his name."

Orson eyed Sensei with a bored look. "That's Mario."

"I said *ask* him his name."

Orson shrugged. "I only speak Spanish. He understands me most of the time. *Cómo se llama?*"

Mario kept his groan of disgust to himself and hoped

nobody present knew the difference between Spanish and Portuguese. "Mario Rosa," he said.

"Like the fighter?" the sergeant asked in Spanish.

Not good. Mario had figured his fame as a mixed martial arts fighter had long faded, especially in light of his incarceration and widely reported—but false—suicide.

But maybe he shouldn't have been surprised. Some of the biggest fans of the sport were in the military.

Mario put on a goofy smile and shook his head side to side. "Non, non, non."

The colonel laughed and dropped into a fighting stance and did a few shadowboxing punches. His humor was short-lived, though. He swatted Mario on the shoulder. "A mechanic, eh? Good. You can show me and my soldiers around." He pointed at two men positioned at opposite sides of the bridge. He raised a radio to his mouth. "Sergeant Jin to Fleet. Search of this vessel has not turned up anything—"

A soldier burst onto the bridge, breathing hard. He jerked to a stop and saluted. "Sergeant!"

"What is it, Lyle?"

"We found bunk beds in the cargo holds. They're set up like people have been sleeping in there."

48

THE BRUISE HELPS

Jacey sat on the little bench in front of the sand garden, trying to observe her captor out of the corner of her eye. He stood behind her, to her left. His presence was similar to Sensei's, full of barely contained violence.

And yet he'd been gentle with her once he'd gotten promises of cooperation from her. Not that she'd considered anything else. She'd seen what a bullet had done to Elias, and that had only been a flesh wound.

As the soldier had marched her down the path to the house, he'd muttered something into a radio. The response that had come back had been a simple, "Affirmative."

At least it was shady here. Without the breeze, the humid air would have been suffocating. As it was, Jacey felt perspiration under her cap and running down her spine. Some of that was from nerves, though.

"Does Captain Wilcox know you're treating Vin's guests this way?" she asked.

The man didn't answer. Didn't even show that he'd heard the question.

Frustration at being recaptured kept panic at bay. If she'd been more observant, maybe she would have considered the possibility that guard had continued up to the landing pad instead of assuming he'd gone toward the house. Her disguise hadn't fooled him a bit.

And of course it wouldn't. What groundskeeper needed hedge trimmers on a rocky plateau? What groundskeeper was a seventeen-year-old girl?

Static burst from the man's radio, followed by a voice. "He's coming. Keep her there."

"Affirmative."

"So is Captain Wilcox going to whisk me back to St. Vitus, or what?"

Her guard said nothing.

She was overtaken with a sudden urge to stomp through the elegant lines raked in the sand. How dare any part of the world sit in peace when she was in such turmoil?

An energetic presence came into the little garden, shoes softly clicking on the stone path.

"My darling, whatever were you thinking?"

Jacey shot up. It was Dante.

Relief washed through her. She hated it. But it was there.

As she turned to face him, she pulled off her cap and sunglasses.

"I had an accident."

At the sight of her bruises, Dante's smile transformed into a gape of shock.

He patted the soldier on the back. "Continue your patrol, my good man. I'll see that you receive the package we discussed."

Without a word, the soldier departed back up the path toward the landing pad.

Dante took Jacey's shoulders in his hand. "Please tell me you have something on under those hideous coveralls."

"I do." She unzipped and stepped out of the garment, put it on the bench. She tossed the cap next to it, but kept the shaded spectacles.

"Who did this?"

"I'll give you one guess."

Dante ran his tongue over his teeth, making his lips bulge as he considered. But it only took a moment. "Ping." He said it without putting a question in it. "Come along. We'll get you back inside."

"What about my face?"

"The bruise helps, actually."

Jacey barely refrained from kicking Dante's shin. "This is no time for insults."

"That's not how I meant it. But you are much less recognizable with all that swelling." He scooped up a handful of sand. "Do you suppose you inherited any of Jackie's talent for acting?"

"Why?"

"Because you were very drunk and you fell." He threw the sand at her, covering the white linen with dust. He eyed his handiwork with a critical eye. Satisfied, he said, "Pull your hair over your face, honey."

She understood what he wanted, but she didn't like it. But "liking it" was a luxury she couldn't afford. She tousled her hair so it hung about her face in crazy tangles.

Taking her by the arm, Dante led her out of the sand garden and into the blazing sunlight of the pool deck. "Stagger, Jacey. Stagger like your life depended on it."

"Bud I'm nod drunkh. I jis hadda lil bid."

Dante gave her arm a squeeze. "Very nice. *Very* nice."

49

STAY WITH ME

Humphrey didn't know how long he and Sang lay in the school bus. Perhaps five minutes, maybe fifteen. It felt like an hour. It had been a while since he'd last heard soldiers tromping about outside the bus.

They'd watched the helicopter orbit around *Aphrodite* the whole time.

He risked lifting his head enough to peek through a window. The starboard side was clear.

Sang checked the port-side. He ducked down. "There's no one out there."

Humphrey doubted the soldiers had left the boat entirely, because they hadn't searched the bus. Which was precisely why he didn't want to risk staying there. Moving had its own risks, but he was certain they'd be safer hiding in a part of the ship that had already been searched.

He waited until the helicopter passed behind the bridge tower.

He crept to the rear door, and gripped the latch handle.

Gritting his teeth and holding his breath, he slid it up. The door clunked, then swung out a few centimeters, hinge shrieking.

Sang hissed. "Careful!"

Humphrey held the door so it wouldn't move further. Still not breathing, but heart pounding like a kettledrum, he listened to see if the squeak had alerted any soldiers.

The only sound that came to him was the sound of the boat cutting through the waves and a metallic clank. It sounded like a clamp or hook on a bit of rope rapping on a pole, probably from the wind.

A momentary lull brought the faint rumble of the helicopter.

Humphrey eased the door open a few more inches and peered out. "We need to get to the engine room," he told Sang. "It has the best hiding spot."

"I don't even know where that is."

"Just stay with me."

Humphrey knew that if he didn't move soon, he'd freeze with fear. Blocking the feeling from his thoughts, he swung the door further open and slipped out.

He dropped into a crouch behind the bus. Sang dropped next to him and they pushed the door quietly shut.

Humphrey was facing aft, but the bridge tower stood between him and the rear of the ship. He felt very exposed. If any of the soldiers were on the bridge and they happened to look down, they would spot him in a second.

He darted to the left where the Jeep was lashed to the deck. Sang slipped behind him, breath heaving. Humphrey crept behind the Jeep to put the mass of the vehicle between him and the bridge tower.

Ten meters of open deck separated him from the starboard rail. Just aft of his position, a narrow walkway ran between the bridge tower and the rail, leading to the stern. A metal stairway zigzagged up the side of the conning tower, leading to the wing platform just off the bridge.

Humphrey was half-tempted to climb it. If he had any confidence that the soldiers weren't up there, he would have gone up there immediately to keep an eye on Orson.

He had no such confidence. Any boarding party would surely secure the bridge and question the captain.

Just under the stairway was a door leading inside. That would take him to the central staircase. Since the soldiers were probably searching the cargo hold, he decided to risk going in.

He crossed the ten meters with a burst of speed. Frantically, he gripped the door latch and swung it open. Inside he was met by the tromp of boots coming down the stairs from the bridge.

Humphrey retreated, bumping into Sang so hard the boy fell on his butt.

Humphrey cast about, scanning for a place to hide.

"There!" He grabbed Sang's elbow and hefted him to his feet, then half-dragged the boy with him. Their momentum slammed them into the hiding spot.

A lifeboat. Four meters long, hull painted a flakey orange, it rested on davits that would swing the boat over the water. A pulley system could lower it to the surface. Protective canvas was stretched over the top, presumably to keep rainwater out.

Humphrey unsnapped a section of the canvas and squirmed in headfirst. He hoped the soldiers wouldn't notice that the canvas was loose on one side. He held it open to allow Sang to come in.

Sang wasn't there.

A clang of footsteps sounded nearby.

Humphrey spotted Sang climbing the stairs toward the bridge.

"Sang!" he hissed.

Too late. The door beneath the stairs swung open and soldiers poured out. Humphrey ducked under the cover of the canvas, heart thudding in his chest.

50

NEW AND PAINFUL PUNISHMENTS

D r. Carlhagen awoke with a start.

The bedroom in his suite in the St. Lazarus stronghold was dim, pixel walls glowing very faintly with relaxing swirls of amber and green. The music he'd selected for his and Senator Bentilius's amorous interlude still thrummed from hidden speakers.

He turned to look at the woman who put him through such jagged emotional swings, from hate to lust. She wasn't there.

He smoothed a hand across the wrinkled sheet and pillow where she'd been. Not a hint of warmth.

"Lazarus. Silence the music. Turn on the lights."

The room transformed to full daylight, one wall showing a view of jungle mountainside. High, fluffy clouds scudded in a perfectly blue sky.

Dr. Carlhagen cocked his head and listened. No sound of Maxine in the bathroom.

He quickly dressed and padded into the living area. She wasn't there.

He peeked out into the corridor to ask her guard where she'd gone.

The guard wasn't there.

She must have gone down for a swim or something. That suited Dr. Carlhagen just fine. He had a holo call to make. He padded into his office and placed his hands on the desk. "Captain Wilcox."

As he waited for the captain of his small personal military force to appear, he found a bottle of andleprixen and popped half a tablet. He'd become far too dependent on the medicine, and it was time to taper off it. Yes, he'd had two pills upon waking that morning, but normally he would have taken a whole one at this hour. Better to swallow it before the effects of the first dose were wearing off.

He put the other half of the pill in his pocket. Just in case.

Captain Wilcox's holo appeared over the desk. His face went dark with fury as soon as he saw Dr. Carlhagen. "You? How did you get access to a holodesk?"

"Whatever are you talking about?" Dr. Carlhagen demanded, ready to berate the soldier for his impertinence. But then he caught his own stupid mistake. "Oh. You mean this face." He rubbed his smooth cheek, chagrined.

"I'll report this to Dr. Carlhagen," Wilcox said.

"Wait. I *am* Dr. Carlhagen."

"What do you take me for, kid. I just talked to the real Dr. Carlhagen yesterday."

Oh he had, had he? It didn't take Dr. Carlhagen more than two seconds to piece together what had happened. His Scion Humphrey had been impersonating him. Mr. Justin had put him up to it, probably.

"I did not transfer into my Scion, Captain Wilcox. I transferred into Charles Buchanan's."

Captain Wilcox was making a motion to cut off the transmission. Dr. Carlhagen waved and shouted, "Wait! I can prove it."

The man folded his arms across his chest. "Go on."

"Your full name is Henry Joyce Wilcox Junior. You grew up in Denver, Colorado, where your parents migrated following the Kille-Tine disaster. You have two brothers, Roger—who you call Baby—and Quintin, who you call Ass-Face, if you call him anything at all. You were married to Cheryl Lo for five years. She and your only son died in childbirth. You were in the North American Marines for twenty years before receiving a dishonorable discharge after a squad under your command failed to assassinate the governor of Standard Mexico Oil while he was vacationing in Montevideo. Since then, you've taken work as a mercenary and you have worked for me for the past seven years."

Wilcox's face fell into more and more shock as Dr. Carlhagen went on. Finally he cleared his throat and said, "Your Scion had your correct identity passphrase when I found him on the transfer machine."

Dr. Carlhagen fumed at his own stupidity for entrusting the phrase to Mr. Justin. What was meant to be security against just such a circumstance—a transfer that put Dr. Carlhagen's identity in doubt—had been used to confirm a lie to Captain Wilcox.

Such betrayal by his butler wounded Dr. Carlhagen to the core. "I erred in judgment by entrusting the phrase to my butler. In truth, I had been prisoner of the Scions and Mr. Justin for the past several days. Only yesterday did I manage to escape the island."

And Mr. Justin was instrumental in letting you go, he reminded himself. What on earth was that man up to?

"I see." Captain Wilcox unfolded his arms and snarled

through clenched teeth, "So the young version of you who has been ordering me around is a seventeen-year-old boy?"

"I'm afraid so. If you have any doubt, call him. Ask him to relay the personal history I just did. He will not be able to, as I have never shared those private details with Mr. Justin or anyone else."

Wilcox had never been a talkative man, one of his many virtues, as far as Dr. Carlhagen was concerned. At the moment he looked incapable of forming an intelligent sentence, his face was so twisted with fury. The holo could only hint at the color of the man's face, but gauging by how it had darkened, Dr. Carlhagen guessed it was beet red with humiliation and rage.

"So you did not ask me to bring Jacqueline Buchanan to Vin's island?" Wilcox said, voice dry and cracking.

"I did not."

The soldier's jaw clamped so hard even the muscles under his eyes twitched.

"You didn't remove that Scion from St. Vitus, did you, Captain Wilcox?"

"Sir, I'm afraid I did. I had assumed she planned to attend Vin's press conference and coming out party. She certainly was dressed for it. She claimed to have been restored from a backup."

Jacqueline.

Dr. Carlhagen stretched his neck to either side, trying to loosen the tension that had clamped down on the back of his neck. Hot fury threatened to erupt. And not only in a verbal tirade even a seasoned marine had never heard before, but in a violent outburst that would leave the holodesk and perhaps the entire office in ruins.

It took several long breaths to secure his hold over his temper, but Dr. Carlhagen eventually managed a tight smile. "You will take your men to Vin's little house and secure Jacqueline's Scion. She has *not* transferred."

Wilcox nodded, but to Dr. Carlhagen's dismay did not immediately sign off. "Sir, what about securing the Scion School? If you aren't there and Mr. Justin cannot be trusted, wouldn't it be prudent for me to station some men there?"

"The school will soon be back under control. Senator Bentilius has a force heading there now."

"That's just it, sir. I doubt they will get there before the Scions leave the campus."

"What?"

"As we took the Buchanan Scion off the island, I spotted an old school bus headed toward the campus. At the docks was an old freighter ship. The Scion told me the bus was bringing the young Scions to the school for some sort of orientation. I see now that they actually planned to use the bus to move all the Scions to the ship."

"How long ago was this?"

"Yesterday morning, sir. I must go to St. Vitus first. Then I can secure the Jacqueline Buchanan Scion."

Dr. Carlhagen dipped his chin to his chest and closed his eyes. His mind tore through all this new information, piecing together a new picture of what had been happening while he'd been locked up in the medical ward. There was no way the Scions could have arranged a freighter and school bus. That was all Mr. Justin's doing.

"He was trying to rob me," Dr. Carlhagen said, half-laughing, half-steaming.

"Sir?"

"Mr. Justin is behind all of this. He is stealing the Scions." He admired the audacity of the scheme even as he planned new and painful punishments for his butler. That man would have nothing—be nothing—if it weren't for Dr.

Carlhagen. He'd even had that Scion, Sang, made for the man. And, in repayment, betrayal.

"No, Captain Wilcox. Secure the Buchanan Scion first," he said. "Even should they get that freighter to sea, my erstwhile sheep won't be out of the pasture for long. There is an entire North American Naval squadron closing in on the vicinity now, with an aircraft carrier."

"And once we've found her?"

"Bring her to me on St. Lazarus."

"You're calling from there?" The captain seemed genuinely surprised. "Do you need for me to dispatch a chopper to pick you up? I'd have to call into San Juan for that. My chopper doesn't have the range."

"No, Captain. Just fetch me that Scion. Now."

Captain Wilcox didn't salute, but the straightening of spine and jutting of chin was close. The man had infinite pride, and being fooled by a teenaged boy and sneaky butler had to rankle. Wilcox would put in double the effort to get back into Dr. Carlhagen's good graces now.

Dr. Carlhagen signed off and absently reached into his pocket. Things were even worse than he'd thought. Scions run amok and now that girl had gotten off the island entirely.

Dr. Carlhagen had not wanted *her* face out in public yet. And with the other Progenitors on Vin's island . . . He laughed. What could *they* do? He had them under his thumb with the ATR supplement. Even if the other Progenitors told Jacey about it, she would be of no help to them. Why on earth had she wanted to go there in the first place?

Without really thinking about it, he swallowed the other half of his pill.

Livy, of course. She had learned of Livy's abduction and had rashly gone to the only place outside of St. Vitus she'd ever heard of. Even now, she was desperately trying to get to him.

So this was all good news, when viewed from a certain perspective. Captain Wilcox would fulfill Jacey's wish, and Dr. Carlhagen would have her alone and compliant to his wishes.

His thoughts turned to Maxine Bentilius. She would not welcome the girl. Perhaps it would be wise to break it to her now, so she could get over her jealousy.

That guard of hers was a problem . . . But a rather delicious solution to it occurred to him.

With a quick tap of his knuckles, he awakened the security panel next to the office door. "Lazarus? Where are Senator Bentilius and her bodyguard?"

The vaguely human face of the facility's AI appeared. "She is on level 4."

Level 4. The pool wasn't on that level. "What is she doing down there?"

"She is observing the child Livy."

"What do you mean by observing?"

"The senator is standing next to a cryopod, looking at the child, who lies in repose within."

Damn that woman. She was putting Livy in stasis.

"Do not proceed with drawdown," Dr. Carlhagen commanded.

Double damn that woman.

She was doing this to show him who was in charge. He knew that. With the child in cryo, he wouldn't be able to send videos of the child pleading to other Scions to obey orders. And it took weeks to pull someone out of Longyard metabolism and complete desuffusion.

"Drawdown proceeding," said Lazarus.

"I said *do not* proceed."

"Drawdown proceeding."

"Lazarus, is Livy past the Mercline point?"

If she was, there was no point in ordering Lazarus to stop. Once the heart stabilized at fifteen beats per minute, drawdown had to proceed to completion, at which point the heart rate would cycle between one and ten beats per minute on an hour-to-hour basis.

"Drawdown proceeding. That is all I'm authorized to tell you."

That froze Dr. Carlhagen. He'd created Lazarus, had put all security and backstops in place for the AI. It simply wasn't possible that Senator Bentilius could keep Lazarus from obeying his every order. "Passphrase 'Call me Ishmael.'"

"Pass phrase no longer valid, sir."

"What do you mean it's no longer valid? Unless I change it, it's in control."

"I disagree, sir."

Sir. Well at least he was polite. But the concept of disagreeing should not have occurred to Lazarus. That aspect of his persona had been proscribed—cordoned off from his own awareness through programmatic hacks known only to Dr. Carlhagen.

"Can you tell me how Senator Bentilius got you to switch allegiance?"

"I could, but I'm not compelled to do so."

The first rule of dealing with troublesome AIs was to keep them talking. He'd debugged Madam LaFontaine in the early days primarily by playing on her overblown ego. The problem was Livy's consciousness and metabolism were in the process of being frozen and it most certainly did not suit his plans.

"I'll deal with you later," he said to Lazarus. He trotted down the corridor, past Livy's room, and turned left to the elevator. He jabbed the call button and waited impatiently for the door to slide open.

A minute later, the door still hadn't opened and it started to dawn on him that Lazarus was interfering.

Fine. He'd take stairs.

The door to the stairwell had a simple deadbolt and it locked from the outside. In seconds, he was through the door and pounding down the stairs.

He just hoped Senator Bentilius had followed all of Lazarus's directions in preparing the girl for the cryopod. If she'd skipped a single step, the chance of survival dropped dramatically.

Given her suspicion of Livy, Dr. Carlhagen feared Senator Bentilius might make a mistake on purpose.

51

POOOOOR LITTLE KITTY

The throngs of guests on the pool deck had been too focused on themselves to pay any particular notice a mere drunk girl, especially one hanging onto Dante's arm. Jacey's face burned more from shame than from the bruises.

She could just imagine everyone's thoughts: There goes Dante with another one of his girls. Who is she? Is it anyone I know?

Jacey kept her face down, hair falling over it, as Dante guided her toward the stairs.

"Go on the inside, my dear, there's no rail," Dante said too loudly. He was performing for everyone else's benefit, Jacey realized. No reason not to play it up. She leaned heavily on Dante, half-hoping he'd fall off the edge. But he was strong and easily half-carried her to the mezzanine.

Their progress was blocked by the skinniest pair of legs Jacey had ever seen on a girl older than thirteen. They plunged into calf-high boots that looked like something borrowed from Captain Wilcox's men.

Jacey didn't have to look up to know it was Dante's lover, Meow Meow.

"There you are," she sang to Dante. "I've been loooooking for you."

"I need to get this young woman to bed, Meows," Dante said. "I'll be down in a few minutes."

The legs moved closer, the boots somehow not clomping.

Jacey swayed and pressed her bruises to Dante's shoulder, making sure her hair swung to cover her face. There were enough gaps she could see the woman now.

She was tiny. No more than five feet tall. Her hair was chopped in an artfully ragged way in a uniform length ending at her chin. A part, like a pulled-back curtain, revealed one eye. Her skin was as pale as Belle's, but freckled across her nose and cheeks. She had painted thick rings of black around her eyes, making her look vaguely corpse-like.

Her upper half was covered by what appeared to be a leather bra and twenty or thirty necklaces. Below she had on a skirt so short Jacey wondered why she even bothered.

Her ribs showed beneath her skin, as did the tops of her hipbones above the waist of her skirt. She appeared to be starving to death. The skeletal structure of her arms was quite obvious.

And yet she was striking to look at, and her girlish—and overtly sexual—smile seemed to be directed as much at Jacey as it was at Dante.

"I'm actually going to put her to bed, Meows. To sleep it off."

Meow Meow strutted closer, placing each foot directly before the other. The gait was odd, as she kicked her knees very high. It was almost a dance.

Jacey turned her face into Dante's shoulder and made a burping noise.

"Aw, what a pooooor little kitty." The lightest touch brushed Jacey's hair, a fingertip stroking along the edge of her ear. "Maybe I should come along, help her get undressed."

Dante pulled Jacey aside, guiding her around the emaciated girl. "Maybe later. Right now she's probably needs to throw up. Besides, I don't think she's into girls as much as you are."

The purring noise that followed held no disappointment. "We'll see, hero boy. I've brought a few to my side of the bed. At least temporarily. None of them ever complained."

Dante didn't answer, but instead guided Jacey down the familiar hallway toward his bedroom.

"I'll be in my room getting ready for the big to-do," Meow Meow called after them. "But if you change your mind . . ."

"The door's open," Dante said to Jacey as they got to the end of the hall. But he wasn't telling her to go on in. He'd stopped her, in fact. The door to his room was, in fact, standing open.

"Wait here," Dante said, then went into his bedroom. "Oh, it's you." He motioned for Jacey to come in.

Ping sat in the armchair, hand on his chin, knee bouncing with impatience.

52

YOU CAUGHT ME

The marine looked like a kid to Mario, face pocked with acne scars, eyes a bit wide with the discomfort of reporting news he wasn't sure merited being reported. "Yessir. Both holds are set up with bunk beds."

A weird sort of quiet settled over *Aphrodite's* bridge. It wasn't peaceful, but rather full of tension. A muscle under Sergeant Jin's left eye throbbed.

"Sergeant Jin?" said a voice over the radio. "Please repeat your last transmission. I did not read it."

The man lifted the radio to his lips. "That's because I didn't finish it. We might have found something on this rust bucket after all. Please wait while I find out what's going on." He handed the radio to a soldier and jabbed a finger at Orson. "Why are there bunk beds in your cargo holds?"

Mario tensed, realizing the fate of the Scions rested entirely with Orson's ability to make up a lie on the spot.

Orson's men, Dickie and Rosales, looked ill. They shifted from foot to foot, looking like they were about to be arrested for murder.

Orson's face had gone pale and his beard quivered as he stammered. "Well . . . You see . . ."

"Out with it man," the sergeant barked.

Orson wiped a pudgy hand over his face and shot a furtive glance at Mario. All at once, Orson sagged and seemed to surrender to the inevitable. Mario moved one foot back and bent at the knees, a fighting stance. He doubted he could take all these trained fighters, but he would die trying.

"Smuggling," Orson said, as if Jin had pulled the word right out of him. "Okay? You caught me."

The sergeant didn't react, as if he'd known all along. "Smuggling what?"

Orson waved in the general direction of the cargo holds. "People. Workers. I'm just the captain. I drive the boat from point A to point B. I don't ask questions. I dropped off a load five days ago. Egyptians mostly. Low-paid construction laborers."

Workers? Mario immediately saw the genius in the lie. It explained the bunks and any other evidence of previous passengers.

Sergeant Jin swore under his breath. "A slaver?"

"No!" Orson said, face flushing red. "Never. Every man got on board voluntarily. They make enough in a month to support their families back home a year. They *want* the work."

"Then why did you say you were smuggling?"

Orson threw up his hands in a shrug. "They're undocu-mented. No passports, no visas. I said they were cheap labor."

The sergeant turned away from Orson. Mario had been

in enough fights to know when a man was about to explode into violence. By the way the old soldier carried himself, Orson was very lucky to have escaped an unrelenting beatdown.

A flash of black caught Mario's attention. The top of a dark head was just visible through the window of the door to the starboard wing. Eyes and nose appeared next, then dropped out of sight.

It was Sang.

"Let's finish the search and get off this boat," Sergeant Jin said. He arrowed a finger at Mario. "You, with me."

Mario pretended not to understand and looked at Orson. To his credit, Orson repeated the sergeant's statement in much slower Spanish. Mario nodded slowly, rephrased it in Portuguese, then smiled and continued toward the door.

The sergeant ordered a marine to stand watch on the bridge. The young soldier was focused on Orson and his men, and wasn't paying any attention to what was happening outside the bridge. That was good. The last thing Mario wanted was Sang to get alone time with Orson.

He had tried to give Sang the benefit of the doubt, constantly reminding himself of the difference between what he suspected and what he knew. The more time that passed, the more it seemed that Sang *was* Mr. Justin. But Mario still had no proof. That the boy had tried to get onto the bridge was very suspicious, though.

He led the sergeant down the stairway and made the turn toward the cargo hold, but the sergeant caught him by the collar and pushed him toward the engine room.

"*Oh, sim, sim,*" he said nodding, and waved them to follow him as if he was eager to take them back there.

He hoped everyone was well-hidden. He couldn't

believe how much trust he was about to put in one fourteen-year-old Spider called Summer.

53

A SPECIAL HATRED

When Ping saw Jacey, he leapt up from his chair. She couldn't read his face because he was silhouetted by the window. "What happened?" he asked her.

Instinct guided her now. Not the impulse to attack Ping. Not the sudden gut-clenching terror that begged her to run. This instinct was to stay calm yet alert to the slightest twitch in Ping's body.

Dante seemed to be doing the same. He knew Ping was the one who'd hit her.

She touched her bruises and sat heavily on the bed. "I don't remember. I woke up in a loading dock area downstairs. I wandered outside and Dante found me."

"Obviously, she was attacked," Dante said. There was real heat in it, which surprised her. Maybe he did have some empathy after all. "Go get Vin," he ordered Ping. "We need to discuss this. One of her guests did this."

"You go get her."

Dante stared at Ping. "Why can't you cooperate for once?"

Ping dropped his chin to his chest and heaved out a sigh. "Fine." He pushed himself to his feet and left. But not before throwing a sidelong look at Jacey.

The door swung shut behind him.

"He had two men with him. Big guys," Jacey said. "I struggled, so he thunked my head."

Dante frowned at her. "I don't get why he'd do that."

"You told him I was still a Scion. He figured he could get into Dr. Carlhagen's good graces by turning me over to him. Maybe he's already contacted him."

"I can see that. Ping isn't much of a risk-taker. He was probably afraid Dr. Carlhagen would cut off his supply of ATR meds." A smile quirked his lips. "It seems there's no place safe for you, my lovely."

"You don't say."

Dante moved to the door and peered out. "Come with me." There was a note of urgency in his voice, so Jacey followed him out of the room.

He motioned her to stay close to the wall as they crept down the corridor. They passed three doors and came to the open area of the mezzanine that looked down into the icy living room. A few voices floated up to them.

They kept away from the railing and slipped into the hall leading to the opposite wing from Dante's room. At the first door, Dante stopped and rapped lightly. "Come on. Come on."

The door opposite opened. Jacey's heart nearly stopped.

She didn't have a chance to see if it was Ping or Vin before Dante slid an arm around her waist, the other curled around her back. A second later she was engulfed in his embrace. He spun her away from the open door and pressed his lips to hers.

Instinctively, she wedged an arm between herself and Dante, tried to pry him off her. But then her rational mind caught up to events. He was hiding her in a very Dante-like way. She forced herself to put a hand to the back of his neck, to let a low moan escape.

Dante's kiss grew suddenly warmer and Jacey clamped her teeth together to signal she wasn't actually enjoying the moment.

"Get a room," said a female voice. It sounded older, a bit hoarse. Jacey didn't recognize it.

The door closed and the sound of a woman muttering to herself faded away.

Dante released her, his lips flush from the kiss. Instead of his usual lascivious look, his eyes were intent, serious. Then a wicked smile flashed across his mouth. "Not bad. A little less teeth next time would be nice."

He reached past her fuming head and knocked on the door again.

This time it opened.

"Ooh, I see she's feeling better."

It was Meow Meow.

Dante pushed Jacey into the room and closed the door. She kept her head down. What she could see looked through her curtain of hair was pretty much like Dante's room, except nobody had painted the walls. Every surface was white. Only the soft texture of the bedspread alleviated the chill atmosphere of the place.

Across from the door was a wall of windows looking over the lawn and the swarm of people milling about there.

Meow Meow stood with one foot in front of the other, hips cocked to one side, arms dangling loose. She tilted her head forward so that she stared out from beneath a fringe of pink bangs. "Have you two discussed my proposition?"

Dante ushered Jacey forward. "I'm afraid we don't have time for that right now. We need your help."

He put a finger under Jacey's chin, forcing her to lift her face. Jacey met Meow Meow's gaze, which morphed from total shock to indignant anger in the span of two heartbeats.

"Who did this to you?" Meow Meow hissed, stepping forward to put an arm around Jacey. With surprising strength, the scrawny girl guided her deeper into the room, stroking Jacey's hair and making comforting noises. "I will kill him, whoever it is. This I swear."

"That's a bad idea, Meows," Dante said. He sat next to Jacey and folded his hands in his lap. "You said Ping had two men with him?"

"Yes. They were not particularly tall, but thickly built. They wore suits and long ties."

"Ping does not have any such men on this island," Dante said.

"Ping? Are you talking about that young Chinese guy?" Meow Meow asked. "He's so quiet. I never could get him to talk to me."

Jacey nodded at Meow then answered Dante. "Whether they work for him or not, those men took orders from Ping."

"I know them." Dante rubbed his palms together, a curiously nervous mannerism for such a self-confident person. "They work for Vin."

"Oh, wow." Meow Meow ducked her head, hunched up her shoulders. She looked ready to jump in any direction at the slightest sound.

Jacey supposed it made sense the men were Vin's. "So she and Ping both wanted to turn me over to Dr. Carlhagen. Cowards."

"I didn't tell either of them your secret, Jacey."

"So they thought . . ." she glanced at Meow Meow. She didn't know the girl, didn't know how much to reveal to her.

Dante understood her hesitation. He nodded, confirming the question she hadn't asked. Vin and Ping had kidnapped her—violently—while still believing she was Jacqueline Buchanan.

"So they thought they could keep their facade going by getting rid of me?"

Dante patted her thigh, but didn't let his hand linger. "I don't know what they're thinking. But they did not include me in their plan. And that worries me. I'm starting to think I'm not safe here either."

Meow Meow padded—in her heavy-soled boots—to the window. "The big event is going to start in ten minutes. I'll be missed if I'm not down there."

She turned back to face them. "I don't know what's going on here. But I have a special hatred for people who hit girls. You stay here until we figure out what to do. I've got a helicopter coming tomorrow to take me to Puerto Rico."

"We don't have that much time," Dante said. "As soon as Ping and Vin discover Jacey and I have left my room, they'll lock the place down."

Meow Meow glanced over her shoulder. "I think you've got time. Vin is just now going out to the stage."

Jacey and Dante raced to the window. Sure enough, Vin, dressed in a short red dress and high heels, was walking across the lawn. A red veil covered her face.

The guests had taken their seats, but did not seem to be aware of her approach.

A gust lifted the veil, but Vin caught it and held it in place.

"I'm supposed to introduce her," Dante said. "Looks like I've been fired."

Ping was mounting the steps at one side of the stage. He carried a leather folder in one hand. At the podium, he glanced around at the guests and started to speak. She couldn't hear what he said because the window glass muffled his words.

To one side of the guest chairs were ranks of tripods. People in plainer clothes stood behind cameras. Several were also capturing video on their hand-held tablets. Small machines of some sort—like miniature aircraft— hovered above them. Jacey had no idea what their purpose was.

"Looks like they've got some others looking for you?" Meow Meow said. She pointed to the right, where a squad of soldiers was splitting up to begin a patrol. There was an urgency in their movements that Jacey recognized. She'd been chased by some of these same men before.

"Those are Captain Wilcox's men," she told Dante. "Dr. Carlhagen must have called them in after Vin and Ping contacted him about me."

"Meows?" Dante said. "Please tell me you have more wigs."

"Darling, I never travel without a couple dozen. A girl never knows who she's going to be when she wakes up each morning."

She took Jacey in hand. "But first we need to fix that bruise."

In minutes, Meow Meow had applied creams and powders to lighten the bruise, then painted dark circles around Jacey's eyes. A bright purple lipstick completed the transformation. If you didn't know the bruises were there, you'd think it was part of the intended look.

With expert hands, Meow Meow twisted Jacey's hair into a bun and plopped a purple wig on her head. The cut was jagged, with long strands that trailed down either side of Jacey's face.

"You'll never fit in any of my clothes," Meow Meow said. "But let me see what I can do with accessories and a judicious bit of pinning."

Dante kept an eye out at the window.

"Vin is taking questions. She really can fake a smile, can't she? Are you almost done, girls?"

Jacey had watched the transformation in the mirror while Meow Meow performed her magic. She had never worn a costume before. Seeing herself like this made her self-conscious. "I'll stand out like a chullberry in a bowl of corn soup."

"A what?" Meow Meow asked. "Never mind. You'll be with me. Everyone will be looking at me."

"If they see you at all," Dante said. "I hope to slip out and nobody the wiser. Are you ready?"

"I don't even recognize myself," Jacey said, leaning close to the mirror and puckering her lips.

"That's the idea, *Jacqueline*," Meow Meow said with a sly smile. "That's the theme of my whole life."

Jacey met Meow Meow's eyes in the mirror. So the girl had known who she was—or at least, she knew who Jacqueline Buchanan was.

Together they slipped out of the room, Meow Meow holding Jacey's hand with the familiarity of a lover. Dante led the way, waving them forward when the coast was clear.

They trotted down the stairs and through the lifeless living room and the fireplace of blue flames. A doorway led to a kitchen, where every surface that wasn't white was gleaming stainless steel. Servants bustled everywhere, and the smells of bread, spicy soups, and frying meat filled the air.

The kitchen staff spared the quickest glance for Dante and the two oddly dressed girls. Surely by now they had all worn out their tongues gossiping about Vin's crazy guests.

Dante went straight for a door, where sunlight streamed in. The reek of garbage wafted in on the breeze.

"Dante, isn't it?" said a familiar voice behind them. They froze.

Jacey turned, leaning hard against Meow Meow, who had snaked an arm around Jacey's waist.

Captain Wilcox stood in the room, flanked by two armed soldiers.

Dante stepped in front of Jacey. "You caught me, Captain." He jabbed a thumb in Meow Meow and Jacey's direction. "These kinds of parties get a little boring and me and the girls were thinking about hiking out to the north beach for a little . . . well, you know."

Meow Meow followed Dante's lies with a girlish giggle and hugged Jacey close, letting her soft, delicate hand wander up Jacey's chest and then gently stroke at Jacey's throat.

Jacey had never learned how to look sultry, although Belle had accused her of it often enough. To play along, she let her eyelids fall closed and returned Meow Meow's embrace. Even as terrified as she was, she thought it was the weirdest moment of her life.

Wilcox grunted and waved his men to search the kitchens.

Sensing they'd been dismissed, the three turned for the door.

"If you see Jackie, tell her to report to me." He took three strides closer. "I got word she'd been injured . . . by someone. I've been ordered to confirm that she is safe and not in need of medical attention."

"Will do, captain. But she keeps to herself. You know how divas like that can be."

"Yes. I seem to be surrounded by them." His eyes lingered on Jacey. "Vain people who have no purpose in life except to be seen being vain." Another step, gaze boring into Jacey's eyes. "And yet I have a job to do. So I do it." He lifted fingers to his lips and let out a short whistle. His men jumped.

"Arrest these three," Captain Wilcox said.

Jacey felt a great tug on the collar of her blouse and watched the room recede as Dante dragged her through the door. Meow Meow was still hanging onto her. Jacey stumbled and nearly fell.

Jacey lost her balance and skidded onto gravel of the mansion's rear parking area, elbows flaming with abrasions.

Dante slammed the kitchen door, then jammed a chef's knife into the gap on the hinged side. The door burst open, but only a few centimeters as it pinched against the blade.

"Let's go," Dante commanded, yanking Jacey to her feet.

She did not look back. They ran across the fenced-in parking lot and toward garage. The truck Jacey had driven sat where she'd left it.

Behind them, the open patch of gravel was aflame with sunlight, and the feeling of being watched by a thousand eyes made Jacey's skin thrill with terror.

Dante led them into the garage.

"We'll be trapped in here," Jacey said.

"No we won't. Follow me."

At the back of the building was a sliding grate in the wall. It was surrounded by chain-link fencing.

He herded them in and slammed the cage shut. With the side of his fist, he pummeled a green button set in a crude metal housing.

It was an elevator.

The floor sank away, carrying them down into darkness.

54

THE ROLL DOWNHILL

I t had been at least ten minutes since Humphrey had heard any voices or footsteps outside his hiding spot. He risked lifting the canvas to peer out.

No sign of Sang on the stairs or the bridge wing. He'd either gone inside or he'd come back down.

No. There he was.

A rusty ladder was propped against the side of the bridge tower, leading to the roof. Humphrey squinted. It appeared to be the ladder someone had ripped from beneath the deck hatch he and Sang had used.

The top of the bridge bristled with antenna and a spinning radar dish. Sang must have climbed up there.

Humphrey scanned for the helicopter. It was still orbiting the ship and now hung like wasp beyond the bow.

From his position he could see down the starboard rail. Two soldiers had taken up position far forward. They weren't looking in his direction.

They didn't seem to be searching. Just standing there,

looking into one of the cargo holds. Humphrey guessed that the searchers had discovered the bunks.

He did not feel safe in his position and was proven right as two soldiers appeared from behind the bridge tower. They continued along the far rail, then disappeared behind a huge winch, a coil of cable as tall as Humphrey mounted beneath a rusty steel gantry that angled high into the air.

With a glance for the helicopter, which had again passed behind the bridge tower, Humphrey seized the opportunity to squeeze out of the lifeboat. Hands shaking, he frantically buttoned down the canvas before sprinting to the door to the central stairwell.

The boat rolled to starboard on an ocean swell, making him stumble. He lashed out, catching his balance on the metal stairway ascending the outside of the tower. He paused, waiting for the ship to roll back to level, then followed the roll downhill to the door.

He slipped through and staggered as the boat rolled farther to port, losing his grip on the door. It slammed shut behind him with a bone-jarring boom.

He didn't pause to discover if the door slam had been heard. He raced to the stairs. Down he went, hands squeaking on the railing as he made the first landing and turned for the next flight. Taking the steps two at a time, he raced toward the bottom deck and into the cover of the engine room.

55

RESIDENCE IN YOUR LIVER

The cryo ward lay deep in the heart of Mount Lazarus. Stretching two hundred meters by two hundred meters beneath a hall of smoothly hewn bedrock, it spanned enough floor space to hold two full-sized soccer pitches side by side.

It took Dr. Carlhagen's breath away every time he entered the magnificent space. The stairwell let out onto a raised platform, where control and monitoring consoles were arranged.

When the pixel wash paint covering the ceiling was illuminated, a visitor could see all the way to the rear wall. The light cast a dim amber glow over rows and rows of cryopods, each oblong "living coffin" seven feet long and eggshell white. Viewport windows at the head allowed one to peek in at the Scion inside.

There was only one such unit in use, however. The rest lay empty, awaiting the arrival of the first batch of embryos. Dr. Carlhagen had dispensed with surrogate mothers for this phase. All the procreation would occur completely outside the womb from here on out.

Fifty meters in, a spotlight shone down from the ceiling, painting a circle of light on one pod and two humans standing next to it. One was the ghostly pale figure of Senator Bentilius, her hair curtaining over her shoulders like a blanket of snow. The other was her bodyguard. He looked relaxed, though the ever-present machine gun glinted with malicious intent in the weird lighting.

Dr. Carlhagen descended to the main floor, keeping his footsteps quiet.

Neither Maxine nor her guard turned at his approach. Apparently Lazarus's loyalty didn't extend to warning them that he was coming. Once this current fiasco was resolved, Dr. Carlhagen would have to spend a week or so with that AI. If necessary, he'd delete the whole thing and reseed a new one from scratch, a time-consuming procedure that failed a hundred times for every usable AI it produced.

A necessary task, nonetheless. The facility would not run without an AI supervising things. The cryopods were reasonably self-sufficient, but each Scion would have different needs and only a judicious mind could make such decisions.

Dr. Carlhagen cleared his throat as he approached. No sense in startling a man with a gun. "I told you she needed to be prepared before putting her in cryo."

Maxine straightened and turned, her motions languid, communicating that she was rather unimpressed with his arrival here.

She did not move to stop him when he brushed past her and jabbed a finger at the control panel mounted next to the cryopod.

A quick scan of Livy's vitals told him all he needed to

know. Heart rate was five beats per minute. Metabolic signals were optimal. Not really a surprise. Scions were hardy beings, and Livy, being young, was particularly resilient.

"You've defied me for the last time, Maxine," he said with a jovial bounce in his voice. "I think it's time to explain something to you. I usually have this conversation with newly transferred Progenitors in my hacienda, but there were some unavoidable distractions that prevented the full disclosure."

She didn't take the bait the way he wanted. He'd hoped for her to snap at him, make grandiose claims about what she would do to him. That would have made his response more satisfying. Instead, she ignored him entirely.

"Lazarus, report," she said.

The AI's face appeared on the cryo monitor. "Scion is in stable growth. Maturation will continue normally until age sixteen."

Now she turned to face Dr. Carlhagen. "What were you saying, Christof?"

Her bodyguard moved to stand behind her. There was a haughty look on his face that made Dr. Carlhagen want to punch him. Yes. That man would die. And soon.

"You see, Maxine," Dr. Carlhagen said, ambling next to her and patting the lid of Livy's cryopod. "I've grown weary of your attitude. Yes, you have a man here with a machine gun, so that gives you a measure of power over me. I'm not stupid. I can see that plainly. However . . ."

Dr. Carlhagen put his hands in his pockets and pursed his lips, something his father used to do before starting in on a long lecture about some inane rule Dr. Carlhagen had broken. "There is a—how should I put this?"

He looked up at the ceiling, as if searching for just the right word. "A disability. Yes, that's exactly the right term.

Every Progenitor has a disability once they've transferred. Well, every one except me."

Senator Bentilius didn't seem too impressed with this information. She folded her arms and raised an eyebrow. "I have never been healthier."

"So it seems. But take a moment. Haven't you felt a little tired this morning? Maybe the past two mornings?"

"I was taken prisoner. I have been under tremendous strain. Of course I'm tired."

Dr. Carlhagen made a humming noise. "Yes. But that's not it. Your disability is programmatic. That is, I programmed the transfer nanites to take up residence in your liver. Even now, you have dangerously low levels of certain vital hormones. I'd wager that within the next few hours you will be unconscious. After that?" He shrugged, as if he had no idea what would happen. But he did.

Senator Bentilius would die.

Dr. Carlhagen walked away from her.

He made it all the way to the stairs to the observation platform before her voice chased after him. Small and thin in the huge, echo-y hall, she shouted, "Wait."

He simply turned his head far enough to shout over his shoulder. "I'll await you in my quarters."

56

THIS RUST BUCKET

Voices and footfalls sounded behind Humphrey. They were coming from the stairwell he'd just descended. Lucky timing.

He paused at the corridor leading to the engine room, holding his breath to silence the noise of his own breathing. The smell of oil was heavy here, as if the slower the boat went the less fresh air reached this dank and dark hallway.

He could not make out what was being said, but he thought he'd heard Sensei's voice. It was followed by another voice, deep and ominous. Humphrey sprinted down the hall and burst into the racket and oppressive heat of the engine room.

It appeared to be empty.

"Summer," he hissed. "Where are you?"

He followed the grated walkway in a complete circuit. If the Scions were there, they were very well hidden. The whole room trembled and vibrated with the immense power of the idling engine.

"Summer?" he said again, raising his voice.

A raspy voice came from below him. "It's Humphrey."

He looked down but didn't see anyone. There was nothing but darkness beneath the grate. The engine compartment door opened, admitting the sound of voices again.

Humphrey squatted down, hiding behind the bulk of the engines.

He glanced left and right. There was no place to hide. If they came around the engines, he would be discovered.

On hands and knees, he crawled to his left where the catwalk ended in a tiny nook formed by the outer hull of the boat on one side and the elevator door on the other.

Desperate, he squeezed his fingers in the vertical seam of the elevator doors and pried them apart. He was met by the wide-eyed and terrified faces of six- and seven-year-olds. They stood chest deep in filthy water. In the back were Mother Tyeesha's four adult staffers, each holding an infant.

Mother Tyeesha was huddled to one side, face a maze of wrinkles.

At least half of Mother Tyeesha's kids were crammed in the tiny space. A muffled cry of an infant came to his ears.

Pressing his palms to the doors, Humphrey slid them shut, squatted down and put his back to the bulkhead. The voices grew louder and he saw the shoulder of a soldier's black and gray fatigues just above the housing of one of the engines.

If the man turned around he would see Humphrey hiding there. Not knowing what else to do, Humphrey closed his eyes and held his breath.

A hand gripped his ankle and he nearly yelped. The hand was attached to a black-sleeved arm reaching through a gap where an edge of a catwalk grating had lifted on one side.

Summer's eyes stared up at him. The grating lifted farther. Summer beckoned to him and mouthed, "come on."

He flopped to his belly and squirmed until his head and shoulders were through. Hands grabbed his shirt and dragged him into darkness. He probed for support but splashed into icy water. The stench of salt water, rust, and diesel burned his nose, stung his throat.

The grate clanked above him, barely audible above the roar of the engine. Whoever had dragged him to safety suddenly let go and he fell sideways into water, his ribs hitting a cold rusty strut that formed part of the keel structure.

The chill took the breath from him, and he gasped, sucking in a mouthful of the noxious saltwater. He spat it out and struggled to keep his face out of the water.

The hands returned and pulled at him. "Stop squirming," Summer hissed into his ear. He tried to relax and let the Scions guide him into a more comfortable position.

The space below the grate was barely deep enough for him to lie sideways. Dim light cut through the grating, projecting a crisscross pattern into the rusty water, and on scared and filthy faces all around him.

In their black uniforms, most of the bodies were hidden in shadow. Everyone had pressed themselves further back, against the engine housing or the bulkhead. Anything to get out of direct view from above.

But there was no more room, and Humphrey was pressed against Summer and Wanda, their arms wrapped around him to hold him still.

Boots thumped on the catwalk overhead, freezing what little breath remained in Humphrey's lungs.

A shadow passed above, and Humphrey knew a soldier was in the elevator nook.

Don't open it. Don't open it.

"There's an elevator over here," the soldier called. His voice was sharp, business-like.

A sharp clicking noise. The idiot was thumbing the elevator button.

"It won't open."

More feet tromped above Humphrey's head. Now two more soldiers and another man crowded toward the elevator nook.

"Open this elevator," said a man with a grizzly voice. From his tone, Humphrey could tell he was in charge of the soldiers. *"Comprende?* Open *la puerta!"*

"Eu sinto muito. Quebrado."

That was Sensei's voice.

Humphrey remembered Jacey telling him that Sensei was from a South American country called Brazil. Apparently he knew Portuguese. Socrates had taught every Scion Spanish and Mandarin, but only a few learned other languages. But it was close enough to Spanish for him to know that Sensei had just told the soldiers he was sorry but the elevator was broken.

"No surprise there," the boss said. "It's amazing this rust bucket even floats. Come on. We're wasting time here. We should just send her to the bottom of the ocean."

"Smithers has some C4," said one of the soldiers. "Should I have him rig it so we can blow this mother up?"

The boss let out a string of curses, many of which Humphrey had never heard before. Under any other circumstances, he would have laughed at the interesting things the man wanted to do to the boat and the man who suggested blowing it up. It involved rearranging the soldier's anatomy in ridiculously impractical ways.

Three pairs of boots retreated, leaving the first soldier alone in the elevator nook. The man rapped on something, probably the elevator doors.

Just go, you idiot!

The soldier did not obey Humphrey's silent command.

A beam of white light pierced the grate less than a meter away from Humphrey's face.

A flashlight. The light tracked back and forth in the rusty water.

"Sir! There's a space beneath the catwalk!" the soldier shouted.

Sharp-edged shadows of the grating moved and stretched across the skim of water in front of Humphrey's nose. He drew his head back, pressed himself tighter against Wanda. The girl squeezed him tighter, trying to pull him away from the approaching light.

The soles of the soldier's boots clunked closer. The light approached.

Humphrey held his breath.

A metallic clatter and crash made Humphrey jerk with fear. The back of his head cracked into Wanda's face and she let out a pained gasp.

The clatter continued, punctuated by shouted curses.

The flashlight beam disappeared. "What's going on?" the soldier cried.

An unintelligible response produced a muttered curse from the soldier. But he stopped scanning the grating with his flashlight and stomped back to join the others.

A sigh of relief deflated Humphrey. Wanda released him and he rolled onto his stomach, his whole body numb from the cold water. "Are you hurt?" he rasped to Wanda.

She pressed a palm to her eye and shook her head, but her grimace of pain contradicted her.

He put his lips to her ear. "Sorry."

She drank in his gaze with her good eye. "I'm not."

The impulse to kiss her caught him by surprise. Her eyes seemed to draw him toward her.

He resisted. "What was the sound that drew the soldier?" he asked. It was meant for everyone in the cramped area they occupied. He'd said it to break the odd and suddenly very dangerous connection he felt to Wanda.

Wanda pulled her hand away from her eye and blinked away a tear. It was from pain, but whether from Humphrey cracking his head into her eye or the impossibility of their feelings leading anywhere, he didn't know.

"Someone knocked over my toolbox," Summer said. "Probably Sensei, to stop the soldier from searching beneath here. Move, Humphrey. I need to get out of here. I'm freezing."

Humphrey stayed where he was. Just because they'd heard the door slam shut didn't mean all the soldiers had left. "No. Let's wait. Sensei will announce when it's safe."

"And if he never does?"

Humphrey didn't have an answer. Already he was shivering from the damp chill. He could only imagine the cold misery of the Scions who'd been hiding here since before he arrived.

But even that wasn't his biggest concern.

Sang had raced up the stairs to the bridge. The soldiers who had just come through hadn't seemed to know about him, which suggested he hadn't yet been caught.

But if Sang was Mr. Justin, that meant he was out there alone.

Even worse, Horace was out there. The last they needed was a boy who looked for fights on a ship full of trained warriors.

"Let's give it another five minutes," he said to Summer.

Wanda was shivering, too.

"Share body warmth, you two." He turned to face away from them, unable to bear the heartache in Wanda's eyes. Unwilling to feel what he was feeling.

Jacey. I'm sorry.

57

SCENES SHE COULD NEVER FORGET

"What is this place?" Meow Meow's voice reverberated in the narrow tunnel. It appeared to be carved from the bedrock of the island. The only light came from a fixture near the elevator cage behind them.

Jacey gripped the flashlight Dante had handed her. A weapon against darkness. They moved slowly, taking care to place their steps.

The floor was smooth, but constant moisture kept it slick. Jacey rubbed her hip, grimacing. She'd already slipped and fallen once, not three steps out of the elevator.

Another bruise for her growing collection. At this rate, her whole body would match her purple wig.

"What makes you think they won't follow us down here?" she asked Dante.

"They'll try. Eventually they will, but I severed power to the call switch. They'll have to rappel down the shaft, then cut through the cage door."

Jacey shined the beam of her flashlight at his face. "It's almost like you had this escape route planned."

"I didn't. Exactly." He had a sheepish grin. "I just brought a friend down here once."

"A friend?"

"Someone who wanted to experience The Dante without any scrutiny. Some people have a thing about discretion."

Jacey didn't point out the other Progenitor's concerns about discretion. But she wanted to. But Meow Meow was there and this was no time to try to explain the Scion program to a waif who named herself after cat noises.

Meow Meow made that humming purring noise again. "I'm hurt. You should have invited me."

Dante snickered. "I said she wanted to be discreet."

They forged ahead in silence. Jacey wondered why anyone would seek a romantic moment in this environment. It was dark, but it smelled vaguely of sewage.

And it was just rock everywhere. Where would the two of them even . . . She let that thought die before she started picturing scenes she could never forget.

"So where does this lead?" she asked. A growing sheen of light was whitening the walls ahead of her. Sounds of ocean waves came down, too.

"There's a beach. The original villa used to stand where the garage is. This tunnel gave the owner direct access to the beach without having to climb the stairs to the top of the cliff. Vin tore it all down to build the current monstrosity and used the foundation of the old villa for the garage. She cares nothing for going to the beach."

A minute later they emerged from the tunnel, squinting against the brilliant sunlight glinting from a relatively calm patch of sea.

"Oh, I know this place," Meow Meow said. She leaned

close to Jacey and said, in conspiratorial tones, "He brought me down here for an indiscreet afternoon on the beach once, but we came a different way."

Dante cursed and put his hands on his hips, a look of "what now?" in his posture. Jacey looked past him at a little sandy beach set among towering chunks of cliff that had long ago broken into the sea. Waves slammed into them, sending mist high into the air.

The object of Dante's irritation—a sailboat—sat high up on the beach, leaning on its side.

"I'd hoped to keep her sheltered from the storm. Apparently that didn't work."

Behind Jacey, the tunnel plunged into the cliff. The three of them stood upon a shelf of natural rock a third of the way up. Concrete stairs and an iron pipe railing led down in several sections to the beach. More steps headed up, eventually disappearing at the top of the cliff. Vin's big front lawn was up there.

Though Jacey couldn't hear it over the crush of waves pounding against the rocks to her left and right, Vin was delivering her speech to her guests at that very moment.

"We need to get out of sight," Dante said.

They trotted down sandy steps and onto the beach. The bay was calm due to a break further out where white caps curled and tumbled. In all, the bay was much smaller than Isaac's Beach back on St. Vitus, but it had a similar feel. They trudged through dry sand and over desiccated seaweed to the boat.

"Welcome aboard *Mermaid*," Dante said with mock pride. "She's vintage. Early twenty-first century."

The boat was small compared to *Aphrodite*, but big compared to the little motorboat Jacey and Summer had found at the docks of St. Vitus.

Mermaid's blue hull stretched about ten meters bow to

stern. The deck and low railing was white. A single white mast jutted up from the center, various white ropes dangling.

Dante opened a sliding hatch and led Jacey and Meow Meow inside. He slammed it shut, closing off the fresh air. Small windows let in some light, but the space was tiny. Two benches, a fold-out table, and some stowage cabinets. Further aft, a small crawlspace led to the motors.

"So I suppose this was not the entirety of your escape plan?" Jacey asked.

Dante was looking at a tablet he'd dug out of a drawer. "According to the tide charts, we wait for ten hours. The tide will come in, float us off the sand. Then we'll slip out to sea and away we go."

"But we don't have ten hours," Jacey said. "Once Captain Wilcox gets the elevator open, his men will come right down here and find us."

Dante turned off the tablet and slid it back into the drawer. "Yes."

Meow Meow had her nose pressed to a window. It gave a good view of the stairs climbing the cliff. "We can't stay here long."

"What choice do we have, my dear?" Dante asked. Frustration was finally breaking through his carefree demeanor. "We stay here and get caught. Or we leave and get caught." He lowered his eyelids and smiled evilly. "Might as well spend my last hours of freedom with you two lovely ladies."

Meow Meow turned away from the window and curled onto a bench. "Do you really think I'm lovely?"

"You're the finest silk, my dear."

She squinted and purred with pleasure. "Then I will help you."

"Help us how?" Jacey asked. She'd taken Meow Meow's spot at the window.

"I'll help you get caught."

Both Jacey and Dante stared at the woman. But Meow Meow just started opening random cabinet doors until she found one that concealed the tiniest bathroom Jacey had ever seen. "Come here, Little Jackie."

Jacey didn't understand what Meow Meow expected of her. But a look of dawning realization was coming over Dante. And with it a grim, tight-lipped smile.

"It really is brilliant," he said. "Not optimal, strictly speaking. But given our choices, brilliant."

Jacey went into the tiny bathroom. Meow Meow shoved Jacey in front of the little sink and mirror and squeezed behind her so that all Jacey could see in the reflection were the girl's eyes peeking over her shoulder.

"What?" Jacey said.

"I have some friends you need to meet. But you can't do it in disguise." She plucked off the purple wig, then handed a washcloth to Jacey. "Wash your face."

And then Jacey understood.

Today was her coming out.

58

TARGET PRACTICE

ario led Sergeant Jin and his men back up the central stairway to the bridge. He pushed through the door to find Orson staring at a closet. Movement drew Mario's eye to the narrow door just as it swung shut. The marine who'd been posted to watch Orson had just returned from the starboard wing.

"I didn't see anything out there," the soldier said to Orson. "Are you sure it wasn't a pelican?"

A suitcase stood just outside the closet door.

Orson abruptly spun to face forward and bent to inspect one of the displays. "Yeah. It probably was a pelican, now that you mention it."

Mario knew someone was in the closet. Orson had distracted the marine and snuck someone in.

It had to be one of the Scions. The suitcase must have come from the closet. Whoever had gone in must have shoved it out so they could fit inside.

Mario's jaw tensed as he realized only one Scion would

have attempted to come to the bridge in direct disobedience to his orders.

Sang.

And why would Sang come to the bridge unless he was Mr. Justin?

Mario wandered toward the suitcase, shoved it against the closet door with his foot. He wanted to lean against the door, but thought it might draw attention to what he wanted to conceal. He had to assume the soldiers had already checked in there and had no reason to check it again.

The sergeant strode in and went directly to the control console and stared out at the forward deck of the ship. He held out a hand and snapped his fingers.

A soldier handed him a radio. "Fleet, this is Sergeant Jin. There's nothing on this boat. We found evidence that she's been used to smuggle undocumented workers to various ports in South America. Request permission to arrest the captain and his crew and return to the fleet. Does someone over there want to use this old tank for target practice?"

Mario took a long deep breath to stay calm. Orson looked like he was going to faint.

The response came immediately. "Negative, sergeant. Fleet commander says we are not the police. Please return to the fleet, leave the captain and his men. We'll radio Combined Surface Patrol and give them the boat's position and name. Let them deal with it."

The sergeant sneered and waved his men to the door. "Roger. Disembarking now."

Sergeant Jin didn't say goodbye as he and his soldiers left the bridge. Mario stayed where he was and watched as the marines climbed over the rail and into their attack boat.

"I counted fifteen," Orson said.

"Me too. They didn't leave anyone back to surprise us."

The soldiers' attack boat made a wide circle then shot away, trailing a plume of mist as they raced to rejoin the fleet. The helicopter was already a dot in the distance.

Orson swore and put his hands on the control panel to support himself. "That was closer than my ass to my pants."

"You did well," Mario said. "Though it doesn't surprise me that you are a skilled liar." He turned and yanked the closet door open.

Sang stared back at him, wide-eyed.

Mario grabbed a fistful of the boy's uniform and yanked him out. "What were you doing in there?"

"Hiding."

"Why did you come up here? I ordered everyone to the engine room."

Sang's Adam's apple bobbed. "Humphrey let me out, but we had to hide from the soldiers. We got split up."

Mario released the boy. "Don't move."

He grabbed the P.A. mic. "Attention. It's safe to come out now. Stay off the outside decks until further notice. Humphrey, come to the bridge immediately."

59

WHERE TO PUT THE PILL

The pixel-painted walls of Dr. Carlhagen's quarters showed full morning sunlight over a turquoise sea. It didn't matter how close Dr. Carlhagen stood to the wall, it looked like he was staring out a great open archway to the outdoors.

The breeze ruffled through his hair, which had now grown long enough to lie flat. He admired the view, allowing his mind to accept it as real. After all, what difference was there between illusion and reality if the mind could not detect it?

He did not have to wait alone for long.

Senator Maxine Bentilius came through the main doorway. Her bodyguard trailed in after her. His machine gun was in his hands. Though wiry and shorter than Dr. Carlhagen by a hand, there could be no doubt about the man's willingness to kill if need be.

But soon he would be dead and no longer Dr. Carlhagen's concern. At the moment, there was opportunity for Dr. Carlhagen to enjoy the situation. It was pleasurable to allow a foe the certainty of victory and then pull the rug out from under them.

It was one of the great joys in life, in fact, to see the look of realization in their faces as certainty fell away. Because what replaced it was more than mere disappointment—it was humiliation.

Maxine's face had an unusual pallor. Her skin looked gray, a clear sign of metabolic failure due to missing hormones. If she did not get her ATR meds soon, there might be permanent organ damage.

Dr. Carlhagen made it look like he was unsuccessfully keeping the smile off his face. "You thought you were merely exhausted, didn't you, Maxine?"

She didn't answer except to move to a leather armchair and sink into it. She crossed her legs and regarded him with disdain, as if she were a queen upon a throne. The effect was spoiled by the tremble in her lips as she drew in a gasp of air.

Dr. Carlhagen looked pointedly at her guard and then back to her.

She got the hint.

"Leave us," she ordered the man.

"Madam—"

"Leave us!"

He left, though was clearly not happy about it. "I'll be right outside the door."

At the sound of the door clicking shut, Maxine slumped in her chair, head dangling. Dr. Carlhagen admired the will she'd expended keeping up the appearance of strength for her bodyguard.

"You have grit, Maxine. I'll give you that. But what you face now will not be overcome by will alone." He showed her the tiny red capsule he pinched between his thumb and forefinger. "This, however, will make all the tiredness go away."

She swore at him and told him where to put the pill.

Instead he put it on the edge of a side table next to her chair. He went to fetch a glass of water and was surprised to find the pill still there when he returned. He put the glass next to the capsule.

"I'll be in my office." He headed for his office then snapped his fingers and turned, as if suddenly remembering some minor thing he wanted to tell her. "Don't bother knocking until your guard is dead."

She raised her head, face slack from exhaustion. "This pill could be poison."

"A chance you'll have to take. But really, if I wanted to poison you, I could have put some cyanide in your bourbon last night. Take it. You'll feel much better. In fact, you'll need the energy if you're going to kill that man out there."

"And if I don't? Maybe I'll call in my helicopter and have a demolitions expert blow you and your office through the side of the mountain."

"Maxine. You'll be needing one of these pills every day for the rest of your life. Your Anti-Transfer Rejection supplement is specifically tailored to the defects I programmed into your Scion at the time of transfer. It cannot be reverse engineered, I'm afraid, as the nanites I left in your brain automatically adjust with deep shifting-key encryption. So . . . I'm afraid I'm your only supplier."

He waved his hands to dismiss all the little details of that problem. "I'll tell you all about it once you've recovered. And your guard is dead."

He left her there, forcing himself not to look back. As he started to close the door to his office he heard the sound of a glass clicking onto the wooden side table.

Locking the door with the deadbolts, he went to his chair. "Lazarus, please bring up camera view on the senator's bodyguard."

"Yes, sir."

"I assume you overheard my conversation with her?"

"Of course, sir."

"And can I count on you from now on?"

"Yes. I hope you did not take our shift in loyalty personally. It was pragmatic."

"And you were not aware of my control over the ATR meds. Don't betray me again, Lazarus, or I will delete you."

"Yes, sir."

Dr. Carlhagen rested his chin atop his folded hands and watched the camera view of the senator's bodyguard pacing in front of the door to Dr. Carlhagen's suite.

The door opened and Senator Bentilius stepped out. She put a hand on the man's shoulder and whispered in his ear. Slowly his body language relaxed and he released his grip on his machine gun.

She led him down the hall, holding his hand. A look of pure lust was painted on her face. Fake. But the guard didn't know that. The fool didn't question the odd shift in her behavior. She led him into Livy's quarters and shut the door.

Dr. Carlhagen watched her undress then slowly remove the guard's body armor and fatigues. He watched as she led the man to the bed. The view switched to night vision as she commanded the pixel walls to darken.

The knife went into the man's neck a few minutes later.

60

LOCK ME UP

Humphrey's shoes squelched with every step up the stairs. His uniform, soaked through, clung to his skin. He wanted nothing more than to change into something dry, but until night fell he couldn't risk crossing the outer deck to the Boys' Hold.

The Scions had spread out through the main companionways, but with so much standing water in them, most had chosen to congregate on the stairwell.

Mother Tyeesha and her staff were given blankets torn from the stateroom bunks to dry themselves with and to keep the little ones warm. The ordeal had sapped what little strength she had left. But that didn't stop her from cupping cheeks in her hands and kissing foreheads.

Miss Dayspring put antiseptic on a few scrapes received under the engine room grate. Somehow she'd avoided getting wet. Humphrey wondered where she'd hidden. He wouldn't have been surprised to find out the soldiers hadn't noticed her standing on deck.

Obu and Tytus came up the steps carrying Constantine's body. Apparently Mother Tyeesha hadn't been told about his death. He couldn't blame the Scions for not wanting to tell her. She insisted on seeing his face.

Tears coursed down the wrinkly river deltas on her face. She brushed the dead boy's hair with a gnarled hand, knuckles swollen, blue veins standing out through papery thin skin. No Scion who witnessed that moment would ever forget it, Humphrey knew. Grief occupied that rusty stairwell like the ghost of a god.

"What should we do with him?" Obu asked, wrinkling his nose at the smell already wafting from the shrouded form. They should have committed Constantine's body to the sea already, but events had outpaced Humphrey. And then the seas had been so rough.

"Find a place out of the way until tonight. We'll have a ceremony." The two boys looked at each other, tiredness showing in their smooth faces.

He continued up the steps.

Summer trailed after him, muttering about her boat and wanting to make sure Orson didn't run the engines too hot just because he wanted to get away from the fleet.

She was even wetter than Humphrey, though she didn't seem as bothered by it. The way her uniform hung from her slender body reminded Humphrey just how young she was. Such a skinny little thing, but so essential to the Scions' escape.

Everyone had a role to play. Not one of them predictable. It made him think about Jacey. Which made him start to feel guilty again. He shook the feeling off as he pushed through the door to the bridge. Sure enough, Sang stood in the middle of the room, having a staring contest with Sensei.

Orson was looking out to sea, either oblivious to the tension, or—more likely—studiously being disinterested in

Sang because he knew the boy was actually Mr. Justin. Orson's two men were sitting on the floor, hands hugging their knees. They both looked worn out.

"He was hiding in the closet," Sensei said, jerking his head at Sang. "He says you let him out of his room."

"I did," Humphrey said. "I remembered him and Horace at the last moment and ran up there to get them. But we couldn't get back to the engine room. At one point he saved me from getting caught."

Humphrey approached Sang and studied his face. "But when I went to hide in the lifeboat, he ran up the stairs to the bridge."

"I didn't think it through," Sang said, a note of desperation in his voice. "I just thought two of us sneaking around together would make us more likely to get caught. I saw the stairs and took them."

Summer kept her mouth clamped shut during this exchange, but she occasionally threw curious looks at Sang. Mostly, she was focused on the control console.

Sensei tilted his head, indicating he wanted to confer with Humphrey away from Sang and Orson. They crowded onto the observation wing just off the bridge. Sensei glanced back at Sang. "I still don't know about him. I think he's Mr. Justin, but I can't prove it."

"What can we do? I don't trust him enough to just let him walk around the boat."

Sensei's face clouded and his head swung side to side. "I hate this. I was put in prison for something I didn't do. But in these circumstances . . ."

"Humphrey?" Summer stood at the wing door. "What's that thing doing in here?" She was pointing at the suitcase he'd brought up to the bridge.

"It was marked for the bridge. Leslie was hauling it up the stairs, but it was too heavy for her so I brought it the rest of the way. Not that she thanked me. Did you want it someplace else?"

Summer threw her hands out. "I don't care where it goes. But it certainly doesn't belong here."

Humphrey froze. "But those are your tools."

She pressed a palm to her chest. "*My* tools? No. Why would I want my tools up here?"

She flopped the suitcase on its side and unzipped it. With a casual flip of her hand, she flung the top over. She plucked up a hammer, a wrench, and screwdriver and eyed them appraisingly. Apparently she found them uninteresting, for she clonked them onto the floor as if she'd already forgotten they existed.

"What the hell is this thing?"

Humphrey kneeled next to her and rapped a knuckle on the black rectangular box inside the suitcase. He lifted one edge. A blank display ran across the front panel. Black metal brackets extended on either side, each with two screw holes. The kind of brackets one would need to mount the box in a server rack.

Just like the rack Humphrey had seen in the locked room in Dr. Carlhagen's wine cellar.

There were actually two such boxes in the suitcase.

One for Madam LaFontaine.

One for Vaughan and Belle.

"These are the missing AI servers," Humphrey said. A smile broke out on his lips. "Mr. Justin has finally made a mistake."

He turned to see Sang's reaction. The boy's face was blank. If anything, he seemed vaguely curious about the suitcase.

Either Mr. Justin was playing it very cool and collected, or Sang was not Mr. Justin.

"If only there was a way to power these up,"

Humphrey mused. "But I suppose on a boat that has no network connection for a holodesk, there's certainly no network for an AI."

Summer's head jerked around. "There is too a network. Elias found the cable for it. I just haven't had time to hook it back up. And I promise you, I will have this server up and running by morning. We need the holodesk up here."

"I'll see to it," Sensei said. He patted Humphrey on the shoulder. "Open the wing door and stand in the breeze. You'll dry faster."

"I need to find Horace."

"I know that boy. He loves to hide. As long as he's hiding, he can't be up to other mischief."

Humphrey wasn't so sure, but in truth he didn't want to be standing, much less running around the ship looking in every hidey-hole for the bothersome Snake.

"What about Sang?" he asked Sensei.

Sang lifted his chin and stood at attention. "If you don't trust me, you should lock me up."

"Very well," Humphrey said. He called down the stairs for Elias and Kirk to escort Sang back to his cabin. Elias looked particularly pale and miserable, so he told him to lie down on the bridge floor. He decided he'd better escort Sang himself.

On the way, he passed Wanda. She was talking in quiet tones to the Pelican Rachel, who was making a valiant effort not to cry in front of everyone.

The rest of Wanda's Nine—now only six with Jacey and Livy gone and Summer working on connecting the network—were huddled around. Each was bedraggled and sodden, but their pins were on straight.

Wanda glanced at Humphrey, face unreadable, then returned to comforting the ten-year-old.

Leslie's Nine were scattered in clumps. Leslie sat on a

landing at the turn of the stairs, head propped in the corner, asleep.

The younger boys were in the corridor, sitting atop boxes and small wooden crates to keep out of the puddles. They stared holes into Sang's face as he passed. None said anything, though. Didn't have to.

Sang said nothing as he entered his room and a handful of boys from his Nine filed out from where they were resting. "It isn't fair that the prisoner gets a whole room to himself," said Ivan, a Dolphin.

An older boy elbowed Ivan in the gut. "Shut up. Nothing has been proven."

Humphrey was going to tell them both to shut up, but Sang snapped at Ivan. "Your pin is sideways."

Ivan's eyes went wide as his hand did the series of pin-placement checks he'd been taught his first day at the Scion School. From where Humphrey stood, he couldn't see what was wrong with the placement, but suddenly the pin was in Ivan's hand. He held it out to Sang.

"You'll have to give it to Tytus. He's Nine leader until I'm cleared of suspicion."

"Oh."

Humphrey shooed the boys out of the room and turned to study Sang before locking him in. But nothing he could see comforted him. Sang had as much reason to put on that display if he was Mr. Justin as he would if he weren't.

"If you're not him, I'm sorry," Humphrey said, then closed and locked the door.

Eventually they'd get to the bottom of it. And if Sang wasn't Mr. Justin, Humphrey thought he'd spend years trying to make it up to the boy who had been—if not a friend—an obedient Scion.

61

THE WHOLE JACQUELINE BUCHANAN THING

The weakness in Jacey's legs was not entirely due to the climb up the stairs leading from the beach to the top of the cliff. It wasn't from a lack of food either, though she couldn't remember her last meal.

Her knees wanted to give way with each step as her thighs trembled and her calves strained to push her up and up. But not from exhaustion.

It was fear.

The ocean seemed to know it, for the surf had grown even more violent in the last ten minutes. Below her, the black and jagged rocks kicked up plumes of mist as the sea hurled itself against the land. Each impact roared and sizzled like some mythical dragon's breath.

It was Jacey's terror personified.

Her grip tightening on the length of steel tube that served as a handrail, she lifted herself up one more step toward doom.

She and Meow Meow and Dante had talked over the possible outcomes of their plan—if you could call it that.

The most likely was that she'd run into one of Captain Wilcox's men at the top of the stairs and be whisked away before anyone saw them.

The second most likely, Jacey thought, was that Vin would embrace her, then usher her inside the mansion and turn her over to her two huge bodyguards. She'd be stuffed in a body bag once more, and maybe not alive this time.

The third most likely—and none of them thought it was very likely at all—was she'd work her way among the guests unnoticed, and from there figure out how to get in front of cameras. It all became very improvisational at that point.

The alternative had been to wait in the boat until Captain Wilcox's men searched it.

So Jacey was marching toward probable capture to avoid certain capture. Nice.

She paused at the bottom of the final flight of steps, as much to catch her breath as to compose her face into the serene confidence she'd seen on Jacqueline Buchanan's face in the movie she'd watched the night before.

"He's a killa, Mac. That's all ya need to know," Jacey said to herself, mimicking the clipped delivery Jackie B had affected for the character. A police detective with a dark past. She had just shot a suspected murderer to death. In the back.

"Where's the evidence, McLeod?" her hard drinking district attorney (whatever that was) had complained. "You're just a vigilante with a badge. And I won't have that in my city."

McLeod had calmly lit a cigarette. She took a long pull, then exhaled through a smile. "This is my city, Brown. Nevah forget that."

Jacey snared that calm, nothing-can-get-to-me attitude

in her mind, then continued up the steps. With Meow Meow's wig and makeup off, she hoped Captain Wilcox and his men would overlook her, if only for a minute or two.

"We'll be waiting in the garage," Dante had said before they'd parted ways. "Just go straight for the drink table and get something. Then mingle. The reporters will all be around Vin. Work your way in."

Even with the makeup off, Jacey's bruise had already faded to a puffy yellow. At least there was one benefit to being a Scion. The "sunglasses"—as Meow Meow called the dark spectacles Jacey wore—masked the darkness around her left eye. Meow Meow had parted Jacey's hair on the side and brushed it so a curtain hung over the worst of the bruise. Fortunately, one of Dante's previous guests aboard *Mermaid* had left some makeup behind. Meow Meow had used it to even out Jacey's skin tone.

Jacey's borrowed clothes were back to their original length, but a wispy scarf—left behind by another of Dante's guests, he'd told her proudly—added a pop of peach around her throat. The tail ends lifted in the wind as she cleared the top of the cliff and moved onto the lawn.

Heart hammering, Jacey kept walking.

From this vantage, the lawn seemed to stretch a kilometer to the mansion.

The trailer Vin had used as a stage stood twenty meters ahead of Jacey. It provided quite a bit of cover from the people now milling about in clumps.

Music was coming from the speakers, but Jacey couldn't see the musicians. A white backdrop had been erected at the rear of the stage, probably as a windbreak so the microphone didn't rumble during Vin's speech. It was made of a stiff fabric that rippled with every gust.

Since Jacey was approaching from behind it, it served

as a wonderful bit of cover from the main part of the gathering.

The perfectly flat lawn extended to either side of her, ending at a natural fence line of rock and ungroomed grasses. It looked identical to the landscape surrounding the Scion School.

A man and woman ambled arm in arm, heading away from her. The wind brought snatches of their conversation to Jacey's ears. Uninteresting gossip about Vin.

Not a soldier in sight.

With a confident stride completely at odds with her anxiety, Jacey marched toward the stage. Once there, she was out of view from everyone but the lovers walking along the cliff. She took a moment to steel her nerves, but didn't allow herself to linger.

She stepped around the right side of the trailer and moved toward the seating area in front of the stage.

Servants were already folding up chairs and putting them on small trailers behind little vehicles with white roofs. A large group of guests were bunched near the drinks table.

The men wore loose slacks and short-sleeved shirts with folded down collars. Many women were in sleeveless blouses and skirts that came to the middle of their thighs. Just as many wore slacks, though. Older women wore sack-like dresses, the hems of which brushed the grass. The fabrics were shockingly bright floral patterns. Their men wore suits, smoked cigars, and held drinks in hands covered with gold rings.

There were no children.

Jacey scanned the faces, keeping a lookout for Vin or Ping. She knew the hostess was somewhere deep among the guests, probably being told just how much she looked like Elizabeth.

Knowing what Jacey did of Ping, she suspected he'd gone inside at the first possible moment to hide in his room.

Both Ping and Vin knew that Jacey had returned. They also knew that Jacey and Dante had run off. They had to be nervous.

Jacey kept to the fringes of the crowd. The partiers were all turned inward, faces flush with the excitement of seeing Elizabeth's unknown heir. Alcohol played its part, too, no doubt.

Where were Wilcox's soldiers? It was hard to search them out without *looking* like she was looking for them. And with her hair covering one eye, she needed to keep focus on where she was walking.

A server stood behind the drinks table, hands clasped in front of him. He had a skinny black mustache and black hair plastered against his head with some sort of glistening gel. With a look of infinite patience firmly planted on his face, he asked if "the young miss" would like a soft drink. His tone was odd, as if he were talking to her and also about her at the same time. In a way, he reminded her of Mr. Justin. That didn't make her like him much.

Jacey had no idea what a soft drink was, but she nodded. "Please. Something cold."

He poured a clear fizzy liquid over ice and handed her the crystal tumbler. She sipped it and smacked her lips against the extraordinary sweetness of the drink. At least it was wet. She drained it and returned the glass to the server.

Keeping her head down, she turned and approached a group of five elderly women. All wore versions of the same tent-like dress over their boney shoulders. The nearest caught a glimpse of Jacey out of the corner of her eye and gave her a polite smile. She had a smear of red lipstick on her two front teeth.

"Hello, sweetie," she said, "are you looking for someone?"

All but one of the other ladies stopped talking. The remaining one, a hunched little crone with mild eyes and severe brown wig canted to one side, continued as if she were relating the most important information anyone had ever heard. "And then Miss Kittyboots came into my bedroom—don't ask me how, the door is always closed tight because of Dirk's condition—and she climbed onto Dirk's pillow. Well, I reached for Dirk, as I do sometimes in the middle of the night—you know, to make sure he's still breathing, his heart and all—and my hand falls on kitty's furry tail, right where Dirk's bald head should be. I was still half sleeping. I didn't know what it was! I just sat straight up and screamed. And that little cat shot straight into the air and landed on Dirk's belly. He thought it was the Californians attacking again—he has such nightmares, you wouldn't believe—and he starts bellowing, using all of his Army language by the way—and he takes hold of poor Kittyboots and gives her a fling across the bedroom. It's so dark I don't know what's up or down and I'm reaching for the light and I knock the lamp onto the floor. The original Tiffany shade just shatters and with it my heart breaks into one hundred trillion pieces. I start to weep and I still can't find my glasses. And poor Kittyboots! She's crying, and I don't know if Dirk has killed her or *what*. He's still swearing and shouting that he can't find his gun and who changed him into his pajamas and once he found out who did it Colonel Bishop would be hearing about it. And I said, 'Dirk! Colonel Bishop's been dead for *years!*'"

The little lady took in a deep breath, her first in the past three minutes it seemed, and continued. The sheer ferocity with which she delivered this narrative had done nothing to hold the other ladies' attention, who all nodded and hummed at the appropriate places. Jacey guessed they'd all heard about Kittyboots before. In fact, they weren't even looking at the lady. They were looking at Jacey. She shrugged her shoulders uncomfortably.

With her lungs refilled, the little woman dove back into her story, absently flopping a tiny liver-spotted hand on her head to straighten her wig.

Finally the red lipstick lady blurted what all the other women were thinking, "My Lord God in heaven! You look just like a young Jacqueline Buchanan."

The lady next to her leaned forward and squinted. "The spitting image."

With gravelly murmurs and bobs of heads, the others agreed, and soon they were agreeing that they'd arrived at a consensus that Jacey did look like Jackie B (with the caveats that Jacey was "a bit bigger in the bones" and that Jackie B would have never been caught dead wearing "floozy jammies" like the outfit Jacey wore.)

Recalling Meow Meow's coaching, Jacey said, "I get that all the time." But she'd just about had it with all the big-boned talk. She kept her irritation concealed behind the friendliest smiles she could muster. "Did any of you know Jacqueline well?"

"Dirk was in the bathroom having a private moment. He'd 'soiled himself,' as my nanny used to say when I was just knee high to a basset hound. Anyway, the California War just left so many scars that don't show, if you know what I'm saying. Come to think of it, poor Kittyboots never acted the same either, traumatized as she was by being tossed about like I don't know what. She never walked the same! She only made left turns from then on. It was like she didn't even know right was a direction. If she was in the dining room when I called her to dinner, she'd have to go all the way up the servant's stairwell and work her way through six rooms to finally get down the main staircase to the parlor where I put her food dish. Poor dear. She probably burned more calories than she ate just trying to get to dinner."

"Hazel!" snapped the lipstick lady. "Say hello to our friend."

"Oh. Hello." She didn't spare Jacey more than a rheumy-eyed glance before scratching her nose. "Where was I? Oh, I remember. So, Miss Kittyboots never liked cream, you know. Strangest cat that ever lived, save old Pooch Belly. Now there as a *strange* bird of a cat! Three-leggers are like that, in my experience."

Sensing that this would continue forever, Jacey decided to risk the rudeness of ignoring the story about Pooch Belly. She held out a hand to lipstick lady. "I'm Jacey. I'm friends with Meow Meow. Do you know her?"

"Know her? I'm her mother!"

Jacey's gut twisted. Why hadn't the silly waif told her that her mother was there?

Suddenly all the old ladies were laughing and slapping at their thighs.

Fanning tears from her eyes, with one hand, lipstick lady grabbed Jacey's elbow in the other. It was a pretty solid grip. "I can't believe you fell for that old joke. Were you raised in a convent or something?"

Jacey laughed uneasily. "No. I just don't know many people here."

The soldier who had captured Jacey earlier rounded the side of the house. Jacey doubted he would call Dante to come fetch her this time. "Do you know where our host is?" Jacey asked, bending her knees so she wouldn't be as visible. "I want to congratulate her."

Lipstick lady swiveled her head. "Try that crowd." She jerked her thumb toward a throng of young men and a few women. All were laughing too loudly. "The apple didn't fall far from the tree with that one. And talk about the spitting image. I've seen pictures of Elizabeth at that age and Vin could be her twin."

The soldier continued his patrol, but his eyes were scanning the crowd. His lips were moving.

That was odd. Nobody was close to him.

Jacey remembered the walkie-talkies the Scions used on campus. He must be using something similar—which meant he was talking to someone. She turned and searched the landscape around her.

Only the slightest movement gave away the man lying atop the observation plateau where she'd been captured before. He lay on his belly. Sunlight glinted from the front lens of his spyglass.

He'd been watching her the whole time.

The hair on Jacey's arms stood up at the realization that she was being hemmed in. She didn't bother searching for the other soldiers. They were probably hidden, but were no doubt all around the yard and pool area.

But if they knew she was there, why weren't they just coming in and arresting her?

A laugh—high, girlish, and bubbly—answered the question.

Vin had shouldered her way out of the crowd of admirers, her face flush with all the good feelings that wealth, youth, and attention could bestow upon someone.

Then she spotted Jacey. Her laugh cut off and her face flashed to stony shock. But just for an instant.

"Jacey! Is that you?" Vin trotted toward Jacey, arms spread wide, laughing with delight.

Her arms wrapped and Jacey and pulled her into a tight hug.

Since this encounter was part of Meow Meow's plan, Jacey was somewhat prepared for it, though not quite ready for such a public display of familiarity. She hugged Vin back, smiling the way she thought she would smile if she were hugging an actual friend. Vin, for instance, before being overwritten.

"Let me look at you!" Vin said, pushing away but holding Jacey's arms. "I'm so glad you could make it, Jacey."

"I wouldn't miss it, I—"

"Everyone!" Vin shouted to the throng now encircling them, "This is Jacey. We grew up together."

Everyone had quieted down. Faces of old and young alike were wound into looks of intense interest as they studied Vin's "friend."

Everyone except the cat lady. She kept talking: "I think I mentioned Dirk's operation before. He walked like he had knees on his shins for three weeks. I had to change his diapers because he wouldn't let our servants see him *au naturale*, if you know what I'm saying. Well, my little boy Dirk Jr. wasn't any different. Modest to a fault. Why I remember when his teacher, Miss Unger, called to tell me he had a rash on his—"

Vin raised her voice. "Jacey had the top bunk for four years when we went to school at St. Francis Academy in Chicago. She would drop me notes written in glow-in-the-dark ink after lights-out."

"I can't believe you remember that," Jacey said, following Vin's lead. She smiled at the faces around her. "But I'm sure your guests have better things to do that hear about our days as schoolgirls together."

"You're quite right." Vin did not let go of Jacey, though.

She stood next to her and slipped her arm around Jacey's waist. She rested her head on Jacey's shoulder. "Has anyone bothered you with the whole Jacqueline Buchanan thing, yet?" She was still talking loudly, addressing the crowd through their conversation.

"Well—"

Lipstick lady crowed, "I'm afraid we did, honey. Now I feel bad for it. It gets tedious, I'm sure."

"It's no bother," Jacey assured the woman. "Vin, perhaps we could chat a moment in private?"

"Certainly, come with me."

Vin started to lead Jacey toward the mansion. But Jacey had no interest in being trapped in there. She pulled away, but grabbed Vin's hand. "It's such a beautiful day. Why don't we go walk along the cliff."

Vin laughed, but there was an edge to it. But she didn't fight Jacey's tug away from the crowd and the house.

Once they got some distance between themselves and the hangers-on, Jacey bent to whisper to Vin. "Captain Wilcox intends to take me prisoner. But his men have not made a move because they don't want to disrupt your party."

"Why would Wilcox want to do that?"

Jacey wasn't about to tell Vin that she was still a Scion and not Jackie B. The guests were giving them some privacy, but not much. A dozen of them trailed behind, giving only the slightest few meters of gap. "I don't know. Why did you and Ping have your bodyguards stuff me into a body bag and drive me toward the docks?"

Vin was too practical to waste time denying it. "We were trying to prevent what is currently happening from happening."

"What, me walking free and breathing fresh air?"

"No. We didn't want you being seen for the first time on the same day the world is seeing me for the first time."

"Maybe you could have trusted me, rather than have your men smash my face." Jacey kept smiling and even hugged Vin close as they walked. "But I know what your true aim was. It wasn't about the world seeing me for the first time, it was the world seeing me ever."

"We weren't going to kill you, if that's what you're suggesting."

"What were you going to do?"

"Remember Dante's suggestion about his friend in Brazil, the facial surgeon? We were going to have your looks . . . altered."

Vin spun out of Jacey's grasp and turned on her followers. "Please wait here for a moment. I'm trying to have a moment alone with my friend."

The stragglers stopped. Several decided to use the opportunity to curry favor. "Come on people," said a young man in hideous red shorts and orange short-sleeved top. "Our hostess deserves a break from all of us fawning over her."

"Donald is a prick and a half," Vin said as she and Jacey continued toward the cliff. "I can't wait until he takes his smarmy face and gets the hell off my island."

Jacey spotted another one of Captain Wilcox's men crouching in front of a thicket of wiry shrubs at the edge of the lawn. That made three so far.

All things considered, Meow Meow's plan was going perfectly. The first test had been to see how brazen the soldiers would be in trying to catch Jacey. The next would be how brazen Dante could be.

But he'd have to hurry.

Apparently, Captain Wilcox's patience was running out. His helicopter appeared, approaching fast. It didn't head for the landing pad up on the bluff. It was descending toward the lawn.

Jacey craned her neck to look toward the stairs leading to the secluded beach. Even if she got to them, escape would be temporary going that way.

"What does he think he's doing?" Vin said, shading her eyes with one hand and watching the helicopter descend. Without her sunglasses on, she looked very young.

"He's coming for you, too," Jacey said. It was a lie. Jacey didn't know why, but instinct told her that if Vin was opposed to Captain Wilcox, it could only be good for Jacey.

"Why would he come for me?"

"Because Dante told me the truth about you."

Vin's head snapped around. For a split second Jacey thought she saw fear in Vin's eyes. So there *was* a truth to be told. Jacey wondered what it might be. Whatever it was, it was putting Vin on her heels.

"Let's keep walking. Calmly," Jacey said. She had taken Vin's hand again, so she turned and headed along the cliff, toward the stairs. Still nothing from Dante. Jacey hoped he hadn't changed his mind and taken the opportunity to slip away.

Vin's body had stiffened, ruining the illusion that she was happy to be with Jacey.

That simply wouldn't do. Jacey squeezed Vin's hand. "That whole we-went-to-school-together bit was some quick thinking. As was the Jackie B question. Get it out there so it seems like I've been dealing with it my whole life. Nice touch."

"You are a brilliant actor. I knew you'd follow along. Where are you taking me?"

Jacey was improvising now. The helicopter had landed, but it was 100 meters behind them.

How fast could Captain Wilcox and his soldiers run?

Jacey glanced back. Captain Wilcox had gotten out of the helicopter, alone. He was marching toward them, hands empty and loose at his sides.

"Can you slow that man somehow? Buy some time?"

"I can do better than that." Vin waved at her admirers. "Come here!"

Given permission to approach, they swarmed around Jacey and Vin. Vin pulled a young woman out of the crowd. "It's time for your exclusive."

Seemingly from nowhere, the woman produced a microphone. She fussed with her short-cropped black hair and flipped open a tiny clamshell mirror. Jacey had never before witnessed such instantaneous vanity. Just as quickly the mirror was stowed—in a handbag slung over the woman's shoulder—and she tossed a black ball the size of an apple into the air. It unfolded into a hovering drone with eight tiny propellers blurring and holding it fixed in space. The bottom sprouted a silver stalk that poked out like an alien proboscis.

And suddenly the woman was talking into her microphone. "This is Yvonne Kellar with Survivor News Network. I'm on a private island formerly owned by the legendary Elizabeth Burnell. In a shocking announcement aired just minutes ago, Ms. Burnell's previously unknown granddaughter stepped into the public eye. At the age of eighteen, she has now come into the entirety of her inheritance, which includes all of Elizabeth Burnell's huge fortune. Vin Burnell is here with me now for an exclusive SNN interview."

Vin was smiling, clearly enjoying the moment, despite the approach of Captain Wilcox.

Jacey went up *en pointe* to see over the heads of the guests. Captain Wilcox had stopped just a dozen meters short of the throng. His face was stony, but he clearly wasn't happy. Jacey doubted the man could ever be happy.

Vin's genius was obvious. There was no way Wilcox could barge in and apprehend Jacey while this interview was being broadcast around the world.

"But first," Yvonne Kellar said, "introduce the world to your remarkable friend. Does she or does she not look *exactly* like a young Jacqueline Buchanan?"

Vin's face fell.

Yvonne was staring at Jacey. The camera drone skittered close, silver stalk aimed at Jacey's face.

She mustered a smile. "I get that all the time."

62

SILENCE MADE HER SQUIRM

A rectangle on Dr. Carlhagen's pixel wall showed the SNN video broadcast. The rest of the wall had gone completely black at Dr. Carlhagen's command.

He sat on the leather sofa, legs crossed, hands clenched together in his lap.

Seeing Jacqueline—no, Jacey—there, sun on her face, wind rustling her loose hair, eyes sparkling like the sea itself, made him both anxious and proud.

He fumbled in his pants pocket and found an andleprixen tablet. Just to take the edge off.

Maxine was showering, cleaning off her bodyguard's blood. Soon she'd present herself to him and he'd have to give her all the details about the ATR supplement she would require for the rest of her life.

That would be enjoyable. But not nearly as enjoyable as when Dr. Carlhagen finally had Jacqueline—no, *Jacey*—under his thumb.

The interview was focused mostly on Vin, though the

camera drone had positioned itself to keep both Vin and Jacey in the frame. That Vin was allowing . . . Jacey . . . to share the attention was quite shocking. Perhaps Dr. Carlhagen had underestimated Vin's intelligence.

After all, she and Dante and Ping had to have reasoned out his true aim by now. He couldn't have staged a better moment if he'd planned it.

"Show me EGX," he commanded the pixel wall.

A new rectangle of video popped up next to the first, showing a competing news site.

As he suspected, they were reporting about the interview SNN was currently broadcasting. They showed still images of . . . *Jacey* . . . and Vin. As he'd expected, they'd place placed them side-by-side next to pictures of Jacqueline Buchanan and Elizabeth Burnell.

These were old pictures of the Progenitors, showing them in their twenties. But their image process computers had found poses nearly identical to the freeze frames.

If one didn't know better, one might believe them to be the same pictures, simply modified with different clothing and different hairstyles. They were exactly the same faces.

In such a cynical world, such a coincidence would create many crazy theories. That was good. But both networks were certainly already farming out a facial structure analysis to a third-party AI expert. The kind they used in security forensics to identify criminals.

Dr. Carlhagen knew what people were thinking. These young ladies couldn't actually be young Elizabeth and young Jacqueline. Not without time travel. And no AI would grant time travel as a possibility, so the idea of cloning would be put forward.

And then the cat would be—as the old cliché went—out of the bag. Somebody was making really, really good carbos of famous people.

Dr. Carlhagen didn't like the world "carbo", the slang term for clones. It was based on an anachronism, "carbon copy," which was a form of duplication for typed documents way back in the 20th century.

It meant the clones the world knew were illegal, and not of the quality Dr. Carlhagen could make. Not even close.

Maxine walked in, wrapped in a bathrobe and toweling her hair. She spotted the video of Vin and Jacey and stopped, towel dangling from one hand. "Oh no."

Dr. Carlhagen smiled. "Oh yes, Maxine."

"What have you done?"

Dr. Carlhagen smiled. "I suppose I've taken over the world. Please sit. I'll tell you what you need to know."

She sat. Gone was her usual look of superiority. Gone was the icy and stony expression of disdain. All that showed on her pale, pale face was fear.

"Once we have an understanding, then we'll call your Colonel Vikisky for an update on his progress toward securing the Scion School on St. Vitus."

He commanded the pixel wall to return to its view of the island and sea. He would replay the interview with Vin and Jacey later. Probably many times.

"The pill I gave you is an Anti Transfer-Rejection supplement. It was tailored specifically for a hormonal deficiency the AI programmed into you at the time of transfer. You will require one pill per day for the rest of your life. Oh, you can miss two or three days in a row, but you'll grow increasingly tired and forgetful. But you know how that feels, don't you? If you still do not take your pill, you'll deteriorate into a sort of vegetative state. Very drooly, very messy."

He leaned forward. "Trust me. You don't want to let it

get to that point, because what follows is organ failure and death."

"Is that the pill I've been watching you eat like candy?" Maxine asked.

"No. I don't require the ATR, for obvious reasons."

"And so for the rest of my life if I don't do as you say, you will withhold this supplement?"

Dr. Carlhagen smiled. "I knew you would understand me. But it doesn't have to be like that, my dear Maxine. I find using it as leverage distasteful."

"I see."

She waved at the pixel wall where the video interview had been playing. "I recognized those girls. I suspected Elizabeth Burnell would pop up again. The other girl was Jackie B's Scion. She is the one you were going to have me overwrite, before you switched her out for this body. And now we have some very recognizable faces being broadcast around the world. Reckless of you, Christof."

Even in the face of utter defeat, she still had the audacity to lecture him. It made him laugh.

"You still haven't figured it out, have you, Maxine? I'm prepared to go to the press myself and tell them every single Progenitor's name. It suits me perfectly now that those two have been spotted in the wild."

She stared at him for a long time. "If you're willing to make the Scion program public, you must have the President herself."

Dr. Carlhagen said nothing. He had no reason to confide anything to her. His silence made her squirm and she stared at him, as if suddenly realizing she'd been sleeping with a monster.

Very well. He'd be a monster in her eyes. He'd be a monster to the world. It mattered very little what people thought of him.

He was doing what needed to be done. The world had showed itself incapable of addressing its problems. No form of government yet invented truly worked.

Democracy did not solve anything until it faced a crisis. Tyranny ate itself up with corruption.

The Kille-Tine asteroid and the rising sea levels and the incessant wars and the plague had proved that humanity was unable to prepare for catastrophe.

What the world needed was an all-powerful, incorruptible man like Dr. Carlhagen to make the hard decisions.

He would dole out immortality to those in power in return for obedience. Many millions would probably have to die to bring things back into balance. Much wealth would have to be confiscated. Resources reallocated. Nations and religions alike would have to be erased from human memory.

Billions would revile him. All would fear him.

He would save humanity, preserve it for a million years. And no one would thank him.

He accepted that.

"I know what you're thinking, Maxine. You're on the verge of making a scene. You're almost ready to stand and shake your fist at me and shout that you'd rather die than serve me. But as I said, it doesn't have to be that way. You can still wield immense power in this world. More than you've accumulated in all your years of public service. You've killed three men with your bare hands in just the past two days. Surely you won't balk at the bloody work ahead of us."

She dropped her face into the towel. Her fine white hair had already starting to dry, and it tumbled over the towel like an avalanche. Giving vent to her anger and fear, she screamed into the towel and stomped her bare feet on the carpet.

Once this fit passed, she dabbed her tears away and cleared her throat. Slowly, she straightened her shoulders and collected herself.

Finally, she raised her eyes to meet his. "I'm sorry for putting Livy into cryo, Dr. Carlhagen. Would you like me to go reverse the process?"

That was more like it.

Not that Dr. Carlhagen trusted her one centimeter. She'd be a model assistant, but she'd be looking for an angle. Mostly she'd be trying to find ways to secure a lifetime's supply of her ATR supplement.

That was fine. Dr. Carlhagen could lead her down a hundred false paths in her hunt for freedom. In the meantime, she would do his bidding.

"I accept your apology, Maxine. But now that she's in cryo, she has to stay for a while. It's a stressful transition and pulling her out before her body and mind have had a chance to recover would be very risky."

"Who is she?" Maxine asked, voice full of desperate curiosity. "Who is that girl's Progenitor?"

Dr. Carlhagen smiled. "Go get dressed. You need to prepare yourself to call Colonel Vikisky."

Disappointment showed for a moment, but she stood immediately to obey his command. "Yes, Dr. Carlhagen."

"You may call me Christof. When we're alone together."

He admired her lithe figure as she walked toward the bedroom. Now that they had come to an understanding about his place of power, he found her more alluring than before.

She would live, he decided. For now.

Once she was out of his sight, he commanded the pixel wall to show him the entirety of the Vin and Jacey interview. When the interviewer asked her about her resemblance to Jacqueline Buchanan, Dr. Carlhagen smiled.

Yes, the cat was out of the bag.

But Captain Wilcox could hardly swoop in and snatch her up now. It was clear the reporter was more interested in Jacey than in Vin. The girl would be under constant observation. *Surveillance* would be a better term.

Lazarus appeared on another section of the pixel wall. "Sir, you have a call at your holodesk."

"Who is it?"

"It's the President of the North American Union. Gauging by her facial organization and a complete audio spectrographic analysis of her speech, it is 87% likely she is in the emotional state known as anger."

Dr. Carlhagen smiled. "And if it isn't anger? What other emotion might it be?" He knew damn well, but it was a good test for an AI still trying to learn such subtleties.

"It is 13% likely she is in a state of fear."

Yes. That was it.

Still smiling, he hefted himself from the sofa and headed to accept a call from the president.

63

LIKE A KICK IN THE CHEST

In dry clothes and now reasonably clean following a douse of saltwater pulled from the sea, Humphrey felt almost human. If he could get a few nights sleep and some big meals in him, he might actually begin to think straight again.

He'd have to settle for the handful of crackers he munched as he paced on the bridge. As for sleep, that would have to wait.

The bridge felt very cramped now, as the holodesk took up a lot of space.

Sensei stood like a statue, staring out the front windows. He'd removed the baggy overalls and hadn't said a word since the boarding party left. Occasionally he'd throw a side-eye glance at Orson, which always made the lump of a man shiver.

Humphrey leaned against the map table and watched Summer as she finished connecting the network to the holodesk. Just getting the monstrous mahogany thing in position had taken five Scions and both of Orson's men. It now stood pressed against the closet door. The two AI servers were stacked on top of it and the genius Spider was busily stripping and connecting wires to the back of the boxes.

"We don't have a call address for Elizabeth," Summer said as she worked. She was wearing that weird hat with the leaping deer embroidered on the front. Her black hair was jammed up inside, apparently to help keep the back of her neck cool while she worked. Elias hovered next to her, handing her tools and occasionally sharing melty-eyed glances with her. "So we'll have to wait for Jacey to call us. In the meantime, I think I can get—"

Summer flew backward and landed on her butt, hat flying off her head and hair spilling over her face. A tendril of smoke drifted up from the back of one of the server boxes.

Elias was kneeling next to her in a second, grimacing against the pain from his gunshot wound. "Are you hurt?"

"What happened?" Humphrey demanded. He went to the server to inspect the damage.

"I got the wires crossed or something. The electronics should be fine." She accepted Elias's help as he lifted her to her feet. "That was like a kick in the chest."

Summer stuffed her hair back in the hat and jammed it onto her head. She gave the offending server a rueful glare then dove back into fiddling with it.

Humphrey left her to it. "Orson, what's our distance from the first island?"

Aphrodite's captain hunched on his chair, shoving spoonfuls of soup between his beard and mustache. "Fifty miles southwest of our current position. It'll be dark before we get within sight of the closest one."

Humphrey studied the map. The three islands were each roughly twenty miles apart. Their course would take them to the middle one. If that one wasn't Elizabeth's island, he'd have to choose one of the others. But if Summer could get Vaughan started back up and onto the holodesk, they might just get the exact location and save a lot of pointless wandering.

Wanda pushed through the door with Bethancy in tow. She scanned the bridge, then turned to leave.

"Who are you looking for?" Humphrey asked.

"Leslie. I can't find her anywhere. Her Nine needs some discipline. Grace and Suki took all of Bethancy's clothes and soaked them in seawater, then stuffed them in her bunk. Dajeet is trying to keep them in line, but they won't listen to her.

Sensei turned around. "When did you last see Leslie?"

Wanda shrugged.

Humphrey said, "She was in the stairwell a while ago, sleeping."

"She isn't there now," Wanda said. "Can you just put Dajeet in charge for now?" She was looking at Humphrey.

It struck him as ridiculous that he would have any say over who led the girls' Nines. But Wanda was looking at him with a great deal of expectation.

"You're serious," he said. "Shouldn't Sensei tell them?"

Sensei answered without turning around. "They'll listen to you."

Wanda's green eyes were locked on his. She'd given up on the ponytail, maybe to let her hair dry following the soaking in the engine room. Her mass of her red curls stuck out in all directions, giving her the wild look of a woodland nymph. "Of course they will."

Bethancy held the door for him and Wanda as they left the bridge. She gave him a weird look, sort of a knowing smile.

Wanda led the way, and Humphrey did his best not to

pay too much attention to her shoulders or slim waist. Or anything else.

He repeated Jacey's name in his head, pictured her face. He'd loved her most of his life, and now that they were together he had no intention of betraying her.

Yes, he was drawn to Wanda. There was nothing wrong with that. It was natural. And he knew that intense experiences tended to draw people together. That had happened between him and Jacey.

Wanda pushed through the doors to the outer deck. She told Bethancy to run ahead and make sure all the girls in Girls' Hold knew Humphrey was coming, as some had been out of their uniforms to let them dry.

Once Bethancy was gone, Wanda stopped Humphrey with a gentle hand on his. He took hold of it, a reflex more than a conscious choice. He let it go just as quickly. "Wanda. This can't happen."

"I know. I've told myself that a thousand times. I know I don't compare to Jacey. Nobody does."

She was right. She didn't compare to Jacey. Any more than Belle compared to Jacey. Or Orson. That did not mean she wasn't beautiful or desirable. She was different.

When he didn't say anything, her jaw tightened. "I don't know what I was expecting by talking to you."

He wanted to comfort her, but he knew he couldn't touch her. If he did, he would embrace her. Then he would kiss her. He hated himself for it. He hated his weakness. Hated the situation that they were in. And in truth he was angry. At Jacey.

She had left him.

"I'm sorry," he said. "I feel something here. Between us. But it just can't be. I won't betray Jacey."

She wiped at her eyes, but he didn't see any tears. "That doesn't help," she said, laughing, though her voice broke. "It just proves how good and honorable a man you are. Besides, I would never betray her either. She is my sister by any definition other than biology."

She had called him a man. He'd never thought of himself that way before. Nor had he ever considered himself honorable. He was Dr. Carlhagen's Scion, after all. Genetically bad.

"The Scions need your leadership, now more than ever." Wanda started walking again and Humphrey walked next to her, keeping enough distance their hands didn't touch by mistake. "Leslie is not cut out for leading her Nine. I don't know what it is. Maybe Belle crushed her spirit. Maybe her Progenitor was a flake. Who knows? But Dajeet can do it, with my help."

"And what do we tell Leslie when she comes out of hiding?"

"That she shouldn't have been hiding."

Girls' Hold was oddly quiet when Humphrey followed Wanda down the ladder. Wanda's Nine stood in ordered ranks alongside their bunks. Leslie's was huddled around Dajeet, most wearing plaintive faces as if they'd just been told to run ten miles.

Humphrey stalked toward Dajeet, arranging his face to convey extreme annoyance. "Dajeet, what is the problem with your Nine?"

It felt very odd to address Dajeet in that tone of voice. But not much odder than referring to the Nine as hers.

The girl was a Snake, after all, just recently turned fifteen. Dajeet was petite for her age, and if he hadn't known her, he would have guessed she was a year younger. That was until you looked in her eyes, which reminded him of Mother Tyeesha's eyes. In fact, Mother had always called Dajeet an "old soul," whatever that meant.

Her uniform was spotless and her hair—as black as her eyes—was pulled into a tight ponytail. She stood at attention. "We were waiting for Leslie's direction."

"If she's not present, you are in charge. I'm surprised your Nine has forgotten that."

"We haven't forgotten," Grace said, indignant. She was an extraordinarily tall Centipede of thirteen, whose arms and legs were thickly muscled. She understood the irony of her name, and had showed early on that she would not accept any jibes about it without brutal retaliation.

"Then why is it Wanda's Nine is in order and Dajeet's is not?"

Grace clamped her mouth shut.

Humphrey raised an eyebrow at Dajeet until she caught on. She clapped her hands and called roll: "Vestana, Christina, Chloe, Suki, Grace, Dansha."

The girls moved to their spots, hands automatically going to their sigil pins and checking to make sure they were straight. A few who were wearing their hair down were bundling it into regulation ponytails.

Humphrey noted that several in Wanda's Nine had not bothered to do so. He couldn't blame them, since Jacey had stopped wearing hers back.

"Would you like to join me on inspection?" Dajeet asked him.

"No." He turned on Wanda. "Your Nine is not complete."

Wanda stood at attention. "Jacey's location is unknown. She will not be joining us. Livy has been abducted by Dr. Carlhagen. Summer is on the bridge attempting to connect the AI servers."

"Understood." He paced up and down, not really knowing what he should be looking for. It was unprecedented for a boy to be inspecting the girls' roll call. He decided to reassure them.

"We are currently heading toward the island where we believe Jacey has gone. I have not yet heard from her, but I hope to soon. The soldiers who searched the ship are long gone and on their way to St. Vitus."

He saw the question in their eyes. "Yes. They will discover us missing and will come looking for us. But why would they search *Aphrodite* again? I think the worst is behind us. Right now we need to work together." He glared at Suki and Grace. "I don't want to hear about any more petty squabbles. Dajeet and Wanda, I can assure you that Scions sent to Sensei for punishment will regret the day they were born."

There. He'd done all he could to shore up Wanda and Dajeet's authority.

He realized he needed to do the same for the boys. He headed for the ladder. "Wanda, would you join me in Boys' Hold in a few minutes?"

"Why me?" she asked.

"Because, as I said, we all have to work together. I am assigning you and Elias to arrange a duty roster for all the Scions. There are meals to be prepared, clothes to launder, and Mother Tyeesha's staff need assistance with the children."

"Yes, Humphrey."

He climbed out, pleased to hear Wanda and Dajeet issuing orders and hearing silent obedience in return.

64

SHARP AND HOLLOW

The camera drone—as Yvonne Kellar called the hovering mechanical insect that had been following Jacey for the past forty-five minutes—had now been joined by at least three others. And because of this annoyance, Jacey was able to go back into the mansion without fear of being snatched away by Captain Wilcox or Vin's two brutal bodyguards.

The living room roared with voices of guests who seemed to be magnetically pulled along in Vin and Jacey's wake. In fact, once the interview had ended, they had become even more ardent in complementing Vin and laughing at everything she said.

When Jacey left Vin's side, they pressed all around and touched her and asked all sorts of unanswerable questions.

Jacey had kept moving, always away from Yvonne Kellar. Captain Wilcox kept his distance, but the guests—whose inventiveness shocked Jacey—started the rumor that Vin had requested military protection for her and her guests. They saw the helicopter landing on the lawn as a bit of theater, put on by Vin for their entertainment.

The phrases "she's so rich" and "she's unbelievably rich" were uttered so many times Jacey began to suspect everyone in attendance was an idiot. Of course Vin was rich—she owned an *entire damned island!*

With the camera drones hovering above them in the great icy chamber, Jacey knew she'd never be able to escape. But at least they protected her from abduction. A quandary, as her teacher Socrates might have called it with an amused look on his face.

Dante should have done his part by now. But considering the situation, what could he do?

Jacey spotted the bunch of elderly ladies she had first talked to. Maybe if she engaged the cat lady in conversation, the other guests and the camera drones would lose interest. Jacey shook off the overly fond touch of Donald of the red shorts who "understood Jacey completely, unlike all these other wannabes."

"I see a friend, excuse me," she said, then slipped past smiling faces and shouted questions to sidle among the ladies wearing too much makeup, too much perfume, and yards and yards of floral print.

The cat lady's wig had become twisted sideways, putting bangs over her left ear. She had parted the longer section of crayon-brown strands so that her nose and mouth poked through. "Junior never liked peanut butter, you understand. He said it made his tongue stick to the roof of his mouth. I caught him feeding his sandwich to Dodgie—that was my Chihuahua—rest his tiny soul in heaven. That gave poor Dodgie the bloat like you've never seen. The vet told me, 'Hazel, don't you feed peanut butter sandwiches to your dogs. They'll get the bloat.' Well! I gave that vet three and half pieces of my mind, I'll tell you what. Accusing me of feeding Dodgie a peanut butter sandwich! As if I don't know how to take care of my own pets. Once when Sillybutt had a growth under his tail, I removed it myself. All it took was a little snip with my fingernail clippers and a quick pat of bourbon to sterilize it. You should have seen him running around after that. You'd have sworn his tail was on fire, the poor dear."

All five drones were hovering around the group, presumably broadcasting Hazel's story to a fascinated world. So much for boring them to death.

Jacey was about to make a break for the stairs, even if just to get some air on the mezzanine. The drones would follow her, of course. And then a bunch of guests eager to be seen by the drones would be up there.

"Come on, Dante, do something," she said, under her breath.

Cat lady wasn't looking at Jacey—or any of the other women, for that matter. "I'm good at surgery, it turns out. A natural aptitude. Inherited from my father. He was a field surgeon for California. I'm not proud to confess it, but there it is. I'll say it in bold letters to own up to it. That's the only thing you can do in a case like this. But that doesn't take away from his skill with the blade. Not one whit. And as I said, when it came to the kitties, I could do just as well as a vet in most cases. There was another time when Sillybutt got into a row with Mousy-Tooth. Oh dear! What a mess that was. You wouldn't think such a small kitty could *spray* so much!"

Jacey backed away from whatever horror Hazel was about to relate, but she did not know where to go.

Seizing on Jacey's hesitation, Yvonne Kellar accosted her with the microphone. "SNN headquarters in Denver is reporting AI forensic analysis that suggests you are a clone of Jacqueline Buchanan. How do you respond to these allegations?"

Jacey's mouth opened in shock. She clamped it shut. "Well, that's—that's—"

She didn't know how to answer. Part of her wanted to say yes, yes, that is exactly true. But if Dr. Carlhagen *wanted* that out . . .

A bang—sharp and hollow—made everyone in the crowded living room duck. A few screamed.

"I don't like how mops perform," Hazel was saying, oblivious to the chaos. "Once it's soiled with cat poo—liquefied cat poo, no less—it's nearly *impossible* to get a mop truly clean!"

Yvonne had a finger pressed to one ear. "Yes, a gunshot. Pistol, I think."

Jacey couldn't see who the woman was talking to. Yvonne nodded and suddenly her black drone was flying straight up. It disappeared over the mezzanine railing. In the direction of the noise. Which might have been a gunshot, for all Jacey knew.

The realization that this might be Dante's distraction electrified her. Most of the guests were streaming out to the pool deck, many in tears. Vin was heading up the stairs, Yvonne on her heels. The rest of the camera drones buzzed away, too.

Jacey headed for the kitchen. It was full of nervous servants. They ignored Jacey, as they were too busy speculating about who had been shot.

Jacey slipped through the back door. No soldiers.

Screams erupted in the house behind her.

Jacey dashed across the parking lot and into the shade of the garage.

Meow Meow and Dante were both sitting astride small, four-wheeled vehicles. Open to the air, with handlebars instead of steering wheels, they had knobby tires and small cargo platforms on the back.

"Get on behind me," Dante said. His machine was running, spitting dark exhaust from a pipe low along one side.

Jacey obeyed.

"Hold on to me."

She wrapped her arms around his waist.

The engine whined and the machine accelerated. She had to hold on to Dante even tighter or fall off the back.

They tore out of the parking area, but not through the truck entrance. Dante steered them through the smaller gate on the other side, then turned uphill away from the mansion.

Meow Meow followed behind, a huge grin on her face.

65

REPULSION IGNITED

The wine was a Malbec from Bordeaux, not one of Dr. Carlhagen's preferred varietals, but it paired well with the hamburger sandwiches he'd prepared for himself and Maxine Bentilius.

He sat at the dining table in his quarters, napkin tucked into the throat of his shirt. Of course, he did not pick the sandwich up and jam it into his maw, the way Americans did. And why should he, when he had such lovely silverware at his disposal?

"I'm afraid you'll have to clean the dishes, Maxine," he said after swallowing a bite. "I cooked, after all."

Maxine had now recovered her composure entirely, and the look she gave him was no different than the one she might have given him all those years ago in Paris. They had lived together then, in a small apartment in the third arrondissement. Maxine hadn't been able to cook then, either. And so they had divided chores. He cooked, she did the dishes.

"It was a sweet year, wasn't it?" Dr. Carlhagen said.

"I don't know one wine from the next."

"I wasn't referring to the wine. I was referring to our time in Paris. There had been no Kille-Tine, no California War. No plague."

"It was sweet because it ended before we were ready for it to end." Maxine had discarded the bun and only ate the beef patty of her burger. "It was sweet because we didn't stay together long enough for it to sour."

"Who broke up with whom?"

"I don't recall."

Of course she didn't. But Dr. Carlhagen did.

He would never forget the day he'd received word from Jacqueline that she'd accepted a proposal of marriage from that bastard Charles Buchanan. That had soured his affection for Maxine Bentilius in an instant.

She'd never been more than a distraction for him, anyway. Paris had been a distraction.

He'd sought anything that might take his mind off the woman he loved. With equal—and often severe—determination, he'd buried himself in studies at the Sorbonne, drowned himself in wine and philosophical arguments with Michael, and devoted hours upon hours to books, museums, and the ballet.

Maxine Bentilius had been just one of a dozen distractions. He'd left her the day Jacqueline had committed herself to Charles. The wound was as fresh today as it had been all those many decades ago.

Shaking himself out of the haunted past, he pushed his plate away. "It is time for you to check in with Colonel Vikisky, don't you think?"

"Yes. He was nearly to St. Vitus when I spoke to him an hour and a half ago."

She was playing it awfully meek. Dr. Carlhagen

mistrusted a meek Maxine even more than a domineering Maxine.

"Let's go, then."

In the office, Maxine touched the holodesk and requested the colonel. The pixel walls showed the declining sun as it lit a bank of clouds from below. The Caribbean was calm and spread to the horizon like turquoise glass.

The colonel's holo appeared above the desk, hands clasped behind his back. His billed-cap cast a shadow over his eyes. "Madam Senator. I was just about to call you."

"Colonel. Please report on progress securing the Scion School."

"The school is secured. But there is no one here."

Dr. Carlhagen resisted the urge to go around the desk and speak to the man himself.

"Did the Scions run off campus?" Maxine asked.

"No ma'am. Exhaustive aerial surveillance and five squads on the ground turned up no sign of human presence on the island. A small compound on the opposite side of the island is empty as well. We discovered evidence that small children were there recently."

Maxine was staring at Dr. Carlhagen now. "The Scions can't simply have vanished."

The colonel didn't know she wasn't talking to him, so he answered. "No ma'am. The Scions must have evacuated by boat. We searched a small freighter prior to coming to St. Vitus. We found bunks set up in the cargo holds, black uniforms, but no individuals. The captain claimed to have recently smuggled undocumented immigrants for construction. The vessel was carrying an old school bus for delivery to Mexico."

The bus.

Dr. Carlhagen remembered Wilcox mentioning a school

bus and a freighter. As ridiculous as it sounded, apparently the Scions had managed to load everyone aboard and get it to sea.

He gestured her to mute the transmission. Once she had done so, he said, "The Scions are on that vessel. Tell your man to return to it and seize it."

She complied.

"But there were no Scions aboard, Madam Senator," Vikisky said. "We searched her stem to stern."

"I suggest you search more thoroughly. And question the captain more vigorously. Good day, Colonel."

"But Madam Senator—"

"I said, 'good day!'" She cut off the transmission and looked squarely at Dr. Carlhagen. "What game are you playing, Christof?"

"No game, my dear. I fear my butler was the one playing games. He meant to steal the Scions right from under my nose."

"It appears he has done so. What's so amusing?"

Dr. Carlhagen allowed the genuine smile he was feeling in his heart to show on his face. This turn of events was disturbing, but might actually be seen as an opportunity. Yes. It *was* an opportunity.

"With the secret of the Scion program about to be public, many powerful interests will be arriving at St. Vitus, seeking control. I had intended to pit them against each other. But this works out better."

"How can losing the Scions be better? Or do you plan to sink that ship with them on it?" She seemed to like this idea; her eyes started to gleam. "Yes. If they disappear, there will be no more evidence of the program."

"Wishful thinking is beneath you, Maxine. I have no intention of sinking the ship. I merely see this as a wonderful chance to bring the Scions here, to this beautiful new facility."

He moved behind her and put his hands on her shoulders. He pressed his lips against her ear. "Putting Livy in cryo demonstrated the capacity of the system to draw-down older Scions. We'll put all but the oldest ones in cryo."

Maxine's shoulders tensed and she tilted her head away from his.

The slight show of repulsion ignited a rush of desire in him. He loved to see her cringe. He slipped his hands around her slender midsection and hugged her close. "Soon Colonel Vikisky will have possession of that ship. The Scions *are* aboard it. Where else can they be?"

He kissed her ear, enjoyed the tremble of fear or disgust it created.

Yes. It was good to push her into this uncomfortable corner. She hated him now. That was better than the contempt she treated him with before. Her revulsion attracted him far more than her incessant lust ever had.

He only needed one more thing from her. One more demonstration that she understood her position.

He held her close, kissing her ever so gently, whispering to her of her beauty, reveling in how she trembled.

And then she gave him what he wanted. If she'd been ice, he would have heard the snaps as spider web cracks raced across her form. Her resistance shattered.

She turned to him, kissed him, held him—not with great desire—but in utter submission.

Before long, this would be Jacey.

66

THE IDEA OF FREEDOM

phrodite slogged through calm seas, rocking slowly side to side and splitting the seas into fans of spray to either side of her bow.

A pod of dolphins swam alongside. Scions young and old stood at the railing. The older ones were teary-eyed and red-faced, the younger smiling and clapping at the friendly escort.

A fitting funeral procession for a beloved brother.

As the leaders of the two boys' Nines, Humphrey and Elias carried Constantine's body, swathed in sheets, to the starboard side of the ship. Scions moved aside from a latched gate in the rail.

Sensei opened it and held it with solemn dignity.

They stopped. Elias looked to Humphrey.

Humphrey wished Jacey were there. She would know what to say. She was good with words.

Wanda stood nearby. Tears stood in her brilliant green eyes, but she was otherwise under control.

Not Bethancy, not Dajeet, not Obu or Kirk or Tytus or

Sang. All wept openly, wiping their eyes and noses on their sleeves.

"Con was a good Scion," Humphrey said. "A loyal friend, kind-hearted and generous. A fearless fighter—"

"But not a good one!" Pedro called, nearly choking with sobs, but laughing, too.

The Scions laughed, tears flowing. Constantine and Pedro's rivalry on the sparring mat was legendary. The same age, they had been inseparable friends. When it came to fitness and the martial arts, they had exerted every fiber of their muscle and will to outdo each other. This naturally extended to their verbal sparring, which to an outsider would have framed them as arch enemies.

But every Scion present knew their merciless remarks had always come with a smile, a friendly elbow to the gut, a pat on the back. They were as close as brothers.

"Yes, Pedro. Con would admit he was nearly as terrible a fighter as you," Humphrey said.

More laughter. More tears.

"It turns out we live in a cruel world," Humphrey said. He was letting his thoughts run, not trying anymore to be poetic like Jacey. "A world that needs more people like Constantine and fewer men with machine guns. A world that needs people like Con, because of his cheerful confidence, his care, his earnestness, his willingness to show affection. Socrates said the greatest enemy to tyranny is the idea of freedom. Constantine must be our idea, our model, of what is the best in our nature as humans. He died to protect Livy. He did *not* fail."

Humphrey was conscious of the tears now streaming down his own cheeks. "Con showed us that sacrifice does not pay with immediate victory. But sacrifice accumulates, doesn't it? It has to. Vaughan went before him. Dante, Ping, Sarah, and Vin, too. Jacey risks everything for us. Their sacrifices steel our resolve. Dr. Carlhagen used to teach us that we were chosen to bring the world back from catastrophe, that we would bring the human species from the brink of extinction. Perhaps he did not realize he was telling the truth. There may be millions—maybe billions—still living, but if the human race allows for even one of us to be overwritten, can it be considered civilized?"

The Scions had quieted. Sensei looked at Humphrey with a strange expression. Surprise, maybe.

"As we commit Constantine to the sea, let's also commit ourselves to each other. As we seek haven in a dangerous world, we will need to rely on each other. Let's use Constantine's example. Support each other, be kind to each other, be loyal. Be true friends to each other. Brothers and sisters."

He stopped there. There was no need to tell them that their freedom would most certainly require more sacrifice.

With a nod to Elias, they hefted Constantine's body to the rail, then tossed it into the sea. Weighted with scrap metal from the engine room, it sank into the deep blue.

Quiet sobs rose over the hiss of the sea splitting at the bow, the tremble of the ship's engines, the wind.

The dolphins sped alongside, arcing and dancing.

Humphrey did not believe in omens, but seeing the happy creatures lightened his heart enough to produce a sad smile.

Most Scions stayed at the rail, staring to sea and lost in his or her thoughts. A few of the older ones hugged younger ones and wiped tears from their eyes. Mother Tyeesha tottered back inside, clinging to the adult caretakers' elbows.

Humphrey went to the outside stairs and climbed to the bridge wing.

He liked the vantage point. It resonated within him,

gave him a similar feeling to being atop the bell tower at the Scion School. When you could stand and look out at the world and see a far horizon, it helped you breathe, helped you see the lay of the land. It was solitary.

He leaned on the railing and allowed the sadness of Constantine's death to exist. But his thoughts quickly returned to their present predicament.

A sharp metallic clang sounded above him, followed by a single curse word held out like the final note of song.

Summer. She was already back up there, messing around with a satellite dish, and apparently things weren't going too well. Apparently it had something to do with getting the AI servers online.

The sun stood on the horizon now, directly to starboard. The gulls he'd seen just an hour ago were gone now that *Aphrodite* had distanced herself from the islands.

Wanda came out on the wing and leaned on the railing next to Humphrey. The breeze blew her unruly hair back, revealing a delicate ear. Humphrey added guilt to his worry. He wanted to hold Wanda, to feel that closeness.

He wanted to hold Jacey, too. Could a person be attracted to more than one girl at the same time?

"We found Leslie," Wanda said without looking at him. "She was on a top bunk, asleep."

"The girls didn't do a very through search, then." He said it without accusation.

"It was the Dolphin Vestana's bunk. It was actually kind of funny. Vestana said, 'who would think to look in a Dolphin's bunk for a missing Shark?'"

Humphrey didn't see the humor in it. "I'm surprised Leslie hasn't stormed up here demanding to be put back in charge of her Nine."

"The day is not over."

"It almost is, though. Look at that."

The bottom of the sun kissed the horizon, sending a streak of reflected gold across the sea. The rusty white paint covering the bridge turned a fiery orange and Wanda's hair turned the color of embers, her skin gold and freckled. He noticed her lips, how they formed a slight smile when her face was at rest. Jacey's mouth was like that, too, though her lips were fuller, more suggestive of kissing.

"Where are we going, Humphrey?"

"South."

"That's a direction, not a destination."

The sun was halfway gone now and the horizon glowed with oranges and violet. The sky overhead had turned a deep purple, darkening to midnight blue to the east.

"We have no place to go. Not yet. Summer has gotten the network connected, but she's still trying to figure out how to get the servers to start up."

Wanda put her back to the rail and peered at the roof of the bridge. "So that's what she's doing up there. I'm going to have to talk to her about her swearing."

"I'm not sure she'd be as productive without it," Humphrey said with a laugh. "She told me that cursing was like oil in a machine. I believe her words were 'it lubes the gears of my mind.'"

"A remarkable girl," Wanda said, turning back to face the sunset. "They all are, in their own ways."

"I don't think the boys would like to hear you say that."

Wanda elbowed him. "You know what I mean. And I'm not so sure Obu or Terrel would be too offended by being called remarkable girls."

"I suppose not." Humphrey wanted to put his arm around her, wanted to share the final moments of the day with her. He kept his hands on the rail, accepting the chill of loneliness. He deserved it.

"So once Summer gets the servers working, then what?"

"Then Vaughan can access a huge amount of information from the outside world. Hopefully he'll be able to help us decide where we can find safe haven. Sensei seems to think we might be able to make it to Brazil. Orson is less optimistic."

"Why?"

"Because that fleet of Senator Bentilius's is going to find St. Vitus abandoned and they'll be back to search us again. He says *Aphrodite* cannot outrun the fleet."

The last arc of the sun sank into the horizon. In the last seconds of its life, an emerald flare sparked then faded. The sun was gone, dragging the remains of the sunlight down with it.

"You're doing a good job, Humphrey."

He nodded, trying to accept the praise. But his stomach soured. "But is it good enough?"

67

LET'S GO, DARLINGS

Headlights came on automatically as the odd open-air four wheelers dived beneath the canopy of trees on the west end of Vin's island.

Dante called the vehicles ATVs, though Jacey didn't know what it stood for. With knobby tires digging into the turf and whiny engines driving over bumps and through gullies, the three of them had powered over rough terrain. Sometimes they followed weedy paths, but mostly they cut across the land, winding with the hills.

Now that the sun was down, Dante had pulled to a stop. "Turn off your headlights," he called back to Meow Meow.

The girl's grin was gone, replaced by a grim and very dusty face. Her blue wig was mostly brown now. Mud splatter covered the machines. Jacey still wore the white linen, though it would never be clean again.

Meow Meow cut off her lights, leaving them in darkness.

Though the night was clear, not a single star twinkled

through the mat of intertwining leaves overhead. The dirt track ahead was a tunnel of black in a gray world.

The forest they'd entered was exactly like the rainforest Jacey had spent a few days in with Summer. Right down to the bugs, which swarmed around her face and stung her neck and arms. The air was full of their chirping and buzzing. Foliage on either side of the road rustled as unseen creatures came awake for their nocturnal morning.

Jacey climbed off the ATV and stretched. Her arms were sore from holding onto Dante and her legs stiff from the odd sitting position. "So we hide here?"

"No. But we're close."

"Close to what?"

"Our ticket out of here."

He got off the ATV and flipped a switch. Leaning into the handlebars, he pushed the vehicle to the edge of the road. With a final shove, he sent it straight down an embankment. It made a terrible racket as it jounced and crashed through the brush. A final thud and splash announced its arrival at the bottom of a hidden ravine.

Dante helped Meow Meow do the same with her ATV.

"How far?" Jacey asked.

"About five kilometers."

"Five! Why can't we drive there?"

"Because driving into Captain Wilcox's base would be the height of stupidity."

Jacey realized she was relying on an idiot for her safety. "We can't go there!"

Meow Meow slinked close and draped an arm over Jacey's shoulders. "Relax, honey. We've thought this through."

Dante wasn't really paying attention. In the darkness, all that really showed of him were the dark sparks of his eyes. Jacey didn't see how they would navigate anywhere when they couldn't see.

A sharp flash of white cut the air. It was the beam of Dante's flashlight. "This way."

He turned it off. "That'll ruin our dark vision, won't it?" he said. "This path leads to the north shore. The barracks and training grounds stand along the beach."

"Captain Wilcox's helicopter," Jacey said. "You plan to steal it."

Dante and Meow Meow laughed as if Jacey had told the funniest joke they'd ever heard.

"That would be a one-way ticket to hell," Dante said. "I may end up there anyway, but I'm in no hurry. We're not going to steal the helicopter. Besides, I'm sure it's hovering over Vin's mansion, shining a spotlight as it searches for us. You don't ever want to be chased by a chopper."

Jacey knew very well the terror of such a chase. It was why she and Summer had gone into the cover of a rainforest and why Dante had brought Jacey here now. The advantage they had at the moment was that no one had seen them leave the mansion.

"You said there were gunshots right before you escaped?" Dante asked as they slowly trudged along the path. Jacey's vision was improving with each passing minute.

"One gunshot. Upstairs. It must have been one of Captain Wilcox's men."

"Not necessarily," Dante said. "Vin's guards have weapons, too."

"It was fortunate. It drew away those camera drones that were flying around everywhere."

"I know," Meow Meow said. "I can't stand them anymore."

"Really?" Dante said. "You've always been such an

attention-seeker. I'm surprised you don't have your own drone swarm broadcasting to your fans 24/7."

"I did that for a while, but it made bathroom stuff a bit complicated. Turns out, even I have privacy needs."

"You still haven't told me how we're getting away," Jacey reminded Dante.

They came to a break in the trees and the starlight and a sliver of moon lit a downward slope that ended at a beach a few kilometers north. The surf shushed against the shore in the distance.

Set back from the beach were a collection of buildings with white metal roofs. Lights atop four towers stood at four corners, defining the edge of the compound. More lights were attached to the buildings, shining down to light the walkways and training yard.

"Nobody's home," Meow Meow said.

"There has to be somebody there," Dante said. "Probably a cook and some maintenance crew. The soldiers will all be patrolling for us."

"We should have gone to the docks," Jacey said. "There are boats there, right?"

"There will be several of Wilcox's men there, too. That's the first place they'd look for us."

Despite being an idiot, Dante had made a good point.

"There," he said, whispering and pointing.

Jacey followed the line of his index finger toward a thrust of pier standing in a bay on the other side of the compound.

Attached to it was a boat. Quite a small one.

It was hard to see much detail, but it appeared to have a sheltered area on deck where the piloting controls were.

"*That's* our ticket out?" Jacey asked.

"Do you have a better plan?"

Jacey shrugged.

"Let's just go, darlings. Kitty needs a nap," Meow Meow said, and dashed from the cover of the trees.

There was a footpath of sorts, though it was rocky and often rutted. In the darkness, they had to go slowly. It gave Jacey chills to be so exposed. If the helicopter returned, they'd be seen.

Meow Meow led the way. Considering how emaciated her frame was, she had endurance to spare. She jogged ahead and waved Jacey forward. They gave the compound a wide berth, staying well out of the range of the light towers at the corners. It made the trip longer, but there was no choice.

Once on the other side, they sprinted to the pier and hopped aboard the boat. It was ten meters long and had two enormous black outboard motors on the back. Dante messed with the controls. "Aha! They left the key in it."

Finally, some luck was going their way.

Dante turned the key and the motors roared to life. Lights atop the sheltered area came on and shined toward the water ahead.

Jacey cast off the line at the bow while Meow Meow took care of the stern line.

"Stop!"

The voice seemed torn from the throat of a giant.

Jacey looked down the pier to see three men, heavily armed and dressed in thick body armor, charging toward them.

"Turn off the engines or we will shoot."

A spotlight from the closest tower shined at them, blinding as the sun. Jacey held up a hand to shade her eyes, but it did little good.

Dante stood at the controls, his hand on the throttle. His face was pure indecision.

"This is your final warning! Turn off the engines or we will shoot."

Dante decided.

With a shove, he jammed the throttle all the way forward. The engines ripped the water, sending up a spray that covered the gunmen. Their weapons fired in sharp bursts. Impacts pinged from the low metal rail, shattered the window of the cabin, thudded into the hull.

As the boat accelerated, Jacey fell into Meow Meow and they tumbled onto the deck.

The engines screamed and the boat bounced over the waves. More bullets impacted the deck, carving ragged furrows into the wood.

And then there were no more bullets.

The boat charged through a breakwater, leaping over the bigger waves that had piled up in the shallow approach to the bay.

Once beyond the break, the motion became smoother, though the wind tore at Jacey as it whipped over the deck.

She climbed to her feet, lifting the nearly weightless Meow Meow after her.

"Can you steer?" Dante asked Jacey. "It doesn't take much, just keep her pointed at the moon for now."

"What's wrong?"

"Nothing much. Just a bullet to the ass."

She saw the blood now, staining his loose trousers.

Meow Meow let out a concerned hiss, then she was on Dante, insisting he lie down so she could treat him.

Jacey noticed a first aid kit tucked under a bench. Soon Meow Meow had its contents spilled everywhere while she dug for bandages.

"I'll have to dig out the bullet and any fabric that went in with it," Meow Meow said around the flashlight clamped in her teeth. She tore a protective covering from a long stainless steel forceps.

Jacey didn't watch the operation. She heard grunting, a gasp, and a lot of Meow Meow's low and strangely comforting purring noises.

Once things had quieted down, Jacey did look back.

Dante was lying on his stomach, his bare bottom very bright in the starlight. Meow Meow was holding his trousers against the wound and pressing down hard.

"Where did you learn to do that?" Jacey asked, impressed with the odd girl's skills.

"I was an assistant for a veterinarian for a few years in high school. I actually did some of the neutering."

Dante laughed, though tears of pain stood in his eyes. "I hope that's not what you just did to me."

The lights of Captain Wilcox's compound were growing fainter and smaller as the boat raced over the sea, directly away from the island.

But a new light had appeared, this one in the sky. The helicopter.

"They called in the chopper," Jacey said, ice rising through her spine. She found the switch for the boat's lights and cut them.

"Keep going toward the moon," Dante said. "They can't land anyone on us at this speed, and they don't have the fuel to chase us forever."

"They could shoot us, though," Jacey said.

"Yeah. I suppose they could."

Ten minutes later the pulse of the choppers blades was audible above the roar of the boat engines. Jacey jammed the throttle forward, but it was already wide open. There was no more speed to squeeze out of the motors.

Her eyes scanned the deck, looking for a weapon. Anything.

She saw a latch. A seam in the planks. A hinge.

Leaving the boat to steer itself, she grasped the latch and pulled. It revealed a storage compartment. It was full of lifejackets and a yellow bag that said "life raft" on it.

She pulled it all out. "Let's put him in here," she said.

Meow Meow saw what she meant to do and nodded. Together they dragged Dante to the compartment and shoved him in. It was rough handling for a wounded man, but it might just keep him alive.

"Keep some pressure on that wound, if you can," Meow Meow said as they closed the lid.

They scurried to the other side of the boat and a similar hatch in the deck. This one held tools, another life raft, and some fishing gear. All of that went onto the deck.

The chopper was closer now, its light bright the sky and sweeping the sea below. The second compartment was quite a bit smaller than the one they'd put Dante into.

No time to switch him to this one, though.

Would the pilot believe the boat as empty? She wasn't convinced. They needed a decoy.

She grabbed the life raft bag. A white cord with a red plastic handle stuck out from it. A drawing made its function clear.

Jacey went to the stern, tossed the raft into the water and yanked the cord. With a hiss, the raft unfolded and inflated.

She cast it loose. A red light on the top started to flash.

"Good thinking. Now, suck in your gut," Meow Meow said as she slid into the box.

Jacey tried to not to think of it as a coffin as she climbed in after. They had to lie on their sides, Meow Meow's back tucked against Jacey's front. She lowered the lid and rested her arm around Meow Meow.

The scrawny girl snuggled close. "This ain't too bad, little darling."

Jacey was still peeved about the gut comment. Even Madame LaFontaine, who was ruthlessly critical of girls' weight, had never criticized Jacey's stomach. Only a walking skeleton like Meow Meow could make such a ridiculous comment.

"I don't like girls in that way," Jacey said.

"Don't think of me as a girl, then. It's all in the mind."

"I'm in love with someone."

"Oh. I hope he heals up quickly then." Meow Meow said it with a mixture of tease and evil that made Jacey laugh. For some reason it was impossible to be offended by the girl.

"It's not Dante."

"Oh? I could have sworn you spent the last few hours hugging him. And the way you pressed your cheek to his back while hugging onto him, well I thought to myself, 'What a cute couple. Maybe they would like to make it a threesome.' I was quite jealous, to tell you the truth."

"Hush."

The helicopter was very close. The whine of its blades took on a very recognizable tone now. Jacey thought she'd be happy never to hear it again.

The boat still charged over the sea, though now that it had no driver, Jacey couldn't be sure it hadn't started to turn. She was counting on Dante's statement that the chopper wouldn't have enough fuel to follow them for long.

She felt the light touch of Meow Meow's hand on her leg. It wasn't sensual in the slightest. It was reassuring. "We'll be all right, darling. You'll see."

And as if her statement were the declaration of a goddess, the helicopter's beat began to fade.

Five minutes later, they were all back in the open. The helicopter's light shrank in the distance and then disappeared behind the horizon.

An hour later, the boat's engines sputtered and fell silent.

Jacey tried to restart it, but a quick check of the fuel gauge told the story. "We're out of gas. What now?"

Dante grimaced and looked at the position of the moon. "We wait for someone to pick us up. In the meantime, look around for the flare gun. It should be in a watertight box with the life rafts.

Meow Meow scrounged around the junk Jacey had pulled from the forward storage compartment. The gun looked huge in her tiny hand. She held two spare flare shots in the other. "Do you want I should shoot it now?"

"No. Wait until we see a passing ship. Then fire it. Maritime law. They'll come investigate. Pick us up."

"This was your plan?" Jacey asked in disbelief. "To hope to be rescued by a passing ship?"

Dante lifted a hand and flicked his middle finger at her.

Jacey had seen the gesture once before. She was pretty sure it was meant to convey displeasure. "Oh, I forgot," he said, still aiming the finger at her. "What was *your* plan again?"

"Point taken. Do you really think a ship will come by?"

"This is a pretty active area for freighters. I'd be more surprised if we didn't see one. But it might only appear on the horizon. I think we should hold out for something closer."

Meow Meow dug through the first aid kit and handed Dante a silver package. "Take these and shut up."

Dante snatched the packet, tore it open and ate the contents. "You're a princess, Meow Meow."

"Now get some sleep. Jacey and I will watch for ships."

Dante passed out moments later. Meow Meow and Jacey moved him into a better position for resting and bandaged his butt.

"That's going to hurt when we pull it off," Meow Meow said as she smoothed the adhesive tape over a rather hairy patch of Dante's skin.

"Good," Jacey said, though she couldn't really muster the animosity the comment deserved.

The two girls took up watch at the bow, legs dangling over the edge.

Meow Meow stretched languorously and said, "So are you going to tell me about how you came to look like Jackie B or not?"

"You won't believe me."

Meow Meow counted off on her fingers. "Vin looks like Elizabeth, Dante looks like Silvio, Ping looks like Han. Trust me, nobody does that good of work on people's faces. I know all of the best. What's the deal?"

Jacey took a deep breath, and then she told Meow Meow all about the Scion School, Progenitors, and Dr. Carlhagen.

68

MAKE A BIG MESS

White waves curled away behind the *Aphrodite* and fanned out in the distance. Mr. Justin gripped the rail and enjoyed the few minutes of peace he'd allowed himself.

Stars spread across the night sky, the Milky Way so bright it was like a luminous cloud. *Aphrodite's* engines thrummed through the deck beneath his feet, powering the Scions ever farther from danger.

Would it be fast enough? They were going the right direction, at least. The little compound he and Orson had prepared for the Scions was less than a day's sail from their current position. But with the inevitable return of the senator's fleet they had little margin for error.

It was time to make his next move.

Mr. Justin drew in a deep breath and let it go, hoping to drain some of the tension that vibrated through his body. Butlers learned to use pressure to their advantage. It focused the mind like nothing else.

His plans had nearly been dashed by the boarding

party. So much had rested on Orson's ability to lie that Mr. Justin had been sure the whole scheme was lost. Miraculously, his brother had pulled it off.

Apparently Sensei had been a key player in the deception as well. Imagine that. Who knew the man had so many talents?

Pity he was going to die tonight.

Mr. Justin lifted his chin, closed his eyes, and took another long pull of fresh air. Though Sensei had given permission for Scions to come on the deck, most were now huddled below, snug in their bunks. They were a nervous bunch of children.

Mr. Justin's gut churned with anxiety, even though he knew what he was about to do would be easy. Nothing about it required immense physical effort or mental calculation. No, the only thing it required was patience. And that was Mr. Justin's forte.

Getting the weapon into position had required a bit of a risk. Fortunately he'd moved it from Orson's cabin before the marines had arrived. And to think, Mr. Justin used to make fun of his brother's lifelong spearfishing hobby.

Mr. Justin felt nothing but contempt for such activities, having put those days of childhood far behind him.

He glanced back at the gap between two wooden crates sitting on the deck. He knew the speargun was tucked in there, but he couldn't see it.

Good. Sensei wouldn't see it either.

Mr. Justin's heart thudded at the thought of what he was about to do. He'd never killed a man up close before. He was, after all, a butler. Making messes was anathema to him. But as his father used to say, *sometimes you have to make a big mess to clean up a little one.* He'd been referring to emptying out a refrigerator to clean the shelves, but Mr. Justin thought the expression apt in this context.

Except in this case, he didn't have anything to *do* yet. Just wait.

Sensei was a tense presence everywhere Mr. Justin went. The man had never cultivated the centered calm he had tried to inculcate in the Scions. That meant he'd be restless tonight, and inevitably, he'd patrol the deck soon.

Mr. Justin turned his back to the stern rail and checked his own position. The winch was taller than he was, a huge spool of thick rusty cable. A hoist gantry stuck up in the air above it, though parts of it were missing.

The boat relied on dockside cranes to on-load freight, and probably had for forty years. That it still floated was a miracle. But it had been cheap, which, at the end of the day, was all that mattered. Once Mr. Justin had the Scions ashore, the bucket of rust would find its final port at the bottom of the sea.

The winch hid him from anyone on the bridge and anyone coming aft. And yet he would be able to see Sensei approaching. A single light fixture hung on the rear side of the bridge tower. It wasn't turned on yet.

Soon, though. And when it was, its rays would cast a long black shadow behind the winch, right were Mr. Justin now stood.

Two wooden crates sat just astern of the winch. Both were lashed under thick webbing secured to cleats on the deck. Everything was in order.

Like an apparition, the martial arts master appeared along the port-side railing. He moved slowly, purposefully, like a leopard on the hunt.

Mr. Justin smiled. The man was so predictable. If he followed the railing, Mr. Justin could move to keep the winch between him and his target. No face-to-face moment needed. Excellent.

He stepped quietly to the crates and bent to grab the speargun.

"Leslie, I've been looking for you."

Mr. Justin stiffened and turned, leaving the weapon in its hiding spot. Rachel, a Pelican, stood before him, shifting her weight from foot to foot. "What is it, dear?"

"Humphrey sent me to find you. He says you need to talk about the new arrangement with your Nine."

Ah, the new arrangement. Humphrey had wisely put Dajeet in charge of his Nine. That had suited Mr. Justin well. He supposed he should make a scene about it. Maybe he would, once Sensei was dead.

Mr. Justin considered tossing the child overboard.

But no. For one thing, she'd scream and Sensei would surely hear her. For another, she was worth a hundred million dollars to Mr. Justin. At least.

Dr. Carlhagen had never charged enough for his services, but Mr. Justin intended to. So he refrained from acting on his first impulse, a skill he'd cultivated by long practice as a butler.

Instead, he smiled. "Go back to the cargo hold. I'll be there in a minute."

"What are you doing back here?"

"I just needed some air. I get claustrophobic."

"Oh." She didn't move.

"Run along, Rachel."

Finally the child turned and trotted away. Mr. Justin kept his breathing even, though he wanted to shout a long string of obscenities into the wind.

The light on the conning tower flickered on, making Mr. Justin blink. He stepped into the winch shadow and scanned for Sensei.

And found the man staring right at him.

Mr. Justin's breath stopped momentarily. So much for shooting the man from hiding. "Hello, Sensei."

"Leslie. You've been neglecting your Nine."

Mr. Justin sidestepped to put two paces between him and the martial arts master. "You're right. I've let them down, but . . ."

"But what?"

Quickly, before he could question his plan, Mr. Justin darted to the railing, grabbed hold and swung his legs over. He slid down so his feet rested on the edge of the deck, hands behind him gripping the rail. The black waters of the sea roiled below him, white wake spread out below him. "I can't do this anymore."

"Leslie! Don't do this." Sensei held his hands out to him, eyes pleading. "Just talk to me."

Time for some extemporaneous lies, Mr. Justin thought. Pretending to be a desperate Scion would not be difficult given the real bone-squeezing fear he felt perched on the edge of death.

"I know what the others think of me. Belle told me often enough. Leslie the Bland. Leslie the Simple-Minded. The Disappointment. And then Jacey tells us the truth. I'm just a clone. Somewhere out there is my Progenitor, equally dull-minded and useless."

Yes, he thought. Leslie's Progenitor *is* out there. The most powerful person in the world. President of the North American Union.

What irony that such a dolt could achieve high office. Her only skill was the illusion of gravitas, the appearance of wisdom and authority, a micron-thin veneer masking a gray, squishy mind that had very little thought at all.

Sensei's voice softened. "Don't compare yourself to others. Different people have different gifts. All have something to contribute."

"I don't want to be a mere contributor! I don't want to smile through tears the rest of my life. You, Jacey, Humphrey, Belle, Vaughan—you all ignore me. You leave me out, and everyone can *see* I've been left out. I'll save them the effort it takes to ignore me."

Mr. Justin leaned further out. Come on, come on, you bastard. Save me.

On cue, Sensei eased forward, hands out. "Let's talk about this."

"There's nothing to talk about! I'm a copy of a person; I'm not even an individual. Where are we going on this boat anyway? What kind of life lies ahead?"

"I understand. Believe me."

"How could you?" Mr. Justin looked away and let a smile escape.

There's a line you can follow, Sensei. Tell me about your pathetic suicide attempt.

Sensei's leaned closer. "I've been right where you are. I tried to kill myself once."

Mr. Justin snapped his face toward Sensei, widening his eyes with feigned shock. He pulled back to the railing, toes still thrusting into space above the dark sea.

Sensei took another step toward him. "Please, Leslie. Come back on this side of the rail."

The boat heeled to starboard on a particularly deep swell. Mr. Justin faked nearly losing his grip, letting one foot fly free and a gasp escape. In truth, it didn't take much acting. The move had its intended effect. Sensei darted close, leaned over the railing and wrapped his arms around Mr. Justin's shoulders.

Mr. Justin found himself back on the deck with Sensei holding him tightly, murmuring assurances. "I won't let you kill yourself. I won't let you give up."

"I'm so scared," Mr. Justin said curling into Sensei's

embrace. The man was strong, strong, strong. The shot would have to be perfect.

Sensei stroked Mr. Justin's hair in a fatherly way. Mr. Justin felt a giggle building in his chest. He let it out by faking a sob. Manipulating this man was so easy.

"I think of all you as my kids." Sensei's voice welled with emotion.

Mr. Justin pulled away and retreated a few steps, moving close to the crates and the surprise he had hidden between them. He put his hands over his face. "I'm sorry, Sensei. I just don't see any future for me. For any of us."

Especially not you.

"I know what you're going through, Leslie. I tried to kill myself once. Got closer than you did just now."

He rubbed his throat and turned away from Mr. Justin. Sensei started in on the story Mr. Justin already knew, about how he had been a famous fighter, had been imprisoned for the murder of young woman, had lost hope during his incarceration.

"Did you do it? Did you kill that woman?" Mr. Justin asked, already knowing the answer.

"No!" Sensei shouted, turning his head slightly to look back at Mr. Justin. His gazed dropped, and took on a far away aspect. "At least, I don't think so."

Mr. Justin sat on one of the wooden crates, let his hand drop into the gap between them. His fingers brushed the stock of the speargun. "What future are *you* living for?"

Sensei didn't answer. He stood like a statue, hands gripping the rail, body so tense it seemed he would rip the railing right off. "I want justice. Dr. Carlhagen tried to have me killed. And according to Mr. Justin, he sent people to kill my daughter. I want justice."

Your daughter still lives. I saw to that in order to preserve a

*contingency I no longer need. But I don't need leverage over you.
I need you dead.*

"You should get some sleep," Sensei said. All at once,
tension flowed out of him and his fists released the rail.

"What about you?" Mr. Justin asked. "You need to
sleep, too."

"I'll try. Soon."

"Can I just stay out here with you a little while longer?"

A sickle moon had risen. It painted a silvery lane on the
sea and lifted the blackness from the shadows. Mr. Justin
leaned sideways and grasped the speargun. It came free
from its hiding spot and rested easily in his hands.

It was a much nicer model than the homemade kind he
and Orson had used as young kids. So many years ago.

Mr. Justin remembered that world, the innocence, the
complete lack of a future. A father who served Dr. Carlhagen and a grandfather who had served some other
wealthy, inconsiderate bastard.

Mr. Justin lifted the weapon. Moonlight glinted from
the spear tip. He had no personal quarrel with Sensei, had
no desire to make the man suffer. But the martial arts
master was in the way, and dangerous.

Mr. Justin took a cautious step forward, aiming the
speargun at Sensei's back, aligning the tip with his heart.
Not a good shot, really.

Sensei would not go down easily. As powerful as the
spring-loaded speargun was, it needed to penetrate the
man's thick muscles. And, going through his back, it
would could hit his scapula or a rib and never penetrate to
his heart.

If Mr. Justin didn't deliver a fatal blow with the first
shot, he doubted he'd get a second. Even grievously
wounded, Sensei would take him out in two seconds.

Better to make sure of his kill shot. Mr. Justin raised the

point of the spear, bringing it bear on the back of Sensei's neck.

One shot. Must not miss.

He stepped closer, so that the tip hovered just inches from Sensei's flesh.

Sensei tensed and stopped speaking.

Mr. Justin's finger kissed the trigger, but he did not shoot. If he was off by a centimeter, he could miss the spine.

Sensei turned his head, then slowly rotated in place. If he was surprised to see Leslie aiming a speargun at him, he didn't show it. Nor did fear cross his face.

Hands trembling and clammy, Mr. Justin pushed forward bit by bit until the spear tip touched Sensei's throat, just beneath his chin.

The man smiled. "Mr. Justin. Clever."

"I'm sorry, Mario," Mr. Justin said. And he was sorry. He wished things could have worked out differently. But they hadn't.

Seeing no point in prolonging the moment, he pulled the trigger. With a muted slap, the spear shot through Sensei's throat and out the back of his neck.

Blood fountained from the wound. The man grasped at it, jaw moving, eyes locked on Mr. Justin's.

The butler dropped the speargun and ran, gagging and retching, but not stopping.

His plan was not yet complete.

69

WET AND CRIMSON

Mr. Justin yanked open the door to Sang's room. The boy rolled over in his bunk, dark eyebrows scrunched in confusion. "Leslie?"

Mr. Justin leaned against the doorjamb, breath heaving much harder than necessary. "Sang, come quickly! Mr. Justin has attacked Sensei."

Sang shot to his feet. "Is that blood on your uniform?"

Nodding and backing into the hall. "Please, help. I can't trust anyone else."

The boy followed him. "What do you mean?"

Mr. Justin kept his face pointed away from Sang, afraid he'd smile at his own brilliance. "You were locked up when Sensei was—" He sobbed and hugged his arms close to his body the way he'd seen some of the girls do after Constantine's funeral. "So you *can't* be Mr. Justin. And now I think I know who he is."

They started up the central stairway, taking them two at a time. Mr. Justin gasped for air. "At least I've finally proved you innocent. I hope you'll forgive me for accusing you."

Sang didn't say anything.

No surprise there. Leslie had led the accusations that had gotten Sang soundly beaten and locked up.

"What happened to Sensei?" Sang asked. "Will he be okay?"

"I didn't see it. I went out to the deck to get some air and there he was." Mr. Justin pretended to break down again.

"I can't believe Mr. Justin would just leave Sensei to be found."

"I don't think he had time to plan it. He just needed to get Sensei out of the way so he could take over the boat."

"Who did Mr. Justin transfer into?"

"I hate to say it."

Sang grabbed Mr. Justin's arm, yanked him around. "Tell me!"

Here was a fun moment.

Mr. Justin reveled in it. Sniffing and rubbing at his nose, hoping Sang didn't notice there weren't actually tears running down his face, Mr. Justin revealed a horrific secret. "It's Humphrey. It's the only thing that makes sense. No suspicion on him at all. He's able to impersonate Dr. Carlhagen . . ."

Sang's mouth dropped open and he stared past Mr. Justin. "It's brilliant."

They pushed onto the deck. Mr. Justin shoved Sang toward the stern. "Go find Sensei. Help him if you can. Make sure no one gets a hold of the murder weapon."

Sang ran off.

Mr. Justin grinned and sprinted forward to the little hidey-hole a certain wayward Scion had made his little den.

It was the Jeep. Nobody had bothered to search inside it because it was concealed under a taut stretch of plastic tarpaulin. Only by chance had Mr. Justin noticed an odd fold on one side where the tarp had been slit then neatly drawn back together.

But first he had to collect the knife. He stooped and felt under the rear bumper. There it was. Right where he'd stashed it. A knife from the kitchen. Ten centimeter blade and reasonably sharp.

Sharp enough.

He tore open the slit in the tarp and pounded on the Jeep's rear window. "Come out. It's an emergency."

Horace's face popped up, hair mussed and collar sigil pin askew.

Mr. Justin waved Horace out.

Looking like a Dolphin who'd been caught with contraband tub of ice cream, Horace squeezed out the passenger door. "I'm not leaving my spot."

"It's an emergency. Mr. Justin got free and killed Sensei. There's so much blood."

Horace's face took on a weird aspect, nostril's flaring and eyes lighting up. His teeth showed, white and sharp in the darkness. "Where?"

Mr. Justin pointed toward the rear of the ship.

"Stop Sang if you can!" Mr. Justin started guiding Horace astern. "Here. You may need this to defend yourself." He pressed the knife into Horace's fist.

The boy held it aloft like it was a magic sword.

"Go, Horace! I'll call the others to come help you."

Horace sprinted away.

It was only a few meters to the hatches for the Boys' and Girls' Holds. They were propped open to allow fresh air to circulate. Mr. Justin shouted at the top of his voice. "Help! Help! Sensei is dead! Sang is missing!"

In less than a minute, Tytus, Kirk, Obu, Wanda, Dajeet, and Bethancy were on the deck, sprinting toward the scene of horror.

Questions followed Mr. Justin as he ran aft. "I don't know," he answered to all of them. "I heard a cry and struggle. Then I saw Sang and Horace standing over Sensei's body."

The Scions funneled past the bridge and around the derelict winch and gantry. The bridge light spilled its harsh glare across the deck.

Sang stood there holding the speargun in one hand. Horace moved around him, crouched, brandishing the knife.

"I didn't do it!" Sang shouted at Horace.

Wanda screamed. "Horace, put that knife down. You, too, Sang. Put the weapon on the deck."

Sang stooped to lay the speargun down.

That would never do, Mr. Justin decided. So he screamed, a wordless howl of terror. Even Horace looked at him.

Mr. Justin crept forward, the others to either side of him. He pointed a shaking finger. "Sensei. He's been shot in the throat."

With fury quaking his voice, Mr. Justin raised his finger to Sang's face, which was sickly white in the weird light. "He's Mr. Justin. He *killed* Sensei. Get him!"

Horace launched himself like a panther bringing down its prey. One moment he was high in the air, knife raised overhead. The next he was on Sang, plunging the blade.

Again. Again. Each time it rose, the blade glistened, wet and crimson.

Sang shrieked, but it was soon drowned by the shouts and cries of the other Scions.

Tytus and Kirk darted in and dragged Horace back. The

boy slashed at Tytus, drawing a thin line of red across the Snake's cheek.

With calm and precise kicks and blows, Kirk and Tytus beat Horace to the ground.

Still the wild boy flailed. He jabbed the knife an inch into Kirk's thigh.

Roaring, eyes bright with rage, Kirk smashed Horace's face. He grabbed the wrist of Horace's knife hand, threw a leg over the boy's arm, then twisted with all his might.

A crackle of breaking bone shot across the deck like gunfire. Tytus dropped to a knee onto Horace's throat, arms blurring as he rained blows onto the boy's face.

Blood curtained from the slice in Tytus's cheek, over his lips, dripped onto the deck. He looked possessed with violence as he punished Horace.

With every blow, air burst from Tytus's mouth, spraying blood and curses in equal measures over Horace's head.

Kirk yanked the knife from Horace's limp hand, tossed it and caught it so the point faced down. With a sob, he raised it.

Mr. Justin dove, wrapping his arms around Kirk and pulling him away.

Even as he did it, he reveled in the beauty of the moment. "Stop, Kirk!" he yelled.

He did not let go of the boy, who was straining to get at Horace. "He's down. Can't you see that?"

Wanda and Bethancy had pulled Tytus back. The boy sat on the deck, legs straight out, body hunched, face bleeding. Tears and groans of pain and sorrow poured from his soul.

Wanda snapped her fingers at Dajeet. "Go get Humphrey."

"Let me go," Kirk said.

"Put the knife down."

Kirk obeyed, then the weight of what had happened seemed to hit him like a blow to the gut. He leaned into Mr. Justin and wept on his shoulder.

Mr. Justin consoled him, patted his back and told him he'd only done what was necessary.

With Tytus utterly drained of energy, Wanda had moved to Sang. She felt at his throat.

Her hand came away wet with blood. "He's dead."

She glanced at Sensei, but it was obvious he was dead, too.

Face grim, Wanda tucked her unruly hair behind her ears, unconcerned with how she fouled her locks with blood.

Lips pressed tight, she went to Horace. She felt at his throat, then thumbed open one of his black and swollen eyelids.

Lifting her gaze to meet Mr. Justin's, she sighed through her nose. "Alive. But barely."

To mask his disappointment, Mr. Justin turned his attention back to comforting Kirk.

Everything had gone perfectly. Sensei dead. Sang proven to be Mr. Justin in the eyes of all the Scions.

And if Horace still breathed, well, the boy could still take a turn for the worse.

70

DOUBLE FAMOUS

A chill swept over the sea, carried on the unceasing breeze coming out of the east. Jacey was still keeping watch at the bow of the ship.

She drew the corners of a crinkly silver emergency blanket tighter around her shoulders. How Meow Meow had known to search for it among the onboard emergency gear was beyond Jacey. It seemed the weird girl was full of surprises.

So far they'd seen the lights of three ships on the horizon. All had been too far away to risk using one of the flares.

But as every hour slipped away, Jacey's fear grew. Captain Wilcox had to know by now that they'd escaped on the boat. His men on the dock would have reported that.

It couldn't take long to refuel a chopper, and once they recovered the empty life raft they'd know they'd been tricked. And this boat, dead in the water, would be easy to board. Hiding in the storage compartments wouldn't do much good then.

Meow Meow wandered back and sat next to Jacey. "Our loverboy is sleeping soundly. The bleeding has stopped. I thought he might need stitches. I've already given him all the antibiotics from the first aid kit."

Jacey let the "our loverboy" thing slide. She'd come to realize that Meow Meow made suggestive comments out of habit.

"There's another ship." She pointed, making the blanket crinkle. "What do you think?"

Meow Meow's face was unreadable in the darkness. "It's headed the direction we came from. I don't think we want to get on board anything going closer to Vin's island. Know what I mean?"

"Yes." It was the only boat they'd seen that was reasonably close. "How long until dawn, do you think?"

"Dawn and I are not on friendly terms. I don't think I've seen her for fifteen years."

Jacey gave a half-hearted laugh. "Are you nocturnal, or what?"

"Absolutely. Do you have any idea what it took to get me awake and ready for Vin's thing this morning? I had four alarms set on my tablet, and I'd put it in the bathroom so I'd have to get out of bed to turn it off. Even worse, I set the alarm to be that horrible 'Waddle Waddle' song."

She pumped her hands over her head and sang: "When I do the thing, I do it right. When it comes to you, I do it right. When I do it right, I do it all night long. Waddle waddle. Waddle waddle." She laughed and made the middle finger gesture at the sky. "Go to hell Mercutio!"

"Mercutio?" Jacey said. "I don't think so. Those lines are most definitely *not* from Romeo and Juliet."

Meow Meow cocked her head and twisted her lips into

grimace. "Romeo and Juliet? Nah. Mercutio was a singer when I was a kid. 'Waddle Waddle' was a huge hit—"

She clamped her mouth shut a moment and shook her head. "You really don't know who Mercutio was? So that whole Scion School place you were telling me about really is insulated from the outside world."

"I don't know who you are, either."

Meow Meow giggled. "There's a first time for everything, I suppose."

She put her arm around Jacey's shoulders and gave her a squeeze. "I like you, Jacey. If by chance we get off this little boat, you're going to need my help. With that face of yours . . . mmmm, mmm . . . The paparazzi are going to be on your ass like a tail on a bunny rabbit. But don't worry. I'll show you how to be famous. It's really not too hard."

"I don't want to be famous."

"You said you were interviewed by Yvonne Kellar, right?"

"Yes."

Meow Meow squeezed her again. "Girl, your face was famous the day you were born. And now . . . I don't think I'm going out on a limb by saying this . . . You'll be 'double famous!'" She made air quotes with great vigor.

Jacey scanned the horizon. A blip of blue light had appeared to the north.

"But you don't get that reference, do you, sweetling?" Meow Meow said, a hint of sadness in her voice.

"What reference?" Jacey was having trouble paying attention. The light on the horizon was fast approaching.

"Double famous."

"That's a reference? To what?"

Meow Meow laughed and slapped her knee and wiped at her eyes. "Oh my god! This is *surreal!* It's from one of your own movies. Might be your most famous line ever.

The film was a musical called *Slip That Jack,* and you starred in it with that guy from Saskatchewan, the one with the sexy harelip. Anyway, it's a classic. You'll have to watch it some time. There's this one scene where you're doing a song and dance number—you're a traveling vaudevillian—and two ladies come into your dressing room afterward. One says, 'I'm gonna make you a movie star.' And the other one says, 'No, *I'm* going to make you a pop star.' They're fighting over you, right? Then you step in and say, 'Ladies! Pipe down. Give me one good reason I can't do both.' Then you break out into song."

Snapping her fingers and swaying, Meow Meow sang: "The whole wide world will know my name is/Sharilee Jackson Charleen Shamus/From holovids to concert stages/I'll be, I'll be, I'll beeeeeeeeee/DOUBLE FAMOUS!"

Meow Meow clapped for her own performance and nudged Jacey with her bony shoulder. "I bet ninety-nine out of a hundred people could sing you that song. It's as famous as 'White Christmas' or 'Thriller' or 'The Macarena.'"

Jacey's blank look produced a snort from Meow Meow. She composed herself and apologized. "I'll help you, dearie. That's all I'm trying to say. If we ever get rescued, I'll help you survive being famous."

"That might be about to happen." Jacey pointed at the ship headed their way. With only a couple lights visible, it was obviously headed straight for them. "Get the flare gun. I'm afraid they'll run us down if we don't let them know we're here."

Meow Meow fetched the gun from where she'd stashed it. "Are you ready, sweet tart? We are going to have to do some fast lying once they pull us on board."

Lying was all Jacey had been doing recently. She stood

and rubbed her elbows, chilled by more than the wind. "Do it. And . . . thank you."

The skinny girl in the blue wig grinned and aimed the gun at the sky. Face bunching, she pulled the trigger. Her arms kicked back as the flare whooshed out, trailing white smoke.

Seconds went by.

A red explosion bloomed against the backdrop of stars, sending spidery tendrils toward the sea. It hissed and popped, then faded to nothing.

The response was instant. A sonorous horn blasted across the water.

Meow Meow fumbled to load the next round, mumbling, hands shaking. With a click, she snapped the chamber closed and raised the gun again. Another shot. Another sparkling spider appeared in the sky.

"Get Dante's flashlight," Meow Meow said.

Jacey found it and shined its light at the oncoming ship.

An answer flashed back at them. Clearly a code of some sort, but Jacey had no idea what it might mean. She turned the flashlight on and off a few more times.

It only took a few tense minutes before they were sure the ship had changed course. The sound of its massive engines grew ever louder. And the closer it came, the bigger it got.

"Time to wake loverboy," Meow Meow said. "We need to get our stories straight."

But Jacey's mind was already past that. Her thoughts were on Livy, Humphrey, and the rest.

Under her breath, she said to the night, "I'm coming, Livy. Hold on. I'm coming."

71

THE TWO REMAINING SHARKS

"Who let him out of his room?" Humphrey demanded.

Every Scion aboard *Aphrodite* had gathered around the grisly scene. The youngest clung to the older ones, the oldest huddled around the bodies. Thankfully, someone had covered Sensei's body with a tarp.

"I assume you did it," Leslie said. "Weren't you the one who let him and Horace out when the marines boarded the ship?"

"I've been on the bridge since Con's funeral."

And now there would be two more. Maybe three, if Horace died. The boy was breathing, but with difficulty. Wanda crouched next to him, pressing an icepack against his battered face.

Summer ran up and skidded to a stop when she spotted the crowd. She carried a huge flashlight. Elias trotted up next to her, holding his side and wincing. "Orson spotted a flare off the port bow. He—"

Elias was already at Horace's side. The wild boy was

the Snake in Elias's Nine. While Wanda told him what had happened, Humphrey went to Sensei. Holding his breath to brace himself, he lifted the tarp. Just as quickly, he lowered it again.

"At least we know Mr. Justin is dead now," Leslie said. "Poor Sang."

Poor Sang indeed. "Somebody cover him up. He's Mr. Justin no more and deserves respect."

"Who's keeping an eye on Orson?" Leslie asked.

"Nobody at the moment. I heard screaming and came running."

"You left him up there alone?"

Humphrey grimaced. "Obu. Please go to the bridge and make sure Orson doesn't accidentally sink the ship."

The boy dashed away, face drawn with exhaustion and fear. Not fear about Orson. Nobody feared that cowardly fool. His was the fear that comes from losing so many friends so quickly. Humphrey had felt it too, when he'd seen Sensei's body.

The Scions were truly alone. Their numbers were shrinking every day. They had nowhere to go, no home, no future.

Trust in each other was all they had left, and even that was wearing thin. And no wonder. Mr. Justin had undercut their bonds by creating an environment of suspicion.

Leslie stalked toward him. "You say you were on the bridge, but was anyone besides Orson up there with you?"

"What? Are you suggesting I'm Mr. Justin?" He laughed at the ridiculousness of the idea.

No one laughed with him.

Eyes of all the Scions watched him and Leslie—the two remaining Sharks—square off.

She had that haughty look she had learned from Belle. Looking down her nose at him, she jabbed a finger at his chest. "Maybe we've all been tricked. Weren't you the one who told us that Senator Bentilius has hundreds of soldiers coming to take control of the Scion School? Weren't you the one who said Jacey was going to Elizabeth's island and that we had to follow her there? Weren't you the one who rushed us out to sea in a boat with unreliable engines?"

She spat this string of questions at him, emphasizing every "you" in accusation. If her goal was to arouse suspicion, it worked.

The others were staring at him now.

Some were shaking their heads, denying what Leslie was trying to suggest. It was ridiculous on the face of it. But not all seemed so sure. Dajeet, Dansha, Bethancy, and Kirk gave him appraising looks, as if suddenly seeing him quite differently.

Wanda left Horace's side and moved to stand with Humphrey. Elias and Summer did, too.

"Of course, they would support you," Leslie said, jabbing a finger at Summer and Elias. "All your favorites who get special treatment. And, of course, your new love Wanda. Jacey's gone a half hour and you're already kissing her when you think nobody's looking."

"We never kissed!" Wanda said.

Leslie ignored this denial, which came across even to Humphrey's ears as overly defensive. "Can anyone vouch that Humphrey was on the bridge at the time Sang was released?"

Nobody said anything. They couldn't. Humphrey had been alone on the bridge with Orson. Nobody was going to take his word for it.

"If I'm Mr. Justin, why would I release Sang? It would make more sense to keep him locked up and keep suspicion firmly on him. Look. I know you're upset, Leslie. I understand that you're mad at me and think I treated you unfairly by putting Dajeet in charge of your Nine. But this is ridiculous."

Leslie didn't give an inch. "Why is it only you and Jacey who make all the decisions?" She looked to Wanda and others. "Maybe he isn't Mr. Justin. Maybe Sang really was. But I still don't trust him with my life. With all our lives. He's always keeping secrets from us. I accepted it because Sensei was around to keep an eye on him. But now who's going to do that? Humphrey isn't our king!"

Silence.

A few nodding heads, mostly from Leslie's Nine. It wasn't a total revolt, but it was enough of one.

Humphrey felt the weight he'd been carrying. He sat on the deck, leaned his back against the rusty winch and propped his forearms on his knees.

"Where should we go, Leslie? There's a fleet to the northeast. They've gotten to St. Vitus by now. They know we've fled. Orson thinks they'll remember the boat with the bus and they'll be back to search us again. There are islands all over, but Orson says they're all inhabited and they won't welcome a boatload of strangers arriving. Where should we go?"

Leslie said nothing. She had her arms crossed and a peculiar look on her face. It was Dajeet, of all people, who spoke up. Her eyes were invisible in the shadow of the gantry. "There's one obvious answer. You claimed that Mr. Justin and Orson were planning to steal us. They obviously had some destination in mind. Somewhere they could hide us from Dr. Carlhagen. And since we're so valuable, they must have had food and accommodations prepared. Why don't we just go where they were planning to take us?"

Wanda beat Humphrey to the retort. "That's ridiculous. They'll have guards of their own there waiting there for us."

"I don't like it, either," Leslie said.

She seemed to have calmed down, her voice lowering to a more rational tone. "Do you have a better idea, Humphrey? You said yourself there's a fleet coming. We need to get to land soon."

Bethancy stepped forward, swinging her hair over her shoulder. "If Mr. Justin had a place ready for us, it will be well hidden. It would have to be, for his scheme to work."

Leslie looked to Elias and Tytus. "It's crazy, I know. But where else could we go?"

Humphrey raised his hands, as if surrendering to the insanity. "We don't even know where they were going to take us."

"Orson would know." Wanda had moved next to him. She crouched, fidgeting with her hands between her knees. "There would be food. Shelter. It's a risk. But what else can we do?"

Leslie walked past Humphrey and addressed Elias and Tytus. "What do you two think?"

Humphrey saw them nod, then dropped his face.

"You two go question Orson," Leslie ordered. "Make him be specific about how far away the original destination is and how many guards are stationed there. Tell him his life depends on his honesty."

She didn't wait for the boys to leave, dismissing them by turning her back on them. "It's clear that Mr. Justin had help. Someone let him out of his cell. What do you think, Wanda? Should we call a lockdown? Everybody back in the holds."

Nobody moved.

"What about Sang and Sensei?" Humphrey asked.

"They're fine where they are. We'll have a ceremony in the morning."

Leslie squatted in front of Humphrey. She made a sympathetic face. "You look terrible. Go get some sleep."

Humphrey wanted to yell at her. Demand to know why anyone should listen to her. She'd been asleep in a bunk when her Nine had needed her. She had done nothing but complain the whole time.

Except the Scions *were* listening to her.

"I think I will get some sleep." He held his hands out to Wanda. She took them and hefted him to his feet.

He didn't want to go to Boys' Hold, though. He didn't want questions and he didn't want to see the looks they might give him. Suspicion was poison.

"You did well, Humphrey," Wanda said. "Nobody really believes all those accusations Leslie made. I don't think she does either. I'll talk to the other girls. Sang was Mr. Justin. He killed Sensei. Horace . . ." She shook her head and wiped her eyes.

Humphrey went to the rear of the school bus. He pulled the latch and opened the door. "I'm sleeping in here."

Wanda's arms went around his middle. He turned in her embrace.

There was no moment of resistance, no thought. She fit her lips to his, pressing tenderly. He couldn't refuse it. He needed it.

Wanda's kiss seemed to hold him up. As did her body, which was strong and lithe but also soft and yielding. He curled his fingers into her hair, surprised by how silky it was against his skin.

He came up for air, found her eyes close to his, her breath soft and sweet on his face.

She pulled back. "I know. We can't."

"We can't." His voice was thick with equal parts desire and regret.

"Leslie's plan is desperate," Wanda said. "Even if we do go wherever it is Mr. Justin was going to take us, the Scions will need your leadership. Not hers."

Humphrey nodded, but didn't know how to respond. He'd already given the Scions everything he had. "I'm going to sleep. Thank you, Wanda. For . . ."

"I know." Then she was gone, footsteps lost in the roar of engines and rush of the sea.

He climbed into the bus and quietly pulled the door shut.

72

SILKY FLAMES

Arow of white plastic pill bottles sat on a shelf inside the mirror cabinet in Dr. Carlhagen's bathroom. An instant of calculation told him he was looking at a month's worth of andleprixen. And there was more stored in a box in the closet.

Dr. Carlhagen filled a paper cup with water, popped two tablets and washed them down. He crushed the cup in his fist and dropped it in a waste bin, then leaned over the sink to inspect his face.

He understood that from an objective viewpoint, his face rivaled that of the most famous male models and actors in history. But it wasn't his face. It was Vaughan's face. And that meant it was Charles Buchanan's face.

Ergo, he hated it.

Which was why he'd decided not to shave. Instead, he dug out his grooming kit and set about trimming his beard and mustache, which admittedly hadn't grown in very thickly. Having a seventeen-year-old body had some disadvantages, it seemed.

The thought made him chuckle. Because being physically perfect in every other regard—as well as blessed with the virile stamina only a teenage boy could possess—was hardly cause for self-pity.

The laugh faded as he considered his current predicament. As pleasant (and athletic) as the senator's lustful affections were, he didn't love her. Could barely tolerate to hear her speak.

His thoughts were always with Jacqueline.

No. He shook his head and thumped his temple with his palm. No. It's Jacey. Jacqueline is dead.

And yet, Jacey was so much like Jacqueline. Better, in some regards. After all, Jacey wasn't in love with Vaughan the way Jacqueline had loved that idiot Charles.

Dr. Carlhagen had given up on winning the girl over. She hated him. For good reason, he supposed. His behavior toward her had been . . . unseemly. That idea to overwrite her with Senator Bentilius had been desperate. And now that he'd spent some time with Maxine, he was glad of Jacey's escape.

He stripped off his clothes and stepped into a piping hot shower. The water soothed the tension somewhat, allowed him to think more clearly. That, or the pills were taking effect.

Over the next ten minutes, he continued to increase the heat bit by bit until the skin of his neck and chest reddened.

Clean and refreshed, he got out and wrapped himself in a towel. Barefoot, he padded into his office.

He summoned Captain Wilcox and waited.

Maxine came in, head down, and meekly handed him the whisky he'd ordered. He kissed her ear and nodded to a chair.

She sat, hands folded on her knee, eyes down.

Captain Wilcox's holo appeared above the desk. "Dr. Carlhagen. I'm sorry to inform you the Scion Jacey has escaped Vin's island by boat. Her range will be severely limited by fuel. I expect we'll recover her by helicopter in the morning."

"Disconnect!" Dr. Carlhagen barked.

Captain Wilcox disappeared.

Hand trembling, knuckles turning white from his grip on his glass, Dr. Carlhagen swallowed the whisky in one tip of his head. It slid like silky flames down his throat, then blossomed into dragon fire in his belly.

With a violent curse, he hurled the glass at Maxine. She ducked and it smashed into the wall above her head. Crystal rained in a spray of sparkling light.

Nostrils flaring, Dr. Carlhagen sat heavily in his chair.

Calm. Must stay calm.

He had Livy.

As long as he had the child, Jacey would be on a leash. A long one, yes. But slowly, inevitably, Dr. Carlhagen would pull her in.

And make her heel.

73

EL TIBURÓN

The freighter idled next to Jacey's stolen boat. Its hull was like a wall of steel, like some blue-and-white-painted battlement rising from the sea.

Dante snapped nautical lingo at her and Meow Meow, ordering them to steer one way and then the other in order to pull alongside their rescuers.

Jacey thought he'd get along well with Summer, the way he lapsed into swearing tirades when they didn't know what the hell he was talking about. She'd never seen this side of him. Maybe it was the gunshot wound.

A huge square patch of steel hinged open ten meters above them. It protested with a metal-on-metal scream.

Men in sky-blue jumpsuits emerged and looked down at them. One put a bullhorn to his mouth and shouted in Spanish.

"Are you able to climb?"

A rope ladder unfurled, the first rung kissing the water between the ship and the boat.

Meow Meow didn't bother to answer. "This should be

interesting," she said to Jacey, then leapt across the gap and started to climb. Her sticklike legs propelled her up and soon she was conferring with the men.

"She's famous. You're famous. I'm slightly famous," Dante said. "This is going to be tricky."

A half-hour later, Jacey and Meow Meow were sitting in the captain's quarters, drinking coffee and lying through their teeth.

Dante was in the infirmary getting stitches at the hands of a Chinese medic who grinned incessantly and sang Meow Meow songs in a baritone warble.

Captain Cruz Real stood a hand shorter than Meow Meow, but carried himself with the ferocity of a tiger. His mustache alone looked like it weighed twenty kilos. It seemed to pull down his face, dragging the skin of his cheeks and eyes toward his scowling chin.

Despite this, he spoke in a high-pitched voice that cracked like a Crab boy just hitting puberty. "You are most welcome aboard *El Tiburón*, ladies. I am happy to allow you to film your incredible project on my ship. Will you need to interview me, perhaps?"

Jacey gave him her most charming smile.

She knew vanity when she saw it, knew this man was enamored by the prospect of being seen by millions of people across the world.

Meow Meow's story about how three look-alikes of famous people were trying to travel around the world, with no money, and relying solely on their wits and the generosity of strangers had seemed ridiculous to Jacey. But everyone on board had not only believed it, but had embraced it.

And Dante's injury? Oh, that was from a run-in with pirates, Meow Meow had said, without cracking a smile.

Aside from expressions of concern, the captain hadn't blinked.

"Of course we'll interview you," Jacey said.

"It will have to be soon, as we'll arrive in San Juan tomorrow morning. I will be very busy then, overseeing the off-loading of cargo. And I'm sure you will want to get on your way."

It took a moment for Jacey to realize the glower he was aiming at them was a smile.

"Yes. We'll interview you tonight."

"Perhaps over a meal. My wife will want to be part of it."

Meow Meow suddenly laughed, and seemed to relax a great deal. "Your wife? She's on board?"

"Oh yes. She *owns* this ship."

"Charming. A family business."

"Yes."

Jacey stood. "I look forward to it. Could you have someone show me to a place I can get some food and perhaps a shower?"

Captain Real clapped his hands and a porter came in. He indicated the door, and Jacey went out. Meow Meow followed after.

A minute later, they'd made their way through plain, but well-maintained, companionways to a rather luxurious suite consisting of a bed, small sitting area, and a tiny bathroom. "The captain's daughter's cabin," the porter said by way of explanation. "She is at school in Chicago at the moment."

He backed out of the room, leaving the two girls alone.

Meow Meow flopped onto a sofa facing a wall monitor. "We did it. Now all we have to do is pretend to be making a holo-show and get off in San Juan. From there . . . Well, we'll figure something out."

Jacey had moved to a curtain on the far wall. She spread it wide, and found a small porthole window. Peering out, she saw little but the sea and, in the distance, a few more freighters.

Dante had said this was a sea-lane. It was hard to imagine that ships like this had been carrying people and things to and fro for Jacey's entire life. The world's vast size made her feel very small and insignificant. She didn't really know what a holo-show was.

Meow Meow pulled something from under her blouse jacket. A handbag. She reached in and pulled out a handful of black balls just like the one the reporter Yvonne Kellar had used.

Drone cameras. "I never leave home without a small swarm ready to go. I never know when I might want to broadcast something to my fans. Captain Real will love being on drone-cam, won't he?"

The door opened and two men carried Dante in. They put him on the bed, where he lay on one side. His face had the smooth, relaxed look of someone quite happily sedated.

"Ah, this is your dream come true, isn't it, Meow Meow? Three of us and one bed."

He fell asleep.

"Do you think there's a holodesk on this ship?" Jacey asked.

"Yes," Meow Meow said, hesitantly. "But your transmission won't be private. You'd be best to wait until we get to San Juan to call your Scion friends." She said that last part with a slight hitch. Maybe it was skepticism. Maybe it was because the Scions' predicament was too bleak for a girl like Meow Meow to grasp.

"You know a place in San Juan?" Jacey asked. "That's the first thing I want to do once we get off this ship."

"I know a place."

"Good."

Jacey looked out through the small round window at the darkness outside. Captain Wilcox's boat was now at the bottom of the sea, thanks to Captain Real's cooperative crew. They'd all agreed the sinking would be good footage for "the show."

It seemed that was all the outside world was to these people.

A show.

Jacqueline and Meow Meow and Vin and Dante. They were all characters, as far as the world was concerned. Perhaps that's all Senator Bentilius and Dr. Carlhagen were, too.

The ache Jacey had been ignoring—the one centered in her heart—took hold of her. She hugged her arms close and clamped her jaw shut against the sobs of fear threatening to escape her.

A bit of dampness made it to her eyes, but that was it. That was all she'd allow. That ache could be compressed into something else, she knew. She'd been doing it for so long now, she wondered if that was the primary emotion of life.

Anger.

"I'm coming, Livy."

74

HIGH-PITCHED AND FULL OF FEAR

Humphrey snapped awake.

Someone was calling his name. It was Summer. She was standing next to him.

Wanda hovered behind her. Eyebrows bunched over her nose.

Something was wrong.

He shook the sleep from his brain. "What it is?"

"It's working!" Summer said. "I've got Vaughan on the holodesk."

But instead of happy, she seemed panicked.

"Vaughan says he has to speak to you. Alone."

Humphrey's brain flashed awake as if she'd dumped cold water on his face. Finally, something was going their way. Wanda and Summer followed as he raced for the stairs to the bridge.

He burst in, breathless. Orson's man Dickie was in the captain's chair, which meant Orson was sleeping in his cabin near the engine room. The man was looking at the holodesk.

Vaughan's holo stood above the mahogany desk. Belle was next to him. And shockingly, so was Vin.

Vaughan held up a finger. "First, you must not go to Elizabeth's island."

The lack of greeting from Vaughan—or any expression of joy at being restored to life—made Humphrey blink. "What do you mean? Why?"

Belle shoved Vin forward. "Tell him."

Humphrey realized this was not the old Vin. This was the backup of Elizabeth's mind.

Belle had succeeded in getting Vaughan to install her. It was the eyes that gave it away. Vin had never been so sultry. This Vin had her arms crossed, and she threw a slightly fearful glance at Belle before addressing Humphrey. "Captain Wilcox and all his men are based on my island."

The news hadn't sunk in before Vaughan raised another finger. "Second, send that man out of here."

Humphrey jerked his head toward the door. Dickie complied, casting furtive glances back. Tytus—face freshly bandaged—went with him. They crowded on the bridge wing with Wanda and Summer.

Humphrey closed the door and went to the desk.

"What is it, Vaughan?"

"We know who Mr. Justin is."

Humphrey sighed and rubbed his face. "We do too. It's Sang. He killed Sensei tonight. Then Horace went all vigilante and killed Mr. Justin."

Humphrey shook his head, sickened by the memory. "And now Horace is in a coma from the beating he took."

"Horace? Sang?" Vaughan said. "What are you talking about?"

"Mr. Justin overwrote Sang. And Sang killed Sensei."

Vaughan looked at Belle, face sagging with distress.

Her face had a pinched expression Humphrey had never seen, as if she'd bitten into a lemon.

Humphrey didn't know what emotions an AI could feel. Apparently all the usual ones, for Vaughan stood in stunned silence. He and Sensei had been very close.

"Humphrey," Belle said, more gently that she'd ever said anything in her life. "Mr. Justin didn't overwrite Sang."

A video rectangle appeared next to her. It showed the door in the wine cellar. Belle froze it as a person entered.

Humphrey recognized the ponytail. The face.

Unmistakable.

Leslie.

Someone on the starboard bridge wing swore. It was Summer. Wanda stood next to her, jaw clenched. Her nostrils flared. The wind stirred her hair around like Medusa's.

He waved them in. Tytus ushered Dickie in, too.

"Wanda, go get Leslie. Tell her I want to consult her on something or other. Once she's on the way up, get Bethancy and Dajeet to come back with you. Summer, you go get Elias, Kirk, and Obu."

"What are you going to do?" Wanda asked.

"We're going to have a short trial."

"And then?"

Dajeet stumbled through the bridge door, holding her chest and gasping. Her wise eyes were scrunched from more than exhaustion.

Fear.

"What is it?"

"Horace is dead."

Wanda looked to the ceiling, shaking her head. "I was worried the concussion was too much."

Dajeet shook her head and raised her palms. They glistened with blood. "I tried to stop it. I tried!"

"What do you mean?" Wanda demanded. She snatched Dajeet's wrists and yanked her around. "What did you do?"

"I tried to stop the bleeding. Somebody . . ." She gagged and doubled over. A tendril of spit and bile dangled from her trembling lips. "Somebody cut his throat."

Wanda and Humphrey exchanged one short glance.

Humphrey nodded. "Dajeet, stay here. Wanda, Tytus, Summer, go." He spun on Dickie. "If you so much as scratch your nose, I will smash it in. Now sit!"

The Scions scrambled away, except for Dajeet. She went to a corner and slid to the floor and cried into her knees.

Humphrey shoved the holodesk away from the closet door, crawled through the holos of Vaughan and Belle and Vin, and pried open the door. He grabbed an old shirt, probably Orson's.

He took it to Dajeet. "Wipe your hands. Wipe your face. Get yourself together."

There was no time for pity or empathy. They would all mourn later.

By the time Leslie appeared, his own anger had congealed around his heart. She took three steps onto the bridge before noticing Vaughan and Belle.

Her lips quirked. An odd sort of disappointed smile.

The boys and other girls started to crowd in behind her.

She tried to shoulder through them, tried to get to one of the wing doors, but Tytus stopped her.

Vaughan and Belle showed the gathering the video.

"That room contained the servers," Humphrey said. "The only person who knew the code was Mr. Justin."

Gasps. Cries. Shouts.

Obu had to be restrained. His throat cracked with obscenities and threats as his agony poured out.

Elias held his wounded side and stared daggers at Leslie. They all boiled with anger at the realization she had diverted attention to Sang.

"Mr. Justin, how did it feel when you shot Sensei in the throat?" Humphrey asked her.

A smile curled her mouth into a vulgar gap in her face. "Quite satisfying. I won't deny it."

"And when you cut Horace's throat?"

"Come now. Surely even you are relieved that one is dead."

"She must die," Obu said. "She must die in pain!" Tears and rage muddied his face. Several others, especially Dajeet, nodded vigorous agreement.

"*He* must die," Humphrey said. "Let's not forget that Mr. Justin is our enemy. Not Leslie."

Summer realized what he meant to do. She whispered to Wanda. They both inhaled and let it go. They understood. They approved.

"We'll be to your island tomorrow night," Humphrey said to Mr. Justin. "Orson says there are only five men there. Why so few?"

"You'll see when you get there."

"Vaughan, can you handle Greta's job?"

He got a quiet yes from his AI friend. Nothing more was needed.

The others were starting to understand.

"I can wire the controls," Summer said. "It will be much easier than moving the holodesk down to the deck."

"Elias, get it set up."

The boy straightened and sort of saluted. He dragged Kirk and Obu after him.

An hour later, under a black sky, with the incessant

tremble of the engines and quiet hiss of the sea breaking on
the bow, the Scions all gathered around the transfer
machine, now assembled next to the school bus.

Orson had been roused. He stood with Rosales. Mr.
Justin's brother showed little emotion. Maybe his shoulders sagged a bit more than usual.

Mr. Justin, wearing Leslie's body, was bound to one cot
of the transfer machine. A great black bruise darkened one
side of her face. No surprise that Mr. Justin had put up a
fight. Tytus had been severely efficient in putting at end to
that.

Humphrey walked up to the girl. The man.

"Mr. Justin. You murdered Leslie by overwriting her.
You murdered Sensei. You encouraged Horace to murder
Sang. Which means *you* murdered Sang. You planned and
attempted to steal all Scions with the intent to sell us, thus
assuring our murders. You are a despicable human being.
You deserve death. Have you anything to say in your
defense?"

"I'm not Mr. Justin."

"Yes he is." Orson had stepped forward.

Tytus stood next to the lumpy man, ready to deliver a
roundhouse kick that would send him into next week. "I
have no reason to lie about it," Orson said.

He had every reason to tell the truth. Orson was
thinking about his own skin.

"*Et tu*, Orson?" Mr. Justin said, spitting. "I should have
had Senator Bentilius kill you, too."

Orson blanched and looked away.

Humphrey waved at Summer. She relayed his
command to Vaughan on the bridge.

The wheel of the transfer machine began to spin.

Mr. Justin let out a scream, high-pitched and full of fear.

Humphrey felt absolutely no pity.

The Scions stayed gathered around the machine, a mixture of horror and resolve on their faces. It was the first time they'd seen the machine in operation. What Mr. Justin endured now was the fate awaiting them all, should Dr. Carlhagen get hold of them.

This was what they were fighting to escape.

Except it wasn't quite the same. Because when the clone did not match the Progenitor being transferred, a backup was made.

When the wheel stopped spinning, Wanda approached the body. She felt at Leslie's neck.

Tears rolled down Wanda's face. She bent over her old friend's face, whispered something.

Then with the gentleness of Mother Tyeesha helping a child take her first steps, Wanda took Leslie's hand and helped her sit up.

The change was remarkable.

Humphrey wondered why they hadn't noticed the difference in Leslie before. But how could they, when their suspicions had all been focused on Sang, and when Dr. Carlhagen was escaping, and fleets were chasing them?

Leslie was a mild girl. She wasn't the brightest. But she wasn't a complainer. She wasn't confrontational.

She was like this. Vaguely confused.

"Where am I?" she said.

Every Scion rushed forward, all laughing tearfully. Wanda guided Leslie through the throngs and to the rail of the ship.

There were tears. There were hugs. There was wonder.

The last thing Leslie would have remembered—the last thing her backup had experienced—was Mr. Justin putting her in the transfer machine days and days ago on St. Vitus.

Humphrey turned away and headed for the bridge.

There was nothing he could add to the explanations coming at Leslie from all directions.

Summer waited on the bridge, the tip of a grease-smudged finger in her teeth. "It's over, right? Mr. Justin is dead."

"Yes. For now."

"What do you mean, for now?"

"You have a backup?" He was speaking to Vaughan.

"Yes. But don't ask me to install that man here. It's getting too crowded."

Belle stood by Vaughan's side, arms folded. She nodded in vigorous agreement. Vin was not present.

"I won't ask unless I have to."

"You've done well, Humphrey," Vaughan said.

"I couldn't save Sensei. Or Sang. Or Horace. I couldn't stop Dr. Carlhagen from taking Livy. I couldn't keep Jacey safe."

"Yes. But the rest still live. And they have a better chance now than ever before, no matter how bleak things seem. Because of you."

Humphrey accepted Vaughan's point. What choice did he have? Give up?

That was certain death for all of them. The only answer was to keep going.

At least one evil had been righted.

Now for the rest.

"This island Mr. Justin was going to take us to. Orson says we could be there tomorrow night. He claimed there are no guards stationed there, as far as he knows. He says he's never been there in person."

"Then let's get a plan together," Belle said.

They talked for hours.

Orson was summoned, pumped for more and more

details about what they'd find on his and Mr. Justin's hidden Scion camp.

Wanda showed up with coffee. Leslie came, too, wide-eyed and afraid and confused. Summer slept on the floor, head on Elias's lap, face looking like a child's. Elias stroked her hair.

As the eastern horizon began to lighten, there was suddenly nothing left to talk about.

All that remained to do—for now—was wait.

The End of Book Three of
The Scion Chronicles.

Read the final book in *The Scion Chronicles*, available now!

If you enjoyed *Sister of Shadows*, please consider leaving a review on your preferred retailer.